PRAISE FOR REX A. EWING'S

Winds of Purgatory

"What a master storyteller! I've read my share of post-apocalyptic screeds (i.e. James Howard Kunstler's works), and this is the best ever. The idea is amazing—a microbe that solidifies the world's oil. His venturing into the metaphysical is never easy, but in this case it works. The characters, the premise, the writing are truly amazing; his narrative description and character definition are equal to the best novelists in the trade."

– NEVILLE WILLIAMS

"The best-written book I have read in years. This post-apocalypse story is exciting, suspenseful, and told with words and descriptions that transcend the ordinary. The weird and wonderful notions of modern theoretical physics play well into this story of bonding, survival and conflict between philosophies. As the story unfolds, human nature is shown to be the same in the new world of an oil-less future. The story is great, the narrative is outstanding, and I recommend it to anyone who enjoys reading."

– JAY WILLIAMS

"An amazingly well written post-apocalyptic book. The characters were intriguing, the pace made it a one-sitting-read. The world-building was utterly amazing, especially if you take into account that the book has some sci-fi elements in it. The plot line is very realistic. Scarily so! The most memorable thing about this book is how exceptionally well it is written. I will definitely read more books by this author."

– WANDA HARTZENBERG

"Imagining a post-petroleum world and its power struggles—political, spiritual and personal—is easy with Ewing's artful prose and subtle cynicism. The characters are complex and appealing, even as they behave wretchedly. *Winds of Purgatory* is an engaging, thought-provoking adventure that left me yearning for more insight into the planet's Renaissance as humanity grapples with its next chapter."

– EINAR JENSEN

"...fresh intrigue and nonstop action when a struggle over secrets to resumed petroleum production, for better or worse for future humankind, leads to a winner-take-all battle set high in the Colorado Rockies, between historically new players. Ewing's players are not the common faceless literary cannon-fodder, but well-developed characters that make this work breathe. This work takes the reader to a different but nearby place and time, and leaves him feeling he was really there. It leaves him with a lot to think about, as well."

– FRED DEMARA, *THE NEW PIONEER MAGAZINE*

"*Winds of Purgatory* is a breathtaking adventure, mixing fantasy and fiction with a gripping commentary on human nature and our society's dependence on fossil fuels. Ewing has written a thought-provoking novel along with a prescient narrative on the outcome of losing our traditional energy supply, while his literary voice and love for nature echo within the pages. I highly recommend *Winds of Purgatory* to anyone who is in need of a captivating, beautifully written book."

– ANNAMARIE HILL

"A big, juicy, satisfying tale of science gone terribly wrong and science fiction that seems all too possible. It will keep your wheels turning long after you've turned the last page. Filled with complex, memorable characters you'll love or hate or fear and more twists and turns than a high mountain road, *Winds of Purgatory* is bound to make you wonder if you'd have the skills and guts and smarts to survive the unthinkable—and what kind of new world you'd create if you did. Carefully crafted, lyrically written and totally engaging."

– LINDA MASTERSON

"An engaging, believable, can't-put-it-down read about an all too possible future. This is a compelling work of fiction, and I hope Rex has a few more gems like this up his sleeve. *Winds of Purgatory* is fun and tough to put down. Highly recommended."

– DOUG PRATT

"A post-apocalypse book that is a page turner. *Winds of Purgatory* is a well written captivating story. The characters are great and you will hate to finish the book. I can't wait to read another book from Rex Ewing."

– HEATHER BENNETT

Winds of Purgatory

REX A. EWING

EASTLAKE BOOKS

To LaVonne Ann,
for showing me the way out of purgatory

WINDS OF PURGATORY

Published by
Eastlake Books
PO Box 149
Masonville, CO 80541 USA
www.WindsOfPurgatory.com

Kindle ISBN 978-1-936555-49-9
epub ISBN 978-1-936555-51-2
print ISBN 978-1-936555-50-5

Late Winter 2037

She woke him in the night and demanded what she claimed he had stolen from her. He'd been expecting her; had, in a sense, summoned her, so he was not really surprised to find her looming over him as he lay alone in his small bed. But he was taken aback by her beauty; even in the pale moonlight that streamed in through the skylights, he could see she truly was as beautiful as they said.

She's a sorceress, Carlos reminded himself, *a sorceress of the new world. She can appear however she wishes.* He pulled himself slowly upright, old joints objecting to every small movement. When he looked up at her a second time he saw what had escaped him a moment before; a darkness lurking beneath the façade of beauty and grace. No sooner had he thought this than her sea-blue eyes flashed, and for a moment they became dark as obsidian, matching in hue if not in sensuousness the glistening locks of jet-black hair that had fallen across her face and shoulders.

"What do you want, Salia?" he asked, although he already knew. He rose slowly from his bed and covered himself with the bathrobe hanging by the headboard.

From her coat pocket she produced a small leather-bound notebook with a tarnished brass clasp. "Isaiah's diary," she announced, studying Carlos's face for any small betrayal of the book's provenance, "sent to me anonymously. By one of your old enemies, perhaps?"

"I thought I had outlived them all," he said, sliding his feet into his slippers. "But what is that diary to me? Your father's been dead for nearly twenty years."

"Yes, twenty years. And for all that time I believed the COTO protocol was lost." She paused for only a moment to gauge his response, then held up the diary and said, "But now I've come to understand that Dobry Robak died from a bullet wound."

"Pity," Carlos said, "I rather liked the thought of him dying in the fire."

"Don't play coy with *me*, old man!" she roared. "Dobry died *before* the fire, meaning that whoever killed him torched the lab and made off with the protocol. And I'm quite certain it was you."

"Protocol?" Carlos said.

"The way to stop Tar Baby!" she fumed, then took a breath to compose herself. "As if you didn't know."

"I don't have it," he told her.

She must have sensed a half-truth, for she smiled sweetly and said, "But you will tell me where I can find it, won't you, Carlos?" Her voice was warm honey. And though he was beyond her powers of seduction, he knew there was little he could hide from her if she wanted it badly enough.

"I knew your father, Salia. Did you know that?" He cast the words over his shoulder as he trundled down the twisting stair. "He was very different from you, wasn't he? Isaiah actually believed the nonsense he preached."

"He was a pulpit-bound idealist," she said dismissively. "In the end the poor old fool just didn't have the stomach to wield the power given to him."

Carlos fetched a match from the table and lit the lantern on the wall behind him. The alabaster light of the gibbous moon mingled with the lantern's soft blue flame, creating a contrast in light and shadows that gave an austere depth to Salia's refined features.

He said, "Perhaps he just discovered he had a conscience...once he realized what he had turned loose in the world. It's a problem you don't seem to have."

"No," she agreed.

She paused to reflect on something that gave her no pleasure, but quickly her focus returned to him. As if to a lover she whispered, "Where *is* it, Carlos? What have you done with the protocol? Tell me, dear, and you may yet live to see tomorrow."

With an effort he eased into in a chair at the kitchen table and clasped his rough hands together in front of him. For decades he'd been holding old age at bay, looking and acting like a man twenty years his junior. It had been a source of great unspoken pride for Carlos. But once the depredations of time found their way into his bones they had been quick and merciless. Now, it seemed, time had begun to punish him for his sins of vanity.

Salia slid into a chair across from him, studying him like a predator sizing up its prey. His death was coldly written in her eyes and the cast of her face, which was set like stone beneath the supple beauty she presented to his still keen eyes. But he'd prepared for this night in ways she had not yet divined. He replied, "The knowledge of its whereabouts is hidden."

Her voice developed a crisp edge. She said, "Oh, but you forget, dear Carlos. I still have *you*."

"It doesn't matter," he lied. "The protocol is far removed from me now."

"We'll see."

In his day, Carlos was a man to be feared. He'd always had a way of making others uncomfortable, as much by his physical strength as by his haughty demeanor. But sitting across from this woman—this witch of the Turning—he felt frail and vulnerable.

He couldn't fight her; not with his body, and certainly not with his mind. But it was not his intention to send her away empty handed. He just wanted to make it difficult for her.

As she fixed her gaze on him he felt the threads of her will weaving through his consciousness, mapping out the landscape of his mind. He tried to distract her by focusing his concentration on all the ways he would like to kill her, for he truly did wish her dead. It was a not unpleasant exercise, but it was of no use. The more he resisted the harder she pressed on, not merely opening doors and peering inside, but leaving fragments of herself in each hidden recess of his mind as she proceeded from one loculus to the next, like someone rummaging for a lost ring of keys. But it wasn't an insignificant key Carlos was laboring to hide; it was the depth of his treachery.

At the rate Salia was tearing through his mind, it wouldn't be long before she found more than he was willing to reveal. She wasn't merely searching; she was affecting his thoughts in ways that would shortly make him believe she had a right to his most closely guarded secrets. And all the while she sat quietly across from him, wearing the look of a concerned daughter doting over her aging father.

That was the worst of it, that look.

In an effort to thwart her prying, he balled his hands into fists and shouted, "Leave me be, witch! I will give you nothing!" His outburst caused her to withdraw for a moment, and he knew it would be his last chance to escape. If what he had planned could rightly be called an escape.

Leaning toward him from across the table, she said, "Tell me where it is, Carlos, or I'll rip your fragile mind from its moorings."

He clutched his chest tightly and let out a breathless gasp.

Her eyes narrowed suspiciously. "What's the matter? Are you ill?" she asked.

"My heart," he groaned. "I have pills in my pocket. May I take them, please?"

Uncertain, she said, "Let me see them."

With a trembling hand he removed a small glass bottle from the pocket of his robe. She took it from him and read the label, hand-written in the cryptic script used by doctors and healers in the hinterland. "Nitroglycerin?" she said, handing the bottle back to him.

He nodded. "It relaxes the blood vessels...around the heart...so the blood can flow."

Conciliatorily, she filled a glass with water from the kitchen faucet and handed it to him. He murmured his appreciation for this small kindness and quickly downed not nitroglycerin, as she believed, but several pills made from monkshood root powder. A lethal dose, if his reckoning was right. He'd be dead within ten minutes and Salia would have nothing more than what he'd meant to give her all along. Ending his own life to protect the world from Salia Warchez wasn't really his idea of a good death, but perhaps it was fitting. In any case, if the local sawbones could be believed his remaining days were dismally few. He might as well die for a reason.

He felt a tingling in his mouth and on his tongue, and the beginnings of the nausea he knew would accompany such a large dose. He quickly screwed the lid back on the bottle and sat calmly back in his chair.

"Better?" she asked.

"Yes."

"Good."

Outside, a strong gust of wind whistled through the eaves and rattled the panes of the greenhouse roof. A fitting dirge.

Salia rose and glided behind him, caressing the top of his head with her smooth cheeks. The strength that flowed through her was nothing he could ever hope to resist in his weakened state; the rhythm of his heart was slow-ing toward its final, meager beat and his breath grew shallow. This didn't concern him; he had already embraced death and now looked forward to it with a child's curiosity. But he was beginning to feel lightheaded and he feared that he might, in his final moments, reveal more than he should, for the things of this world were quickly beginning to appear petty and insignificant compared to what awaited him.

"Where *is* it, Carlos?" she cooed. "Where is the protocol?"

"Die...witch."

"Oh, but you will tell me, dear," she whispered, "because I feel that you are dying—" he tensed with surprise "—yes, I know you are. Just as I know the dying always reveal their secrets to me." He felt her lips open into a lusty smile against the side of his head as she continued probing the evermore detached consciousness that swirled within. Her hot breath clouded his vision. Or maybe it was the just the poison.

It didn't matter. She was right. As he began to sink through the welcoming layers of the next world he felt his will to resist diminish in this one. And with his awareness ebbing, he knew it was time to give her what she wanted, lest she find that which he did not wish to reveal in the shining moment when the spirit cleansed itself of the things it would soon have no need for.

He closed his eyes, and as he did he felt himself transported to a meadow. It was bathed in soft light from the morning sun filtering through a dreamy mist. The air was sweet with the scent of flowers and he hoped to linger here for a time. Salia stood beside him; radiant, enticing...and mesmeric. It was sorcery; sorcery with a single purpose, but the peace he felt was very real. With a small, innocent smile she beseeched him to speak, and in his mind he said, "I'll tell you only this, my lovely witch. I've hidden the key to what you seek in the mind of one who is beyond your charms and your sorcery, and even your threats of torture. His mind is broken, you see, and not even you can fix it."

"Oh, we'll see about that..." he heard her say, as if from the other side of a great chasm. And then he heard no more.

Words no longer held meaning. As he prepared to forever sever his ties with the familiar, his rheumy eyes gazed up one last time at Salia Warchez and he peered beneath her outward beauty. There, for just an instant, he saw her for the hideous, parasitic creature she truly was, and he felt deep and profound pity for her.

Then, like a man emerging from a murky pond into the light of day, Carlos withdrew his lingering foot and the waters drew quickly together, revealing nothing of what lay beneath them.

It no longer mattered.

1

"Sure Sounds Like Religion to Me"

Tar Baby was the greatest dirty trick ever played on mankind. Not even in His flashy Old Testament heydays could Yahweh have topped it. In terms of pure destructive force, it far exceeded the firestorm He rained down on Sodom and Gomorrah, and made the Ten Plagues of Egypt seem amateurish. And while the Great Flood came closer to driving humanity to extinction, it did so only by a pretentious, overblown display of divine force. In every respect it lacked the sheer cunning of the Tar Baby bacterium.

FROM THE UNPUBLISHED MEMOIRS OF CARLOS HERRERA

He drove into Purgatory early in the fall. It was a pleasant time of year, just before the leaves began their slow and colorful descent into decay, when the mornings were sometimes frosty but the first snow was still weeks away. For most of the trip he'd had the curious feeling he was driving into destiny, though he didn't know what that meant, exactly. It was an unusual feeling for him, but one he'd had since dropping down out of the High Sierras into the barren deserts of western Nevada and finding the night sky at once so black with nothingness and so bright with stars that the universe seemed precisely as inevitable as it was impossible. And for one fleeting, illogical moment, he felt that he was at the center of it, on stage and stripped of his anonymity. At the time it didn't seem like much, but it was a feeling that refused to go away.

His dog Jazzman rode on the seat beside him, staring through the windshield with rapt attention, as if their destination were of considerable importance to him. He was a handsome creature of coyote/German-shepherd ancestry, with greenish-yellow eyes and large ears that looked all the larger for the fact that they rose ramrod straight from the top of his broad head, eager to capture any errant sound that might stray their way. The eyes gave the dog a decidedly wild look, while his thick coat of blended gray, tan and brown fur conspired with his enormous size to make him appear, at first glance, to be a timber wolf.

Everything Jack owned was haphazardly packed in the back of a small gray Toyota pickup that had seen all its better years back before the Turning. It was a four-wheel-drive affair but he had only owned the truck for two weeks and had no idea if the front-wheel drive train even worked. But the drive batteries had been replaced recently and they held a good charge. An old canvas tarp was roped down over the load to deflect what rain there might've been between California and Colorado, but the skies had remained clear.

He stopped in the middle of town to get a bite to eat before driving farther up the mountain to the place he had recently inherited from his birth father, a man he had known nothing about until several months ago. He wished he could have met Carlos Herrera but the old Spanish expatriate had a previous date with his Maker.

The news of his inheritance was timely; his marriage to a woman he thought he knew was over and his career as a professor of quantum physics in a world that no longer cared for the peculiarities of the very small was on the rocks. For now his resignation was pending, but he'd never go back. From early childhood the blood of an Oklahoma cowboy had flowed in his veins and the fine aroma of horseshit he'd been smelling since rolling into town was exciting his nostrils like the scent of a border-town bordello.

He was ready for a change, and Purgatory seemed a fitting place.

The small restaurant was quaintly named The Daisy Mae, and it was all but empty. He took a table by the window where he could see the street and enjoy the warmth of the afternoon sun. And watch Jazzman, who sat in the pickup with his stately head stuck out the rolled-down window, staring expectantly at his master. The waitress was short and slim, and cute in the homey way a lot of waitresses raised in small towns were cute: cute enough to enjoy looking at, but not cute enough to dream about. He supposed she had been out of public school no longer than two or three years, if indeed there was a school in Purgatory which, now that he'd looked around, seemed doubtful. He imagined that if he were to ask her what she intended to do with her life she would say she was still considering her options, though she probably didn't have many. But he didn't ask; he just wanted to know if there was a place in town where he could charge up his truck.

"No public power 'til the wind picks up again," she answered. "When it's calm like this all the hydrogen is saved for other things. But once the big turbines up north kick in, they'll start up the electrolyzers. At least that's usually how it works."

Her nonchalance was not surprising. Daytime electricity was more a luxury than a necessity in the hinterland, so people came to rely on other means to heat and light their homes, like wood or alcohol, or hydrogen. Solar panels were easy enough to come by—every occupied house had several. They'd mostly been scavenged years ago from the homes of the dead. But with no batteries to store the power, the energy was converted to hydrogen gas in the daytime and back into electricity at night, by way of the same dual-purpose apparatus, namely an electrolyzer/fuel cell stack.

Thinking he had enough charge to make it to his father's acreage a few miles west of town, he asked her what sort of fresh meat they offered.

"Rabbit," she answered. "That, or chicken."

"No beef?"

She shook her head then pulled away the few strands of golden blonde hair that had fallen across her face. "Refrigeration is sort of a luxury around here."

He nodded his understanding. Without reliable refrigeration, it was hard to keep big carcasses fresh. But a chicken or a rabbit could be eaten the same day it was killed.

He ordered a sandwich of pulled rabbit meat with French fries on the side, and a glass of cold tea which she served without ice in a tall glass with a wedge of lemon straddling the rim. The lemon surprised him. "The owner's got himself a greenhouse," she told him, with no particular emphasis on the man's achievement. "Thinks it gives him an edge on the competition," she added with a wink.

She brought his food then sat down across from him and asked his name. Jack Vara, he told her. She smiled the practiced smile waitresses so easily conjure as part of the tip-hustling trade and replied that her name was Susan, but her friends just called her Sue. Since he was twice her age he couldn't imagine that her interests were anything more than mere curiosity, and he liked it that way. She then asked him where he was from and what had brought him to town—"If you don't mind my asking," she added politely—and between bites of a stringy sandwich on a crude dry bun and fries carved from unpeeled potatoes, he provided her with answers as brief as he could make them.

There were only two other customers in the café at that hour, old men with dirty straw hats who exchanged infrequent words with one another at the lunch counter, where they sat separated by three empty stools. He watched her as she sashayed over to fill their cups with hot chicory that might have been mixed with a little coffee. Her small hips moved nicely beneath a pink dress with white, frilly lace and the remnants of food stains that would most likely outlast the garment, and he supposed it was a talent that served her well.

She returned without invitation and asked him what he did for a living. He recalled Steve McQueen's answer to a similar question posed by Eli Wallach in the old 2D classic, *The Magnificent Seven*—"We deal in lead, friend"—and though it wasn't exactly true, he told her that he dealt in the infinite. "Oh," she answered, narrowing her eyes, "you must be some kind of preacher." There were two types of religion these days: the old and the new. Most rural folks were rightfully leery of the latter. Its leader was a woman named Salia—Salia Warchez—and her reputation for beguiling the guileless had been ruthlessly earned.

He smiled without parting his lips. "No," he answered, "Mine is a different game. I don't preach to anyone anymore...nor does anyone preach to me." His ex-wife and her unfortunate conversion came to mind when he said it, but it was not a thought that lingered.

"What, then?" she persisted.

He thought it was Albert Einstein who'd once remarked that it should be possible to explain modern physics to a cocktail waitress, and he saw this as his chance. The short version, at any rate. He doubted she'd want to know that new worlds were forever springing into existence as the logical extensions of probability waves that refused to collapse, or that everything she considered real was nothing more than the vibrations of tiny strings several orders of magnitude smaller than an atom's nucleus. And if he were to tell her that her rock-solid notion of time was only a convenient illusion she would probably walk away.

So he asked her if she believed that the stars in the night sky went on forever without end, and after a moment's contemplation she replied that, yes, that was exactly what she believed. He then told her that if such were the case, she could rest assured that somewhere in the vastness of space there were doppelgangers—copies of her, exact right down to the unique letters of her DNA—too numerous to be counted, many but not all living on worlds that resembled this one in all of its particulars. Many of these other Sues were having this same conversation in the same restaurant and they were all thinking the same or similar thoughts. What's more, he claimed, everything she had ever done in her life was forever being done again and again, and all the things she had yet to do had already happened a million billion times. Furthermore, he went on, everything that might have happened in her life but didn't had already happened somewhere else and was still happening now. She had, he said by way of conclusion, never in her life conceived a thought or a dream or a fantasy that would not somewhere come true if it were physically possible for it to do so.

"Sure sounds like religion to me," she replied.

He shook his head and said, "No. It's just math." He told her it was a mathematical certainty based on the probable distribution of matter in limitless space, and he could easily demonstrate the certainty of his words with a sufficiently powerful pocket calculator. But she didn't appear interested in his numbers or his proof. His words seemed to be enough to set her to thinking in a way he would not have expected from someone of her age and education. Her face grew pensive, and she asked him, "What do you suppose it all means?" He was embarrassed to admit that he hadn't been able to put it all together and probably never would.

Considering his reply, she stared for a very long time into the nothingness just beyond his left shoulder. Then she met his eyes and said, "But somewhere you know; isn't that right? Somewhere you've already solved the riddle."

2

Cruising Purgatory

*When Wal-Mart abandoned their store in 2017, it was like they had
left the town a great gift. We first removed the inventory, then we tore
it down, brick by brick and saved everything that could be saved. The
concrete was smashed into pebbles and used to hold the dirt on the
roads; the rebar and glass that was salvaged made many greenhouses.
Most people wanted bricks and glass and steel for their homes, but I
would not put anything of Wal-Mart in my house. Still, there were
things I wanted for other purposes...*

FROM THE UNPUBLISHED MEMOIRS OF CARLOS HERRERA

The main street of Purgatory followed a narrow swift stream that
obliquely bisected the town like a jagged wound. It was known to the
locals as Old Scratch Creek, a name Jack thought both amusing and ironic.
In the old Catholic tradition, purgatory was the halfway house for those too
tainted with sin for immediate entry into heaven, but not so spiritually lost
as to be deserving of eternal damnation in the realm of—who else?—Old
Scratch. Thus was purgatory the carrot on the stick for which the sinful sal-
ivated, while a consuming fear of Old Scratch was the stinging whip lashed
against the sinner's indolent ass. Together, they had been deftly employed
throughout history by a dogma-mired clergy for the purpose of herding the
strays from God's flock back to the harp-string-straight path to salvation.

Everyone who had lived through the Turning knew the taste of hell, so
no one found purgatory a worrisome concept. In any event, the Church of
Rome was in shambles and the few remaining adherents had formed into
regional sects that fought amongst themselves. Or so it was said; Jack dis-

trusted anything that hinted of organized religion and so didn't follow what he perceived to be the inexorable decay of outdated institutions. It was the more recently created cults that concerned him.

Huge cottonwood trees grew along both banks of Old Scratch Creek. Some had been dead for so long all the bark had fallen off and they stood austere and white as bleached bone. He passed a place where a park had once been, but now the grass was long and tangled, and hopeful saplings with waxy leaves had sprouted in its midst. A solitary mule, its pin bones sticking out like the prongs of a hide-draped hat rack, grazed lazily in the tall grass, plump seed heads tickling its full belly.

Most of the street surface had been returned to the original hard-packed dirt and gravel, but in the places where patches of pavement remained the potholes were deep and hungry. He came upon a section of road toward the north end of town where a small crew of men was breaking up the old tarmac with bars and picks and loading the pieces onto a horse-drawn wagon made from the bed of an old Chevy pickup. The men, three in all, were lean and muscular, and their tanned bodies, naked from the waist up, glistened with sweat that ran in muddy rivulets down their faces, arms and chests.

Jack stopped beside the work crew, bringing the men's labors to an instant standstill. Two of the three smiled half-heartedly. The other, a man in his mid-twenties with a tousled shock of dusty brown hair, let his pick drop to the broken pavement and ambled over to Jack.

"Need some help, there, mister?" the young man asked. As he bent down to face Jack eye to eye, Jazzman craned his muscular neck across Jack's chest for a closer look. The young man instinctively drew back. "Whoa! That's a some dog; kinda wild-looking, if you don't mind my saying."

"Not at all. He likes it that way," Jack told him.

Jack imagined the young man a perfect match for Sue, the waitress; a little older with boyish good looks that would probably begin to fade within a decade. There was a simple, easy sense about him that Jack appreciated.

The other two bent down for a better look at Jazzman, and with a wink Jack said, "Careful. You don't want to make him feel self-conscious."

"No," the young man agreed, "I s'pose not."

Jack said, "I'm looking for the Old Lacuna Road. Does this lead to it?" The older men positioned themselves around their young amigo as if Jack's question were complex in nature and would require a lengthy consultation.

"Sure does," the first man answered, pointing north. "Turn left at the crossroad on the north end of town. After a mile or so it meets up with the creek again and follows it more or less for another five miles."

A man with a sweat-soaked bandana around his balding head, said, "You'll think it's the end of the world...like driving into nowhere." He was the heaviest of the crew and probably the oldest.

"Nowhere sounds about right," Jack said.

"Hope you like wind," said the younger man, "because there's no end to it up there."

"No end at all," agreed the bandana man, who, though heavier than the others, was not much older than Jack and appeared to be in better shape.

He was ready to drive away when the third man, shorter than his companions, leaned against the fender of the truck. He had the broad shoulders of a wrestler, with the chest and arms to match. "You're the guy, aren't you? The islander who inherited the old Herrera place?" Jack eyed the man carefully. 'Islander' was generally a slur in the hinterland, in the same sense 'barbarian' was a slur in ancient times. But his tone was not accusing; it was merely a question posed by a man who didn't see many outsiders in his dead-end town.

"The same. Carlos Herrera was my father." He was looking at the wrestler, who removed his hand from the fender.

The wrestler smiled, exposing a few dark places where teeth had been lost. "Well then, welcome to Purgatory," he said.

"The edge of the map, you could say," offered bandana man.

"Have any trouble on your way from out west?" the younger man wondered.

"None to speak of," Jack answered. "The inter-island corridor's smooth as silk. Can't say the same for the road between here and the Denver island, though. That one's a bit rough." In truth, it was one of the worst roads he'd ever been on; several times he thought certain his journey would end miles from Purgatory in a washed out bridge or a newly formed gulley.

There were snickers all around. The wrestler said, "There're some who'd like to fix the road, but most of us like it the way it is."

"The less communication between here and there the better," bandana man agreed, crossing his arms and drawing his lips into a resolute smile that conveyed a proud species of stubbornness.

"They've got nothing we need, anyway," said the younger man by way of conclusion.

Jack was hardly surprised at their distrust of the Denver urban island. Why should they feel any different? If they thought it was such a hot place, they'd already be there. As it was, there probably wasn't much they couldn't do for themselves. He thought of the Old-World bureaucrats running the islands, with food and manufactured goods in one hand and a social contract in the other, and concluded these earthy men of Purgatory were wise to be leery of anything from the urban islands.

"No, I don't imagine they do," he said.

He was ready to drive off down the road when a thought occurred to him. "What's the best watering hole in town?" he asked. "I'd be honored to buy you boys a beer sometime." *Never hurts to have friends in a strange town.*

"And we'd be honored to drink it," the wrestler told him. He turned to his companions and found ready affirmation. Some things never change.

Bandana man bent down, looking carefully at Jazzman, and said, "The Blue Fox. Ol' Harley brews up a pretty decent brew in the back." The others nodded as he added, "And on Saturday nights it's usually cold."

Then, just above a whisper, he said, "Watch your back up there in the hills, son of Carlos. Lots of things can happen to a fellow who isn't paying attention." He gave Jack a knowing wink, then stepped away from the pickup.

He thanked them again and touched the accelerator. The old Toyota's powerful Westinghouse motor whirred softly as he continued down the street, watching for potholes and whatever else might be lurking just out of sight.

A couple of blocks down he saw a faded wooden shingle announcing the entrance to The Blue Fox. It was a hole-in-the-wall sort of place tucked into the corner of the block. The façade was in need of paint, just like the rest of the town. Squinting in the bright sunlight, he tried to see over the tops of the barroom doors, but only darkness stared back at him. There were a couple of horses tied to a hitching post and a small electric fuel-cell ATV that had been pieced together from god-knows-what parked outside. He thought about going in, then thought better. He still had some miles to go. Besides, he had a few bottles of Budweiser he'd brought from California. He drove on to the rusty bullet-riddled stop sign on the north end of town and hung a left on Old Lacuna Road.

An interesting town, he thought, as the dusty road began to climb in altitude. It still reverberated the faint echoes of the past, but with undertones of a misplaced irony. No one missed the cultural necrosis that had infected the flesh of civilization in the days before Tar Baby had brought the Old World to a screeching halt. It was something those still scurrying for normalcy in the urban islands found difficult to comprehend, and yet it was so damned simple. Life here had shed all its former pretensions, leaving nothing exposed but necessity. Life had become the point of living, and it was an aspiration that had engendered an easy directness in its people. Purgatory was a place where evil would have a hard time hiding behind fast talk and subterfuge. Evil would require new sorts of cunning.

* * * *

The men watched in silence as Jack's pickup rolled down the street, making no noise they could hear other than the crunch of gravel under the tires. It headed past tethered horses with well-worn saddles, mules with sawbuck pack frames girded to their sunken backs, and draft animals pulling buckboard wagons. There were other, motorized, conveyances parked along the dusty street as well, but none was nearly as 'stock' as Jack's old Toyota.

It made Turney, Jack's 'bandana man', wonder just how well Carlos's heir would fit in in a place where new things were as rare as old whores. Life in Purgatory required a man to be good with horses and good with his hands, able to cobble together something that worked out of a lot of things that didn't.

Oh, the man was smart enough, Turney knew. Intelligence shone in his dusky blue eyes. But intelligence had a way of stifling imagination, getting itself wedged in between a good idea and its proper execution. In any case, Jack Vara would soon be rubbing elbows with some handy people up at the old Herrera place. If he was worth his salt, Tay and Luke would be the first to know.

Still, his handiness was the least of his problems. There were people about who would be watching him closely. Along with Carlos' property, he had inherited the old man's enemies. And his secrets.

He paused in the middle of his ruminations when he felt a coolness creep around him; felt it several seconds before he heard the clop, clop of horse's hooves and saw himself and the others bathed in the shadow of the mounted man looming behind them. The coolness was sepulchral, like the breath of a ghost exhaled from a tomb. He turned and said, "Good afternoon, Sheriff Primm," without really meaning it.

"Turney...Boys," the sheriff said, nodding. A wide-brimmed black

Stetson rode low on the sheriff's head, giving him the appearance of an old-time cowboy, or perhaps even a gunslinger. But he was neither, and everyone knew it, including the sheriff himself. It made him more dangerous than he otherwise would have been, as he was plagued with an obsession to prove he was a man he did not possess the attributes to be. Turney had heard it called the 'little man complex', and it seemed to apply well enough, though in terms of stature Sheriff Prygor Primm ("that creepy horse's ass" to those who knew him best; "snake eyes" to those only recently acquainted) was taller than most. He was also thin as a rail from his slender, pointy boots to his long, narrow face, from which there sprouted a thin-lipped mouth few had ever seen ratcheted into a smile. The man had no friends, though every month or so he roughly entertained various lady friends, delivered all but gift wrapped by Sturm Baker, an old school chum of the sheriff's who currently played politics in the Denver urban island.

It was a liaison that was hard to make sense of. Sturm Baker was a wealthy politician with an affable personality, and the fact that it was thin as snake skin did not diminish in the least his large circle of friends and cronies. It was Sturm who had arranged for a sheriff's position in the first place, even though the town didn't feel the need for one and certainly wouldn't have chosen the likes of Prygor Primm if it had. But it was all part of some half-baked 'renormalization' plan whereby the State of Colorado—what little was left of it as a geographical and political entity—would grant certain future and as-yet unspecified services to Purgatory, provided the town agreed to place itself under the 'oversight' of a 'deputized observer' who would ensure the good citizens of Purgatory were conducting themselves in a 'productive and lawful manner', rather than behaving like a rogue band of outlanders. Or (and on this point Turney almost agreed) to make certain that the town was not unwittingly harboring a militant nest of Apocalyptic Warriors—Poxes—a radical Christian movement hell bent on finishing what little the Turning of 2017 had left undone.

It might almost have seemed on the level, had Baker not been the mastermind of the program. But since he was, the only conclusion anyone with a lick of sense could draw was that Baker and Primm were up to something.

It's just that no one knew what.

Turney said, "Fine day, sheriff." *You self-important prick.*

Prygor said, "That was him, the man who just drove off?"

Turney sensed the sheriff was worried. Carlos Herrera had long been a thorn in Prygor's backside. Like before the Turning when he'd gotten fresh with the thirteen-year-old Teague girl. Carlos had cuffed him good that day and practically killed him a few years later—again on account of Jennifer Teague. There could be no pleasure for Prygor in knowing that the pup was taking over what the old dog left behind. Particularly since the pup was about to become the fair Miss Teague's closest neighbor. Turney answered, "And who would that be, sheriff?"

Prygor leaned down until his chest rested on the saddle horn and his small dark eyes bore into Turney. Little as he would like to admit it, Turney felt their sting. "You know who I mean, Turney," Primm hissed. "I'm talking about the son of Carlos Herrera."

"Didn't give a name," Turney answered. He turned to his compatriots, who looked at each other and shook their heads. "Just a fellow out looking for a place to get a sandwich and a beer, it seems. Of course, you could maybe ride him down and ask him for yourself. Might be he's a Pox spy; probably traveling incognito, looking for a place to burrow in and stir up trouble."

Primm regarded them each in turn, then said, "It may all seem like a joke to you three right now, but when it's all said and done you won't see much in this conversation that's funny."

"When *what* is said and done, Sheriff?" Turney asked, feeling the chill return. The sheriff might have a natural knack for deluding himself, but that didn't mean he wasn't dangerous.

"Never mind what," the sheriff said. "Good afternoon, gentlemen." He tapped his boot heels to the horse's flanks and walked the mare off down the deserted street.

3

Vientos de los Dioses

Few men would live where I live; they could not endure the wind. Myself, I find it a welcome companion. It sings me to sleep and provides me always with air fresh from the high mountains. It whispers nature's secrets into my soul and fills it with anticipation...

FROM THE UNPUBLISHED MEMOIRS OF CARLOS HERRERA

A mile northwest of town Jack came upon the wind farm the waitress had mentioned. Or rather, what was left of it. It was perched on a bluff that stood out from the surrounding terrain like a solitary wrinkle in an old carpet, and appeared to be the highest spot for a mile or two.

He counted seven turbines in all, small commercial jobs of maybe half a meg each, but only two turned slowly in the mild breeze. The other five were in varying states of disrepair; three with one or more missing blades, one with its nacelle partially removed. The last turbine in the row lay chained to railroad ties on the ground beside the tower. It resembled a wild beast, captured, bound and readied for transport.

By the looks of it, this was once part of a larger regional utility that had withdrawn from its rural operations when almost overnight all the world's oil had turned as thick as taffy. Much like a spider retreats to a corner of its web when threatened.

It wasn't just the utilities that had truncated their operations. The abrupt end of oil had thrown the whole world into chaos. For all the hype proclaiming the "greening" of energy and the bright future that lay ahead with the development of sustainable biofuels and clean solar, wind and geothermal technologies, the day the hammer fell practically every conveyance used by mankind still ran on petroleum.

The beginning of the end came without warning in late December 2017. The carefully orchestrated assault began in the Iranian oilfields, but quickly spread to Iraq, Libya, and the vast fields under the endless sands of Saudi Arabia. Venezuela was next, then Mexico, Russia, the offshore reserves in the Gulf of Mexico, and Alaska. By New Year's Day, 2018, there was not a drop of oil to be pumped anywhere on the planet. It was like trying to suck cold molasses through a two-mile straw. Only later was it determined that the damage had been caused by a bacterium so perfectly engineered that it actively resisted all subsequent attempts to subvert its genome to a more benign purpose.

At least ninety percent of humanity was doomed to starvation. It was a fact that had been known and written about for years prior to the Turning. It's just that no one expected it to happen overnight. But fast or slow, the math was inescapable: it took ten calories of oil to produce one calorie of food. When the oil ended nine of every ten had to go without.

An easy formula anyone could follow.

What wasn't figured into the calculations were the desperate things starving people will do to survive. Without oil the world governments were helpless to enforce laws. But that was the least of it. Law quickly lost all meaning when eight billion people lived on a planet that could not sustain but a fraction of their number without oil to sow, reap, and transport the harvest.

In the United States, the military—the authoritative arm of government that controlled the strategic oil reserves—tried to keep order through the National Guard. Their efforts amounted to a cruel joke. Starving people, they quickly discovered, are impossible to control. In the end, the military did the only thing it could do: it seized control of all the coal, natural gas, and biofuels, and all the food it needed to ride out the storm. Then it left the civilians to their fates.

The generals just wanted to make sure the military would be around to pick up the pieces.

The carnage was worse than anyone could have imagined. Predictably, the cities were hit hardest. Essentially parasitic, American cities drew water and food from the surrounding countryside while producing little of value in a hand-to-mouth world. Starving people fighting for survival had no need of financial planning, legal services, food catering, construction contractors, car dealers, furniture warehouses, or restaurants that no longer served food. Almost everything that could aid in the production of food, shelter and warmth had long since been produced offshore and was not to be had in a world where ships and planes were all built to run on a fuel that could no longer be pumped from the ground, or synthesized from coal and biomass in sufficient abundance to restore order.

What was now called the Denver island was actually an entirely new community built from the ground up near the former prairie town of Bennett. Old Denver was slowly but inevitably being reclaimed by nature, although it still maintained an unofficial population of society's dregs and misfits, down-and-outers and have-nots, this being because the islands were picky about who they would let in.

By the most optimistic estimates, nineteen of every twenty people alive on the planet in December of 2017 were dead by January 1, 2020—half by starvation, the rest at the hands of others who were starving. Jack was twenty-two at the beginning of the Turning. He'd seen his share of hard times and had no more taste for it.

It quickly became corporate policy for any company that survived to abandon all outlying operations and concentrate their efforts in the newly formed urban islands where supply lines were as short as they could logically be and potential markets were concentrated into a few square miles. Towns like Purgatory that lay deep in the hinterland had been cut off as a matter of policy and left to fend for themselves.

Whether from lack of resources, lack of resolve, or predation from roving bands of raiders, most towns had eventually died. But a few, against all odds and expectations, held on. By strength of will, Jack thought; pure defiance. Because nothing in this world feels quite as good as saying fuck you to someone who thinks you can't live without them.

About a mile west of the wind farm the dusty road met back up with Old Scratch Creek and entered into a winding canyon that grew progressively narrower as it ascended in altitude. Pines and cottonwoods hugged the road on either side. In many places the upper branches met above the middle of the road to form a dark archway. The wind was stronger here, and gusty. It playfully tossed the treetops and grew progressively more businesslike farther up the hillsides.

The narrows went on for little more than a mile before emptying out onto a rising, tortured plain. Dense coniferous forests grew several hundred yards distant on either side of the road, but directly in front of him the landscape supported little in the way of vegetation beyond short grasses, scraggly shrubs, and stunted pines that grew mostly on the lee sides of hillocks, granite outcroppings, or other deformations in the highly uneven terrain. It was a half-mile wide Dalian dreamscape broken only by the creek running through the middle of it and the rutted dirt road. Dust devils buffeted the pickup and scoured its fading paint with gritty air.

A half-mile ahead the creek split off from the road, making an oblique cut toward the trees to the south. The road followed after a couple hundred yard's hesitation and Jack soon found himself beyond the desert wasteland on a mildly rolling grassy plain, skirting the edge of a coniferous forest. At this point the creek disappeared into the trees while the road paralleled the tree line.

The wind had quieted considerably, though whether it was due to geography or meteorology he couldn't say. Just a mile or two ahead he could see towering peaks rising toward the distant clouds behind a north-south ridge. They rose nearly straight up for a thousand feet above the plain along its entire length, which went on for many miles in either direction. There was but one gap—a lacuna—in this impenetrable natural rampart, a narrow opening to the northwest bounded by sheer cliffs on either side. He reasoned that the water in Old Scratch Creek originated from the jagged mountains beyond that forbidding slit. As did the wind that had sculpted the tormented landscape he'd just driven through.

Jazzman was sitting up in the seat beside him, panting lightly and staring straight ahead with the focused eagerness nature reserves exclusively for dogs. He jabbed his companion lightly in shoulder with his elbow. "What do you think, kid? You like this place?" The dog groaned impatiently while regarding Jack with loving, untamed eyes. Then he stepped up the pace of his panting. It meant that he either had to pee or he'd seen a rabbit in need of chasing. Or he just wanted to run around with his nose to the ground and take in the new smells. "Don't worry; we're running out of real estate. We'll be there soon enough, if we don't drive off the end of the earth first."

And so they were. Just over a gentle rise, the road terminated into a single pair of rutted tire tracks continuing on toward the mountains in a snarl of sharp, unfriendly weeds. On his left a well-worn gravel driveway passed between two weathered timbers, spanned at the top by a smaller log that arched as severely as the back of a frightened cat. A hand-carved wooden sign wagged lightly in the breeze. On it the words *Vientos de los Dioses* were emblazoned. Winds of the Gods, if his Spanish served him. The rusty chains holding the sign squeaked in an oddly prescient way.

He turned and drove under the arch.

The Girl Next Door

When I crossed the river from Juarez into El Paso in the spring of 1984, I thought I might have been the first Spaniard to illegally wade across the Rio Grande from Mexico into the United States. But it was not for anything so noble as the need to earn money to feed my family, or to escape the shackles of political repression. I did it for love, and only love...

FROM THE UNPUBLISHED MEMOIRS OF CARLOS HERRERA

Jennifer's hand closed tightly on the curtain as she watched the gray Toyota turn into the main drive. The old pickup bounced and threw up plumes of dust as it labored through the potholes in front of Carlos Herrera's house of timbers and stone. She'd been waiting for some time for Jack Vara to arrive, and though she told herself she wasn't anxious, she knew it was a lie confirmed by her white knuckles. This made her laugh at herself, a nervous sort of laugh that did little to change her mood, which was formed from a mixture of dread and excitement (and hope, of course), all tangled up in a snarl.

She was spying through a narrow window on the north side of the small house she had lived in most of her life, a house Carlos had built for Jennifer's mother after her father had been killed in an "accident"—a mishap involving a large caliber handgun and a jealous husband. Situated south and east of Carlos' house, it was partially protected from the wind by large fir trees on the east and west sides, while the large south-side greenhouse was afforded full sunlight.

Jennifer had few memories of ever living anywhere but *Vientos de los Dioses*, and no recollection of her father, which was just as well. Everything wonderful in her life of thirty-four years had come to her through Carlos Herrera's generosity.

The thought of Carlos prodded her to move, to step outside with a rat-cheted smile on her face and welcome the long-lost son of the man she owed her life to. But she hesitated. It was not that easy; was, in fact, maddeningly complicated. Though she had never met Jack Vara—never seen more of him than a photo Carlos had somehow acquired; an unflattering snapshot taken in secrecy in which he scowled disparagingly at the *(pretty)* woman *(the unhappy woman)* beside him—she knew things about him; things that aroused her and filled her with dread. Things the winds of fate were even now entangling in an uncertain future involving Jack Vara and her invalid brother. And another man she wished had never been born.

The son of Carlos stepped out of the pickup. As Jennifer had feared, he looked pretty damned good. *From a distance, anyway,* she thought, adding a critical footnote to her observation as if upon closer inspection he might prove to be bucktoothed and pig eyed and thus make her life easier by re-moving from it any unwelcome temptation. But she doubted it. He looked a lot like she imagined Carlos—always handsome and stately—must have looked, long before she was born. Clad in faded jeans, a denim shirt and scuffed leather boots, his garments seemed the antithesis of what she had always supposed men in the urban islands would wear, though never having been to an island she couldn't say for certain. But this pleasingly dark-com-plexioned man who now stood erect with his hands on his hips appeared to be the strong self-assured type most of the women around Purgatory drooled over. The local expression was "A real man ought to be able to eat anvils and piss nails." Colorful imagery. And though many of the local belles might disagree, Jennifer knew it didn't wash with this guy. He was far more complex that your garden variety anvil-eater. Despite the height, the shoul-ders and the dark, unruly hair which all conveyed the rugged countenance of a guy who'd been in a few scrapes in his time, she sensed he was a man who would attack a problem with his mind before slashing blindly through it with his ego.

No sooner had she thought this than he turned his head and looked right at her. His eyes closed the distance between them and caught her com-pletely off guard as she stood *(like a sitting duck, for crying out loud)* directly in front of the window staring back at him. *He sees me watching him, and now I feel like an idiot for spying,* but just as quickly he turned away.

As a gentleman would.

He bent down into the cab of the pickup, made a motion with his hand, and a second later a large dog bounded out and made a beeline to the wood post that held Carlos' rain gauge. After lifting his leg and peeing for several seconds the dog pranced playfully back to Jack, who by now had begun to explore the grounds. Jennifer wondered how well Sasha, her Alaskan malamute, would get along with the large beast that had just peed all over *her* real estate. Either splendidly or not at all, she concluded, by way of concluding nothing.

As if summoned by the thought, Sasha awoke from her mid-afternoon slumbers on the rug by the chair where Silas sat lost in another time and place. At the moment Jennifer's twin brother was mumbling to himself and drawing abstract constructions in the air with unnaturally bent fingers.

She turned away from the window momentarily and regarded Silas with a heartfelt mixture of admiration and sadness. He had been such a gifted child before the War of the Turning; before an errant bullet had sped through a breach in a makeshift street barricade where her brother had been reloading their father's old 30.06...

The instant the bullet struck the side of his head, Jennifer had felt Silas's burst of pain as if it were her own. Perhaps that empathic sharing of pain had saved his life, like an airbag cushioning a fall. She didn't know. What she did know was that the episode intensified the psychic bond that had existed between them from before birth, and sealed it for all time. Nothing could now happen to one without the other knowing. Unless, as he sometimes did, Silas chose to lock her out while negotiating the strange worldscapes accessible only to someone of his extraordinary abilities.

Like now. She could sense him no better than the faintest wisp of smoke from a distant fire. It meant he was adrift in a place far from the objective world most people recognize as reality.

Occasionally he would talk to no one in particular in a word salad that seemed both random and nonsensical, though it was neither. Silas spoke from a unique perspective from within strange realms (*worlds; worlds unto themselves, each as real as this one*) Jennifer found both fascinating and confusing. And so she usually listened in those rare moments when her brother descended but lightly back into the objective side of reality, but now she turned away from Silas and watched curiously as the big malamute slowly ambled to the window to see what it was that had her mistress so entranced.

Like a pair of dutiful sentries, the dog's ears jerked pertly forward, and the growl that began rumbling in its throat at the sight of the other dog termi-nated in a bark that left Jennifer's ears ringing. *To hell with it; let them kill each other*, she angrily resolved, but she knew it wasn't going to happen that way *(nothing like that at all)*, and that's why, amidst Sasha's tortuous whines, she opened the door.

As she did, she heard her brother say, "Careful, Jen. Now begins the madness."

His voice was crisp and clear, a sharp departure from his customary blunt-edged murmuring. In a whisper she replied, "It's about time."

Jack decided the big house was Carlos' (now his, he thought with uneasy pride), while the smaller one belonged to Jennifer Teague, the executor of Carlos' estate. And the two sleek horses grazing in the pasture to his east? Hers; definitely hers. Eighty-seven-year-old geezers had no need of well-groomed saddle mounts, did they? He was forming a discordant men-tal image of an octogenarian horseman when the heavy wooden door to the distant house opened in a jolting rush, and a large, gray, wolfish crea-ture bounded across the threshold. He instinctively reached down to grab Jazzman's collar, but the big coy dog was already five long strides closer to the threatening animal than Jack was. He thought to call out to Jazzman, but instead just shook his head. He could sooner sweet-talk a bullet back into the breech. *Maybe they'll meet head-on and knock each other cold.* At the moment it was the best he could hope for.

A number of peculiar things happened in the course of two or three seconds, though that seemed impossibly short as Jack later pondered the scene in the darkness of his father's bedroom. First, *she* appeared in the doorway. Even from the considerable distance between them—a distance Jack was endeavoring to close with some haste—he *felt* there was some-thing different about this woman. Later he would see she was beautiful, but subtly so; in the way a lily was beautiful: serenely, and with soft-spoken elegance. Later still, he would realize that he had fallen in love with her in that first moment.

The two canines, silent and locked in a mutual focus, seemed destined for a bloody clash—one to defend its territory, the other its honor—and no more than ten strides apart when *she* stood on the stoop and cupped her hands around her mouth as if to magnify the command to call her dog back from the imminent encounter. The problem was, there were two dogs (as

Jack had concluded the other creature was not a wolf, after all), and the second of the two—namely Jazzman—was at that point about as likely to take orders from a stranger as he was to jump up on his hind feet and dance a jig.

But she didn't shout; not exactly. What Jack heard was not a sound in the sense of vibrations moving through the air, but rather a directive that had arisen from within his own head, booming out simultaneously from inside every neuron in his brain. Except that it wasn't his brain. It was someplace deeper; someplace...primal.

Wherever it came from or passed through, the command acted on the malamute like a tranquilizing dart. In an instant the dog dropped down onto its haunches and seemed almost to grin as it panted heavily, its tongue drawing slightly in and out with a dozen quick breaths. It was a position of vulnerability Jazzman could have easily seized.

But he didn't; his actions instead mirrored those of the malamute. He dropped to his belly, panting like a dog who'd grown tired of a game of fetch-the-stick. Inexplicably, the storm had fizzled. While Jack and Jennifer closed the distance, Sasha and Jazzman got peacefully acquainted. Noses and nudges. Expectant whines and friendly yips. In a lifetime spent in the company of dogs, Jack had never seen anything quite like it.

And then the man and the woman stood face to face. Jack tried to ignore the earlier avalanche of wild thoughts and unfamiliar sensations, and act like any man would when meeting a *(clearly extraordinary)* woman for the first time. But he still wasn't sure he'd find his voice, so instead of pressing his luck and making a fool of himself, he said, "Nice trick," and left it at that.

With a coy smile that showed her bemusement *(at my stunning loquaciousness, I'll wager)*, she answered, "Thanks. I practice this sort of thing all the time. It usually ends up in a bloody mess, but I guess I got lucky this time." Then she gave a nervous little laugh. Her face was flushed and he thought she must be embarrassed by her display of control over the uncontrollable.

"Practice makes perfect," he said, thinking, *except in the quantum world, where it really doesn't matter, since everything that can happen does, whether you want it to or not.*

"If you say so." There was a trace of condescension in her voice, though not in her bottomless blue eyes. There he found a desperate sort of conflict that confused him.

He said, "Anyway, I'm pleased to meet you, Jennifer Teague."

"I trust we both are...pleased, that is." She said this with a shy coquettishness he thought maddening. Then she held out her hand and Jack took it; took it with some reservation, considering her little trick with the dogs. Perhaps he expected sparks and neon lights to go off in his head. Or the answer to Life, the Universe, and Everything. But it was only a hand; warm and stronger than he thought such a delicate hand could be. After holding it longer than was strictly proper, though not so long as to cause either of them undue embarrassment, he released her hand and regarded the whole of her.

He found no one thing about her particularly sexy or compelling, but it only drove his curiosity. Lightly built and no more than five-six, she was not outstanding in any exact way, and yet the sum of her resolved into woman of rare, understated loveliness. He was entranced with her gossamer blonde hair and the skin of her face, so delicate he thought if he looked close enough he might be able to discern the underlying web work of capillaries beneath the skin. It was like looking into the core of her. The fact that she was dressed in worn garments of faded cotton only added to the many pleasing incongruities of this woman.

"Are you tired from your trip?" she asked, perfunctorily.

"No, not really," he told her, finding his weariness had indeed left him, though he'd have answered the same had he been dead on his feet.

"Good. I could show you the land, if you'd like." She looked him up and down, as if to take the measure of him. Inside and out. "You're from Oklahoma, right? Around Purcell? Good horse country, or used to be, at any rate." She nodded toward a small barn and said, "Do you still remember what it feels like to have a horse between your legs?"

He smiled. "It's not something a ranch boy easily forgets."

She returned the greater portion of his smile and said, "Even in the hallowed halls of Berkeley?"

"That's in the past," he replied, failing to add that he'd taken an indefinite leave from his position shortly after his wife had decided to burn the narrow little plank that spanned the chasm between piety and lunacy. Yessir, he'd launched himself into a whole new life because of Deborah's unilateral decision to sail away on a doomed ship that by all rights should have sunk long ago. "A mere twenty-year side trip," he added.

"I see," she said. "In that case, follow me."

5

Primm and Baker Ham it Up

The loss of the ability to communicate instantly with anyone, anywhere drove many to the prattle-prone sanctuary of the urban islands. For the rest, those few of us who stayed, the pulse of life slowed, and we inevitably joined in with the natural tempo of the Earth and sky. Some still use old radios to listen to news from within the islands, of course, but it is implicitly understood that it is impolite to discuss what they hear in public...

FROM THE UNPUBLISHED MEMOIRS OF CARLOS HERRERA

"He just made it into town; he's headed up the mountain as we speak." Sheriff Prygor Primm was talking into an old-fashioned telephone handset. He sat stiffly erect in the bare metal chair in the unadorned office the Colorado Department of Seditious Affairs had provided him on the south end of town. From the dirty window looking across the empty street to the west, an orderly row of old foundations protruded from the weedy ground like the ruins of a lost civilization. Primm was talking to the man who had created and currently managed the DSA (Desa, to those who liked their bureaucracies to have a feminine touch). The handset he held was plugged into a radio-phone transceiver by a stretchy pigtail cord. The transceiver, in turn, was wired to a large yagi antenna mounted on top of an 80-foot lattice tower in a bare lot behind the building. It wasn't as good as the old hard-wired telephones he remembered as a kid, and it was a damned far cry from the smart phones all the kids *(all the kids but me)* had used before the Turning, but it worked well enough.

At least it was better than the days before Desa, when communication

between Purgatory and anywhere else in the world was, at best, an iffy proposition. The remains of the Internet had become the sole province of the
military after the Turning. All the satellites in the sky before then had long
since ceased to function, and none of the new ones could be accessed for civilian communication. As for hard-wired communications, all the overhead
wires between the islands had been pulled down over the years and sold for
their copper and aluminum content, and the fiber optic phone cables connecting the urban islands to distant outposts such as Purgatory had been
dug up by outlanders and sold back to the phone company through circuitous black market networks. Ever pragmatic, U.S. Communications found
it cheaper to buy back their own scavenged cables than to manufacture new
ones, and they needed all the cable they could get to strengthen their communication networks within and between the islands, where uninterrupted
phone service was expected by a pampered and unforgiving populace.

For those outside the auspices of the urban islands, the only real way
to talk to someone at a distance was with an old ham radio set, using a
spectrum of frequencies between two and eighty meters. The military allowed these bands to operate as they had before the Turning, but they were
closely monitored for nefarious activity. Supposedly, Sheriff Primm's communications with Sturm Baker at Desa were on a secure frequency that was
instantaneously scrambled and unscrambled by the paired transceivers. But,
considering that high-tech communication's encryption was now the sole
province of the military, one never really knew who might be listening.

"Did you give our new friend a proper welcome into town, Sheriff?"
Even through the crackly transmission, Prygor could hear the cutting sar-
casm in Baker's booming voice.

"Negative," Primm answered flatly. "He was on his way out before I got
the chance to introduce myself."

A pause, then: "Maybe it's just as well. You're not exactly the type to be
running the welcome wagon." A beefy chuckle.

"No, I imagine not," the sheriff agreed after a brief hesitation. His limitations were a constant source of amusement for Baker, but Prygor couldn't
argue the fact that he had the personality of a lizard.

Sturm said, "The important thing is not to make him suspicious. Be
patient. We've got plenty of time. Let him get settled in and make friends
with your old girlfriend." Primm bristled at the reference to Jennifer Teague;
bristled particularly because of the lewd inflection in his boss's voice. But, as

always, he let it pass. Sturm went on. "Hell, chances are he doesn't even know where they are yet. Carlos was a secretive old bastard; you've gotta hand him that. And even if Vara does know, what's he gonna do? Dig 'em up and put 'em in the vault at the Purgatory Savings and Loan?"

Again Baker chuffed at his own little joke. There hadn't been a bank in Purgatory since First Community Savings was ransacked for cash and coin during the first month after the Turning. Prygor started to reply, but Baker cut him off.

"Anyway, I'll be up this weekend with some fresh entertainment. We can discuss it more then."

Baker's 'entertainment' was Prygor's biggest weakness and they both knew it. It tempered the sheriff's excitement with a smoldering contempt for Baker, who always found a way to dangle the sheriff's inadequacies in front of his face. And yet he knew he'd be unable to resist. The very thought of a new carnal escapade caused a brief stirring between his long bony legs. But a stirring only, unfortunately; never a complete awakening.

"Are you going to tell Tharp about Vara?" Prygor asked.

"That cutthroat bastard? He's the last person we need running around stirring up trouble. It's better he doesn't know. Understood?"

It was clear as crystal. And to Primm's satisfaction. Hadrian Tharp was an unprincipled loose cannon who moved around outside the Western islands with his small band of misanthropes. His specialties were black-market trading, thievery and sabotage, but it was also speculated that he was responsible for moving Salia Warchez, the Pox leader-in-hiding, from place to place. No one knew for sure, but it only made sense. Warchez's known followers were closely watched by the military, but nobody had the slightest idea where the elusive Tharp would be from one minute to the next. Baker used Tharp's talents from time to time, ironically to strengthen his own position as head of Desa: practically everything Tharp did underscored the need for Baker's new agency.

Primm hated him.

"Affirmative," Prygor answered officiously. "See you this weekend."

He heard the words, "Same time same place," before the connection went dead in a sharp crackle of white noise.

6

Witchy Woman

*...Salia is such a strange child. Sometimes she worries me. That the Lord
has graced her is a truth I cannot question, but neither can I fathom
it. Today I found her alone in her room with her bible, reading quietly
from Judges. I thought she might be reading to herself, but then I saw
there was a gathering of children huddled outside beyond the window.
They could not have heard her; Salia spoke too softly. And yet their lips
moved with hers as they murmured to themselves. I fear for her...*

FROM THE DIARY OF ISAIAH WARCHEZ, APRIL 12, 2009

I *study their faces. They plead and hope and dream, though some, I see, regard
me with scorn. These souls I mark.*

Then I speak.

*"The Turning, we are told, was the Devil's work. The Devil gave us the oil and
the Devil took it away. Isn't that what is whispered among your friends and in
your churches?"*

*Under my breath I say, "Fools." It is heard by all, and all eyes become my
conduits.*

*"Listen to me," I say, "there is nothing wicked about oil, and the only devils
are those who conspired to take it from us. Scientists. Politicians. Men with no
faith in anything beyond their own godless aspirations. They are the ones who
stole your freedoms and profited from your misery, and they are the ones who
even now control you like so many rodents in a maze."*

*A great uproar ignites within the crowd, but I quell it with a single glance.
Then I tell them a parable, one that Jesus himself gave to his disciples, the parable
of the man sowing seeds. It is apt because every one of these lost souls is a seed,*

and none of them wants to fall on barren ground. They all wish to grow. And grow they will. Some today, some tomorrow, some in a year or two. Some will grow straight and true while others will bend and twist like creeping thorns. But grow they will. It's what they want; to grow into soldiers.

And so to my army I pose a simple question: "What if the Turning were unturned? What if the Lord gave the oil back? Oh, not to the scientists and their political minions, but to us, the faithful, so that we may have the power to smite our enemies and build an earthly Paradise? Would this not be the just war?"

I revel in the thunderous affirmation.

But still they wanted more, insatiable rabble that they are. They all came with private desires, things they could not procure for themselves, whether hope, or lust, or revenge, or assurances that there is indeed some profound, mystical purpose to their small confused lives. Some came to spy, others came to confirm their own skepticism. But most came to the gathering with ravenous longings gnawing at their hearts; desires that only I can sate. Whatever their reasons, the spies and the doubters and the faithful all left that day feeling that every secret prayer they dared not utter had been answered.

Saving souls for their own sake is not my craft, however; I leave the business of salvation to lesser prophets. Me? I provide purposeful direction to the lost and beguiled.

Like the beautiful Deborah Vara who so needed comfort that day. I might have given her death, poor fool, for the things she sought could not be found on this Earth, but I instead bestowed to her the mindless comfort of peace and serenity, and enduring happiness. She embraced it like a warm puppy, never sensing the raw savagery of the dog within.

And to her husband Jack Vara, son of Carlos, who dared to glare at me as if I were an aberration? I gave him something very special, indeed.

Salia Warchez sat up quickly in bed, long locks of ebony falling loosely over smooth round breasts. She'd felt something; something slight, yet possibly of importance. There was a change of aspect to the quest.

Jack Vara was in Purgatory. And Silas Teague was stirring.

Gritty footsteps on the stones outside the door. A knock. "Are you decent?"

The voice was as condescending as it was insensitive. Cocksure. Or, as Isaiah might have said, fallibly proud. She disliked the man it belonged to as much as she needed him.

For now, at least.

Hadrian Tharp was her facilitator. He made it possible for her to move from island to island without fear of capture. The man knew every badger hole and underground warren big enough to hide a person from Kansas to California. And in the comfort that was her due. Mostly, at any rate. He had safe houses everywhere (which were often no more than cleverly concealed rooms underground or, in some cases, high in the trees), and he knew the seldom-used routes that connected them.

She was currently in the master bedroom of an underground Earthship a few miles southeast of what had been Salt Lake City before the Turning. Like the city, the Earthship had been mostly reclaimed by the desert sand. Tharp's people had completed nature's work by removing the solar panels and covering the exposed south side with sand and earth. Nothing remained for the eye to discern but an inset doorway that could be easily camouflaged between occupations.

Tharp's people were few but ubiquitous, and fiercely loyal. As the hereditary leader-in-hiding of The Church of Jesus Christ in the Ultimate Days, Salia knew firsthand how powerful a currency loyalty could be.

It was an uneasy partnership she had with Tharp, but one that served both their purposes.

"What does it matter?" she replied.

The door opened and a dry breeze caressed the smooth skin of her face and mingled with the air inside, which had become thick and stale, smelling faintly of sex and candle smoke. Bright desert sunlight washed into the windowless room and danced off Tharp's silhouetted form in shimmering sprites. Shadow man. The aptness of it almost made her smile.

"It doesn't," he said in his habitually domineering way. "But I'm sure you appreciate my deference to Christian decency."

She couldn't hold back the bitter laugh that erupted in her throat. "You're so full of shit, Tharp."

He stepped to the side, allowing her to see his efficient, compact features. He was somewhat short for a man, no taller than she, but powerfully built in a way that other men must have found threatening. It was a theme that moved seamlessly from his thick thighs and wedge-shaped torso, up to a jaw that seemed inexpertly carved from some manner of impervious stone. His eyes were small and dark and set in deep sockets below a heavy brow that made it impossible for anyone to tell what was going on behind them.

Anyone but her.

She remained motionless just long enough for his eyes to adjust to the poor light and give him a good look at her milky-white breasts. Then she pulled the covers up to her neck and watched with cryptic amusement as a ripple of disappointment scurried across his otherwise emotionless face.

"Cock tease."

Another man might have taken her then *(tried, at least, to his ultimate disappointment)*, out of spite, if nothing else. But she knew Hadrian wouldn't. There were unspoken rules to their uneasy liaison: civility was expected, tenderness (so far as it applied to one such as he) was amply rewarded, and wantonness was punished.

Besides, he had other things on his mind.

"I think it's best we prepare to move on," he said matter-of-factly. "A military patrol is nosing around to the north."

He can shift gears at the drop of a hat, I'll grant him that much, she thought with a measures of admiration.

"Colorado. We need to go to Colorado," she told him, with no particular urgency.

His eyebrows formed arches above the crest of his brow. "I thought you had business in the Reno island."

"Change of plans," she said dismissively.

Tharp smiled, showing a mouthful of thick, tightly packed teeth. They seemed designed to crush bones. "Smell something on the breeze, do you?"

It was pointless to try to hide anything from him. They each knew what the other was thinking. Depending on the circumstances, it either simplified things or made them more difficult. She liked to think (though, admittedly, she wasn't certain) that Tharp's talents were categorically different from hers; hers being of a more divine nature—gifted from God—while his were instinctual and

(devilishly)

...beastlike.

She knew his thoughts in the way the angels knew hers.

He came to his preternatural knowledge in the way snakes and toads divined earthquakes.

We both toil for a greater purpose, she consoled herself, *even if only one of us knows it.* Her loose and cavalier means were nothing her sainted father would approve of, certainly, but Isaiah was gone and these were different times. Time that required cunning and compromise as well as faith. In the end, God would read every heart and cull out the unbelievers. Until then, Tharp had his uses.

"Perhaps," she answered flatly.

Tharp's jaw tightened reflexively when Salia slid out of bed, naked and unashamed. She was a rare pleasure to look at. A complete package. Naturally warm sea-blue eyes that could turn to ice with a word. Expressive lips that turned confidently up on the edges. An assertive but purely feminine mouth. Attentive breasts with nipples that begged to be fondled. Curves that could make a eunuch grow weak in the knees.

Desirable.

Maybe too desirable. She clouded his thinking, sometimes. He should be used to her by now, he told himself. Women had always be disposable pleasures. Once, twice, three times at the most. Then *adios, chiquita*. But Salia was different; she used him as much as he used her. It was maddening as hell. He wished to be rid of her, but he could not discard what he did not possess. So he did her bidding, securing her safety and moving her from place to place, while she paid him in hard silver. And doled out sex like meat scraps to a starving dog. But he gobbled them up, just the same.

As if reading his thoughts, she tossed her head to the side and her hair brushed against her bare breasts like black silk caressing fine art. Before it fell back across her face she gave him an impishly seductive smile. He hated her for it. Just as he knew she hated him.

It was a good working relationship.

7

A Ride of Discovery

When the oilfields became unworkable after the unleashing of Tar Baby, most thought it would be the end of humanity. But when all was said and done, and the warring and the starving finally ended, we who remained came to realize it was only the end of the madness—of the feverish pace the entire world had become addicted to in its mad rush to consume itself. That is the lesson of horses. You cannot hurry a horse; the horse will resent your haste make you slow to its rhythm. Oil made us deaf to that rhythm and caused us to abandon for a hundred years the strongest link we had with our nomadic heritage. I'm glad the oil is gone.

FROM THE UNPUBLISHED MEMOIRS OF CARLOS HERRERA

To watch Jennifer Teague—the small, almost frail, Jennifer Teague, he might have mistakenly said to himself—saddle a stout mare that stood fifteen-three at the withers was to watch art in the making. Every motion gracefully evolved from the one before in such a way that efficiency was not only served but glorified. It made Jack realize just how rusty his skills as a horseman had become. While Jennifer's pad, blanket and saddle had all landed squarely in place, Jack had to fuss with his gear for interminable seconds to find the proper repose. She drew her cinch to the perfect tightness on the first pull; Jack checked his three times before he was satisfied. Her mare took the bit like it was molded from sugar; his gelding took it only by force. The worst of it was, it was entirely his fault for trying too hard. The horse quickly sensed his impatience and made him pay the price. *I've been away too long. I've forgotten how to appreciate things that breathe air and stand unquestioningly beneath the stars every night.*

It wasn't that he intended to compete with her as they saddled her two high-bred steeds in front of the loafing shed east of her house. He just wanted to hold his own. For the purpose of upholding his proud upbringing as a horseman. But then he saw just how good she was and it turned him into a bag of thumbs. It was embarrassing as hell and he appreciated how Jennifer acted completely ignorant of his clumsiness, though acting it must certainly have been.

It was only when he pulled himself into the saddle and felt the twelve hundred pounds of vibrant horseflesh beneath him that it all came back. Every breath, every heartbeat, every twitch of every nerve in the horse's body pulsed through the saddle and into him, and it translated into a quiet joy that only a horse can impart on a receptive human.

Jennifer smiled as if to say *nice save*, then rode ahead of him on a trail that led into the trees west of his father's peculiar house of black granite and seasoned timbers. The dogs trotted along beside them as though they were litter mates.

Jack was indeed a horseman, despite his initial fumbling while saddling his horse. He rode with a sharp eye and a soft hand Jennifer appreciated, for it meant he respected the power of the horse as well as the individuality of it: he treated his mount as a being rather than a thing. She'd given Jack the bay gelding—Coco was his name—while she rode a black mare called Negra. The gelding was more even tempered; not liable to buck, bolt or rear when startled, unlike the mare, who was often a slave to her hormones. Besides, the mare was in foal and Jennifer didn't want her to have to endure the unfamiliar idiosyncrasies of a strange rider.

But quickly she saw that her concerns were unnecessary; Jack would've been fine with the mare. She was especially pleased with the way he and Coco communicated with each other, responding instinctively to the other's body language. Anyone could be taught reigning and posture. They were important elements, certainly, but really not much more than simple mechanics, like riding a bicycle, or steering and braking an automobile.

A true horseman, however, worked in a higher domain; one where feeling and intuition became perception and thought was freed from the cumbersome act of thinking. Horsemanship was unspoken communication between human and horse, each knowing what the other was going to do before actually doing it. It was reading the horse's mind and allowing the horse to read yours, both of you buoyed by a mutual bond of trust.

Much like true lovers, she imagined, though in truth she didn't know.

Watching Jack through the corner of her eye, she concluded he was more than she expected. And less; agreeably so, as he was hardly the archetypical academic—either too fat or too thin with too little common sense to temper too much knowledge about too many things with too few practical applications. He appeared, instead, intelligent in a worldly way, and good humored, and Jennifer had no difficulty imagining him growing progressively disenchanted with the patterned life she imagined people embraced in the islands. He had too much of the country in him.

He was fairly tall and nicely built, and with the breeze blowing through his unruly brown hair and his pleasing face set against an azure sky, he didn't look at all out of place. Overall, a rather good-looking man; expressive, yet cryptic. Secrets lurked in his deep-set gray-blue eyes, and unacknowledged sorrows that were not at all hard for Jennifer to sense. But there was also a simmering excitement just below the surface, perhaps even a quiet desperation. *A desperate man looking to survive in an unfamiliar land.* It was enough to crease the corners of her mouth into a smile, and for just a moment she felt slightly guilty for knowing more about him than he thought she did.

After stepping their horses gingerly over the slippery round stones in Old Scratch Creek they rode to the top of a treeless rise and paused to take in the view. The dogs slogged up behind them, pausing every few feet to shake off the water from their heavy coats. "Whew!" Jack exclaimed, with a lengthy exhalation of thin mountain air. "This is spectacular. Are we still on our property, or is this government land?"

"Oh, this is still...ours," she told him. She thought the word awkward, although Jack had used it properly. "There are four parcels making up the original *Vientos de los Dioses*. Together they are surrounded on all four sides by National Forest, forming what's known as an in-holding."

It was land that was originally granted to the Union Pacific Railroad by the Bureau of Land Management, back when Colorado was still a Territory. The former owner, a well-heeled hermit by the name of Ezekiel Jordan, had purchased a section of land—one square mile, or 640 acres—from the UPRR back in the 1950s when the railroad was divesting itself of holdings it no longer found profitable. The railroad subsequently sold most of its remaining sections back to the U.S. Forest Service, leaving Jordan in the middle of a large chunk of government land with an ironclad guarantee he would never be bothered by neighbors or real estate developers.

"Your father acquired the land from Jordan in 1985. Ezekiel's health had gone pretty far south by then—probably from of a steady diet of poached meat and rotgut whiskey. Carlos, you know, was originally from Spain. He snuck into the United States illegally through Mexico."

A spontaneous chuckle burst from Jack's mouth. "You're telling me my old man was a wetback?"

"Crude, Jack, but accurate. His family was living in Mexico at the time."

"Why Mexico?"

She replied, "Your grandfather, Juan Ramon, worked as a minister for the fascist Franco regime in the 1940s and early 50s, but never could warm up to the monarchy Franco declared after the war. Probably found it too pretentious for his plebian tastes. So in 1957—Carlos would have been seven, then—he resigned his post and emigrated to Mexico." She waited for a response that never came. He simply looked at her expectantly as if she had stopped to catch her breath. Just as well; there was more to the story, but Jennifer wasn't yet of a mind to tell it.

"So Carlos was raised in Mexico?"

"Right. Until 1984, when he fell in love with your mother."

Jack smiled broadly. "I sense we're getting to the good part."

She rolled her eyes. "Carlos was thirty-four, Marisa was the sixteen-year-old daughter of a wealthy landowner. You could call it kidnapping with an international flair. But somehow they pulled it off. You can imagine the rest."

"Except the part where I was given up for adoption."

"For eleven years they loved each other fiercely, Jack. But when she died giving birth to you, well…"

"Something snapped?"

She shook her head. "Not exactly. But I think every time he looked at you he missed her all the more, so he gave you up and moved on. That was his way. It was a decision he later regretted, I think; one of the few things he ever regretted."

Before Jack could comment, she said, "Anyway, we're close to the southwest corner of your land. Everything west of here belongs to the U.S. government, which means you can hike it or ride it anytime you please, so long as you leave it the way you found it. Or don't get caught doing otherwise."

"Caught by whom?" Jack asked, steadying his mount after the two were slapped by a playful burst of wind from the south.

"Forest rangers, except these days they're more military than civil service. Special Forces in training. Tough hombres. They patrol the forest on foot and horseback, living off the land. A scary lot, but respectful of the old laws...for the most part. They're a lot like mountain lions—you know they're there but it's very rare to see one."

Jack said, "With so few left—people, that is—why should the government care about maintaining the National Forests? I mean, with so much land unoccupied, it's not like anyone is going to overpopulate the hills and upset the natural balance of things."

"Let's just say there are nefarious sorts outside the islands, more than you think. For many, the War of the Turning isn't over. It's best not to let the hard-core troublemakers burrow in where they can't easily be dug out."

"I s'pose," he replied, his attention now drawn to the area's peculiar geography. The saddle leather creaked sharply as he turned in every direction to take in the view. The general lay of the land to the east was downward. The meandering path of Old Scratch Creek was easy to follow by the light-colored leaves of the aspen and cottonwood trees that grew in thick stands along its banks. Numerous hills cascading one after the other seemed like ripples of earth on an immobile sea. They were mostly covered with a thick blanket of evergreens, though the trees were occasionally displaced by frozen bubbles of pink and black granite protruding from the hillsides like proud flesh from unattended wounds. Far down the valley lay the northern edge of Purgatory, barely visible before dipping behind the easternmost ridge of the Front Range.

Jack drew his eyes slowly up the valley until they caught the movement of a trio of wind-turbine propeller blades several hundred yards to the southeast. "What the hell...?"

Jennifer laughed. "Call it our personal power company."

"Wind turbines?"

She nodded. "And a whole lot more. You'll see."

He thought to insist on the rest of the story, but he was too captivated by the strange geology of the place. The mountains directly to the west were steep and jagged, and towered high above them. Jack had noticed them on the way in, but up close they were truly formidable. They formed a natural barrier for miles in every direction. The only breach was the deep slash through which Old Scratch flowed from its source somewhere in the high Rockies. Jack was staring at it now. "That must have been quite the waterfall at one time," he said, nodding toward the nearly vertical granite walls looming high above the creek on either side.

"Way back when horses had toes," Jennifer agreed. "Now it's the source of wind beyond your ability to imagine it."

"Of course!" Jack exclaimed. "Cold air from high in the mountains blows downhill, picking up heat, speed and momentum as it descends, until it reaches the backside of that monolithic mountain in front of us...at which point it has nowhere to go but through the canyon. And when that giant volume of air is forced into that narrow little opening, it just goes faster and faster," Jack finished with a self-satisfied smile. "It's the classic venturi effect."

"It's the wind from Hell," Jennifer countered. "You don't want to be anywhere near the mouth of that canyon when the wind is feeling frisky, believe me." As if to buttress her point, a blast of wind came out of nowhere and buffeted the two riders and their mounts hard enough to make the horses lower their heads and widen their stances. Then it was gone, like a wraith moving swiftly by on its way to perform some sepulchral deed. With a shiver, she added, "Sometimes I think it hears me bitching about it."

Jack traced an imaginary line from the canyon mouth to Carlos' house and outbuildings, a distance a little shy of a mile. Seen from their elevated position it was clear that the wind dictated what grew in its path. Beginning at the opening and spreading out in the shape of a funnel, there was little vegetation over a few inches tall in the wind's immediate path. He looked farther north and east at the surreal landscape he'd passed through on the way in, then back to the narrow slit in the mountains to the west. It all made sense: the slit worked like an air nozzle, directing its strongest spray at what lay immediately in its path. Carlos' buildings were beyond a sharp drop at the south edge of the plume; Jennifer's house and barn lay a little beyond it, at the edge of the tree line. "Carlos was wise to put his house on the lee side of that granite wall," Jack observed, "and to build your house in the protection of the trees."

"Don't kid yourself; the wall and the trees don't help much when the wind decides to pitch a fit. But the worst of it is in the first mile or so, as you can see. It can snatch a man right off the ground and send him flying—until it tires of the game and slaps him back down again." She spoke as if she'd had some experience in the matter. "Anyway, you'd do well to not take the wind lightly."

He believed her.

The four 160-acre properties Carlos had carved out of his original acreage were laid out roughly in squares, one half mile on a side. Jack's house, corrals, outbuildings and pasture were crowded into about five acres in the northeast corner. The creek ran diagonally across Jack's land before bending east and zigzagging back and forth across the southern border of Jennifer's. The two properties to the south were out of the wind funnel and mostly forested.

They stepped their mounts down and back across the creek, making their way through the pine and spruce forest along one of many game trails that wove between the trees. They came across a pile of mine tailings at the base of a small hill. Shards of quartz-encrusted granite and feldspar, ranging from coarse sand to fist-sized chunks, littered its slope. Ever curious, Jack coaxed his mount up the side of it to peer into the tunnel. Sasha and Jazzman both ran into the old mine a few feet, then stopped when they reached a pool of standing water. Jazzman tested it with his tongue, but stepped back after a taste of the stagnant water.

"This is a considerable excavation," he hollered down to Jennifer, who waited at the base of the tailing pile. He sounded like a kid who'd just discovered an opening to another world. "Anyone ever find any gold here?"

"Doubtful," she called back, "but who knows? A smart miner listens more than he talks." Jack took one last look then gingerly stepped his horse down the scree.

They followed a meandering trail through a dark forest of towering ponderosa pines. Many had trunks two or three feet in diameter. Shimmering shafts of sunlight danced wildly on the forest floor as the wind tossed the tops of the trees in sporadic gusts, then all grew quiet again. Only the *clop clop* of the horses' hooves on the needle-strewn trail invaded the perfect silence. It was rhythmic; almost as if the forest were a single entity, alive and breathing, and wholly aware of their presence. Jennifer thought it a magical place where ancient energies converged. She glanced surreptitiously at Jack and saw his eyes float to the treetops, searching with no preconceived notion for anything, or nothing, as he and his horse breathed in the piney air. His ears seemed attuned to the tiniest of sounds. Perhaps he shared her feeling. But maybe, she thought cynically, he was just taking in his new surroundings in the curious but shallow way scientists examined all new phenomena: purposefully searching for proof that nature had no purpose.

She wanted to believe that Jack was naturally inclined to look beyond that false little wall, but only through a little mental trespass—a passing glance through Jack's windowpane, as it were—could she know for certain. What could be the harm?

She dropped back a few paces, closed her eyes, and allowed her mind to do what it did so easily, and quickly she found herself tangled in complex thought patterns and arrays of mental energy that nearly overwhelmed her. *Who is this guy? How can anyone's mind be so damned busy?* And yet however discordant it was to her, she knew it was all harmonious to Jack. Abstractions were his instinctual refuge; his way of processing the world through myriad filters until it all came together to become comprehensible on every level.

This is amazing.

But did he *feel* the forest? Was he *in* it? Oh yes; somehow, despite the apparent busyness, the pure enchantment of the place flowed through him to his very core—a clear and quiescent sanctuary she could not (nor would not) violate.

It's what she needed to see before she could ever fully trust him. He turned and met her eyes. He offered a wry smile. She answered with her own before looking away. As she did, in that last instant of eye contact, she caught something else; something she'd missed. Something very small and ever so dark, no more than a mote. She shook her head; *probably just my imagination.*

The trail followed a dry drainage out of the protected valley where the giant ponderosas grew, emptying into a broken plain where small juniper trees had been artfully twisted and shaped by the restless air. As soon as they entered the path of the wind plume the junipers relented, giving way to low-standing mountain mahogany bushes on a dry and rocky terrain. Even their low branches had been twisted by the wind.

The peak of Carlos' house was visible a couple hundred yards ahead. They followed the trail north, around the backside of the protective granite wall.

"Did you stop in Purgatory for food before driving up this afternoon?" Jennifer asked after they dismounted and tied their horses to the hitching post.

He shook his head, as she knew he would. Though not exactly absent minded, he didn't seem to expend a lot of effort thinking about the little things most other people doted on. "I stopped for lunch, but not for groceries," he answered.

"Then I don't suppose you have much in the way to eat?"

"Let's see...I have granola bars and cheese crackers, sunflower seeds and hard candy. Might even have a warm beer or two back there somewhere. Does that count?"

Jennifer made a sour face. "Not for much. I didn't know they still made junky stuff like that."

"One of the perks of living in an urban island. The principle of instant gratification is alive and well."

"How depressing. Would you care for some real food?"

He grinned. "I guess I could handle it."

"Good. You need to meet the others. Dinner's the best time to get together."

"A banquet in my honor?"

"Don't get cute. We do it all the time. We have a common interest."

"Which is..?"

"Survival, Jack. Life out here is not without risks."

8

Codes and Memories

It was hardly surprising when people with extraordinary abilities began to appear so soon after the Turning. The paranormals who came before them had been ridiculed by scientists for over a century, and feared and persecuted by eighty generations of papists and Protestant fanatics before that. But with the Turning came an awakening, and an understanding that biblical literacy and reductionist sciences had led us nearly to ruin. The new culture was receptive and willing to embrace things that did not fit into the old paradigms—things they had always been told were either scientifically impossible, or the work of the devil...

FROM THE UNPUBLISHED MEMOIRS OF CARLOS HERRERA

Jack stood in the shower, a soothing downpour of warm water cascading over him. He had no idea where the water was coming from, just that the sun had heated it; he'd seen the solar hot-water collectors mounted on the south-facing eyebrow roof during the ride down from the mountain. As for the inside of his father's house, he hadn't gotten far in his explorations. Not that it mattered. It was enough to know that there was water and it was warm. The rest was of little consequence, including the hundreds of questions he had yet to ask about Carlos and...well, about Carlos. Everything revolved around his father, yet what Jack knew about the man would fit neatly on a postage stamp with ample margins around the edges. Besides what precious little Jennifer had told him and what he had gleaned from Carlos' handwritten will, there was but a single letter his father had penned just a few days before he died. It was written in a shaky scrawl by a man who still possessed a surprisingly lucid mind:

To my son Jack Vara –

An apology, before all else, but a small one, for you have lived a good life by your own efforts, and I suspect a better life than if I had raised you amidst the grief of losing she who bore you, my darling wife Marisa. It is a grief that haunts me still, and in your absence I have tried to fill the hole in my heart with the needs of others not of my blood. I have followed your life and your career, and you have done well without me. Of that I am curiously proud. You are my son.

Soon, I will die; probably by the time this letter reaches you. It is just as well; I have spent enough time on this Earth. I am ready to move on to fresher worlds. How I know of my own passing is not your concern. Not yet, anyway. But to you I leave all that I feel is yours. It is more than you might think; certainly more than you now have.

I am sorry for your marriage. Misguided faith is a venomous thing. You were wise to leave her, for she was lost to you. Perhaps you can start anew, in a town named for the cusp between Heaven and Hell. You might say it is my dying wish.

With a father's love,

Carlos Juan Herrera

PS: $6 \subset 79 + (14 + (8 \times 2))$

Memorize it, and destroy this letter.

Not exactly the teary apology he thought it might be, but perhaps all the better for it. It at least gave him a glimpse of Carlos Herrera. He was especially curious about the way it ended with an equation and an admonition. But it really wasn't an equation at all, at least not in any number system he was familiar with. Disallowing the possibility that Carlos was simply bad at math, it meant that the clever old man was giving him information that could not be easily deciphered; neither by him nor the bad guys, whoever they might be. In any event, he couldn't bring himself to destroy the only communication he had ever received from his real father (*call me a sentimental fool*), so he'd hidden it in the lining of an old sports jacket he had no intention of ever wearing again.

He dried himself off and dressed in a soft cotton shirt and a clean pair of denim jeans (*thank God Levi Strauss didn't go tits up at the Turning*). Jazzman watched him patiently with catlike eyes that sometimes showed more intelligence than Jack was comfortable with.

It was obvious the house had been prepared for him. All of Carlos' personal belongings (and they were few) had been neatly stored in a small closet downstairs, leaving the loft closet for Jack's things. The tile floors had been mopped, the bathroom scrubbed, and the log bed made up with linen so new and fresh it had either been bought at great expense or stored unused since before the Turning.

From the loft railing he was able to admire the tight, efficient design of the house. The entire south side was a greenhouse, two stories high and fifteen feet deep, separated from the main house by a window-studded concrete wall designed to absorb heat in the daytime and give it back at night. Judging by the quality of the materials, it must certainly have been built back when the wheels of commerce were still greased with OPEC crude, though he couldn't discount the ingenuity of certain people who had, for the past twenty years, been highly motivated to recycle the Old World into the new.

When he'd first seen the house from the outside, he thought it resembled a cave that had itself been chiseled from a rocky hillside and put on display with a glass front. All sides but the south were made from stacked granite slabs that tapered from five feet at the base to two feet where the top of the wall met the log roof beams. The sheer mass of the walls seemed like overkill, and Carlos may have done it for aesthetic reasons, but Jack doubted that was the whole of it. If he'd learned anything about his old man thus far, it was that he didn't do anything just for the hell of it. So the walls were either built to store heat from the sun and the wood stove, or—and this was scary—protection against the wind. Perhaps that was why the greenhouse glass was framed with stone and the whole affair X-braced with inch-thick steel rods.

He treaded down the spiral stair to see what he'd missed in his earlier haste. Not that there could be much hidden in a house as wide open as this one. On either level, only the bathrooms were sequestered; everything else was separated by bookshelves, rock planters or, in the case of the kitchen, a stacked-rock bar topped with a thick slab of polished pine.

A pair of kitchen appliances caught his eye: a gas range and a propane refrigerator that certainly had been refitted to run on hydrogen, since the few remaining natural gas reserves had long ago been seized by the military. He turned a knob to light one of the stovetop burners and was not surprised to see it instantly light up with a ghostly blue flame. He opened the fridge. It was cold inside. He smiled when he found a one-gallon mason jar on the top shelf, filled with a dark amber liquid and crudely labeled "Purgatory Lager, proudly brewed by your new friends at Vientos de los Dioses."

The beer would have to wait; now he was curious. He found the door to the mechanical room and peered inside. A hydrogen-fueled boiler plumbed to augment the solar hot-water system rested quiescently on a stand of concrete blocks. On the wall behind it was a complicated nightmare of pipes and valves assembled to run a hydronic heating system. It was all Old World stuff that was little used these days, particularly in the hinterland where wood and agricultural wastes were the common fuels and combustible gases were as rare as coffee.

Satisfied for the moment, he fished through the cupboard and found a simple glass mug for the beer. He told himself not to expect much. Most folks in the boonies brewed beer with bread yeast, a bottom-fermenting fungus that made homebrew taste yeasty. (Most islanders described hinterland beer as tasting like cow piss, though he doubted many spoke from experience.) He braced himself for the worst and took a mouthful. It was frothy, full-bodied, and tasting of hops.

He threw down another swallow, then sat at the small kitchen table and silently toasted Jennifer and the others he had yet to meet—the resourceful people who lived in relative luxury in Carlos Herrera's wilderness.

But mostly he just thought of Jennifer...thought of the way she moved when she thought he wasn't watching her—and then he contrasted that with the stiff twig she became when she knew he was. She feared him.

Yet she liked him; that was clear enough. Was she afraid of liking him?

Another swallow of Purgatory Lager erased the question. And as the next mouthful spilled down his throat, her strange behavior was forgotten.

He wanted to hold her as he would hold a hummingbird trapped in a snowstorm. Except he knew if he did he would never set her free.

*   *   *   *

In her entire life Jennifer Teague had known only two lovers. Prygor Primm had killed them both. The first he drowned. The second, from what could be determined from the remains, he had nearly decapitated.

Not that Prygor had ever been brought up on charges, or even officially accused. What justice there was in Purgatory at the time of the first murder—that of Jennifer's teenage lover, Kip Moran—was unorganized and not so keenly focused on the principle of finding a villain for every presumed misdeed as it had been before The Turning. There weren't any witnesses; there wasn't even any real proof a crime had been committed. Just the body of a young man

who could swim like a fish

washed up on the shore.

His laughing blue eyes were open when she found him, but they weren't laughing anymore. Just cold and still like a blue-eyed bass that had suffocated in anoxic water. She tried to close those eyes, tried to make them stop regarding her with that deaf, blind gaze. But they were swollen in a watery stare, gazing at nothing she would ever want to imagine.

They'd been swimming—skinny dipping, really, as kids did down by the horseshoe bend in Old Scratch Creek south of town where it flattened into a deep, shimmering pool—after having made love; the fumbling breed of love made by teenagers in the bushes when they think they're alone but suspect they soon might not be. The sweaty, frantic, grasping sort of lovemaking that begins with the sharing of breath and gazes so intense that eternity could not erase them from memory, then builds to an electric ecstasy that can only be felt by bodies just a few seasons past puberty. Then, when they could bear no more, it was over, like the conclusion to a symphony carrying such pleasure on each note that its end was a death both feared and sought.

Then rebirth.

She remembered how pink his backside was as he ran to the water, whooping his delight (*his conquest*, she thought with a wry smile, since it was hers too), and how smooth and fine his skin was, draped tight to his muscular body as it was, and she wondered—though only in passing—if he would get fat and wrinkly as their years together unfolded. She supposed he might—someday. In a thousand years. She had laughed then; laughed at their youth and its invulnerability.

And the hollowness of her laughter scared her.

Something was just a little not right...

Not so wrong, she intuited (*badly, God, forgive me*), that she could not cover herself before chasing after Kip, who had by now let the current carry him far beyond the pool into the cover of the scrub willows and towering cottonwoods. Just wrong enough to cause her to slip back into her swimsuit on the fly and run across the hard uneven rocks in bare feet without giving a thought to the pain it caused her.

She found his body a couple hundred yards downstream, beyond the rapids that began where the creek narrowed and descended just after the pool. He lay on a sandbar where the stream slowed and he looked so peaceful she hoped to think he was napping. But it was a hollow hope. He was dead. Dead as a doornail, as the old expression went; one she'd always thought funny in a dim and blunt sort of way. Until now. Until she saw firsthand the sharp edges of dead. As a doornail...

...saw his face when she rolled him over and saw the sand on his lips spilling into his mouth a few grains at a time, as his face dried in the sun.

She might have tried to revive him.

But dead was dead. And she knew it without taking a pulse, or listening for a heartbeat, or pausing to feel a breath against the tender skin of her face. She knew it because it was so.

There were footprints in the sand

(they may have been there for days, she was later told)

leading away from the body—from Kip—but nothing was ever proven.

Why, after all, would anyone want to kill a likeable kid like Kip Moran?

Three days after the funeral she saw *him* on the street. He shook his finger in admonition and froze her with a crocodilian leer that told her everything she needed to know: he would see her dead before allowing her to ever be with another man. That look scared her half to death, but it couldn't diminish her rage. Even if there was no way on God's green earth to prove Prygor Primm had murdered her fiancé, he was as guilty as hell was hot and he would pay for what he'd done. She ran to confront him—to slap and bite and claw out his eyes—but he disappeared like a ghost under the cover of darkness.

She told Carlos what she suspected *(knew; I knew it then, and I'm sure of it now)*, though looking back on it now it might not have been the wisest thing to do. Even though he was seventy and therefore at a point in life where most men might reasonably consider alternatives to direct physical confrontation, Carlos hunted down Primm like a rancher on the trail of a rabid cougar. He found him on the streets of Purgatory where he descended on the lanky twenty-year-old like a drop hammer.

It took four men to pull old Carlos off the young man, and not before he had bloodied his mouth and nose, and turned his left eye into a black, swollen slit. Through it all, Prygor never fought back.

And he never quit smiling.

It was then she came to understand that Prygor Primm had lost the fundamental elements that make a person human.

Two days later she awoke in the dead of night to find Prygor sitting on the edge of her bed. She was so terrified she was unable to move. He sat so quietly and proper—like a devout Christian in church—that she could not even sense the sound of his breathing, and she knew by the deadly glint in his one good eye that he would strike her down if she tried to cry out. When he saw that she understood the rules of the confrontation, he leaned forward so far she could smell his stale breath, and he hissed, "If that meddlesome old man ever crosses my path again, Jennifer, I'll cut his throat in his sleep." To emphasize his point, he produced a gleaming barber's razor from his jacket pocket and deftly flipped it open with one hand. He seemed fascinated by the way the lethal blade reflected the soft moonlight falling through the window, the same moonlight that had illuminated Kip's smiling eyes the first night they'd made love. "He'll wake up choking on his own blood, but he'll see me just the same, and he'll know."

She saw the focused madness in his eyes, and all her anger left her. She began to tremble, and tears rolled down her cheeks in distinct droplets that fell off her chin onto her white linen nightshirt. In her fear and frustration all she could utter was a feeble, burbling, "Why?"

Perhaps he felt pity for her in that moment, because he grasped her tiny hand softly with his long, skeletal fingers and pressed it to his lips, still split and swollen from Carlos' assault. In a cold, slithery voice that made her break out in gooseflesh, he said, "Because I love you, Jennifer. I always have, and I always will."

But it wasn't true. He didn't love her; he couldn't. There was no place within him where love could take hold.

It was then that she found herself looking into his mind (*his soul, you saw his tortured soul*) and all the blood drained from her face.

His past lay before her like a faceless desert where his cruelties lay buried beneath a sea of black sand; sand in which she could not force herself to dig. And his future, in its dark and multiple incarnations, appeared to her as a jagged shard of time that would remain lodged in her mind, waiting to someday shatter and drive her insane. It was the first time she'd ever looked into another person's mind, and at the time she hoped it was the last.

She never again spoke to Carlos of Prygor Primm. Weeks later, when all his attempts to initiate a formal inquiry into Kip Moran's death had failed,

Carlos appeared to finally let the issue rest. But that wasn't Carlos' way. He was watching him, she knew; waiting for the younger man to step across the invisible line he'd drawn between Primm's world and Jennifer's. And if he did, Carlos would kill him.

Ten years later, after she had forced herself to forget what she knew to be true, a man's body was found in a ravine. He had been dead for several weeks and his body was so ravaged by scavengers that the only evidence he'd been murdered was a deep score on the inside of the third cervical vertebrae.

Jennifer never told anyone, least of all Carlos, that the unfortunate young man had been her second—and last—lover.

9

Dinner at the Malloy's

As I began to grow older, I realized I could no longer do for myself what I had done in the past, nor could I expect Jennifer, whose talents lay elsewhere (and who was also burdened with Silas's care), to tend to the continual task of securing energy for our homes. With some misgiving, I decided to use my own land as incentive to attract the expertise I needed to make Vientos de los Dioses the self-sufficient oasis it remains today. It was fortuitous a decision...

FROM THE UNPUBLISHED MEMOIRS OF CARLOS HERRERA

Jennifer stood waiting for him at the corner of the wooden fence enclosing the small yard in front of her cottage. Sasha sat expectantly at her feet and Jazzman sprinted to greet his new best friend. By the distant look in her eyes Jack sensed that she was troubled about something. But then she smiled and said, "Evening, Jack," and though the distance remained, he felt the gap close a little, so he thanked her politely for the beer without bothering to ask how she knew of his fondness for it.

Not certain if it was his place to ask, but willing to risk a moment of awkwardness if that's what it took to find out, he said, "What about your brother? Don't you have a twin brother? It seems I read something in the estate papers..."

"That would be Silas. He had dinner a little while ago. He'll be fine for the short time we'll be gone."

"He's a...an—"

"An invalid? You could say that; Silas took a bullet to the side of head during the last year of the war. The bullet glanced off, but not before sending bone splinters into his brain."

"Jennifer, I'm sorry." It was all he could think to say.

"Don't be," she answered, her eyes gauging his for sincerity, "Silas makes the best of it. Really he does."

They followed a narrow dirt road into the forest and crossed a log-trussed bridge spanning the creek. To the south stood the wind turbines he'd seen earlier on their ride. From perhaps eighty or ninety feet up, the blades were turning briskly in a wind that was only a slight breeze on the ground. The propellers made a rhythmic *whish, whish* as they sliced through the air. Beneath the turbines were a dozen large lozenge-shaped tanks of the kind that used to hold propane back in the days when such fuels were still available and delivered routinely by truck. He guessed their capacity at 1,000 gallons each. Beyond them, on the far side of the lattice towers that held the turbines, stood a vast photovoltaic array, at least 100 feet long and 10 feet high. Beside it was a shop building with a large overhead door facing the road. It appeared to have been made from scavenged wood and steel, but no less stout for it. The entire installation was surrounded by a circle of large quartz stones, as though it were sacred.

"Cool setup." Jack observed. "How does it all work?"

Dramatically, Jennifer waved a delicate hand across the installation like a queen flaunting the breadth of her realm. Then she chuckled. "Wind. Solar. Hydrogen. Want to know more? Ask the guys who built it."

They took a narrow gravel road on the other side of the bridge and headed toward a squarish little log house-front with an arched door. The house was built into a natural hillock which hid from view all but the windowed outer rooms. Numerous skylights protruded from the top of the hillock, providing light for the inner rooms buried beneath the dirt and rock.

A young woman and a little girl appeared in the open doorway, each carrying a dish to a weathered slab table in the grassy yard. The woman smiled when she saw Jennifer, but the smile was melancholy.

The girl was another matter. She was a child of boundless enthusiasm. Seeing Jennifer and Jack approaching, she quickly and inexpertly ditched her serving dish—meat of some kind; Jack hoped it was beef—on the edge of the table and ran to greet them. Sasha bounded out ahead, capturing the girl's complete attention. She threw her arms around the dog and Sasha rewarded the child's affection with smothering licks across her tanned face.

The woman walked past her daughter to meet them. She was tall and athletic with silky olive skin. A long braid of jet-black hair fell to the middle of her back. She gave Jack a trace of a smile and offered her hand. "Catalyn," she said.

Jack shook it lightly. "A pleasure. I'm Jack."

The girl, whose unruly sandy-blonde hair contrasted starkly with her mother's sleek ebony locks, was far less reserved. She stepped up and thrust out a small soiled hand. "I'm Cassie!" she announced. Jack gave her hand an easy shake, and thought to ask her age when Cassie said, "I'm six. That *was* what you were about to ask, wasn't it?"

Catalyn raised her eyebrows and said, "And perhaps next time you might have the courtesy to *let* someone ask?"

Ignoring the rebuke, Jack said, "Actually, I was going to ask if you would like to meet my dog, Jazzman."

Cassie gave him a scowl that said *no you weren't*, but glanced at her mother and decided to hold her tongue. Jack whistled and Jazzman appeared from amidst the undergrowth where Sasha had joined him in a fruitless attempt to shag out a rabbit or a squirrel. Without prompting, Cassie smiled and said, "Com'ere, Jazzman." Promptly the dog trotted over and dropped to his haunches, gazing adorningly at Cassie. As she'd done with Sasha, Cassie fell to her knees and gave the dog a bear hug. Jazzman raked his big pink tongue across her face. Cassie giggled with delight, and held out her hand. "Shake, Jazzman. Shake," she said. The command wasn't spoken in the sharp, snappy voice most little girls use when trying to sound authoritative. Instead, she spoke slowly and deliberately, with more self-assurance than a girl her age should possess when ordering around a carnivore twice her size. Jack was about to tell her the dog didn't know that trick when Jazzman lifted his right forepaw and offered it to her. The girl promptly shook it.

Catalyn gave a little nothing-unusual-about-this laugh that didn't really work. She was clearly uneasy with Cassie's unbridled display of talent. She said, "He's a coy dog, isn't he?"

"So far as I can tell," Jack answered. "He came from a breeder outside the Bay island who was more than a little secretive about his breeding stock."

"You can see it in his eyes," she went on. "Cunning and playful, like a coyote. He's too intelligent to be just a dog."

A man appeared in the doorway. His hair was wet, as if he had just showered, and his simple clothes were freshly laundered. He offered a good-natured smile. Cassie ran to him and pulled on the thick fingers of his left hand. "C'mon Daddy! You've got to meet Jack and Jazzman!" She sounded like a little girl, again.

Again, Jack got beat out by the mutt. Cassie led her father to the dog and told him to shake his paw. The man smiled and shrugged, *What can I do?* Jack liked him immediately for it. Jazzman sat politely but refused to shake until Cassie gave the order, at which point the dog offered his paw as if hand shaking had been drilled into his canine brain from puppyhood. The man shook it, saying, "Pleased to meet you, Jazzman. You're a helluva dog...if that's what you are." He stood to shake Jack's hand. "Hey there, Jack. Luke Malloy. Glad you finally made it. I guess you already met the women in my life?"

The hand was big and rough. Luke, himself, was neither. With an easy smile and a face that harbored neither wrinkles nor dark secrets, he reminded Jack of an overgrown kid. A casual mop of blonde hair falling to his shoulders completed the illusion. "Two of them, at least. Are there more?"

"Trust me—two's all I can handle."

Catalyn said, "Tay's not here yet, but the food's getting cold. Maybe we should just go ahead and get started without him." Jack and Jennifer took their places at the log-slab table, sitting side-by-side, facing the house. Luke, Catalyn and Cassie took up the bench on other side.

The food was good country fare: fresh carrots and celery; boiled potatoes; a salad of crisp lettuce, ripe red tomatoes, cucumbers and onion. It was the kind of homegrown food most islanders could only enjoy in the summer months, either from their gardens or from truck farmers who sold their produce on the island outskirts.

A block of white cheese sat alluringly on a cutting board in front of Jack. He cut a slice, tasted it, then cut another. Suddenly he was famished. Catalyn poured mugs of cold frothy beer for both him and Luke without bothering to ask if he would prefer tea (with real ice cubes, he noticed) or thick milk from a glass pitcher. Jack washed down the cheese with a long swallow of the same tasty brew he'd found in his fridge.

The meat in the serving dish turned out to be grilled elk steak, which in his estimation was even better than beef. He hadn't tasted elk since before the Turning, but it wasn't a flavor easily forgotten and he attacked it greedily. The fact that it was not dried and heavily salted meant it was either freshly killed, or had been frozen. Considering the size of the *Vientos de los Dioses* power station, freezing would be no problem.

"What's the capacity of the little power plant down the road there?" he asked Luke.

"You want it in kilowatts or Btu?" Luke asked.

"Kilowatts would be fine," Jack answered.

"Okay...let's see here...the photovoltaic array is made up of those super-efficient nano-crystalline jobbies that convert light from three separate bandwidths. Carlos and Tay scavenged them from the old Wal-Mart store nearly twenty years ago, but never got around to doing anything with them 'til yours truly came along.

"Anyway," he went on, "we've got nearly 70 kilowatts of capacity, producing over 300 kilowatt hours on a sunny day."

Jack let out a breath and whispered, "Jesus."

"The wind is another matter. Each turbine can put out better than 20 kilowatts in a good steady wind. We fabricated them from spare parts and scrounged material. Made the blades from poplar trees. Combined with the solar array, it's a kick-ass system, believe me. Beats the socks off anything around here, public or private."

Jack said, "I'd think you'd have trouble with looters and thieves."

Luke shook his head. "Still lots of good solar panels there for the taking on the derelict houses of the, uh...previously living. And more than that stuffed away in garages and barns and cellars. Same goes for most everything else. But generally folks around here are happy with the old ways; they're distrustful of anything of a technological nature and avoid electronic devices whenever they can."

It reminded Jack of something a colleague at the university had once told him: "The islands are for those who see their salvation in the twenty-first century; the outlands for those who'd rather live in the nineteenth. No one has much stomach for the years in between." The Age of Oil, ironically. Most people had lost all faith in any form of energy that came from below ground. Seeing everyone you care about starving or being maimed or killed in a brutal civil war can leave a real bad taste in your mouth.

"Of course," Luke went on, "it doesn't mean there aren't those who'd like to shut us down; sabotage our little power plant and make us live like everyone else. God knows your old man had enemies; more than his share, really." Luke looked up and smiled. Jack heard a faint rustling behind him as Luke said, "But he also had friends..."

Before he could turn around, Jack felt a hand with vice-like fingers on his shoulder. He heard, "Hello, Jack," in an accent that was not quite Mexican. Then the man sat down beside him and regarded him with dark eyes and a gunslinger's smile. There was a trickle of fresh blood from a scrape on the side of his face, next to a heavy scar that ran from his right ear to his chin. It appeared to be an old scar, perhaps from the War of the Turning, but it was smooth and much lighter in color than the man's brown skin. He was smaller than Jack, and older; 50, maybe more. His long salt and pepper hair (more pepper than salt) was tied in back and fell past his shoulders. He was handsome in an unfinished way, though less so for the nose that appeared to have been broken more than once. A large hunting knife in a fringed scabbard hung from his horsehair belt.

But perhaps the most curious thing about this man was that he was neither fat nor muscular, but neither was he scrawny or thin. *He seems to be made of wire,* Jack thought, with a touch of awe.

The man reached for Jack's hand and Jack saw the knuckles were raw and bloody, like the scrape on his face. Jack smelled a trace of whiskey on his breath. He shook the hand with some reluctance, having felt what those steely fingers could do. "Otaktay Ortega Villa. Just call me Tay." He ran his sharp eyes across Jack's face while giving his hand a firm shake without causing further pain.

Jack started to repeat the name, "Oh-Tak..."

Tay finished for him. "Otaktay," he voiced with heavy inflection. "From my mother's side."

Grinning, Jack replied, "Tay, like you said," and left it at that.

"Trouble in town?" Luke asked, eyeing the scuffed knuckles.

Tay smiled, showing teeth that appeared unusually white when contrasted against his dark skin. "Not what you think."

Luke dropped the subject—whatever or whomever the subject might have been. It reminded Jack he was still an outsider, and probably would be for some time.

Seeing Jack's querulous look, Tay said, "my girlfriend's mare did not want a new set of shoes."

Luke turned to Jack and murmured, "Everything Tay does involves bloodletting in one form or another."

"Better than letting it grow stale in my veins, *amigo*." He took the small glass of whisky Catalyn had poured for him and sipped it lightly before stabbing a piece of meat with a knife and slapping it on his plate.

Following a brief silence, Jennifer said, "Luke; you were explaining the power setup to Jack?"

Luke said, "Right...let's see here...well, we rectify all of our incoming electrical power to low voltage direct current, and run it through electrolyzers to break down water into hydrogen and oxygen gases. Of course we have some big conversion losses going from electricity to hydrogen and then back to electricity, but we've got more than enough capacity to make up the deficit. A series of electrolyzers kick online as they're needed, and the same with the fuel-cell stacks and power inverters. The big tanks hold hydrogen and oxygen separately. We mix the two gases together for heating, cooking and refrigeration, and use pure hydrogen and oxygen in different stages for the stationary fuel-cells stacks and the vehicles."

"Vehicles?"

"That's mostly what Tay does," Luke said, poking his thumb toward his friend across the table. "At least when he's not otherwise engaged."

Vehicle maintenance and modification struck Jack as peculiar talents for a man whose most obvious qualification was scaring people shitless. He asked, "Fuel cell cars, or gas jobs?"

"Good old-fashioned ICEs," Tay said, at last looking up from his food. "You know, V-8s, V-6s? It's just a matter of bypassing the intake valves with direct ports, and tinkering a little with the injection system. Luke could probably even do it with a little help."

Luke retorted, "Sorry, ol' pal. Too busy keeping the lights on in that shop of yours to get my hands greasy."

The irony of hydrogen fuel was obviously not lost on these two. In the years before the Turning, hydrogen's detractors had all but killed serious research into methods to produce the energy-dense gas, and to store it and use it as fuel. Instead, industry had focused on what it understood best: liquid fuels such as ethanol, methanol, bio-diesel, and Fischer-Tropsch synthetic fuels, all of which could be easily stored and synthesized from virtually anything with carbon in it. In their scramble to perfect the manufacture of these almost-like-gasoline fuels, however, one salient point that was earlier overlooked became painfully clear the day everyone woke up to find the world's oil reserves solidified and the military keeping the nation's coal and natural gas supplies under lock and key. With the exception of ethanol, which could be made in small quantities with a backyard still, the more energy-dense liquid fuels required half-billion-dollar installations for their manufacture. Pure hydrogen gas, in contrast, could be extracted from water by anyone with a $1,000 electrolyzer and a source of electricity to run it.

Hydrogen very quickly became the fuel of choice for people in the hinterlands who had lost all faith in anything that smacked of government control. Recognizing the simplicity of producing hydrogen fuel from water and solar electricity, people took up home-scale hydrogen production wherever clean—which was to say, ash-less and smokeless—energy was needed for things that formerly did, or could have, run on natural gas.

Jennifer asked, "What about the islands, Jack? What do people use for energy there?"

Jack shrugged. "Electricity, as much as possible; from wind and solar, and nukes—mostly the new-generation nukes that run on atomic waste from the older generation plants. Electricity runs the rail systems most people use to get around, and the private vehicles they drive, which aren't used that much. Of course, alcohol is used mostly for heating and cooking, synthetic diesel to run the heavy equipment. Solar arrays and wind farms line the corridors between the islands to provide power for the trains and the electric vehicles that venture out, so the corridors are constantly patrolled for vandals and saboteurs."

"Like interlanders and Poxes?" Catalyn asked.

"Right. The interlanders steal anything that isn't nailed down, then sell it back to the rightful owners through a thriving black market. The Poxes, of course, want nothing more than to restart the war."

Catalyn shivered. "They're deranged. Every last one of them."

Jack thought of his ex-wife. She had somehow gotten sucked into the giant Pox network to the sudden and irretrievable ruination of their marriage. Overnight Jack had gone from loving husband to the devil's liege, simply for refusing to buy into her cabalistic beliefs. He replied, "No argument here."

"Perhaps it's true that they're the ones responsible for the...the Turning," Jennifer suggested, "and now they just want to finish the job."

The nagging truth of the matter was that no one knew for sure, though there was no question about the engineered nature of the Tar Baby bacterium. Like a one-celled Frankenstein, it had been ingeniously cobbled together from a number of extreme-environment microbes and endowed with a ravenous hunger for the high-energy molecular bonds that made crude oil such an energetic fuel. The *pièce de résistance* was the virus living symbiotically within each bacterium. Like a junkyard dog, it would attack and kill any bacterium whose DNA differed from that of its benefactor, making Tar Baby immune to all attempts to destroy it with other, newly engineered, microbes.

Upon being introduced into a well—through contact with drilling equipment—Tar Baby went on a feeding frenzy while reproducing at a prodigious rate. It quickly turned immense volumes of liquid crude into a dense, energy-depleted tar that could not be extracted in any way that produced a positive energy balance: to get the sludge out of the ground required more energy than could ever be extracted from it. The fact that all the major oil fields in the world were infected at practically the same time pointed to a conspiracy of considerable complexity. The remarkable part was that no one had ever broken the silence, even after twenty years. It was the kind of loyalty that suggested an intensely secretive group.

Was it the Poxes? The movement wasn't new, after all. They were the same bunch of "Christian" radicals that had been spouting Armageddon since before the turn of the century and later organized into a cohesive sect a few years before the Turning by a shadowy figure named Isaiah Warchez. When Isaiah died around the same time the oil fields became unworkable, his daughter Salia stepped up to continue the family business, so to speak. Possessing a charisma her father did not, she quickly turned the movement into a personality cult; a cult whose adherents multiplied daily, despite the fact that Salia herself had been branded an outlaw and an Enemy of the State.

As for the theories that pinned the Turning on the Poxes? It was the best one Jack had heard yet.

Luke, who didn't strike Jack as one to spend a lot of time pondering the philosophical peculiarities of virulent religious sects, said, "Why in God's—or anyone's—name would they do such a thing? I mean, what's the fucking point?" Catalyn kicked Luke in the shin and threw her head toward Cassie, whose expression said, *Wise up, Mom; I hear that word all the time.*

Jennifer answered. "It all goes back to bible prophesy and judgment day. I think they really believed only the faithful—*their* faithful—would survive the Turning. Fortunately, things didn't quite turn out that way."

Jack added, "Tar Baby was supposed to cause worldwide anarchy, leaving a power vacuum the Poxes could then fill. They got the anarchy part right, no question there. What they didn't count on was the military's unilateral decision to quickly seize all the unaffected energy reserves. He who hath the coal, hath the power, as it were. It left the military in charge of things, unfortunately, but it's still better than living in a radical theocracy whose only goal is to destroy their enemies. We had enough of that thinking with Al Qaeda "

"Who's to say they haven't infected the military?" Luke wondered. "God knows they've spread everywhere else."

"They have, certainly," Jack agreed. "But not in the numbers they had hoped, owing to the unforeseen little setback they encountered upon discovering that they were as vulnerable to the ravages of global chaos as anyone else. But they seem to be regrouping."

Catalyn shook her head, "After the damage they've already done, how can they go on, spreading their sick insanities about bible prophesy and Armageddon? Haven't they had enough?" She opened her mouth to say more, then exhaled deeply and crossed her arms.

Jack swallowed a mouthful of beer. "If you're a Pox, it ain't over 'til it's over."

"But the war was over seventeen years ago!" she exclaimed, suddenly becoming animated again. "What is there left to destroy?"

"Simple," Jennifer said evenly. "The forces of evil. Meaning us."

"But can't they *see*? *They* are the evil, the so-called soldiers of Christ; them and these 'end of the world' prophecies they dredge up out of God-knows-where."

Jennifer asked, "Would it help to know that most true Christians feel the same way you do?"

Catalyn snipped, "Do they now?" then put her hand to her mouth.

"Of course they do, Cat," Jennifer answered, reaching across the table to entwined her fingers with Catalyn's. Slowly the tension and anger drained from her face. "This is nothing Christ would condone, no more than the Crusades or the Inquisition, or the burning of witches. The Poxes are violent fanatics and most true Christians know that."

Catalyn said, "I'm sure you're right, Jen. It's just that sometimes the illogic of it overwhelms me."

In a whisper that bordered on silence, Jennifer mouthed, "I know, Cat. Me too."

Luke grabbed Catalyn's right hand and put it to his lips. She gave him a crooked smile, and he said, "Yeah, well, gee...this is one damned cheery subject. What should we talk about next, rattlesnakes and rabid skunks?"

"At least they're natural," Tay offered.

"And manageable," Jack chimed in. "The skunks, anyway."

"Skunks? You can keep 'em!" Cassie offered with a sour face.

Catalyn kissed her daughter's forehead and chuckled in spite of herself. "Maybe we should toast Jack's arrival," she suggested.

"Damn straight," Luke said. "Welcome, Jack, to the *malagente* of *Vientos de los Dioses*." Everyone raised their vessels and touched them to Jack's.

Jack poured himself another beer and said, "I really hate to play the devil's advocate here, but how do you know you want me as part of your circle? I mean, maybe I'm not who you think I am."

Jennifer said, "Trust us, Jack. We know you."

Probably that was true. Seems his old man had done his homework. In any case, he had the spooky feeling that it would be impossible to hide anything from Jennifer and Cassie. "Okay," he said, "You can count me in, as long as someone explains to me what 'ma-la-HEYN-tay' means."

Luke answered. "*Malagente*...It's a word Carlos used to describe us, himself included, which was good, because if any of us was *malagente*, it was your old man. Literally, it means 'bad people,' but it really means something closer to 'bad asses,' except in a positive way, like, say, Superman."

"Or Crazy Horse," Tay said.

"Or David," Jennifer added. When Tay gave her a puzzled look, she said, "You know...the kid who slew Goliath."

Unimpressed, Tay said, "*That* little shit? He just got lucky. It doesn't count."

Jennifer reached around Jack's back and slapped Tay's shoulder.

"*Malachiquita*," he said.

Jack downed another swallow of frothy homebrew and silently rolled the word around in his mouth. *Malagente*. He liked it.

10

Hand in Hand

If we are ever to find extra dimensions beyond the tiny ones we believe to have been rolled up in spacetime since the very early universe, we need to look elsewhere. And with different eyes. These hidden dimensions are not beyond our current concept of space, but they are fundamentally different from it. They exist concomitantly within our own three dimensional space, and yet they cannot be occupied by matter and energy as we currently understand these concepts.

So what moves within them, ladies and gentlemen? Why, everything we've always believed couldn't possibly exist…

EXCERPT FROM A SPEECH DELIVERED BY DR. JACK VARA
TO THE RANDALL RESEARCH INSTITUTE, JULY 14, 2037

It was growing dark by the time Jennifer and Jack made their way back. The moon was rising in the east and its soft light illuminated the gravel road before them. Long shadows fell behind any stones or low vegetation they might otherwise have stumbled over. Jazzman and Sasha studied every one as if demons might be lurking there.

Tay walked with them as far as the bridge. Jack felt safe beside him, which was funny, since he was obviously a dangerous man. It was evident in his quick, fluid stride, and in the way he seemed always to be watching. Looking. Seeking. But mostly the danger was in his eyes. The moonlight glinted off them now and as Jack studied them, Tay smiled and glanced his way.

"You wonder about me," he said.

"Yes," Jack answered. "It's hard not to."

"If I were you, *amigo*, I would wonder about me too." After another step he said, "I knew your father well; long before the Turning."

The Turning was the definitive dividing line between the Ages of Man, like the birth of Christ, 9/11, and the first voyage of Columbus, all rolled up into one. Knowing someone on both sides of the Turning was like having gone to hell and back with them. It meant that Tay knew more about Carlos that anyone now alive.

Jack prompted, "You were in the military before the Turning, right? Before you came to Purgatory?"

Tay nodded. "The Marines. I was with the Rangers in Afghanistan in '14 when the lid blew off the pressure cooker in Farah."

"Jesus," Jack murmured. He recalled seeing the gruesome aftermath of the fighting on the evening news, from the comfort of his freshman dorm room on the Berkeley campus. Ten thousand ragtag insurgents, all falling over each other for the chance to die for Allah, rose up from the hills to the northwest and descended on the Marine stronghold, wielding a panoply of military technology spanning thirty centuries. The Marine artillery couldn't knock them down fast enough. Half-billion dollar planes with bombs and napalm only slowed the onslaught. In the end the fighting was hand to hand. When the smoke cleared, 87 of 1,200 Marines were still breathing.

"You're lucky to be alive."

Tay smiled coldly. "I like to think it was more than luck, *amigo*."

His reply caught Jack off balance. He muttered, "Uh, yeah, I—"

"Anyway, it was not so bad as the War of the Turning."

Jack had missed out on that one, too. All but the first two weeks of it anyway, before the Military deemed him an asset that might prove useful in rebuilding civilization after the conflict played itself out. They held him in a protected compound in Marin County for the duration. Which was fine with Jack; two weeks was enough.

Veering away from an uncomfortable subject, Jack asked, "So how did you end up in Purgatory, if you don't mind my asking?"

"The same way we all end up in Purgatory. Fate."

Jack chuckle and said, "So it seems." For the first time since he'd arrived, he began to feel the weight of the place.

Tay stopped in the road and faced Jack, saying, "You do not really know why you are here, do you?"

He quipped, "Not really. But I'm beginning to think this may not be the quiet little retirement village I hoped it would be."

Tay smiled but didn't laugh. He said, "Carlos was involved in things of importance, Jack. Things that may soon affect us all."

Jack felt a chill creep up his spine. "What things?" he asked, not certain he wanted the answer.

"Maybe it's better that you don't ask. At least not until you are ready to hear the answers."

A glance at Jennifer told Jack she was nearly as confused he was. He thought of the little riddle Carlos had left him—the equation that wasn't really an equation—but decided not to mention it. "How did my father die?" he asked.

Jennifer answered. "Natural causes...as far as we can tell; heart attack, probably. He died sitting at the kitchen table. But who's to say? In Purgatory death is simply death. No one bothers with autopsies around here. I found him in the morning when I went to take him his milk. It was like he'd fallen asleep." A pause, then, "I remember thinking it strange that he would be smiling, but he was."

"And why is that strange?"

Tay said, "Carlos was not one to smile without good reason."

"Then he must have had one."

"Apparently," Jennifer agreed, "but what would a dying man have to smile about?"

They walked on to the bridge and watched in silence as Tay disappeared in the deepening night shadows on the road leading east toward his own home. Led by the two dogs, Jack and Jennifer took the bridge north across the creek.

"They're... interesting, the others," Jack said, when they reached the far side.

Jennifer chuckled. "That's a judicious assessment. Most people would say that Catalyn's a bitch, her daughter's a witch, and Tay is just downright scary."

"Actually, I think Catalyn's protective, Cassie's precocious, and Tay—and Luke, for that matter—are the guys I'd want on my side when things get dicey. But my point was that they're a far cry from normal islanders who are usually so dull they make mud look interesting."

"Sounds dreadful," Jennifer said.

"Positively painful."

"Cassie is far more than simply precocious."

"I know," he said. "Like you."

"Did you meet anyone in town before you came up?" she asked.

"A girl. A waitress named Sue. And three guys on a road crew. The one doing most of the talking was a little older than me, and wore a headband."

"That would be Turney. He's a good guy."

"I take it, then, there are bad guys?" he said.

"A few," she replied, then asked, "Did you see a tall, slender man wearing a wide-brimmed hat? He would have been riding a dappled gray mare."

"Sound like Wyatt Earp."

"This man is anyone but."

"So he's a bad guy?"

She said, "That's a nice way to put it."

He motioned with his hands for her to go on, so she said, "Let's just say that Carlos had something—something of value—that we would all prefer didn't fall into the wrong hands."

"The wrong hands being those of the skinny dude on the horse?"

"Among others," she confirmed.

"Why not just report them to the State?"

"Report what? That we *think* there are people who want to take something...something we suspect is valuable, though we don't really know what it is or where it's hidden?" In a low voice she added, "Besides; they *are* the State."

"Could be a problem," he agreed.

"Fortunately, no one knows where Carlos hid anything, and that's good. Because as soon as one of us finds out, all hell is going to break loose."

Jack's eyes lit up with recognition and she knew, without 'exploring,' that Carlos had given him a clue. He said, "As you probably know, Carlos wrote me a letter before he died. In the postscript there was a sort of equation that really wasn't an equation at all."

"Six equals seventy-nine plus fourteen plus eight times two?" She rattled it off in the same practiced fashion that people used to recite their Social Security numbers, back when they still meant something.

"Been reading my mail, have we?"

"Not hardly. Carlos showed the equation to all of us; made us memorize it while he passed around the paper it was written on. Then he burned it. Frankly I'm surprised he would write it down in a letter."

Jack said, "Must've wanted to be sure it wasn't lost forever. In case something happened to all of you after he died."

When Jennifer made no comment he said, "The curious thing is, 'equals' wasn't the symbol; Carlos used a different symbol, one from set theory. It means 'contained in'."

"Any idea what it all means?" she asked.

"None whatsoever."

"Me neither," she replied, not quite truthfully, "and I hope I never do."

"And if I should figure it out...?" he prompted.

"Forget it," she said. "I mean it. No good can come of it."

"Just tell me this: are you and Tay talking about the same thing, or is this a riddle that comes in layers?"

"Yes. No. Hell, Jack—I don't really know what Tay and Carlos were up to back when I was in pigtails. Ask Tay."

Jack decided to let it rest. They walked on in silence, their footfalls mingling with those of Sasha and Jazzman who now trailed behind. The wind was still; even the shadows splashed across the road from the treetops high above did not move. Usually such calm air was a harbinger for a big blow; the proverbial calm before the storm. It was inevitable; abrupt changes were a way of life in Purgatory. Changes in the atmosphere, changes in peoples' lives—they seemed to mirror each other. Ask someone what was going on around them at the time a memorable event occurred, and if nothing else they could tell you if the wind was up that day or not. It howled for hours after Kip Moran *(was)* drowned, was gusty and blustery the day they put him in the ground, and dead calm the day Carlos almost beat Prygor Primm to death for a crime no one else would believe he had committed. It was a peculiar way to mark time, but here it came naturally enough.

Wind was a potion for insanity. A nervous horse could forget its training and throw its rider when the winds came down out of the gap, and a dog surprised during a hard wind might turn and bite its master. People, on the other hand, could go either way. Most were simply more edgy or more inclined to act on impulse. Other, more iniquitous sorts, found people's averted attentiveness during windstorms a perfect way to hide their dark deeds. It all depended on one's nature.

She inched a little closer to Jack as they lazily ambled up the path. She couldn't remember the last time she had walked in the moonlight alone with a man, except of course for Carlos and Tay, which was hardly the same thing since they were both like fathers to her. But Jack was different; different enough to be dangerous. He was only a few years older than she, single, and not at all unpleasant to look at. It excited her as much as it filled her with dread. She wanted nothing more in this moment than to take his strong hand *(then do it!)* and hold it to her face, just to know, if only for a moment, the feel of another human being. The mere thought of it made her ache inside.

She took a deep breath and composed herself. Jack took notice and asked her if she was alright. *Oh, yes, fine*, she said, thinking her thoughts were again under control *(just as you like them, Jennifer: flat and composed)*, but as they walked on a little more she found herself wondering what it would be like to feel his hands touching her where her flesh had so seldom been touched by another. To lie naked with Jack Vara in a long embrace of shared passion. To see the early morning sun lighten up his sleepy face. And though she tried to put it out of her mind, the seed of the vision *(the feeling; the deep and sensuous feeling)* grew until the desire to be loved bedeviled her body like an gnawing hunger.

Face it; you want him...but you're scared to death to do anything about it. Is this really the way you intend to live your life, as a woman in the anatomical sense only, afraid to look over your shoulder for fear that you might find him *leering at you?*

No, it wasn't. But Prygor Primm had been in her life for so long *(controlling your life, right down to your dreams)* that she could no longer imagine ever being free of him.

Then something odd happened. Unbidden, her arm reached across the narrowing space between them until her hand found his. He seemed almost to be expecting it. He gently squeezed her hand—by way of acknowledgement, perhaps—but never turned to face her. Side by side, hand in hand, they continued on their way as though holding hands for the very first time was the normal course of things.

She didn't know if she expected a jolt of electricity or a mere tingling in her nether regions, but there was neither. All she felt was a sense of belonging, as though Jack had wanted this as much as she; more than anything in this world.

Still without looking at her, *(Oh, and I know why. It's the same reason I'm not looking at him)* he said, "You're a viator, aren't you?"

A viator was a traveler; one who explored places inaccessible to most. Before the Turning viators were called psychics, telepaths or paranormals, but the terms were limiting and seldom used anymore. Psychics could reach into the future and extract information from it while telepaths were simply mind readers, people who could send or receive communications without resorting to speech. Both were one-trick ponies. Viators came with more robust credentials which allowed them to journey through the hidden realms of time and space.

The question didn't surprise her—it wasn't as though she'd tried to hide it. Of course he knew. From the first moment with the dogs, he must have known. But she still thought it was strange he would phrase the question so nakedly.

Playfully, she said, "Is that an accusation, Jack Vara?"

He smiled at her reply and the delight that played on his face was like a melody. "It might be. If I were the Grand Inquisitor."

"Then I take it you're not?"

His sidelong glance was his reply.

"All right. If the word suits you I'll wear it. But it doesn't mean anything, really. It's just a word thought up by someone needing a noun to explain something he obviously didn't understand. The things I feel, and the places I sometimes travel...well, it's way beyond words."

"Have you traveled through *my* mind, yet?"

She chuckled. "*Your* mind? Another's mind is seldom a pleasant place, Jack; disorienting at best, and certainly no place to tarry for long..." For an instant she grew silent. Because she was lying. After a long sigh, she said, "But yes...briefly, this afternoon. I had to know what you were feeling when we were riding through the forest. If you were feeling what I was feeling."

He gave her hand a quick squeeze; this time she did feel the tingle. And then he turned to face her, taking her other hand as he did. She thought then he might bend down to kiss her. It made her wonder if she would kiss him back or pull away. Or maybe even run. But he smiled just enough to crease the corners of his mouth and asked, "Was I?"

"In your own way, yes."

"And why was that so important to you?"

She returned his smile and replied, "A gentleman would not ask a lady such a compromising question, Mr. Vara."

"No, I don't suppose he would. So let me ask a different question: while you were inside my mind did you happen to catch a glimpse of my future?"

His question took her aback. "Your future? Are you serious? I mean, which future would that be, Jack? There are so many ways for things to happen; nothing is ever chiseled in stone."

"But you can change, things, right?" he insisted. "Change the future, the way you did with the dogs this afternoon? Make things turn out differently than they should?"

After a moment's reflection she said, "Oh, they still had their bloody little fracas. It was unavoidable."

"But *where*?"

She shrugged. "I don't know *where*, only that they did."

"How can you be so sure?"

"Because I *saw* the fight, Jack. All I did was divert it to some other place, or plane...or reality. Hell, I don't know *where* it happened. But it did. There's no logic to it. It's just something that comes naturally, whether I want it to or not."

A tingle of excitement ran up and down Jack's spine. He had spent the greater part of his adult life trying to put a logical foundation under the same phenomena that came so naturally to Jennifer, what had come to be known in physics as the many-worlds interpretation of quantum physics. It was originally formulated in the 1950s by a young physicist name Hugh Everett, who had pointed out that the probability wave equation (that was said to "collapse" into a distinct outcome whenever an observation of an event was made) could be more elegantly solved if instead it were allowed to play out unhindered. Mathematically, it was the better solution. But the real-world implications of Everett's idea were a little hard for the scientific community to swallow, because it meant that every possible outcome of any given event was realized, somewhere. But where? A different universe, according to Everett; a fully intact fledgling universe identical in every way to the one from the original, except that in this one you wore the white hat instead of the black one, or you took the left fork in the road instead of the right.

Few took Everett seriously. At least not until the last decade of the twentieth century when new cosmological theories suggested there were indeed an infinity worlds beyond this one. Were they Everett's worlds? No one could say.

But there was a problem: the laws of physics forbade these worlds from interacting with one another. Everett's theory required that each nascent universe should exist alone in the wilderness, so to speak, forever out of touch with the universe from which it arose. Subsequent attempts to allow theoretical communication between universes provided only tenuous and unsatisfying possibilities.

Yet Jack's gut instinct told him that disparate worlds did communicate; that they in fact interacted with one another naturally and continuously. And he had devoted his career to proving it, first as a civilian working for the military and later, after the military grew weary of his lack of progress, as a tenured professor in a university with a hard-won reputation for endorsing kooky ideas.

And now, two decades later, all of his thoughts, intuitions and hard calculations had just been trumped by a woman who probably had no concept of quantum physics. He said, "Maybe I can help, Miss Jennifer Teague. We've got a lot to talk about, believe me."

She cocked her head to one side and gave him a queer look. "Jack?" she said. "What is it? You look like the cat who just ate the canary."

He shrugged. "A long story...for another time."

A clumsy silence engulfed them as they stood face to face holding hands in a game they would win or lose together. Words formed and dissolved in her throat before she could utter them. Jack wasn't doing any better. Neither was ready for what they were pondering, though for very different reasons. Jack wanted nothing more than to hold her and kiss her and make intense love to her, but Jennifer, he sensed, was a woman who needed to be wooed, slowly and tenderly.

Jennifer, for her part, had the crawly feeling they were being watched.

At last Jack broke the silence. "And where does this evening end?" he asked.

She said, "Right here, I'm afraid."

Primm Meets His Match

When I fell in love with Marisa it was like falling under the power of a storm from a direction no compass had ever pointed before. It swept us to its very source, and then demanded payment, for nothing is free. It appeared then to be a love affair we could neither of us afford. But as time went on we discovered an endless source of love's exclusive currency...

FROM THE UNPUBLISHED MEMOIRS OF CARLOS HERRERA

Primm was watching her as she and Sasha came through the door. The wind had begun to pick up by the time she and Jack parted with no more than kind words. She had been relieved when Jack had not tried to kiss her, but a little stung when he had not seemed all that disappointed that she hadn't kissed him. With such little experience in matters of the heart, she really didn't know whether he was being gentlemanly or coy.

So she watched him walk off, braced against the building wind, in a direction opposite of where they both in their hearts wanted him to go, a handsome dog with a beastly pedigree marching dutifully beside him.

Jazzman had sensed the intruder in Jennifer's house, even though he was a good distance downwind when the first low rumble left his throat, and with a couple of walls yet between them. Jack had taken notice and offered to walk her to her door, but she was already certain at that point that things were far from alright and would be even less so if Jack were to set foot inside her house just then. So she told Jack that Jazzman was probably just a little on edge after a long trip and if there truly were any reason for alarm Sasha would also have picked up on it.

It was a lie, of course. Sasha had long ago learned to avoid Prygor Primm as a consideration of her own survival. It was something Sasha had "picked up" from Jennifer, who knew that any assistance the dog could offer would come too late, as it was doubtful the dog would be able to disable Primm before he could draw a razor or a gun, two things that were always at his immediate disposal. And so Sasha avoided Primm not as a thing fearful or revolting, but as nothing at all. It was as if he didn't exist.

Prygor didn't know the dog considered him a non-entity, and wouldn't have been insulted if he had. Not being able to connect with other living things himself, it would seem only natural to him that a dog would be unable to connect with him.

She had to hold onto the door tightly to keep the wind from slamming it against the horseshoe coat rack in the entryway, and even though she knew who was waiting in the dim light just a few feet away, she couldn't help but think how nice it would be have an entry room with a door that opened from the east.

Her nonchalance did not arise from any boldness on her part, but from habit. Prygor Primm—his Christian name, she knew, was really Pryus; Pryus Gordon Primm, and why he had contracted it into the abomination "Prygor" no one knew—was a not-infrequent visitor to her house, always coming unannounced and silently making his way inside. In twenty years she never knew from which direction he came, nor by what path he departed, for he always came and left in the dark. But in all that time he had never once harmed her, or threatened harm to anyone other than Carlos. And while the fear he invoked with that simple threat was enough to ensure her silence and keep her in her lonely celibate state, she had never felt that he was going to hurt her or defile her in any way.

It was enough to make her believe he really did love her in his own empty, perverse way, and sometimes she almost felt pity on him.

But when she at last managed to close the door against the viscous wind, any thoughts of pity quickly dissolved. Even before turning around she felt a tightening in her chest and throat that made it hard to breathe, as if the air in the house had gone foul. But it wasn't the air that had gone bad, it was the room itself. It had been sucked dry of all its vitality.

Trying not to let him see the panic building in her chest, she looked toward him for the first time. He was sitting in a kitchen chair facing the big stuffed armchair where Silas sat during most of his waking life. He was holding her brother's left hand and smiling in way that made spiders race up and down her spine.

In his right hand he held a straight razor, which he waved back and forth just above Silas' wrist as if keeping time to an unheard melody.

Silas didn't seem to mind, or even notice Prygor was in the room with him; Silas was off on one of his 'adventures,' leaving behind nothing more of his mental apparatus than a custodial staff to keep the lights on while he roamed through distant realms where his body could not follow.

Seeing Jennifer, Prygor let the dancing razor dip closer in a long, arcing wave that slid the razor across Silas' upturned wrist. Jennifer gasped as dark blood quickly bubbled up from the wound, flowing in rivulets to either side. Silas appeared not to notice.

It was a small wound, not so deep that it wouldn't quickly heal, but it was enough to cause hot anger to boil up from inside her; anger that threatened to spew out her mouth in venomous oaths. But before she could act, a calmer voice told her to beware of this man, this night, and when he turned his attention away from Silas and met her gaze, the reason became clear.

His eyes, customarily cold and lifeless *(like the eyes of a shark)*, were tonight filled with jealous madness.

"Well, hello there, Jen," he said with a mechanical grin that looked riveted to his face. "Glad you could find the time to come home and be part of the ol' family." It came out in the sing-song cadence she might expect from a machine.

"Hi...Prygor," she said delicately, eyeing the congealing blood on her brother's wrist, and wishing she wasn't so afraid of this man. "What...what are you doing here?"

"Oh, well, gee, Jen. Just thought I'd stop by to see how the new boy was getting on, but I can see he's doing fine. Real fine, actually." This wasn't Prygor's normally composed self. There was a volatile nervousness about him that was disturbing. She had the feeling he was either going to break into tears or fly into a rage and slash her brother's wrist all the way to bone.

Or maybe both.

"He's far from fine, Prygor," she said matter-of-factly, hoping her lie was believable enough to prevent him from further harming Silas. "His wife left him just before he came and he's not taking it very well. I was trying to give him a little encouragement...but...well, I wasn't much use; it just takes time. You know how it goes." She wanted to slap herself for that last part.

But somehow it seemed to appease him, if only a little. His hand relaxed on the razor, causing the tension constricting her chest to ease slightly. He said, "It's a hard thing... for a man to learn a woman no longer loves him." His eyes wandered wistfully for only a second, then stabbed her with frantic intensity. "You know the feeling, Jen?"

"No. I don't."

A small chuckle left his throat as he must have realized *why* she didn't know the feeling. "Sorry, but it was for the best. I hope you know that."

She didn't. But she *did* know she was being slowly strangled in a deadly man's twisted delusion and now her defenseless brother was being dragged into it. Summoning more courage than she thought she had, Jennifer told him exactly what was occupying her mind. "If you harm my brother any further, Prygor Primm, I will see you dead. This I swear to you on the grave of Kip Moran." Her eyes were locked on his and she spoke through clenched teeth.

He apparently hadn't expected such boldness. It caused him to sit back in his chair and look at her almost pleadingly. She said, "Put the razor down and leave my house, Prygor. *Now.*"

She had never spoken to him like this before and it confused him. He was not a man accustomed to receiving orders from a woman he thought he owned. Seeing his momentary indecision, Jennifer slowly reached down and grasped his razor-wielding hand by the wrist, gently working the fingers that seemed to be but partially frozen around the handle. After a tense moment during which Primm's mind seemed to be stuck in neutral, she was able to remove the razor and fold it safely closed.

She had just let go the breath she was holding when Primm dropped Silas' limp hand and folded his now-free hand over hers.

It startled her, and she made the mistake of looking into his eyes. The wind, which had been huffing and wheezing through the trees and rattling the window panes, suddenly ceased. No one breathed; neither she nor Prygor, nor Silas nor even Sasha, who now sat up and regarded Primm with intense brown eyes.

Jennifer's power had always been in her hands. Whatever she could touch, she could control. But Primm's power came from his eyes; eyes everyone instinctually avoided because of the feelings they invoked; not the poet's windows to the soul, but dark caverns leading to stark, barren places.

A thought flew into her mind, clear and sharp as broken glass, and every bit as deadly. With her free hand, she realized, she could flip open the razor she now possessed and, with a single bold stroke, end the tyranny by which Prygor Primm had ruled her soul for half of her life. *It would be so easy; why, there is even a curved finger-hold at the base of the blade, the latch that opens the door to freedom.*

A grin formed on her face, a hungry, unclean grin that made her feel dirty. And angry at being pulled down to Primm's level of baseness and cruelty.

She knew then that hers was not the way of violence, but of gracefully arching subtleties; disparate islands of possibilities converging into a gestalt of potentials where all the many worlds-to-be were carefully layered one on top of another until, with an act of will she could never hope to understand, they all swirled into a volatile matrix in which anything could happen.

Anything at all.

Anything except what happened next.

Primm must have gotten a glimpse of the hair-triggered microcosm about to explode within Jennifer's mind; must have seen the shock wave of possibilities that was about to set him adrift in a strange, unsettling place. The gleaming portals of his eyes dimmed as a multitude of fates unfolded simultaneously in his mind and drew away his vitality like puss from an infected wound.

Jennifer watched his confusion with detached pleasure. His eyes grew rheumy and impotent, and his hand relaxed against hers. It no longer felt creepy so much as it felt dead. He was drowning in doubt, knowing now there were more ways this stalemate could end than there were heartbeats left in his life. And most did not end in his favor.

Until this moment she had never dared to believe she could hold any power over Primm. He had always made her feel a shrinking little girl— weak, defenseless, frozen in her own fear. But now something that had always been hidden to her became brightly obvious: his power was really hers. He'd stolen it from her long ago before she knew it was hers to lose, and he had lorded it over her ever since.

And now she wanted it back.

It was then she felt something she had not felt since she was a teenager except in fleeting pulses so elusive they strained her lingering hopes. It was Silas, her twin; the other half of her, so long dormant there was no more than the breath of a hope that she would ever feel him again. But she did...

The mental glacier in which his body's consciousness had been so long entombed was starting to melt. Rivulets of sensation flowed through the icy cracks now forming in the glacier's frigid mass, invading Silas' private world with pulsing waves of awareness. He felt the full warmth of flesh for the first time in an eternity, and as the sensation seeped through his veins igniting awareness in every cell of his body, he knew he was again becoming a flesh and blood human.

It was a realization both terrible and wonderful. For what felt like eons he had been free of all sensations associated with corporeal existence; what he thought of with no small disdain as the heavy world. He had been joined to his body much as a shadow; unable to enter and seize control, unable to abandon his flesh and explore the wonders of the infinite. But his peculiar bondage to a marginally responsive protoplasmic machine stuck on idle had not been without compensation. He was comfortable in his private realm where matter could not intrude and time was exposed as the illusion it truly was. He had not been living in a vacuum or a cloud, but in a world rich with detail where colors unknown to the boy he'd once been tinted forests and streams and an endless sky, where storms raged and winds howled across a landscape filled with vibrant life of every imaginable form. He had spent all these many years in the midst of an exquisite ever-changing microcosm crafted to guard him from all manner of harm, while filling him with wonder and awe.

And knowledge far beyond the understanding of the young man he once was.

But now he was drifting out of his solitary domain to once again identify himself in the heavy world as the human, Silas. Older now, he knew; much older than the boy of seventeen he vaguely remembered. He would be alone, except for the one who had cared for his damaged body during the years he was unable to. Her voice had been an enduring comfort across the chasm; he had taken into his world the words—the hundreds and the thousands of words—she gave to him each day and from them he'd built a landscape unique in creation, more tangible to him than any world of matter, where the young spirit learned and matured, and nurtured the knowledge that one day he would be called back into the body of Silas.

The warmth of Silas' body slowly enveloped him and pulled his consciousness away from the comfort of his sanctuary. After a moment of hesitation he let go and drifted with the tide that flowed between the two worlds, letting the warm waves wash him toward that distant, unfamiliar shore.

The original brain lesions the body had suffered in battle had healed, leaving a mass of scar tissue around which the nearby neurons had slowly and steadily constructed new pathways for the conduction of electrical energy and the unimpeded flow of nerve impulses. As the damaged brain healed itself, it began sending brief, succinct messages through all the tissues of the body, commanding the muscles to slowly and rhythmically contract—one, two, three cells at a time—and then relax...contract and relax...contract and relax. It had become the music of the body, a quintillion-part harmony that had slowly transformed soft, flaccid, flesh back into toned muscle, readying the body to welcome Silas, as he readied himself to return home after his long and fruitful wanderings.

It was not an easy thing, to occupy flesh that had been largely deprived of activity for so long, and Silas could only enter by slight degrees before the cloying heaviness overwhelmed him and he had to retreat. But like waves on a rising tide, each time he penetrated deeper before receding back into the world of lightness.

It was only a matter of time.

There was a force behind him like a gentle but persistent breeze, coaxing him to rejoin with the body of Silas. It was his sister, eager to see him in the flesh again, drawing him back into the heavy world.

And what would that world be like? It was difficult after such a long absence to separate memories from dreams. There would pain, of this he was certain, but also joy, and love, and desires that could not be easily sated. Desires, yes. And what did he desire most? To look into the eyes of the one who shared his blood, whose spirit had been tightly entwined with his from the moment of birth. Of all the things of the heavy world he missed very few, and of those he only truly longed for one.

His sister. Jennifer. Who now called to him urgently from across the great chasm that had after an eternity begun to close...

Silas was awake.

Primm felt it too. His eyes lit lively with disbelief *(fear; it's fear, stark and beautiful)* and he jerked his hands free from hers only to find them ensnared by Silas's. He tried to pull back but could not, and when Silas opened his eyes and drew Prygor close to him, he quit trying.

Primm was mesmerized by Silas' eyes, which had gone from murky gray to brilliant blue. He was immersed in fear and confusion and Jennifer hoped to see him drown.

Bring it home Silas. Finish it.

With all the will she could muster she joined with Silas to bring an end to Primm's long reign of terror, watching in fascination as Primm's dark eyes became smoldering coals as her energy united with her brother's to make Primm's body convulse.

How easy to end it now. How very, very easy.

Together they could rip Primm's mind free of its moorings and set it adrift where time and place no longer had meaning and self was an untenable concept.

But then Primm, shaking and sweating, wailed, "Please, Silas! Oh God, please!"

Jennifer was now intoxicated by the release of nearly two decades of fear and vexation. She was not of a charitable mind and would have been content to see Primm driven to the edge of madness (*and then pushed into the abyss, by god*). But Silas did not share with equal intensity his sister's long-held desire for retribution. And because he understood all too well the crushing loneliness of living with a damaged mind he could not bring himself to continue against Primm's cries for mercy.

Besides, fate yet had pathways to set before the sheriff and however tangled those pathways might be, Prygor Primm could prove unwittingly useful in the days ahead.

He closed his eyes and let go of Prygor Primm's hands.

Like a man who had been held under water until his lungs were near bursting, Primm collapsed in his chair and drew quick, deep breaths while his eyes tried and failed to draw the room back into focus. He reached for Silas' hands—perhaps in gratitude—then thought better.

At length, he shook his head and fixed his still-cloudy gaze first on Silas, then on Jennifer. The dark power was gone from his eyes, replaced by utter confusion. Abruptly he rose from his chair, knocking it over backwards, and disappeared into the windy night.

12

Meeting Silas

When a man lives for as many years as I have it is likely that he will end up doing many things for which he is neither proud nor reasonably justified. And if he has not, he is not to be counted among my friends. I do not like such "good" men, nor do I trust them. But the Turning made many of them; many who doubtless ascended to saintly status by virtue of their charity. But for every new saint there were made ten new demons. As for my part, I must surely include myself in the majority, although it is curiously true that saints and demons cannot always be told apart by their deeds...

FROM THE UNPUBLISHED MEMOIRS OF CARLOS HERRERA

Jack was dreaming hard when Jennifer rousted him in his bed; had in fact been dreaming of her. It might have been a real humdinger of a dream, the kind you remember fondly for weeks and months afterward. It certainly had all the basic ingredients: a grassy stream bank beneath a somnolent weeping willow tree, a soft cotton blanket, and a bottle of genuine French Bordeaux from before the Turning. But this dream, unfortunately, had gotten twisted in the way dreams often do when something enormously pleasurable is just about to happen. The unwelcome twist had arrived, fittingly enough in the form of Deborah. She had begun to lecture Jack about the sin of fornication, a lecture Jack thought impeccably disingenuous, owing to the circumstance of Deborah herself being naked as a newborn mouse. (He had always liked to see her that way, particularly when she enhanced the visual experience with a suggestive smile. For all her faults, she remained to the end a fine example of womanly splendor.) He was about to point out the inconsistency (and mention in the by that she'd packed on a couple of pounds since he last saw her *au naturel)* when he felt Jennifer tugging on his shoulder.

"Jack, wake up! Something strange and wonderful has happened!" He agreed with the strange part; seeing Deborah so seductively exposed while Jack wooed another woman was indeed strange. But wonderful? Then he recognized the logical conundrum of being awakened by the same woman he was dreaming about. He opened his eyes and pulled himself upright when he saw the pleading look on Jennifer's face.

"What's up?" he croaked. The first few rays of morning sunlight shone through the clerestory windows to east, casting her delicate features into brilliant relief. It made him wish he could finish his dream, here and now, sans Deborah and her sanctimonious commentary.

"It's Silas, my brother," she said, a tone of urgency invading her voice. "He's come back to the world."

Jack was about to ask where else he might be when he remembered she had said that he'd suffered some sort of head wound in the war. What was it she said? *He moves between existential planes, never resting for more than a moment on this one.* Or something like that. He thought it a very odd way to describe someone missing a few cogs in his mental machinery, but then, there was a lot about Jennifer that he found odd

in a compelling sort of way.

Jack said, "I thought he was...incapacitated. Permanently."

"We all did. But now...well, you've got to come see him. He mentioned your name. I think he'd like to meet you."

That got Jack's attention. "Me? How would he even know I exist?"

"I'm sure I told him about you, though with Silas I was never sure if I was getting through to him or not. But he's always known things beyond... well, beyond what the rest of us would consider his ability to know."

Must run in the family, Jack concluded.

"So? Are you coming?"

He said, "Mind if I get dressed first?"

"Oh....Sorry." Jennifer flushed with embarrassment, then turned her back and held her hands to her eyes in an overdone gesture that Jack dismissed as nerves.

He eased himself out of bed, feeling the lingering effects of his first horseback ride in years. His crotch and the insides of his thighs felt like he'd had a rodeo with a humpback whale. A particularly rank one. But after a few abortive attempts he managed to slip on his socks and jeans and stand on two feet. *Just need to move a little, that's all,* he reassured himself. He fished around in a duffel bag where he found a T-shirt—one that didn't smell any worse than he did—and slipped it over his head. Then he hobbled over to Jennifer *(feeling better with every step, yessiree)* and pulled her hands away from her face. "So what happened? Why the sudden change in his condition?"

She took her time answering. "I don't know, really." A long pause, during which she looked at him only fleetingly. "He was gone from his bed when I got up this morning." Another pause. "I found him in his chair in the living room. It was a move he never would have attempted by himself...before. His eyes are bright and...well, he's back. I don't know how else to say it."

He was happy for her, but it was obvious that she was holding something back. There was a nervousness about her; a taut furtiveness he found unsettling.

She's spooked. There's no other explanation.

"What is it, Jen? What's the matter?"

"Just come with me."

He gingerly followed her down the stairs, pausing at the door to slip his feet into his boots before ambling across the yard and down the path to Jennifer's house. Jazzman trotted briskly in front until he met up with an expectant Sasha. After a couple of shared and jubilant spins that translated into "Good morning. How nice to see you!" they were off nosing in the undergrowth.

Jennifer's house was much smaller than his. It had the cozy feel of a stone cottage tucked deeply away in the woods. (Which, he supposed, is what it was, except that it could be reached by road instead of a long winding footpath through an enchanted forest, and this spoiled the warm illusion of being in the fifteenth century). Wind chimes too delicate to endure the often savage winds hung just inside each of the main room's three windows. A bookshelf on the far wall held a few old photos, assorted knickknacks, and several volumes of old, leather-bound books. The faint smell of incense permeated the air, mixing with the food odors—*she seems to use a lot of herbs,* he thought absentmindedly—that so easily accumulate in a small space. There was another odor, as well; the sickly, sour odor that issues from the lungs of someone in the grips of a lingering illness. It explained the incense.

Tay was already there, sitting in a wooden chair. He was facing a worn recliner where sat a gaunt man with long light-brown hair and a day's growth of beard. In addition to the knife Tay wore on his belt, Jack spied, beneath the open shirt, a shoulder holster with a large caliber pistol strapped under his left armpit. It wasn't unusual for men outside the islands to carry weapons. Many carried small boot guns, or simply stuffed their irons inside their belts. Tay's shoulder holster, however, had a businesslike efficiency to it.

The man Tay was talking to sat drinking tea from a bright ceramic mug and mumbling something below Jack's range of hearing. A fresh bandage had been applied to his left wrist.

Tay looked up and smiled perfunctorily at Jack. Then Silas turned his head. "Jack Vara," he said in a steady, friendly voice, "How was your trip? Any trouble along the way?"

"Not really; except for the stretch of dirt and asphalt that used to be the road between here and the Denver island," Jack answered. This brought a smile to Silas's face. The similarity between Silas and Jennifer was immediately apparent. Same delicate features; same striking blue eyes. The main difference was that Silas's face looked as though it had just been thawed after an extended freeze, allowing the blood to finally circulate again. It was happening fast. His skin grew rosier even as Jack studied him in the momentary silence. Jack wasn't a doctor, but he surmised that what he was seeing was probably not normal.

Silas asked, "You've met everyone, then? Tay? And Luke and Catalyn? And Cassie? Now *there's* a girl with talent."

"No argument here," Jack agreed.

"I look forward to getting to know them all," he went on, "or rather, letting them get to know me. I can't even begin to tell you how frustrating it was to persist in a condition where information only traveled one way. It was like communicating through a rogue computer that changed its algorithms from one minute to the next." Silas gave a little chuckle and shook his head. "I never knew what was going to come out."

Jack found this interesting. He said, "But you always knew what was going on around you?"

"When I wasn't otherwise occupied." His eyes brightened and with a smile that almost seemed cunning, he said "It's a big old world out there, Jack. Bigger than all of our dreams and fantasies."

You'd be the one to know, Jack thought.

In the lull that followed, Tay turned to Jennifer and narrowed his eyes. With a mirthless smile, he said, "Your brother was just telling me that that *pendejo* Prygor Primm was here last night, *muchacha*. Care to tell me about it?"

Jennifer suddenly froze, like she'd been immersed in liquid nitrogen and painted up to look warm and alive. Jack and Tay both stared at her as if witnessing something entirely unnatural, which only served to make matters worse. Then her mouth flew open. "Oh, shit, Silas!" she exclaimed. "Did you have to tell him *that*?"

Silas sat up straight and turned to face his sister. The flesh of his face seemed to grow more firm even as Jack watched. With unmistakable tenderness, he said, "Sorry, Jen. But you have to tell them. No good can come from keeping it to yourself any longer." When she began to protest, he held up his hand and said, "Please? Let's get this out of the way. There's a lot that needs to be said, and quickly."

Hearing this, Tay rolled his hand in an impatient motion that said *out with it*. Having no idea what was going on, Jack crossed his arms and watched with interest.

Jennifer took a deep breath. The trepidation she felt was tempered with relief. Finally she could tell it all. Tay, of course, knew what Carlos had known—had, in fact, wanted to kill Primm himself, until Carlos decided on his own to beat him to a pulp—but no one but Primm himself (and perhaps Silas, who seemed to know all sorts of things he shouldn't), knew what Jennifer now revealed.

Wordlessly, she went to the kitchen and fixed them each a mug of tea lightly sweetened with honey, then sat on the overstuffed loveseat across from Silas. Jack eased down beside her. Tay pulled his chair back to a vantage point from which he could watch the three of them.

For Jack's benefit, she began with the death of Kip Moran (leaving out the lovemaking part) and her certainness that Primm was responsible; Carlos's brutal attack, and Primm's threat a few night later as he waved a razor in front of her face. It was a painful history that awakened all of her senses to the pain she'd hoped to forget. And yes, the pleasure too, for to gaze into Kip's dead eyes was also to glimpse the moment before his death to see her lover's laughing face and feel his hands upon her body.

Without giving his name—which in any case she'd forgotten—she told the story of her second brief love affair and the horrific end to which it had come, and Primm's numerous (*countless*) visits to her house under the cloak of darkness to ensure that she would never again be so foolish as to take another lover.

She tried not to cry—told herself she wouldn't—but the harder she tried to hold the tears back the more they flowed. Jack put a reassuring hand on the back of her neck which she acknowledged with a sniffle and weak smile that broke around the edges.

Silas rocked slowly in his chair—sometimes gazing at her, sometimes looking back into the netherworld from which he'd just escaped—nodding often while gripping and releasing the threadbare arms of the chair with his long, delicate fingers, much like a cat sharpening its claws.

Tay sat with his legs crossed, tapping the butt of his revolver with the fingers of his right hand.

Jennifer concluded her tale with the events of the previous night. The telling seemed to have taken hours, though by the clock on the wall behind Tay's head it had scarcely consumed twenty minutes. She was exhausted in every way it was possible to be exhausted. Her hands trembled so she held them together in her lap in hopes that no one would notice. A sigh of relief left her lungs when she was through, but to hear it all laid out for the first time in her own voice, it seemed ludicrous that anyone would endure that kind of abuse for so long. She was ashamed of her weakness, as she had been every moment for the past seventeen years, but at least now she knew her shame would, like her memories of Prygor Primm and his repeated misdeeds, begin to lose their sharp edges.

Tay's reaction was predictable—"For your own safety, I will have to kill him," he announced with a simple finality—though certainly not what she had hoped for.

And Jack was hardly helpful when he replied, "Sounds like fun. Mind if I tag along?" This coaxed a reflexive laugh out of Tay and broke the ice, if only a little. But Jack didn't know Tay; didn't know what the man was capable of. She did. She had loved Tay like a protective uncle most of her life, but she was still wary of him. People who caused trouble for Tay or any of the *malagente* always ended up regretting it; some more than others. It was the reason she had never told him of Primm's not infrequent visits. Carlos had made Tay his confidante for a very good reason, and it wasn't because he was a brilliant conversationalist. Tay *would* kill Primm, and soon, unless she found a way to talk him out of it.

Jennifer spoke before Tay could think any further on his threat. She rose while he was still sitting and put a hand on his shoulder, knowing if she could touch him he would be more likely to listen to reason. "You can't Tay. Really, you can't. And this is hard for me to say, because I've wanted him dead for a very long time. But you can't kill Primm while he's under the protection of Sturm Baker and Desa. You...we...have to leave him alone—for now, at least. Otherwise things might get real complicated real fast."

Tay covered her hand with a steely paw and gave her a reassuring smile. "People have accidents every day, *muchacha. Así es la vida.*"

Jennifer shook her head. "Not Primm. He's too careful. I doubt the man's ever stubbed his toe."

From the loveseat Jack said, "Sounds to me like he's long overdue," and only shrugged *what'd I say?* when Jennifer speared him with an icy glare.

Silas listened to every word. Vara was an interesting man; he liked him and looked forward to getting to know him, along with the other members in this curious confederacy they called the *malagente.*

Tay was the immediate concern. He didn't know what was at stake. Prygor Primm was not the problem. He was the little insect that heralds the arrival of the big smelly beast. If Tay were to swat him he would not be mourned; but he would be missed, and this early in the game that could be troublesome.

Silas raised his hand, something he could have done only with tremendous effort before. "Listen," he said with a voice so strong it surprised him.

They all three looked at him, Tay most intently. It felt good to command attention without drooling, farting, or mumbling syntactically butchered phrases. He would enjoy rejoining this brotherhood of man after being apart from it for so long; enjoy partaking of the many pleasures to be found in the physical world.

But first things first.

Though no one knew it, they were all in danger because of a certain body of knowledge Carlos Herrera had—unbeknownst even to Jennifer—crudely but effectively implanted in Silas's formerly damaged mind. It was knowledge Carlos knew would lay dormant and undiscovered, but not lost. But might, if Fate desired it, be allowed to come to the fore.

As it now had.

A delicate balance had been jarred akimbo by his awakening, and there was no way in Heaven or Earth to set it back the way it had been. Knowledge could not be unlearned, nor could memories be willfully forgotten. How much of this dangerous knowledge could he share with his compatriots? Enough to get their attention, certainly; enough to prepare them for action.

But not a word more.

He turned to his sister and asked, "Do you know the name 'Salia'?" It was a name that had come to him repeatedly as he emerged from his cocoon, and he recognized it in association with things Carlos had told him—things planted in his idling brain and seized by his roaming spirit—not long before the old man died.

Jennifer tensed, as if shocked. She said, "Salia Warchez. She's the leader of the Poxes...the Apocalyptic Warriors...a religious sect hell bent on bringing about the end of the world. She's been a fugitive for years, but it only strengthens her mystique."

Jack added, "She pops up from time to time—no one ever knows when or where—and preaches to her flock. Then she disappears. You can imagine the kind of modern myths and legends *that* creates. Drives the military completely bugshit, which of course works in her favor. Thanks to their bungling incompetence she's been elevated to a status somewhere between plain old run-of-the-mill supernatural being and goddess. But she's an electrifying orator, I'll give her that. She certainly reeled in the former Mrs. Vara, presently one of the hopelessly deluded. And happy as a maggot on the corpus of humanity because of it, I might add."

Silas considered this, then said, "Do you know her, Jack? Have you had many...encounters...with her?"

"Encounters? Well, I've never shagged the bitch, if that's what you're getting at."

Tay snickered, then broke into laughter. Jennifer joined in after a futile attempt to keep a straight face.

"Shag?" Silas answered, perplexed.

Jennifer bumped Jack with her shoulder, saying, "Never mind, Silas. Jack is just being cute. And crude."

Silas smiled broadly and it felt heavenly. He wished that he, too, could be cute and crude, but it had been some time since he had and he suspected it was something he would have to work into. He let the unpracticed smile fade as gracefully as he could and returned to the inquiry. "I'll rephrase the question: have you met her?"

Jack shook his head. "Not personally. But I saw her speak, once."

Silas thought this interesting. "Go on, please," he prompted.

Jack recalled the encounter clearly; it wasn't something he could easily forget. It was a Saturday in the late spring of '36; the day his life changed in a fundamental way. The wildflowers in the reclaimed landscape east of the Bay island grew in thick patches, their delicate sweet scent mingling with a salty ocean breeze. It went right to his brain, filling Jack's head with crazy ideas of love and romance. And why not? He and Deborah were still young and strongly attracted to each other in the most natural and primal of ways. Who was to stop them from enjoying a little roll amidst the bluebells and the periwinkle?

But Deborah's suggestion of an afternoon in the countryside, a long walk in the fresh air beyond the busy island was not for the reasons Jack had hoped. His wife wasn't thinking of a tryst in the tulips or even a heart-to-heart in the heather. Her mind was on salvation, though what she needed saving *from* was something Jack had never been able to comprehend.

Whatever her reasoning (if indeed reason had any part in it), they were hardly alone for long. As if from out of thin air, others soon appeared. Even now he didn't know where they could all have come from. Perhaps the abandoned suburbs that appeared on the horizon beyond the three-mile island perimeter. These were the former homes and businesses of many of the two-point-six million Bay-area residents (give or take a hundred thousand) who had perished during the War of the Turning.

These were stripped, rendered, and razed edifices, slowly being reclaimed by nature and currently home to multitudes of mice and rats and the snakes that feed on them, as well as thriving populations of birds and bats. Coyotes, wolves and feral dogs roamed in packs, sometimes interbreeding to create fearsome canine creatures no god would ever take credit for.

Wherever the people came from—young and old, though mostly young; well-dressed or crudely clad, many in simple white robes; black skin, white skin and every shade in between—their numbers silently swelled into the hundreds. Deborah graced him with a smile—half of one, anyway, and from what seemed a great distance—then took his hand and held it tightly *(to keep me from bolting)*, and he remembered the serene *(empty)* expression on her face, on everyone's faces, as the gathering congregation sloughed wordlessly through the verdant meadows and packed tighter and tighter toward a central point that was, in no way Jack could discern, the slightest bit different from any other point of geography in the engagingly pastoral setting that lay conspicuously placid between the decay of the old world and the spit-shine of the new.

The crowd—*the multitude,* Jack though wryly, as the gathering had taken on a disturbingly biblical aspect—had formed itself into concentric circles with a large hole in the center, perhaps fifty feet across. He turned to Deborah for an explanation, but he saw, beneath a heavenly blue sky against a backdrop so perfect (for romance; for retying loose knots and rekindling feelings lost along the way) that his wife no longer had eyes for him. She, like all the others, stared sightlessly into a naked hole in a mass of humanity.

And even then he didn't know what the gathering was all about. How stupid could he be?

He gently but insistently turned her head to face him. She smiled that distant smile and caressed his face in the pitying way a woman does when she's preparing to say *I still love you, Jack, but not much and not for long.* But she said not a word. Nor did she need to. She just turned back to face the empty clearing, engulfed by a serenity as unnatural as it was complete. Jack let go her hand and watched it fall to her side, like a dead and broken limb with all the nerve impulses severed. He turned and began making his way out through the crowd.

Then he heard the chanting. Faint at first, little more than a collective breath, but growing louder. Deborah was in the front circle—by chance? Somehow he didn't think so—and he had made it but three or four layers back when he was able to discern what they were chanting.

It was "Salia; Salia..."

Back still turned, he had visions of Roman plebeians in the Coliseum, drunk on cheap wine, chanting for their favorite gladiator until their throats turned raw. But this bunch had not gathered for something so earthy as pagan entertainment. He turned and noticed a man whose eyes were milky with blindness, but moving in their sockets as though everything before him were as vivid as a child's dream.

Then *she* appeared in the clearing. Out of nothingness. One second empty space, the next second...Salia Warchez, in the flesh.

"Interesting..." Silas replied, gazing out the window for a long, pensive moment. "And you're certain she didn't just walk out of the crowd? There were, as you said, several rows of people in front of you."

Jack shrugged. "It's possible, I suppose. She might have been out of my line of sight for a second or two. But it's not the way I remember it."

It wasn't the way he remembered it at all. Mostly because—and this was shallow and hard to admit—she was so stunningly beautiful. His eyes would have been drawn to her like a ship to a maelstrom had she merely walked out of the crowd.

Silas stood and began to teeter as he did. Tay sprang out his chair and grabbed him by the elbow even before Jennifer had a chance to gasp. He patted Tay's hand and thanked him. "Just get me a walking stick. It's time to start using these things again," he said, looking down at his legs as if they were rusty parts on a strange conveyance he'd never operated before. Tay grabbed a gnarled cedar walking stick by the door and offered it to Silas. Using the stick for balance, he took one step, then another. Tay followed him closely, hands outstretched without actually touching. Jennifer rose from the loveseat and took her brother's free hand. He smiled up at her and said, "I think I may be wanting my mobility before long. I'd better get in some practice." She helped him for a few ponderous paces before letting go, then watched with a sister's pride as Silas took his first unassisted steps in nearly two decades. Tay remained standing for a moment or two, then sat back down. The speed with which Silas had evolved from tottering invalid to stiff-but-ambulatory pedestrian was remarkable.

Perhaps even a little disturbing.

Who the hell is this guy? No sooner had the thought danced through his mind than Silas, his back turned as he shuffled his slippered feet in the direction of the kitchen, let go a short laugh and turned slowly to face Jack. He was wearing the wry smile that might spread across an old man's face when he's about to teach a young whippersnapper a thing or two about life.

"You answer my questions first, Jack, and then I'll try to answer yours," Silas stated with an undertone of authority. Jack had to remind himself that Silas was Jennifer's twin brother and at least seven years his junior.

"Ask," Jack sighed.

"You said she was beautiful..."

"Yes," he answered, though beautiful was an inadequate word. Salia Warchez was a five-star drop-dead knockout.

Seeming amused, Jennifer asked, "What color were her eyes, Jack?"

"I don't recall."

"Her hair?"

"Blonde. I'm pretty sure she was light blonde." Yet even though he thought he had a clear picture of her in his mind, he couldn't swear to her hair color.

She pondered this answer for a few seconds before asking, "Was she dark skinned, or light?"

"Light. Definitely light." *I think.*

"Hmmm...," Jennifer murmured, then said, "Would you like to know the facts about this woman?"

"Sure; let's hear it."

As if reading from a note card, Jennifer began, "Salia Warchez was born in a small village outside Kutno, Poland, on March 15, 2000. Her father, Isaiah, was an American-born Pentecostal Baptist minister of Czech ancestry, doing missionary work in Poland at the time. Her mother, who died in childbirth, was a Mexican-born peasant woman originally from Chihuahua. Distraught by her death, Isaiah joined up with a radical end-of-the-world sect that he eventually came to lead. Under his fervent direction, the small sect grew into The Church of Jesus Christ in the Ultimate Days. Isaiah and Salia emigrated back stateside nine years before the beginning of the Turning. She was a dangerously gifted eight-year-old at the time."

Jack said, "How—"

Jennifer held up a hand to silence him. "The thing is, Jack, by most reports her hair is black as midnight and, as you might imagine from her ancestry, her skin is light brown. You saw what you wanted to see. Or maybe she showed herself as you wanted to see her." When he began to ask what the point was, Jennifer grinned smugly and answered, "You obviously have a penchant for fair-skinned blondes. She wanted to appear desirable to you."

"How do you know so much about her?" he asked.

Jennifer glanced first at Tay then Silas. "Carlos somehow came into possession of Isaiah Warchez's diary. He never told me where or how he got hold of it, and I've never seen it, if in fact it still exists. But a few days before he died he began telling me things about her past; made me memorize them as if they were important."

"But *why*?" Jack asked, truly bewildered.

"That, my dear, is the question of questions. Carlos became more and more concerned about Salia Warchez with each passing day. On the morning before his death he told me we should expect 'a visit,' as he put it. We're still waiting...and hoping Carlos was wrong."

Jack glanced at Tay, who sat expressionless, then to Silas, who said, "Come and walk with me, Jack."

Without argument—the room had suddenly grown small—Jack followed Silas through the kitchen, out the back door, and into a greenhouse that was at least twice the size of the house itself. The morning sun shone obliquely through tempered glass, illuminating a colorful abundance of life. It was like stepping into the proverbial Garden. "Good lord," was all Jack could manage to say, and it loosened a chuckle in Silas's throat.

He said, "This is where my sister grows the things that make eating a pleasure, apart from the matter of subsistence, which is, of course, provided by the vegetable gardens beyond."

Jack let his eyes roam over the wealth of vegetation he saw before him. Conspicuous were the tropical fruit trees, upon whose verdant branches hung plump oranges, mangos and papayas. Well-manicured bushes grew between them, bright red berries growing in clumps among the dark green leaves. Coffee? Had to be. Elsewhere vines crept along trellises, heavy with red, green and black grapes. Raspberries. Strawberries. Blueberries. Herbs he didn't recognize.

Behind his back he heard Silas say, "There is nothing difficult about living in the world, Jack. It's living with each other that we can't seem to figure out."

Holding a clump of grapes in his hand, he answered, "It's always been that way, Silas."

Silas shuffled up beside him and leaned on his walking stick. He looked tired, but not so tired that he was through with their chat. He was just warming up. "The Turning was our chance. Maybe our last chance, Jack. If we can't learn from that, then we can't learn anything."

Jack said nothing, so Silas continued. "The last time I was as much a part of this world as I am now I was a very young man, hunkered down behind a makeshift barricade in the middle of Purgatory's main street with a bolt-action thirty-aught-six in my hands. I was hungry and freezing. I had just killed a man and I was feeling pretty damn good about it. He wasn't my first, either. I'd gotten others; others who'd killed people I knew as friends. It was hard to blame them, of course. Most of the people we were fighting were living on things a billy goat wouldn't eat. But to feed them was out of the question. We had no food to give them; just enough for ourselves—those of us from in and around Purgatory who'd come to defend the town and its stores of grain. It was kill or be killed; there was no middle ground."

The story was not new. Practically anyone who had lived through the Turning had a similar one to tell, Jack included. When the decent folks in and around Berkeley were told by roving military patrols to park their vehicles and wait for assistance, everyone knew it was a lie; there would be no assistance. The looting began almost at once and continued until every store shelf was empty. Dozens lay dead and dying in the streets, shot, stabbed or bludgeoned. It was only the beginning, but even the elderly turned vicious at the thought of running out of prescription drugs, and new mothers fought like rabid badgers to secure enough diapers and baby food to see them through the bad times they must have known would not soon end. The memory that lingered longest and most poignantly in Jack's mind was the almost comical sight of a frail old man with patches of wispy gray hair on his liver-spotted head. He had fallen dead in the street, apparently from a heart attack, while running from a ransacked pharmacy. His dead hands were clutching a dozen tubes of denture adhesive.

After the initial looting, it only got worse.

In the end, the ones who survived were from rural communities that had the good judgment to band together and fight to the death to defend their collective food reserves. And, of course, those the military thought worthy of protection. These were promising young men and women with the organizational and technical skills it would take to rebuild civilization, piece by piece, once the conflict—which the military merely monitored, since it had horded all the fuel and most of the food to ensure its own survival—was over and balance had been restored.

Jack had been selected as one of those. He said, "You were going to make a point?"

Silas walked on a little more, the sound of his footfalls on the stone pathway growing clearer and more distinct with each step. Jack could almost feel Silas's strength returning, flowing through him like a river now; a river that had begun as a trickle in some distant, unrecognized outpost of his recently mended mind. *Of his spirit, Jack; it always begins with the spirit,* he heard Jennifer say inside his head. Was it peculiar? In every sense of word, yes, it was. Peculiar that a man could return to the waking world with such focus after so many years in a semi-comatose state. Peculiar that he would perceive the Turning—the very vehicle that had brought him to the brink of ruin—as mankind's last great chance.

Most peculiar of all, Jack realized he agreed with him.

At length Silas said, "Each man knew where he stood in those days. There were no longer any contrived cultural conventions to hide behind. Whether a man lived or died, he knew the reason."

"Doesn't it irk you that the Turning was an act of terrorism?" Jack asked.

"In all likelihood perpetrated by Salia Warchez's predecessors? It certainly adds to the irony of it. But of course they got caught up in the anarchy, just like everyone else—"

"—Which can only mean that something went terribly wrong with their plans," Jack concluded.

"Ah!" Silas said holding up a finger, "but was the problem an act of God, or did the devil have *his* thumb on the scale?"

Jack thought *why do I think you already know the answer to that one? And a hell of a lot more.* He said, "Got any devils in mind?"

"Perhaps."

Jack liked this man of secrets. He'd spent the better part of two decades observing the world from beyond humanity, looking in. It was a perspective that would make any philosopher drool. Jack said, "Don't you want to know what Salia Warchez was preaching the day I saw her?"

Silas winced. "Why would I? Would you drink poison out of curiosity?"

While Jack pondered a witty comeback, Silas broke into his thoughts. "Listen, Jack. We can discuss Salia's particular brand of fanaticism some other time. It's a tool she uses to accomplish her ends. Whether or not she actually believes what she preaches is another matter entirely. But Salia the woman goes far deeper than that, and that is the immediate problem for all of us—you, me, and the *malagente.*"

A vague picture was forming in Jack's mind. "Does this have something do with my father? Something he did. Or knew?"

"Right on both counts," Silas answered.

"Really pissed her off, huh?"

Silas nodded somberly. "And then rubbed her face in it."

Jack couldn't hold back a *that's-my-old-man* chuckle. Again it made him wish he could have met Carlos; at least once. But Silas wasn't laughing. He said, "Jack, I hope I can make you understand the danger we are all in here. I didn't just *happen* to rejoin the world the same day you showed up from California. Things don't work that way."

"You *timed* your awakening...your comeback...to my arrival?" Jack asked, incredulously.

"Partially; at least I feel it was of my own volition. It was certainly what I wanted, in any case. But I was also pushed, and that disturbs me."

Jack was confused, again, and it was getting wearisome. He exhaled loudly and said, "Silas, what in God's name are you talking about?"

"If I could tell you, I would. Believe me. But for now, the less you know the better. All I can say is that I have to go away, and I need you to look after my sister until I return."

The request was agreeable enough, but still he asked, "Why me? Why not Tay? Why wait for me to show up on your doorstep?"

Silas graced him with a look he could almost interpret as fatherly. "Tay is a good man, Jack. He has many talents, but providing comfort to the distressed is not one of them. It's better that he continues doing what he does best: keeping his ear to ground and preparing for the worst."

"And where are you going?" Jack asked, far from convinced that Silas was strong enough to go anywhere.

"Away. To where no one would ever think to look for me. And I'd appreciate it if you'd keep this conversation to yourself until after I'm gone."

"Of course, whatever you want. But do you really think you're up for a journey? I mean, sure you're getting better; even as I watch you you're getting better, but... "

Silas raised his free hand and Jack fell silent. "I'll be alright. I have to be." He inched closer to Jack and met his eyes. "I wish I could stress the importance of what I think is about to unfold, Jack. It's bigger than all of us."

"But you still can't tell me?"

"I'll tell you this," he said evenly. "Salia Warchez knows you, Jack Vara, and she is on her way here as we speak. My guess is she intends to get to know you a whole lot better."

He felt gooseflesh rising along his arms and up the back of his neck. Of all the people in the world he had no desire to ever see again, the name Salia Warchez was emblazoned at the top of the list. "Me? Why me?"

Silas put a white hand on his shoulder and said confidentially, "Like you said, Jack, something went terribly wrong for her father and his accomplices at the Turning. My guess is she thinks you can help set it straight. But it's not just you. For better or worse, we'll all have a part to play before it's over. She needs us."

Silas strode down the narrow path that bisected the greenery, toward a row of trees from which hung plump, succulent oranges. He paused for a moment, examining the bright fruit as if it were the embodiment of a miracle. Over his shoulder, he asked, "By the way, Jack...do you even remember what she said to you?"

Strangely, he did not.

13

Breakfast in Loray

Nothing ever happens in isolation. For every possible event there is a multitude of related events, all fated to converge at a specific time and place. We scientists always tell people it is pure chance—a roll of the dice—while the religious faithful insist everything happens by God's will alone. But God wills nothing more than he has to, and the notion of chance is merely a reflection of our lack of understanding. The world only begins to make sense when we acknowledge that it, and everything in it, possesses both purpose and consciousness...

EXCERPT FROM A SPEECH DELIVERED BY DR. JACK VARA
TO THE RANDALL RESEARCH INSTITUTE, JULY 14, 2037

"You don't eat much, do you?" Tharp asked. The question was posed between Tharp chewing a mouthful of fried potatoes and Tharp stuffing his mouth with a forkful of runny egg. They'd had this conversation before, and Salia didn't care to have it again. She would almost rather go hungry than to break bread with this man, who ate each meal as if there might not be another for days, a prospect he was always quick to point out whenever he felt a need to justify his enormous appetite. To his credit, there was hardly an ounce of fat on his dense, rugged frame and she could only suppose that what food he didn't burn outright in the course of maintaining his intense metabolism added directly to his already impressive musculature.

Wherever the food went, its consumption was a process she would prefer not to witness. Not when they were alone at a safe house, and certainly not in a public place. And especially not in a rundown, burned-out, dirt town like Loray, Utah—population forty-seven, if you counted the jackrabbits—

where Tharp and Salia sat in a booth with torn vinyl seats and a flaking Formica tabletop beside a smoky, cracked window in a tiny diner with no name. Having no signage, they might have driven right past it had Hadrian, whose life often depended on his unique mastery of local geography, not already known it was here. So here they sat, Hadrian devouring a plateful of protein, carbohydrates and cholesterol glistening with fat and red-chili salsa, while Salia sipped herbal tea and picked at a slice of buttered toast with apple jam, contemplating the very real prospect of better days ahead.

Just ahead...and just in time, she thought.

Ignoring Tharp's question, she looked over the chipped rim of her tea-cup and said, "When will we be in Purgatory?" She was careful to keep the urgency out of her voice. If detected, Hadrian would lord it over her for the rest of the trip. But feigned indifference might not be the best tack right now; she had the feeling that events were unfolding faster than she had anticipated. It made time a more precious resource.

"Tonight. Around dark, maybe. Depends on the roads, and who we have to avoid. Or outrun. Why?" He paused from his meal long enough to toss down a mouthful of chicory coffee. "Something going on I don't know about?"

Salia chuckled mirthlessly. "Hadrian, there is *always* something going on you don't know about. It defines the whole nature of our relationship. I give you sex and hard silver, and you do what you're told without asking too many questions. I would think you'd be used to our little arrangement by now." His broad face grew sullen at the rebuke. It reminded her just how moody her facilitator could be.

"Anyway," she went on, trying now to sooth his bruised pride, "There will likely be some work for you, once we get there. The kind of work you were made for. I'm sure you'll find it rewarding."

The brooding darkness left his face, replaced by a fearsome display of Paleolithic dentition. "Who?" he uttered expectantly.

"I'm not sure yet, Hadrian. Can we get out of here, now?"

She nodded at his empty plate but Hadrian missed the gesture. His eyes had been drawn to something behind her. She knew without turning her head it was the middle-aged man at the counter with the scruffy grey beard and the hard-case eyes. She'd pegged him on the way in as someone who might be trouble, but after a day and night of traveling the back roads with Hadrian Tharp—a man who drove his modified Trans Am like a teenager with a death wish—her nerves were so benumbed that her usually reliable sense of danger had been muted. Hadrian, on the other hand, was a machine. He never grew tired or even weary. Anytime, anywhere, if there was danger lurking, he'd ferret it out and deal with it head on. And invariably to the other person's detriment. It was one of the many reasons she felt safe with Hadrian and able to suffer his annoying ways.

His coal-dark eyes were clear and locked onto the man at the counter. Salia didn't need to turn around to see what Hadrian was seeing. She knew already that the old couple at the back of diner still sat quietly picking at their breakfast, talking in near whispers between themselves. Out of well-serving habit they were paying no attention to the man at the counter. The waitress waited in the kitchen, also avoiding the man at the counter; He looked like trouble and she wanted no part of it. But it didn't stop her from taking a furtive glance through the open doorway every few minutes...first to the man, then to Salia and Hadrian.

The man at the counter lit a pipe. Through the thick veil of rising smoke he turned his head in their direction, but quickly returned his attention to the the cup in front of him when he caught Hadrian's intense gaze.

This person had no friends or allies in this place, or in this town. Whatever his intentions, he would be acting alone. In the end it would make things a lot less messy, both physically and conceptually. Clearly he recognized Salia and was right now dreaming of all the things he could do with the fifty pounds of silver the military was offering for her head.

But she didn't recognize *him* when she walked in the diner and *that* she found unnerving. It could only mean that he had never been part of a gathering, since she was always careful to mark every face. And she never forgot. If he had seen her before—and doubtless he had—he'd been watching from the shadows, something not easy to do.

The thought infuriated her, and caused her to stab Hadrian with an intense glare. "Are you going to deal with this problem, or should I?" she hissed sharply.

For an instant, Hadrian diverted his gaze to Salia, then looked back to the man. "He's got a hog-leg poking out from under his coat. Saw it on the way in. Right now he's probably trying to decide if he should try to take you dead or alive, but he doesn't know what to do about me." A smile tugged at the corners of his mouth. He was savoring the prospect of a confrontation. Fists, guns, knives—it was all one big holiday for Hadrian.

"You're enjoying this," she accused.

"Immensely," he agreed.

Hadrian carried two guns. One tucked in the small of his back, the other nestled in a pocket inside his right boot. Yet his hands were lightly caressing his coffee cup, about as far away from either gun as they could be.

"He might be faster than you think," She said, goading Hadrian. She knew the man at the counter had thought too long on the subject and lost his nerve.

"Maybe. But I doubt it. Anyway, he knows he's been made. I don't think he's got the balls to start anything now." He glanced at her with a cocksure grin. "Not that it matters. Bullets bounce right off you, or so people say."

Salia blew out an exasperated breath. "He'll see us leave, Hadrian. He'll know what direction we're going and that's more than enough knowledge to make him dangerous."

"So I should just gun him down where he sits?" It came out with the detachment of a rhetorical question and did little to improve her mood. But it gave her a wonderful idea. Glaring at Tharp, she slid out of the booth and headed for the man at the counter.

His name was J.R. Feather, and nothing he could have done when he crawled out of his bedroll this morning would have prepared him for what was about to happen. He'd tied his mule to the hitching post outside the diner about an hour after sunup and wandered inside just a few minutes before Salia Warchez and the stocky outlander. J.R. had been in the backcountry for the better part of two months, dipping his gold pan into every promising-looking creek from the Continental Divide to the Utah border, hoping to find enough glitter to justify further exploration and a greater investment in time. But the trip had been a complete waste of time and resources.

It had been the story of his life for twenty years and counting. Ever since he learned the hard way that having all of his wealth (thirteen point seven million, give or take five hundred Gs) tied up in high-end urban condos at the beginning of a civil war was as ill-omened as being heavily leveraged in freezers at the onset of an ice age. He'd been left with the clothes on his back and a pocketful of change. It was an old story and it was told in one form or another by almost everyone who had found themselves alive on the backside of the Turning. But that didn't make it hurt any less. There was an oft-quoted adage: If you were breathing at the end of the War of the Turning, it was only because God wanted you to be. Because, presumably, no one else did. It sounded good to J.R., even hopeful, and for the first year or so he ran it through his mind like a mantra. *God* wants *me to be alive! God* wants *me to be alive!* But after a while he began to wonder *why* God wanted him alive. Eventually he concluded that God wanted him alive just so He could torment him for a few more years before casting him aside.

He was taking his first real breakfast in weeks and wondering if his luck would ever change when a vintage Trans Am pulled in beside his mule. The trail-weary beast didn't so much as grace the pair with a sidelong glance, but J.R. did, once he got a peek of the woman riding shotgun.

Maybe at long last God had had a change of heart.

J.R. knew at once it was the fugitive Warchez woman. He'd caught a glimpse of her two years ago, outside the Reno island where he'd been scavenging through abandoned houses with a metal detector, an enterprise (he now reflected) that beat the socks off of panning stream gravel that had been panned a hundred times already.

Salia Warchez had been standing on a grassy mound a good three hundred yards distant when he spied her through his field glasses. Even then, surrounded by two hundred or more of her adoring followers, all falling over each other to get close to their savior, she looked right at him. Like he was jumping up and down waving a Roman candle in each hand. It almost caused him to pee his pants, what with all the scary stories he'd heard about this woman. Fortunately, he'd been looking at her through a crack in the siding of a roofless ranch-style house, a place he vacated as quickly and as silently as he could without drawing further attention to himself. She couldn't have actually *seen* him.

But he sure got a good look at her.

And now here she sat, Salia Warchez in the flesh, quiet and unsuspecting and worth more hard silver than J.R. could imagine after twenty lean years.

Imagine that.

The man with her was the problem. He'd looked long and hard at J.R. on the way in and hadn't eased up during the thirty minutes he'd been stuffing down food. *He'll be trouble*, J.R. had thought, back when he was still fantasizing on how he might collect the bounty on the Warchez woman.

But he'd since come to two disheartening realizations: one, he didn't have the nerve or the temperament (or for that matter, the luck) to pull this off; certainly not to shoot a woman in the back, and probably not even to make a citizen's arrest. And two, it didn't matter, because the stocky bastard with the hard cold eyes was probably going to kill him anyway.

Shit.

J. R. was silently enumerating all the different ways his death might occur when Salia Warchez sat down on the stool beside him and smiled sweetly. He was almost relieved.

"Hello there," she said, "All alone?"

"You would know," he told her, without actually looking at her. He puffed once more on his pipe and realized his hand was shaking so bad the stem clicked against his teeth. He laid the pipe on the counter and took a sip of bitter chicory coffee. When it dribbled down his chin he gave up all pretensions of nonchalance.

"Listen, Miss—"

She silenced him with a long sensuous finger to his lips. *No names, please,* the finger seemed to say.

She said, "It hasn't been easy for you, has it?" Her voice was like music through satin. Is this the way death came calling—through the voice of an angel?

"No, ma'am. No it hasn't," Her kindness overwhelmed him. He felt like his legs had been kicked out from under him. He wanted to press his head against her shoulder and beg her forgiveness for even thinking about collecting the bounty on her head. Instead he dared to turn his head and meet her eyes.

That's when his life changed forever.

"I didn't see blood coming out his ears. You must be losing your touch."

Salia smiled coldly at Tharp and slid into the passenger seat of the Trans Am. "His was a different fate."

"So...?"

She huffed her impatience at the question, but when it became clear he wasn't going to start the car until she told him, she gazed through the windshield and said "When he leaves here he'll head back to the Rockies. In a small tributary to the Colorado River he will turn over a rock and discover enough gold in the gravel to keep him solvent for many years. On his way home he'll meet a woman. Not young and not beautiful. But she will love him in her own strange and troubled way until he dies."

"That's charitable. Getting soft?"

"Hardly. This one was for Anna."

"Anna?" he said. "Who the hell is Anna?"

"Never mind. Drive."

"Right. Just as soon as you tell me where that rock is."

"Piss off, Tharp."

14

Night Meeting

I have begun to see in Salia a frightening capacity for cruelty. Does she blame herself for what happened to Anna? Is that why she does these things, to make others feel the pain of her guilt and frustration? I don't know, but today she made blood gush from a boy's ears just by willing it so. And for what? The boy only teased her a little. I disciplined her severely and sent her to her room to pray for her own soul, but she acknowledged neither pain nor insult. With Anna gone I fear it may be beyond my capacity to lead her down the righteous path...

FROM THE DIARY OF ISAIAH WARCHEZ, JULY 14, 2011

The town of Purgatory was roughly square, laid out in a grid that was strained, stretched and routinely broken by Old Scratch Creek, which bisected the community obliquely from the northwest to the southeast. Purgatory's few remaining grand houses rose from the high ground on the west side of the creek. The others had either been razed or torn down and recycled for their windows and bricks, boards and stones.

Sturm Baker's mansion was one of the few still standing, high on a hill above the others, as it had for three generations of Bakers. (Sturm, himself, was the last of the Purgatory Bakers, a once thriving clan of granite quarry-men and stonecutters). A three-story Victorian affair, complete with pointy turrets and showy dormers emerging from steeply gabled roofs, it was a thoroughly impractical edifice for the current age. Built snuggly up against a hillside that veered to the southeast, the house received too little sunlight to be of practical value, either for heating or the generation of electricity. Nor did the land on which the mansion stood offer a single sunlit grove in which to locate solar-harvesting apparatuses, owing to the fact that the entire ten acres was populated by towering cottonwoods and blue spruce trees that kept the earth from which they sprang in perpetual shadow. But Baker could afford to be impractical; he considered his extravagance a privilege granted the very few in this largely pedestrian world without oil.

Down the tree-shrouded hill and across the creek, downtown Purgatory stretched three blocks deep along the east bank of Old Scratch. There a few shops, a general store (boasting that it could get anything you wanted, so long as you didn't want it anytime soon), a pharmacy, and a couple of bars and restaurants with limited menus kept their shingles hanging out front. Most of the stores in the downtown area were "between owners," so to speak, although maintained by the good citizens of Purgatory, at least to a degree that discouraged leaky roofs, rotting floors, broken windows and rodent infestations.

Behind the downtown lay a small residential area where the meat-and-potatoes segment of the town's modest population lived in small, efficient, architecturally diverse houses. Most homesteads took up three or four building lots, though some comprised as many as six, and others as few as one. It was largely a matter of who was left standing when the dust cleared, and who was buried beneath it. The property of those who died without heirs, or those who abandoned their homes and property for the perceived safety of the islands (which were by early 2018 being constructed under joint military and civilian supervision) was redistributed among the small minority of survivors who remained. Payment for the unencumbered property was in the form of community service, for there was much to be done when the food supply and the human population were once again in accord and the time to rebuild was upon them.

Prygor Primm's small but neatly kept house and barn were situated on a parcel of land that consisted of but a single building lot on the southeast edge of town. He could have had as many as three additional lots at the end of the Turning, when at the age of nineteen he found himself in sole possession of the house where he had lived with his father and younger brother before they were both cut down in a bloody skirmish Prygor had skillfully managed to avoid. But he declined the town's offer, feeling his time would be better spent pursuing his individual goals rather than throwing his efforts into the community ring where they would be diluted amidst the sweat and toil of the common rabble. The notion that he, too, might have been as common as those he refused to work beside never entered his head, despite the obvious reality of his modest means and pedestrian upbringing.

For unlike them, Prygor Primm was a man of destiny.

The fact that no one but he recognized his special station in life was a grating annoyance that accounted at least in part for the enmity he felt toward the other denizens of Purgatory, as there was not a soul among them he considered his friend. Some he merely disliked; others he hated with a crimson-ringed passion. Carlos Herrera had been at the top of that list, for reasons too numerous to be recounted, but old Carlos was gone for good *(and good riddance, you meddling old goat)*. This had left Silas Teague as the man Prygor hated the most. Of course, hating a man who, until last night, was thought unable even to nourish himself without his doting sister's help would have seemed strange to most. But not to Prygor. He had always suspected Silas's invalidity to be an act, and last night's surprising display of mental acuity had confirmed it; he'd simply wanted his sister's attention all to himself...

...no, that wasn't quite right; was in fact thin to a fault—

That's because you're jealous. Jealous about a woman who would as soon dance on your grave as grace you with a smile; a woman you have never in your life even touched in the way a lover touches a lover.

—and what he didn't know disturbed him a whole lot more than what he did.

And *now*, no sooner had Carlos Herrera finally gone to the worms and maggots than the whelp shows up from nowhere to take the old man's place.

Right next door to Jennifer Teague.

It was becoming too much. Something had to give. Prygor wanted blood. But not tonight.

Tonight he was dressed in his best finery, which amounted to nothing more than unstained denim trousers, an ill-fitting tweed suit jacket his father had worn to funerals, and the black Stetson he'd snatched off the mummified corpse of an outlander way back in '19 when he'd decided then and there to cultivate the gunslinger image he still clung to.

Trying his best to put his thoughts of Jennifer behind him, he mounted his aging dapple mare and turned her toward town. Baker was at his mansion and Prygor was expected. He hoped the entertainment would be enough to dampen his simmering uneasiness about the situation developing up at *Vientos de los Dioses.*

But he doubted it.

He'd been sideswiped by a lover he'd never known in the biblical sense of knowing and a man he'd always wanted dead. *Sideswiped.* The word was far more common before the Turning, when cars were plentiful and often ran into each other. The irony of it was that he'd gotten his driver's license just a month before the Tar Baby bacterium hit the first oil fields and everyone had been summarily ordered by the National Guard to drive their cars home and park them.

Talk about bad timing. Sideswiped then, sideswiped now, he thought bitterly, picking up the thread of his thoughts.

For years he'd not made a single mistake with Jennifer; always secretly coming and going and watching, and making sure that Jennifer

dear Jennifer

was safe.

From men. All men. Men who would pretend to love her. When all they wanted was to defile her; to touch her and feel her in filthy, carnal ways and drive themselves into her...something that Prygor could never do.

While Prygor was lost in thought, the mare made the turn onto Main street without any prodding. She knew the route, even in complete darkness. Animals and humans were both creatures of habit, and the mare knew there were only two places they ever went after dark; up the hill to Baker's mansion, and up the winding creek trail to Jennifer's house. He headed down Main now, past the two southernmost bridge entrances, now blocked off with railroad ties set on end. The bridges had been ripped out in the flood of '32 and never rebuilt, considering that Purgatory was a much smaller town now—maybe two hundred if you counted the close-in farms—and one bridge was all that was needed to ferry people from one side of the normally quiescent creek to the other.

Main was deserted except for the few horses and piecemeal vehicles in front of the two taverns, The Green Mill and The Blue Fox, occupying opposite corners on the same block. Bawdy places Prygor never entered. Why should he? He had no friends, and liquor only confounded him and opened the gap between himself and the rest of humanity wider than it already was. He passed them both, making a conscious effort not to look inside their batwing doors, feeling somehow superior with his legs wrapped around his big virgin mare, while the common riffraff hooted and hollered and pinched breasts and asses that must, by now, be black and flaccid from so much pinching.

He felt better when he heard the *clop, clop* of the mare's hooves on the bridge planks where High street hooked west off of Main; at least until he heard

Prygor

a voice in his head.

Pryus Gordon

He ignored it and touched the mare's flanks with polished boot heels. A powerful blast of wind wound through the trees on the far side of the bridge and nearly pushed him off the side of his mount. The mare who had no name lowered her ears and whinnied her displeasure at the gusty insult. *Strange I didn't hear that coming,* Prygor thought, steadying his mount. The wind in town was always heralded by the raucous slap of leaf against leaf and the soughing of hurried air through distant whipping branches. It gave people a chance to brace themselves in anticipation. He chalked it up to his preoccupation with Jennifer and

(the voice in my head)

a bad case of nerves

(after being sideswiped).

He continued on, the air becoming more unsettled with every *Clip, clip, clip CLOP; clip, clip, clip, CLOP* of the mare's hooves. And darker. The cottonwoods had not yet lost their saucer-size leaves, and the spruce and fir they mingled with were even denser. What little light there was came as threadlike shafts.

Usually, darkness didn't bother him. It enabled him to move without being seen on errands he would prefer went unnoticed. But this darkness was different; there was a crawling malevolence about it, a slithering conspiracy to which Prygor was not privy.

Then the voice.

Kill her, it whispered.

"Kill who?" Prygor asked the night.

Her.

"Who?" he asked again, this time with more urgency.

Before the voice could say more, something shiny flew across his field of vision within a hair's breadth of his nose, making a solid *thock!* when it stuck in the tree just to his right. The elk-antler handle of a familiar hunting knife vibrated from the impact. It had the immediate effect of pulling the air from his lungs.

A dark-clad figure stepped out of the shadow of the trees to his left. He said, "*Buenas Noches, pendejo*. Nice night to talk with yourself about killing. But tonight, I'm afraid, I will be doing the killing."

Prygor was able to draw just enough air back into his lungs to utter a single word: "Tay."

Tay was tempted to unholster his Ruger Blackhawk and end it here and now, but when he stepped toward the sheriff he was careful not to reveal the iron tucked snugly in his armpit beneath the unbuttoned shirt. Perhaps Primm would think him unarmed and try to draw on him.

Lo siento mucho, Jennifer, but he drew first.

But Primm was too scared to reach for the shiny .38 in his hip holster. That much was evident by the rictus that had seized his face and forced it into a parody of a smile, and also by the way the reins shook in his hands. Like he'd just opened the wrong door and found Death standing on the other side.

Tay was enjoying sheriff's predicament. Primm had no stomach for a standup fight. He was a skulking coward who would only engage a foe from a concealed position.

Tay said, "You would do well to enjoy every breath you take from now until the end, *pendejo*," Tay told him. "Each one comes to you courtesy of *señorita* Teague." He held the mare's reins as he worked his knife free from the tree, careful to keep the outline of Primm in the corner of his eye. "If it were up to me, I'd bury this knife in your throat and watch you drown in your own blood." Primm didn't move; not a finger, not even an eyelash.

He was thinking. Or more likely, scheming. Calculating a move that would put him on top of his delicate situation. Or at least improve his odds. It was amusing; amusing because Tay enjoyed watching a man's eyes as he imagined all the ways he might maneuver from a situation that was hopeless to one that was merely desperate. Once that point was reached, a man had to will himself to action; whether to speak, or fight, or run. What would Primm do?

If it is the wrong choice, pendejo, you may die tonight.

After a moment, Primm's mouth slid into an officious repose, and he proclaimed, "It would do you well not to threaten me, Tay Villa, for as you know I am an agent of the State and any provocation toward me will be considered a provocation against—"

"Enough!" Tay commanded. With a quick thrust he drove the knife through Primm's boot into the soft flesh on the side of his foot. Primm yelped like a wounded weasel and his eyes grew big and round with surprise as he instinctively jerked his foot free from the stirrup. Then he made the mistake of reaching for his gun.

It was a big mistake, but not his last one. Tay snatched the gun from the sheriff's hand before his fingers could tighten on the grips. In response, Primm jabbed his boot heels into the mare's flanks. The mare lurched forward, but Tay held her by the reins as he pulled Primm from the saddle with his free hand.

Primm landed on his back, all the air driven from his lungs. Tay planted a boot on his heaving chest and said, "I think maybe now we should talk. Do you agree?"

Primm did, enthusiastically. He nodded his affirmation and even managed to force a pained smile. Tay removed his foot to allow Primm to suck in a series of ragged breaths, then watched patiently as the sheriff struggled to his feet and brushed the road dust off his black Stetson and his freshly laundered duds. In the patchy moonlight he looked like a badly dress wraith.

Blood leaked through the slash in his boot, but Primm wasn't complaining. He was smart enough to know what happened to people who crossed Tay's path.

And so they had their little chitchat, one-sided though it was. People live and people die and either way life goes on, Tay told him. It was as philosophical as he ever got. Then he explained succinctly what the sheriff could do to stay alive and what he could do to quickly become dead.

The sheriff listened intently, saying little and either nodding or shaking his head at all the appropriate points in the conversation. "You know what you have done, *pendejo*, and though I would prefer to kill you for what you have done in the past, I think that if I kill you it will be for what you do in the future. *Intiende?*"

He did understand.

"So these are the rules. If you ever set foot on *Vientos de los Dioses* again, you will die. If you ever again try to talk to Jennifer or Silas Teague, you will die. And if you breathe a word of this conversation to anyone, you will die.

"Now, listen, *pendejo*, and listen well. I know you think you could find a way to kill me if you dared to try, because you are a coward who lies in wait like a snake beside the trail, waiting for the little mouse. But I am no mouse.

If you try to kill me, you will die. This I can promise you." Primm raised his eyebrows at this, and Tay returned a grim smile. He said, "And now I think you know everything you need to know to keep on living. Am I correct?"

Primm's earlier agreeableness had passed and his face had withdrawn into a sullen shadow that made Tay want to draw him into real confrontation. But he simply repeated, "Am I correct, *pendejo*?"

"Yes," Primm muttered, lifting his head to expose an utterly expressionless face. He took a breath, and when he exhaled the blank expression had evolved into something ascending to the lower limits of compassion. "There's no need for bad blood between us, Tay. I never meant any harm to Jennifer; truly I didn't."

For the first time since Tay had known him, Primm sounded sincere. Perhaps he was; maybe somewhere in his tortured mind he really *did* think he was protecting Jennifer by killing off her lovers; making certain she would remain as celibate as Primm was reputed to be. It made Tay's skin crawl, so he thought no more on the subject. He cared not for what went on in the man's mind and even less for the disposition of his soul, assuming he had one. All that mattered was that Primm understand the precariousness of his situation.

"I will try to remember you said that," Tay told him evenly.

"And you won't speak of this to anyone?" Primm said, more as a request than a question.

Tay could see it was a matter of honor with Primm and decided to leave him with at least the illusion of dignity, since illusion—or perhaps delusion—was all the man had in this world. "Everything that will be said has been said here, *pendejo*. There is no need to speak another word." The acquiescence in the tall man's eyes told Tay his words were believed.

Tay pulled Primm's gun from the front of his pants, spun it quickly by the trigger guard, and held it out it to him, handle first. The sheriff's eyes grew wide with surprise. He took the proffered weapon as if it were a hand grenade with the pin missing. Without another word he returned the gun to its holster, gathered up the mare's reins and pulled himself quickly into the saddle.

Tay watched him disappear into the living darkness and wondered how long it would be before the sheriff met his end. As he walked back toward town the unsettled night gave way to a mounting gale.

15

The Blue Fox Inn

If there is a single person to whom I likely owe my persistent longevity, it would be Tay. It is his gift that he thinks only as far as he needs to before trusting his body and soul to instinct. He then becomes like an animal: cunning, but on a purely genetic level quite apart from the machinations of the mind...

FROM THE UNPUBLISHED MEMOIRS OF CARLOS HERRERA

Jack was on his second pint at the Blue Fox Inn when Tay walked in. He made no special effort to greet him, or to even acknowledge his entrance. Tay knew he was there, at any rate. He'd ridden with Jack into town before heading off on foot across the bridge. Jack hadn't asked where he was going, partly because he remained leery of Tay despite his friendliness, but mostly because he already had a pretty good idea.

The Blue Fox had been a busy place in Tay's absence. Mostly the bar was inhabited by rough-hewn men who perceived their pleasures as something best pursued without restraint. A fight had broken out in the hour that Jack had been sitting alone at the bar and blood had been spilled on both sides of the dispute. It began when a large husky fellow in dirty jeans held up with red suspenders had started a shouting match with a shorter man of equal or greater tonnage. The fight began in the presence of a shabbily dressed woman who might have been worth shouting about twenty years and thirty pounds ago. They each wished to treat said lady to a dance, the music for which was to be provided by a young man in the far corner with a dinged-up rhythm guitar and a singing voice that was a little gritty but not half bad.

For her part, the woman must have been thrilled that anyone would want to fight over li'l ol' her, considering how little effort she expended to stop it.

The initial shouting quickly escalated to pushing, but that seemed about as far as it was going to go until the shorter man made a comment, of which Jack could discern only two words: *mother* and *sucks*. That had earned him an inexpertly thrown roundhouse punch to the side of his nose. Blood flowed instantly, prodding a surprised Shorty to retaliate with a quick jab to Suspender's lower lip, which had the effect of balancing out the blood scale. Then Shorty, who obviously knew a whole lot more about fist fighting than Suspenders, followed his success with two more trip-hammer jabs to the face, connecting one solidly with Suspender's left eye. Surprised by his foe's pugilistic prowess, Suspenders fell back and examined Shorty with a wary eye. Shorty was smiling a vicious and satisfied smile that stretched the breadth of his meaty face, despite the fact that blood ran from his nose into his mouth in such volume that his teeth glistened red and every heavy breath sent a crimson spray out into the room.

Having concluded he probably couldn't beat the man in a standup fight, Suspenders launched himself at Shorty like a meatloaf missile in a flannel shirt. It was a brilliant maneuver that caught the smaller man completely off-guard. They hit the floor in a thundering snarl of meat and blubber, and rolled around in a twisting ever-changing display of full and half Nelson's, single and double chicken wings, head locks, leg locks and a few moves invented on the fly. Their wrestling ring was provided by a three-deep circle of curious and noisy bystanders, none of which saw any reason to try to stop them.

It finally ended when Shorty farted. It was a long, bubbling rip of a fart that set Suspenders to laughing so hard he couldn't fight anymore, which was okay because by then they had both reached the point of exhaustion. So they laid on their backs on the floor, shoulder to shoulder with blood dripping from their lips and nostrils, panting like a pair of fattened boars after a marathon run. And laughing in raucous hoots before finally getting up to have another beer. The withering belle who had ignited the fight joined in the newfound camaraderie by occupying the stool between them at the ancient pinewood bar.

It was both interesting and refreshing. Interesting because a disagreement that had erupted so furiously had come to so little in the end, suggesting there had never been any real enmity between the two; they'd merely seen the chance to blow off a little steam and have a generous helping of fun in the bargain. What consequence was a bloody nose or a fat shiner in the midst of such sanguine revelry?

It was refreshing because everyone there (including the bartender who looked on with no more than mild curiosity) took it for what it was.

Had the same thing happened in an island tavern, both men would've been immediately subdued by a throng of nosey do-gooders and held until the Island Authority could haul them off to a detention area. Probably they would both have spent at least a day or two in detention (as jail was no longer an acceptable word), a healthy fine, and forced counseling to probe the roots of their anger. When it was all said and done they would be angrier than ever and filled with hatred for the Island Authority. But they would *act* like two whipped puppies and that's all that mattered.

Shortly after that Jack had bumped into Turney, the bandana man from the road crew he'd encountered on the way out of town yesterday. *Was it only yesterday?* The other two—the young man and the stout one he'd thought of as the wrestler—were engaged at the pool table in a game of eight ball.

Turney still wore the bandana around his tanned head, but he'd either laundered it or traded it for a fresh one. His shirt was at least as clean as the brightly patterned bandana though of much cruder cloth, the same cream-colored sackcloth material that found its way into so many of the garments country folk wore.

Jack was happy to see him; happy to be noticed, or rather acknowledged. Up to that point he'd felt a little like a guy with his fly open: everyone looked, but no one wanted to break the news that something was a little out of place.

"Well, well. The son of Carlos!" Turney said, taking a stool next to Jack. In the dim gas lights of the Blue Fox the creases in his face harbored shadows that made him look both older and wiser than he had in the bright sunlight, but his genuine smile remained unchanged.

"Jack, actually. Jack Vara." He offered his hand and the man gave it a strong shake.

"Turney. That's the only name you need to know."

"Simple," Jack offered.

Turney winked. "I like simple."

Jack said, "Beer? I'm buying."

Turney wasn't one to turn down a free beer. The bartender, a thin, middle-aged man with a large, spider-web scar on the side of his neck, filled a heavy glass mug from the bar's only tap, leaving a frothy head on top. He slid it down the ten feet of polished bar to Turney. He clinked his mug against Jack's, saying, "To Purgatory, the farthest you can be from anywhere while still being somewhere."

"To Purgatory," Jack echoed.

"So what do you think of our little town, so far?" Turney asked, as if the answer somehow mattered.

Trying not to think too hard on his reply, Jack said, "If she were a woman I just might be in love. But I'd sure never turn my back on her."

Turney snickered in his beer, blowing a cloud of foam off the top as he did. "Well said, Jack. She is a generous mistress, it's true, but always ready to serve up a surprise or two."

"A lady of many secrets," Jack said, feeling now the effects of the strong beer and the local greenhouse tobacco many of the patrons smoked in clay or corncob pipes.

Turney speared him with a hard look. "So she is, Jack. She likes it that way. Better you don't ask her why."

"Better for who?"

"You, Jack. Everyone. You needn't think any further on it than that."

Oh, but he would; he'd been mired in secrets since he got to this place and oh boy was he was ready for a few answers, starting with: what had his father rat-holed away, and why were Jennifer and Silas so afraid of it being found? And how, of all people, did Salia Warchez figure into it?

And finally: did Turney know of Carlos's secrets, or was he discussing a whole new batch Jack knew nothing about?

Jack asked, "Did you know my father, Turney?"

Turney considered his answer for a long moment, all the while staring at a bit of nothing just over the top of Jack's head. Finally he said, "I don't know if anyone did, really; he was a secret in himself. He'd dug himself in out there at the end of Old Lacuna Road before I was born, but everyone—me included, I suppose—always thought of him as an outsider."

"Why?" Jack asked, more than a little curious.

"Because he acted like one," Turney replied, rubbing the side of his bewhiskered face. "Purgatory's a small place, Jack. It was small before the Turning, and it's a hell of a lot smaller now. For good or bad, everyone here knows everyone else's business; that's just the way it is. A boy can't kiss a girl on the north end of town without people talking about it on the south end five minutes later. But no one ever seemed to know what your old man was up to. No sir."

Jack took a long draw on his beer and savored the rich hoppy flavor before letting it slide down his throat. "So you're telling me my father was an outsider because he didn't join in the local gossip circles?"

There was an edge on his voice he wished hadn't been there, but Turney seemed not to notice. He looked Jack in the eye and said, "It was a matter of participation, Jack. Carlos never really acted like he wanted any part of us, so we let him be. For us"—he made an expansive gesture with his hands to indicate everyone in the place—"Purgatory is home; for Carlos it was more of a refuge."

"You think he was hiding?"

Turney shook his head. "More like avoiding being found. Carlos didn't want to draw attention to himself, which was kind of ironic if you think about it, because that's exactly what he did by keeping to his own company."

Jack recalled what Jennifer had told him about Carlos's father; how he had become disenchanted with the old Franco regime. Was there more to it than she was telling him? Had he taken something with him when he 'emigrated' to Mexico? Something of Franco's? And then there was the story of how Carlos had absconded with Marissa *(my mother)* across the Rio Grande. Of course he wouldn't want to draw attention to himself. But that alone hardly seemed like enough reason to "avoid being found" for fifty-seven years. He asked, "Did my father stay here during the Turning?"

Turney barked a quick laugh, then clipped it short. "*Stay?* Jesus, Jack, he did more than stay. He was the one who doled out the guns and bullets that kept us from being overrun by the urban militias who rightly figured a nice little farming community like ours would be well-stocked with food, but badly mistaken in thinking we'd be guarding it with shovels and pitchforks. Oh, everyone had a hunting rifle, of course, and maybe a box or two of shells tucked away in the cupboard, but no one was prepared for war except Carlos. And Tay, of course."

"Of course."

Animated now, Turney continued, saying, "Being an ex-Ranger, I figure Tay had the right connections to get his hands on all the really lethal things civilians aren't supposed to be able to get. And he showed us tactics; where to set up defenses, booby traps, ambushes...the Indian knows the art of war, and that's a fact."

"Yes…he is half Indian, isn't he?" Jack said thoughtfully. He thought it a volatile mixture that would make for a formidable foe, and once again he felt thankful he and Tay were on the same side.

"Pawnee mother, Mexican father. I don't know any more than that. Tay's not a big talker, and neither was your old man. But what they did for us during the Turning saved our asses. It's the reason we all respected Carlos and his eccentricities. Even though he made it clear he wanted to be left alone."

Jack took a long pull and said, "How fortunate that he should be so prepared."

"More like serendipitous," Turney offered. "Probably he showed up in Purgatory expecting a lot of trouble from wherever he came from; just didn't expect it to play out the way it did, that's all. I guess you could say we all owe a debt of gratitude to Carlos's enemies, whoever they were."

Or are, Jack mused.

The guitar player had been working his way through an old Irish ballad Jack remembered from his childhood, a song about lovers whose hopes had been denied them by a cruel fate. *Barbara Allen,* it was called. He paused to listen to the final two verses, thinking, though not wishing to, of Jennifer.

They buried her in the old churchyard
They buried him in the choir
And from his grave grew a red red rose
From her grave a green briar
They grew and grew to the steeple top
Till they could grow no higher
And there they twined in a true love's knot
Red rose around green briar

It was right after the guitar player wrapped his final note around a lilting rendering of *greeeen brii-arr,* that Tay pushed open the doors with the wind howling behind him. Jack expected all the merry making to come to a portentous halt, but the few who took notice did so without any particular sense of alarm, though everyone gave Tay a wide berth as he strode purposefully toward the bar. The big corn-fed farm boy sitting on the far side of Jack vacated his stool without a murmur of protest when he saw Tay coming with that ghost of a smile on his face and Tay slid onto the proffered stool without acknowledging the hefty lad who had warmed it for him. A shot glass of whiskey was waiting for him when he sat down and Tay thanked the bartender in the polite, reserved way he seemed to conduct himself when he wasn't otherwise engaged in the formulation of devilish thoughts. He allowed himself but a small sip while scanning the large smoke-filled room with narrowed eyes, and seemed disappointed when his search bore no results. It was only then that he acknowledged Turney with a smile and a handshake.

"In town on business or pleasure?" Turney asked Tay, perhaps by way of being nosey without appearing to be.

"Is there a difference?" Tay asked wryly.

Turney met his eyes and matched his smile. "I reckon not for everyone," he said.

A blast of wind shook the old building so hard the gas lights flickered in their globes, and pushed the swinging doors full open with a sustained huff of gritty air. "Something blowing in, you think?" Jack said, for lack of anything more intelligent to add to the conversation.

"Nah," Turney opined, "just blowin' for the hell of it."

Tay replied, "No, *amigo*, I think you are wrong. There is something evil about this wind."

Jack turned away from Turney and back to Tay, then to the door where Tay now directed all his attention. Tay was looking at the stout, short man with a Neanderthal jaw and a head of thick, unruly hair who had just strode through the doors. He was unaffected by the wind, though it was still strong enough to push the doors open. The words 'built like a brick shithouse' came instantly to Jack's mind.

This time the music *did* stop and *everyone* took notice. Those near the door shrank away from the man as if he were exhaling ammonia, while the revelers closer to the periphery tried to watch without appearing to.

Everyone except Tay, who locked his eyes on the newcomer and dispensed another sip of whiskey into his mouth, which had formed itself into a most unpleasant grin.

"Who the fuck is *that*?" Jack whispered into Tay's ear.

"Tharp," Tay answered, without taking his eyes off the man. "Hadrian Tharp."

16

Old Enemies

I always give them what they want. It is my gift, my very special gift, given to me by God. But not my father's God. Not the madman of the Old Testament who made men free only to rein them in, again and again, in floods and cataclysmic firestorms; who placed the tree in the Garden, then forbade the apex of his creation to eat its fruit.

That is nonsense, pure and simple allegorical drivel fabricated to keep a multitude of superstitious goat herders from destroying themselves by their own lusts.

Poor Isaiah. Named by his father, Ezekiel, after a Jewish prophet, as he himself had been named.

And each of them, down to the first man ever to draw breath as a member of the family Warchez, an eastern European with a long and proud warring tradition who had never once slept with a Jew!

But no matter. Times change. People die. The world goes on. But confusion persists. The god of the Jews doesn't work for the rest of us.

Sorry, Isaiah. I miss you.

But not enough to wish you were still in the way, thwarting all my plans. You had it all wrong, hardheaded old fool that you were.

But at least you were right about one thing...

God is power. Just not your God.

FROM THE AKASHIC JOURNAL OF SALIA WARCHEZ

It was late when they passed the first of the outlying farms east of Purgatory, a large expanse of field surrounding on all sides a small, neat house dimly lit with gas lights. Moonlight played brightly in the leaves of the towering old trees on the north. Salia caught a glimpse of the flower garden on the south, bordered by stones in front of the greenhouse where she imagined the people grew herbs and vegetables year 'round. She craned her neck from the passenger seat of the jeep to get a better look. Were there marigolds? She thought so, although it was impossible to tell from this distance, in this light, with this man driving.

"Why don't you slow it down, Hadrian?" she asked reasonably. "This isn't the Trans Am, you know."

"Don't I know it," he replied sullenly, never taking his eyes off the road.

They'd left Tharp's mechanical pride and joy at a safe house near the Wyoming border, where a hydrogen-fueled jeep was waiting to ferry them across the last forty miles of rough road. It was hardly capable of the 140-plus mile-per-hour speeds the modified '86 Trans Am could muster, but that didn't stop him from pretending. The man could be insufferable when he wanted to be.

Salia sat back and closed her eyes, rocking with the bumps and potholes Tharp seemed to be aiming for. Two more miles, she told herself. Just two more miles to Purgatory.

Purgatory. She smiled in spite of the uneven road and Tharp' offensive driving tactics. Such an ignorant, innocent place it was. People of the Earth, they thought of themselves; preservers of the old ways. Even now she could feel the consciousness of the town flow through her, like smoke filling the olfactory and alerting the brain to the nature of the embers, be they of incense or flesh. She was here to immerse herself in the place.

She was last in Purgatory the night Carlos Herrera had died clutching his heart *(and smiling; the arrogant goat),* before Salia was able to ascertain what she desperately needed to know: the location of the protocol.

She wouldn't make *that* mistake again.

* * * *

Hadrian Tharp stopped at the safe house just long enough to get Salia settled in before heading on into town. It was an old farmhouse owned by Sturm Baker and leased to Tharp with money paid to him by the ever elusive Ms. Warchez. Were this latter fact ever to be made known to Baker he'd probably use all the considerable power at his disposal to snare the notorious woman fugitive. But it never would be known. As far as Baker knew, Tharp was just a pirate. The thought that a spiritual leader of Salia's repute would use an unbelieving hedonist like Tharp to move invisibly from place to place would have been laughable.

The house was small and Spartan, but her room was more than comfortable and the cellar was well stocked with meats and produce preserved in glass jars, along with containers of coffee, rice, beans and flour. If she got hungry, she could eat. Not that she would anytime soon; she'd spend the next day in fasting and meditation as she prepared herself for whatever voodoo she intended to set loose on the unsuspecting citizens of Purgatory.

Whatever. Hadrian had other things to do.

She'd given him two admonitions before he drove off, the same two he heard every time they landed in a new town together: *Don't draw attention to yourself*, and, *If you can't keep your pants on, don't plan on dropping them at the foot of my bed again in this lifetime.* This one he found amusing. She was demanding monogamy from a man she didn't even like. Just as he was from her. Yet of the two, this was the reproof he always took seriously. If he were to find his way to another woman's bed Salia would know and make good on her threat. And that would be unbearable, to be so close to her without partaking of her considerable pleasures...

Tharp was betting that Baker was at his mansion as he usually was on Saturday nights. Him and that spooky fuck, Prygor Primm. It might be a good time to stop by; pay the rent, shoot the shit, and see what mischief the fat larcenous bastard was up to. Maybe he could even pick up a contract or two—little nettlesome acts of inner-island sedition that justified the continued funding of Desa, much to the benefit of Baker, Primm, and, of course, Tharp.

But first things first; a beer to wash down the road dust and a chance to see how many of the fine citizens of Purgatory remembered him.

*   *   *   *

The man Tay called Hadrian Tharp paused at the door to cast his eyes on everyone and everything in the room. From their faces it was clear there were many in this room who recognized the man—mainly the older Purgatory natives—and he was certain Tharp would not find a friend among them. Not that it bothered him. Seeing the effect he was having on the patrons of The Blue Fox Inn, a smile grew on the man's square, weathered face, exposing a mouth full of thick, crowded teeth of unusual whiteness. It was only when his eyes came to rest on Tay that his smile withered. Nonetheless, he set his course for the empty stool beside him.

"Smells like blood," Tharp said in Tay's general direction.

"What's the matter?" Tay asked evenly. "Getting queasy in your old age, *Hadriano*?" It came out *Odd-ree-AH-no*.

He slid onto the stool. "Top of my game, Villa. How about you? Civilization making you soft?"

"Care to find out?"

"Some other time, maybe. I just stopped in for a friendly beer."

"Then you have come to the wrong place," Tay told him. "You have no friends here."

Tharp motioned to the bartender for a beer. The man with the unsightly scar on his neck looked askance to Tay, who nodded slowly. The bartender drew the beer and set it in front of Tharp without meeting his eyes. Tharp threw a small silver coin on the bar in payment. By Jack's reckoning a man could drink all night for the value of that coin, but when the bartender brought his change in brass, Tharp waved his hand. The bartender gathered up his sizable tip and backed away to the far end of the bar.

Tay took another slow sip of whiskey, then rested his elbow on the aged bar and drew his face close to Tharp's. The muscles in his jaw tightened reflexively and his fingers were curled into fists, but he spoke calmly when he said, "There is another bar at the end of the block, *Hadriano*. Maybe the friends you are looking for are there."

Tharp was ten years younger with at least twenty pounds more muscle wrapped around his bones. *But does that really matter?* Jack wondered. *Isn't it all about skill and technique? If these two go at it they're not going to exchange a few punches or wrestle around on the floor; they'll be breaking bones and causing serious trauma to each other's internal organs. And they sure as hell won't end up laughing and slapping each other on the back.*

Tharp threw back a mouthful of sudsy brew like he'd just walked out of a desert, then said, "The war's over, Villa. It's been over for seventeen years. In case you've forgotten, there was a blanket amnesty at the end."

"That was unfortunate," Tay reflected. "I was hoping to kill you before then."

Tharp touched his mug to the half-empty shot glass in Tay's hand. "And I you, *amigo*," he replied, almost warmly. "Sometimes things just don't work out the way we plan." His smile, which had grown friendly, was sharply contrasted

by the icy glare in his eyes. He wouldn't be making the first move, Jack figured,
but he was more than ready to make the second one.

Tay's attention was diverted when the batwing doors swung open and
his taut muscles gently uncoiled. Tharp saw the change in Tay's demeanor
and spun on the squeaky old stool to see who could have caused it.

As often happens, the fate of the confrontation was laid in the hands of
a woman; in this case an unsuspecting woman of less than forty years who
looked enough like Tay to be his younger sister. Jack heard Turney breathe a
sigh of relief when she appeared from out of the night and this caused Jack
to breathe a little easier. She looked like trouble, though of the kind men
usually welcome. Her silky black hair hung to the middle of her back, though
the wind had blown a few strands across her shoulder where they fell below
the frilly white tank top visible beneath an oversized shirt left open in front.
Smooth brown skin was exposed from just below her economical breasts to
the conclusion of her narrow waist. The woman was short for Jack's liking,
and a little bulky in the hips, but otherwise built of all the right stuff and
skillfully assembled, right up to her face, which was hard and possessing features that seemed small against a large, aquiline nose. A nose very much like
Tay's—hence the familial resemblance—except that Tay's seemed a worthy
contribution to his scarred and rugged face while hers was a distraction.

In any case, this woman was not his sister, as became clear the moment
she set eyes on him. Her hard face softened by several degrees and it made
her look almost pretty. Without a moment's hesitation she sidled up to Tay,
who barely had enough time to set his drink on the bar before she smothered him with her embrace.

Tay didn't push her away but neither did he take his eyes his eyes off
Tharp.

She lay her head over his shoulder and lanced Hadrian with a classic
what-the-fuck-are-you-looking-at? stare that merely caused the stout man
to smile disarmingly. Then she pushed her face into Tay's neck and rattled
off a flurry of words in Spanish. Her tone spanned the spectrum from scold-
ing to pleading. Tay answered firmly but consolingly. The words were spoken
too fast for Jack to understand any of them except for the name Carmen,
but two things were clear without a translator: she'd been feeling ignored
all day, but if Tay were to give her the attention she deserved, she was more
than willing to forgive and forget.

It seemed a generous offer. As Tay considered it Tharp downed the rest of his beer and made for the door without another word. Over Carmen's shoulder, Tay said, "Another time, then, *Hadriano*?" He didn't have to raise his voice; the place was still as silent as a tomb.

"Another time," Tharp agreed without turning around as he walked out into the gusty night.

Jack drove back to Vientos de los Dioses with Jazzman as his only passenger. The dog didn't seem to mind.

17

Silas's First Supper

*There is no feeling more humbling than being seized by the knowledge
that no matter how enlightened you may one day become, the world will
always be vastly more beautiful and complex than we can ever know...*

FROM THE UNPUBLISHED MEMOIRS OF CARLOS HERRERA

As Jennifer fussed in the kitchen to prepare what she hoped would be
the perfect meal to celebrate Silas's awakening, she couldn't shake the
feeling that something big was about to happen. It wasn't the pure inductive
jolt one felt upon discovering a sound conclusion dangling at the end of a
logical thread, but neither was it purely psychical. It was in her gut. Not an
unfamiliar place for others to uncover their instincts, she supposed, but it
wasn't the way Jennifer was put together. Hers was a visual mind and a lucid
psyche. She saw future events as though they were memories. But this not a
vision; only a feeling that something was amiss.

She felt many things, actually, and that might in itself have been the
source of her difficulty, for with so much out of kilter it was impossible to
splice all the psychic film into a mental movie that made sense.

For one thing, Jack had gone into town with Tay, even though she'd specifically asked them both if they would please stay and have dinner with her
and Silas, in celebration of his unexpected awakening. So why did they go?

(Not to kill Primm, that much she *did* know.)

Adding to her unease, Silas was keeping his own counsel in the greenhouse while Jennifer stood at the granite counter and sliced her au gratin
potatoes much thinner than usual so Silas, who surely must be tired by now,
would have no trouble chewing them. She did the same with the radishes

and also the carrots, which she rendered into slivers as she worked farther and farther along a frayed line of reasoning that had so far ceased to produce a single viable conclusion.

In light of the urgency in Silas's voice this morning—an urgency curiously not embellished upon—Tay was probably out getting a feel for what might be happening and where, and doing it silently under the cover of darkness. But Jack? He had neither the training nor the inclination for that kind of work, and she doubted Tay was taking on any students in the dark arts of stealth and bloodletting.

Besides, Jack regretted his decision to go to town. It was easy enough to see—his body language, alone, gave him away on that account—but he went anyway. Without ever really considering *not* going.

And this, she suspected, was Silas's doing; Silas who had taken Jack aside to speak to him of things he couldn't even share with his own sister. (*Are we jealous, Jen?* a little voice whispered from some dark crevasse of her harried mind.) Was he unhappy Jack was off somewhere? Hardly. *Too bad, Jen*, he'd said with an offhanded nonchalance that struck her as a trifle polished for a man so recently returned from the uncharted hinterlands of consciousness, *but I'm sure he had something important to do*. Translation: he's not here because Silas told him to be somewhere else tonight.

Were it not for the dread she felt in the pit of her stomach she could let it pass and trust her brother to know what he was doing. But there was something more. Something that frightened her.

But by then the Malloys had arrived and whatever lurked in the shadows she hoped to put aside, for it certainly hadn't made itself known to Catalyn or Luke, who enjoyed the unanticipated get-together almost as much as Silas. (Cassie, on the other hand, was cheerful, but distant.) They shared a homegrown bounty around the oval table that Luke, ever helpful, had set up in the living room after moving Silas's heavy chair into a far corner.

Silas sat at one end of the table, Luke at the other. Cassie took the seat on Silas's right, next to Jennifer, allowing Catalyn the other side to herself. The room was warmly lit by lantern light that flickered every time a gust of wind from out of the lacuna careened into the house, making all the shadows softly animate and friendly. Luke had brought along a bottle of dandelion wine from his private stock. It was '35 vintage; a good year, Luke boasted (as if he'd ever admit to a bad one), and to his credit it provided a most pleasant way to take the edge off Jennifer's fears. For a while she was able to forget the misgivings that taunted her from beyond the shadows.

Luke was excited to finally meet Silas—the real, unfettered Silas— since he and Catalyn were Carlos's two most recent "acquisitions." Silas was equally curious to learn how they had come to reside at *Vientos de los Dioses*. Luke dutifully regaled him, beginning his tale in the spring of '31, when he and Catalyn wandered into Purgatory after walking for days over roads largely reclaimed by nature.

Recently married, flat broke, and out of work, they shuffled into town with a few provisions and belongings tied to a sawbuck pack frame on the back of an old swaybacked gelding that had just made the trip of his life and wasn't liable to make another. Catalyn was pregnant with Cassie. They were a meal away from starving and very near to giving up all hope.

Carlos spied them in the street when they arrived—dirty, disheveled and bone tired, but happy to be in a living, breathing town where people worked for hard silver and commerce was routinely conducted. It was a classic hard-luck story that struck Carlos in the right way on the right day. Or maybe he was just playing a hunch. Either way, he took them to *Vientos de los Dioses*, fed them, gave Luke a few odd jobs and, as Jennifer put it, "quickly realized his electrical and mechanical talents lay somewhere in the expanse between amazing and divine."

"Obviously," Silas interjected.

Blushing, Luke said, "Once Carlos was satisfied I knew what I was doing, he showed me all the stuff he'd been collecting over the years, some of it from before the Turning." His chocolate-brown eyes grew wide with boyish wonder and he exclaimed, "And holy Christ on a Harley! When I saw what he had I was in heaven. I realized what we could do with it, and...well, that's what I'd like to show you, Silas...when you're up to it, that is."

Silas thoroughly enjoyed Luke's youthful enthusiasm and his awkward but colorful expressions. Carlos had done well in finding him. "I look forward to it." His voice rasped involuntarily, a reminder of how many years it had passed without the simple pleasure of real conversation.

Cassie had hardly taken her eyes off Silas since they sat down. She looked up now and said, "My dad's a pretty smart cookie, all right." Everyone laughed, Luke in particular, who thought his daughter the most precious being in the universe.

Silas placed his hand on the girl's head, and patted her gently. He had no memories of ever trying to communicate with a child (at least not since he'd been one himself), but he sensed in Cassie an innocence he feared the world might have lost, and to have her sitting beside him filled him with hope beyond any that mere reason could provide.

She looked up inquisitively and asked, "What're you gonna do, now that you're not sick anymore, Silas?"

Silas pondered the question for a moment then was taken by an idea. He had sensed something in the child the moment she sat down beside him. *Maybe I'll see if your dad will give me a job,* he thought.

Cassie quickly answered, "Ah, c'mon! You don't wanna work for *him!*" then threw her small hands to her face and said, "Oops!" when she realized that Silas hadn't spoken a word.

Silas cast an eye to Catalyn, shaking his head almost imperceptibly when she opened her mouth to admonish the child. Catalyn cut him with a sharp glance and let go her breath in a huff, but held her tongue. Cassie lowered her hands and smiled; sheepishly at first, then more boldly as she grew certain her mother wasn't going to scold her for doing what came naturally.

Before the moment had a chance to turn awkward, Silas raised his glass—the wine was indeed of good vintage, not that he had tasted much in his lifetime to compare it with—and said softly, "How good that you are all here, to help me reclaim what time and war have withheld from me."

Luke stood and raised his glass high: "Here, here!" then, looked at his wife when he realized no one else was standing. "Did I do that right?"

Catalyn replied with a you-do-your-best smile, then tugged on his shirt in a motherly way. "Welcome back, Silas," she said, raising her glass. "You've been away too long and we're all anxious to finally get to know you."

With tears forming in the corners of her eyes, Jennifer rose and hugged her brother, whispering, "I love you so much, Silas."

Cassie thought, *I love you too, Silas,* her "voice" as loud and clear as crisp mountain air.

He's drawing away from me, Jennifer thinks. *He hugs me, he says without lies that he loves me. But somehow he is even more distant now than before. I have never known a day without Silas, until now. His smile is full of promises but he will not let me near...will not let me feel what he is feeling.*

She draws back and whispers, *What's wrong?* And he says only, *It's heavy.* She thinks for a moment, *what could be so heavy?* but she doesn't know, and it frightens her. Then she feels it; not Silas, nor anyone or anything in the room, though she knows it is through her brother that the unwelcome sensation is coming.

It is indeed heavy. It is a weight on her soul like nothing she has ever felt before; worse even than the years spent in fear of Prygor Primm. It is the emptiness of knowing you have fallen into a pit that has no bottom. She looks first to Luke, then to Catalyn. *(How can they not feel it? The terrible weight?)* They are standing and smiling, and Luke has his arm around Catalyn in that easy embrace a man gives the woman he loves without thinking how much he loves her. Though he loves her endlessly. It is an embrace that Jennifer has never felt in thirty-four years and in that moment the emptiness could consume her.

It's Cassie who saves her from madness—from utter and endless despair. She looks into the child's eyes and sees...tomorrow. A distant tomorrow; maybe days or weeks or months—who could tell?—but tomorrow. The girl knows.

Knows more than

(the woman? what woman?)

she.

Goodnight, Jennifer tells them. She drops to her knees and hugs Cassie as never before.

Then the despair crawls back in to roost for the night.

18

A Purloined Conversation

During the pitched battles that took place during the War of the Turning we came to dread the quiet times; when the winds calmed to a whisper and songbirds could be heard by ears still ringing from gunshots. Such times were the top of the pendulum's swing, when for a short time we could see above the clouds of war as the day broke bright and warm. But never to last, for the pendulum could pause but for an instant before plunging back into death and darkness. This we knew, and the knowledge stole from us the few precious moments we had to be hopeful...

FROM THE UNPUBLISHED MEMOIRS OF CARLOS HERRERA

In the roughly one hundred years before the Turning, granite from the Baker quarry had been shipped to every state in the Union and twenty countries on four continents. Being of a rare quality—a consequence of the extreme heat and pressure under which it was formed over two billion years ago as a molten, pyroclastic stew deep beneath surface of the Proterozoic Earth—it was suitable for many splendid purposes. A number of the Industrial Revolution's movers and shakers rested peacefully beneath headstones carved from fine, black granite taken from the Baker quarry, and many a grand old building had been made even grander with Baker granite adorning its floors and walls. It was an enterprise that had made the Baker family gloriously wealthy in a pedestrian town of simple people for whom wealth was measured by the equity in one's home and the number of roadworthy four-wheel-drive vehicles in one's driveway.

Yet few had ever harbored any real resentment toward Sturm Baker, the last surviving heir to the Baker fortune. Despite his ostentatious wealth

Sturm was a likeable sort who made a point of showing up for nearly every civic function, no matter how puerile in its inception or inept in its execution, and he could always find the time to chat with whomever he might happen to meet on the street, whether or not the fellow had anything to say.

And while the Turning had redefined the meaning of wealth—due to the universal forgiveness of debt, virtually all property was now owned outright, and a man's vehicle no longer carried as much status as his means for producing the fuel to power it—it had done little to change the friendly relationship Sturm had with others in the town. He was still looked up to, since he remained the warmly gregarious soul he had always been. So much so, in fact, that it was hardly noticed that his acts of civic philanthropy had dwindled, and the number of townspeople he employed to maintain his estate had grown fewer, for it was rumored that Sturm Baker had converted a goodly percentage of his wealth to precious metals before the Turning, and now was certainly able to live the rest of his life in customary comfort without ever having to lift a finger to earn another dollar, drachma, denarius or doubloon.

Or so Sturm wanted everyone to believe. In truth, it was an expensive proposition to remain habituated to opulence in a world where luxury had long been out of style, especially since the fabled Baker fortune could not be readily replenished in an age that had little use for fine-grained pre-Cambrian granite. His salary at Desa was considerably less than what he needed to support his lifestyle, and his side deals with pirates like Hadrian Tharp had not borne as much fruit as he had hoped. He needed money. It was a secret he alone was privy to, since nothing he could imagine in life would be more un-Baker-like than to admit that he was nearly broke.

*   *   *   *

Hadrian had a score to settle. During the War of the Turning, after he and his band of urban guerrillas finally tired of eating rats, dogs, skunks and each other and moved out into the hinterland to find proper nourishment, they'd set their sights on Purgatory for its perfect isolation and its reputed stores of corn, wheat and soy. Sodbusters and goat ropers. Easy pickings. But the blitzkrieg-type assault he planned against the citizenry had instead turned into a lengthy siege, then a massacre, courtesy of Tay Villa. Hadrian hated Purgatory and despised his old enemy. But for Villa, at least, he had respect.

Tharp left his jeep parked in front of The Blue Fox and made his way across the bridge and up the hill to Baker's mansion on foot. He was not expected there and would probably not be welcomed, which was fine with him. Hadrian liked surprising people; it threw them off-guard and made them squirm. And gave him a chance to see what they were up to.

Was Baker up to something? Call it a hunch, but the peculiar partnership between Baker and Primm was a strange one and it only made sense if the glue that held it together was money. Why else would a prosperous man like Baker befriend a shadowy character like Prygor Primm? The sheriff was liked by no one, and had little or no money. What he did have were the morals of a black widow and the officiousness of a Gestapo agent. Which made him the perfect choice as Baker's eyes and ears in the sleepy little faux-nineteenth century community of Purgatory.

The night was warm and the erratic wind that had kicked up earlier had fortunately died down. It was easier to eavesdrop when windows were open, and easier still if the conversation of interest were being conducted outside the thick stone walls.

Baker was there with Primm. He'd arrived in a syndiesel-powered state-owned Hummer, Primm on a tired gray mare. For entertainment, Baker had brought along a matched pair of nicely constructed female specimens, one blonde, the other brunette. Neither was older than twenty-five and both were lightly clad in the sort of fine lingerie that was difficult to come by in these hard times.

This much Hadrian was able to discover with a paucity of effort; as he had hoped, the ancient double-hung windows were raised high in their jambs and the interior of the stately old house was brightly lit with hydrogen lamps. He positioned himself beside a large window that gave him a good view of the spacious great room. Inside, Baker sat in a red velvet loveseat, clutching a glass of wine in the hand that wasn't stroking the blonde's bare shoulder. Because of his considerable girth, the loveseat was a tight fit; so much so that the girl's shapely left leg was raised off the cushion and lay over the top of Baker's leg, which was mercifully still stuffed within his trousers. Baker seemed pleased with the arrangement, as did the girl. She too sipped wine—a burgundy, Hadrian imagined, tasting both the wine and woman on his lips—and planted a wet red kiss on Baker's jowl as reward for a witticism Hadrian had been unable to hear.

Primm, by contrast, was having trouble warming up to the spirit of the gathering. He sat conspicuously erect on the other side of the glass coffee table in the twin to Baker's loveseat. Both hands rested in his lap, holding a stemmed glass half-full of ice water. The brunette beside him was every bit as appetizing as the blonde, perhaps more so, since the expression on her unblemished face was a scornful sort of pout that Hadrian thought sexy, even though Primm obviously did not. Because of Primm's rail-like frame the loveseat was almost roomy, and Primm used every extra inch to estab-lish a DMZ between his legs and hers. The sheriff's reluctance filled Hadrian with a gnawing temptation to invite himself in and give Primm a little in-struction in how to get his money's worth from a high-class call girl.

Baker had also taken notice of the sheriff's peculiar behavior. He ex-cused himself to step outside and have a cigar, though it was obvious what he really wanted was a private word with Primm. The brunette was certainly pleased to see the sheriff vacate his spot on the loveseat and follow Baker out the door like a dutiful dog. She blew out a long-held breath and gulped her wine the instant his back was turned.

The porch coming off the first-story great room was ten feet or more above the stone patio below. Hadrian silently made his way down the incline where he repositioned himself in the near-perfect darkness directly under Baker and Primm.

Baker was clearly unhappy. "What is it, Prygor?" he hissed under his breath. "Tell me, please. I'd really like to know what your fucking problem is." He cast a furtive glance through the window at the two hookers to see if they were watching. They weren't; they were too busy gossiping in hushed tones and giggling between sips of wine.

"Nothing," Primm lied in a terse monotone. *Everything* was wrong, and he had no idea how to make it right. He stared coldly at Baker and said, "I'm just not feeling up for this tonight, that's all."

Baker laughed at his unfortunate choice of words; a nasty little chuckle that Primm knew from experience always preceded a slur against his char-acter. This time was no different. "I'm not sure you're ever up for it, Prygor. I won't even pretend to understand why. But somehow, you always find a way to enjoy yourself."

Primm listened obediently while thoughts of killing Baker—Baker with his harlots and his strong drink and his foul mouth—danced across his mind. He said, "I'm sorry. Like I said. I appreciate what you do for me. It's been a bad day, that's all."

It was the most pitiful understatement of his life. Between last night's encounter with Silas and Jennifer and tonight's run-in with Tay Villa, every fine dream in his small-but-manageable world had been shattered into impossibly tiny pieces. His foot—which he'd wrapped in a hanky to stem the bleeding, and which he refused to favor in the least, lest Baker ask about it—throbbed painfully, but that was nothing compared to what had been done to his pride. He needed Jennifer; she was the only human in his small universe he could talk to. But unless he found a way to do away with Tay, Silas, Jack Vara and possibly the entire Malloy family, he might never be able sit with Jennifer again. And that simply wasn't acceptable. He would rather die. For now he would wait and bear his misery as best he could. Then if there was simply no other way he would "disappear" his enemies as neatly and quietly as possible and hope for the best. As for Baker; he might be useful in ways that were at the moment beyond Prygor's meager imagination.

Perhaps sensing the dark machinations churning behind Primm's dark eyes, Baked stepped back and said, "Yeah...all right, Primm. Everyone has bad days. But you have to understand," he went on, suddenly emboldened by the economics of the matter, "these ladies don't come cheap. I expect you to enjoy my little presents"—then his parting shot—"in so far as you can."

He was right, of course. Prygor usually *did* enjoy the ladies. He enjoyed touching them and watching as they warmed to his touch. As though his long, skeletal fingers held the secret to their every pleasure. The thought that they might be acting had never occurred to him. He had once closed his eyes and tried to imagine it was Jennifer's body he was stroking with his fingertips and Jennifer who softly moaned with pleasure beneath his tenuous, exploratory touch, but the experiment ended abruptly when he was suddenly overcome by shame for thinking of the woman he loved as an object of sexual desire.

Baker lit a long, skinny cigar that smelled to Prygor like a stick of dried horse dung. But he dutifully held his tongue on the matter and changed the subject. He said, "Do you think Vara's figured out where the diamonds are hidden?"

Diamonds? **What** *diamonds?* Beneath the porch, Tharp snapped so quickly erect from the slouch he'd settled into that he feared the creaking of his combat-ravaged bones would betray his presence. He held his breath for a long moment, then let it slowly out when Baker replied irritably, "How the hell should I know, Prygor? You're the one who's supposed to be watching him. All I know is what's in that letter you managed to waylay. Good job on that, by the way," Baker said under his breath. Then, "I'm betting that little code in the postscript gives the location of the stones. I mean, what else could it be for? The question is, can Vara make sense out of it?"

Does Salia know about this? Tharp wondered. Is that what she'd been after all these years? At first it didn't make a lot of sense. She raked in so much hard currency from the faithful hoping to buy their way into Saint Salia's Army of Delusion that he couldn't imagine she'd ever need more. Not unless she had something *really* big planned—and on that account he always had to leave room for the unexpected—and she'd somehow gotten wind there was a king's ransom in diamonds stashed under a rock somewhere out at the old Herrera place.

And if there was? It would be just like Salia to play him for a fool, pretending she was after some elusive and mysterious document—the contents of which she refused to reveal—when in fact what she really wanted was some dead Mexican's horde of diamonds. Maybe she had lied to him to all along to keep him from engaging in a little freelancing. She knew Hadrian would never raise an eyebrow over some old long-forgotten document so she'd fabricated a lie to throw him off the trail.

Sorry, Salia my dear, but we may soon be changing the nature of our relationship.

Overhead, Primm said, "Vara will figure it out. That's why his old man made up the code: it's his kid's job to make sense of things that don't make any sense. But are the diamonds real?"

"Oh, the diamonds are real enough," Baker chuffed with an assurance Tharp thought comforting, "don't lose any sleep over that one. Cagey old fart that Herrera was, I've still managed to trace a number of large stones back to him. Those houses and that little power installation out there weren't built on sweat and good intentions, Prygor; there's been a lot of money poured into that place. And whenever old Carlos found himself in need of hard currency he'd beat a path straight to an old friend of mine with a special talent for turning stones into silver."

"Then Vara will find them," Primm said flatly.

"But what if he *can't?*" Baker bellowed. "What if it's so complicated *no one* can figure it out. What then?"

"Then we'll get it out of Silas Teague," Primm replied. "He'll know."

"Teague?" Baker scoffed. "The man's a turnip, for Christ's sake."

A long pause, then: "Not anymore. There's been a sudden change in his condition. He's...better. And he knows more than you can imagine."

Teague, Teague...why was that name familiar? Hadrian wondered. Then it hit him. Teague was the name of the brother and sister who lived in the house next to Herrera's. (*"Be careful,"* Salia had whispered as Hadrian took up his position outside Carlos Herrera's house the night she killed the old man. *"It wouldn't do to wake up the Teagues. They can't know we were ever here. At least not until I'm ready to tell them."* It hadn't taken much imagination to figure out the Teagues were in for a rough time.)

"But *how* would he know?" Baker asked. There was a tone of respect in his voice that wasn't there before.

"He knows. Believe me, he knows."

It seemed they had resolved something. Baker flicked his half-smoked cigar off the porch and they both went back inside. Hadrian didn't wait around to see what a guy with a limp noodle in his pants planned to do with a gorgeous whore.

19

Silas on the Move

My father was a self-disciplined man. He was able to feign loyalty to Franco long after plundering a considerable fraction of the very diamonds the dictator himself had plundered. Had he fled in panic to Mexico it would've been the end of him—indeed the end of us all. But for two years he stayed with Franco, living modestly on his State salary while a sparkling fortune lay hidden beneath the roots of the lettuce, peas, and radishes in my mother's garden. That neither my mother nor I knew of his larcenous deeds until long after we had emigrated to Mexico was a testament to my father's extraordinary resolve...

FROM THE UNPUBLISHED MEMOIRS OF CARLOS HERRERA

It didn't take long for Silas to discover that the legs he'd used to move around on the flat floors and even surfaces in the house and greenhouse were unsuited for the task he had now set them to. Even a rock in the trail no larger than his fist could cause him to trip and nearly fall, and the ups and downs of the mountainous terrain forced him to use muscles that had not been properly exercised since he was a lad of seventeen. Several times his walking stick had kept him from tumbling to his knees.

But the level of difficulty didn't concern him so much as the possibility or impossibility of completing his journey. Difficult he could handle—if he could do it, he would. He just didn't want to discover too late that he'd walked into a landscape he couldn't possibly traverse with his diminished physical capabilities and end up as nourishment for a frightening array of scavengers.

But maybe being buzzard bait was better than falling into the hands of Salia Warchez.

He wouldn't think about it. Visualizing an event you wished not to happen was no different than casting weed seeds into a nicely tended garden: either way you ended up the author of your own defeat. Far better to dwell on what he desired than on what he feared, otherwise he ran the risk of crystallizing into reality the exact thing he least wished to happen.

Fine words and wise, Silas thought. The kinds of words certain to sway an argument in one's favor as armchair philosophers gather with their wine goblets 'round the fire to exercise their aging elbows and tired wits. But his situation was considerably more salient than clever snippets of verbiage strung end to end. The wrong thought might cost him and all those he cared about their lives.

He at least had the comfort, small though it was, of knowing he really had no choice. For the safety of Jennifer and the others—and perhaps for the future of the world, such as it was—he had to remove himself to a place no one would ever think to look for him until he could regain his full strength and act on the information Carlos Herrera had months ago planted in his mind while Jennifer was off on an errand.

At the moment, all he knew for sure was this: if Salia Warchez found him, the game was over. And that wouldn't be much of a game at all.

On his back he carried a small gray nylon backpack. It may even have been the same one he used to ferry his school books. When Jennifer went to share the news of his recovery with the Malloys, he stuffed a few essentials in the pack and hid it behind a bush just outside the greenhouse.

He followed a winding game trail along the wooded north side of the creek until he was well past the dwellings, then crossed the creek before the bank became any steeper. With pale moonlight as his only beacon, he labored along in a more-or-less southwesterly direction, weaving—as his legs commanded—to avoid any direct assaults on hills of more than a few degrees of grade.

His legs burned, a sensation he had not felt for nearly two decades and he found it strangely comforting; as if it were reassuring to know he *could* feel pain.

And cold. As the hours since sunset mounted, the chilly downslope breezes strengthened by perceptible degrees. Every few steps he paused to blow on his hands—if he'd ever had any gloves they were long since packed away in some forgotten place—before lumbering forward again.

He tenuously worked his way through a pine and aspen forest, over a rise populated with dense stands of mountain mahogany bushes and occasional juniper trees twisted into ghostly silhouettes by the ceaseless breezes that nipped at his feet with every step.

Upon reaching the rocky plain that paralleled the north-south mountain chain he headed due south. Once beyond the gusty spout of the lacuna he paused to take stock of his position. It was then, when his own footfalls ceased, that he heard movement behind him. Pebbles crunching underfoot. Claws clicking against rock. Cold fear danced up and down his spine. With no defense other than his walking stick, he would be easy pickings for a mountain lion or a grizzly. Or more likely, one of the fearsome outcrosses that occurred when feral dogs got together with wolves and coyotes for a DNA swap meet. Muties, they were called. Tay had once stabbed a large male that had made the mistake of attacking him. He recalled Jennifer describing it to him, as she did everything that happened at *Vientos de los Dioses*. This memory was especially poignant, however, because of the concern in Jennifer's voice as she told how the mutie had been stalking Cassie before Tay intervened.

He turned a slow circle, but the scrabbling ceased as he did. He took a few more steps. The creature followed, always staying far enough back to keep from being spotted in the dim moonlight. It mirrored Silas's movements like a distant shadow, and after a while his fear was replaced with curiosity. Apparently the creature meant him no harm. Like Silas, it was merely curious, keeping pace from just beyond his visibility, as though it'd had enough experience with humans to know the limits of a man's night vision.

As the night wore on he welcomed the company, whatever the company might be, and his mind moved on to other things. Having no watch, he tried to reckon the time by judging how far below the horizon the sun would have to be to illuminate the moon to its present point of half-fullness. As best he could reckon, sunrise was less than two hours away, and when next he paused for a sip of water from his canteen and a slice of dried apple he saw a muted glow on the eastern horizon, illuminating the sleeping town of Purgatory with diffused light. How peaceful it seemed in the predawn blush; the calm before the storm.

A storm named Salia.

He could feel her ravenous spirit moving through town like an ill vapor, exploring weaknesses in every soul. She was learning, preparing to work her mischief, though mischief was hardly the sum of her intent. It was just one of her many talents. Salia was first and foremost a predator, and tonight she was stalking Silas.

Somehow, she knew he was on the move; he could feel it. Worse yet, she knew what he was hoping to find.

Could she find him, like a compass needle seeking out magnetic north? Perhaps, but he didn't think so. He'd felt her inside his head many times when the pathways that connected him to the rest of world were too dense and murky to navigate through, but she was not inside him now.

Jennifer and the others were his greatest concern. Their ignorance, ironically, was their salvation; they knew nothing of what she sought and harming them would do her no good; not unless she could be sure Silas himself knew her intentions. And *that* she couldn't know for certain unless Silas phoned home, so to speak, something he had no intention of doing until he was perfectly good and ready.

Besides, they had Tay to look after them.

Am I being too smug? Or too hopeful? If she finds me she will have everything she needs. Then God help us, because none of us will be of any further use to her.

He pressed on, leaving a slice of dried apple behind for his new friend. A wet gnawing sound told him his gift was accepted. Shortly thereafter he realized his unseen companion had quietly worked his way around in front of him. Silas now followed, listening carefully as the creature picked out a path for them through the bushes and talus that slowed his progress. Whatever manner of beast it might be, at the moment it was the only friend he had.

20

Woltr and Bil

At seventeen, Silas Teague was a man of extraordinary talents. Then a cruel fate deprived him of his senses. Or so I thought. But as time went on I learned a different truth: Silas had lost nothing; he continued to grow stronger every day he spent beyond the distractions of this world.

FROM THE UNPUBLISHED MEMOIRS OF CARLOS HERRERA

Woltr was not pleased with the scant bounty produced by his trap line this week. He'd been hoping for a rabbit or a tufted-eared squirrel, but all he had snared today was one old porcupine. Still, it was better than nothing, which is what he'd found in his traps yesterday. Porcupine was tough and stringy but he'd eat it anyway; maybe let it simmer all day, with lots of garlic and salt. A few carrots, potatoes and onions from the garden and he just might turn this bristly rodent into a feast.

When was the last time he'd moved the traps? Had it been a week? He knew autumn was beckoning though he wasn't certain if it was still September or if October had sneaked up him. He liked the hot months for the relief the heat offered from whatever high-sounding malady it was that plagued his aging knees and shoulders—and lately his elbows and even his knuckles. But now summer had drifted into fall, and all he had to look forward to were several long months of creaking and aching.

How old am I? He wondered. He'd quit counting at seventy-nine, but that had been four or five years ago. Maybe longer. What did it matter? He'd live until he died, and then he sure as hell wouldn't give a damn.

As he shuffled through the tall pines that obscured the early morning sun, stabbing the trail with his walking stick, he wondered how long it would be before anyone found his body when his time came. A good long stretch.

No one ever came up this way anymore. Not since that big mess everyone called the Turning. He still remembered the day a couple of ragtag devils came up from the south looking to take over Woltr's little hideaway. He dispatched them in short order and hoped the Almighty wouldn't mind that he'd given their bodies to the beasts and the birds. It made a lot more sense than burying them where nothing but worms could enjoy the bounty.

Woltr's homestead lay at the end of an old overgrown logging road. It had been his grandfather's land since before Taft was President and Woltr was the sole survivor of that line. So it was his place and no one could take it away from him. At Woltr's age, a sense of place was his greatest comfort.

Once in a while he'd get lucky and bag a deer, or an elk. The big ruminants had gotten dangerously scarce during that Turning business, but now they were coming back. He knew he wasn't supposed to shoot game animals out of season or without a license, but he did just the same. The military boys who lived in these woods knew what he was up to, but Woltr shared the meat and that seemed to appease them. One of the privileges of age.

He could eat for a month or better on a deer and longer on an elk, if he jerked the meat and dried it in his smoke house. His teeth were worn but he still had most of them, so he doubted his death would come by starvation.

However it came, he hoped the animals got him before someone wandered in from Purgatory to haul his remains back to town and put them in some dark hole in the cold ground. The crows would like his eyes, the four-legged creatures could have the rest. Maybe the old mountain lion that kept close watch on the place, but more likely a bear. There was still quite of bit of flesh left on his bones and he hoped for the bear's sake—for he reckoned it would be a bear and not the lion or the wolves, or the half-breed wolf dogs that had no fear of him—still a bit of tasty marrow inside them.

It would be better that way. The forest had been good to him; it was only fitting that he give something back to it. He always left a window open at night even during the coldest part of winter, just in case he died in his sleep. He didn't want the bear to have to work too hard for his meal.

He emerged from the forest into the small clearing where his crude cabin stood. The stout logs that enclosed its single room were a lot more weathered than they had been in '87 when he'd built the place, but it was home and it always brought a smile to his weathered face.

He noticed the door was ajar as he ambled toward the rough wooden bench in front of his porch where he cleaned and skinned his small game. Maybe he just hadn't closed it tight on the way out. The iron hinges had begun to sag and sometimes the latch didn't hit the striker plate squarely so he usually gave it a little lift until it caught. But had he done so this morning?

He was even forgetting his habits.

Just then Bil ambled out of the cabin. The wily old raccoon brought such a smile to his face he could feel the wrinkles bunch up around his mouth. He'd been gone most of the night and Woltr was afraid a big cat or a coyote might have caught his masked companion unawares.

"Mornin' Bil," he said as if to an old friend, which of course Bil was. "Want some breakfast?"

Bil sat up on his haunches and made a wringing motion with his hands. Then he followed Woltr to the cleaning bench.

In death, porcupines were almost soft; not at all the thorny things they were in life when their spines stood erect and ready to fend off all threats large and small. As he slid his knife into the rodent's soft underside his six crows cawed in the distance. A moment later they took up their places on the branches of the large ponderosa overshadowing the north side of the cabin. Woltr watched them watching him. He didn't know if they had always been the same six crows, but they were always six. In all these years, he still couldn't tell one from the other. Except for Cross. He was the leader of the gang (Woltr thought maybe it was called a *murder* of crows, but 'gang' better described this bunch), and most likely the oldest. Certainly older than fifteen.

Like all crows, Cross was jet black except for two intersecting lines of white feathers in the middle of his breast that formed a crude likeness of a crucifix. For a time Woltr had called him Jesus—pronouncing it Hay-SOOS, like the Mexicans—but the bird never warmed to the name. He liked Cross better, dipping his head whenever he heard the name.

Crows were talkers. Mostly they greeted him with clipped *caws*, but they also cooed. And sometimes they ran off caws and coos and rattles and trills in such quick succession they sounded like sentences. Not that they could really talk, at least not in the way a man does, but they could mimic Woltr's speech well enough that he could make out a few words.

Cross was especially talkative. Thanks to Woltr's tutelage, the big bird had names for most of the animals Woltr trapped, like *raaackit* (rabbit), *baukchah* (badger) and *skkiirrl* (squirrel). He rendered "porcupine" into something like *pawk-peye*. Not at all like human speech, but the big bird got the message across. He was attentive, and he knew what Woltr was up to most of the time, which is more than Woltr could say for himself.

Awk! Pawk-peye. Crawwws. Then he trilled and clicked. Normally Woltr would have tossed the big bird the heart, but pickings had been slim lately. He'd save it for the stew. Instead, he cast a lung in the sky, and watched Cross shoot from his perch to snag it in midair before the bloody organ's trajectory crested. Cross landed on the edge of bench and paced the edge as he gobbled down the tasty treat. The others waited in the branches.

"You're a pig, Cross," Woltr told him.

Awk. Crawwws iiig, the shiny, black beggar agreed.

Woltr pulled the other lung from the chest cavity and held it out for Cross. He yanked it away, as Cross nipped at it. "What do you say, my friend?" Woltr asked.

Awk! Crawws awnks!"

"Close enough." Woltr handed him the lung, before shoeing him away. Cross returned to his branch to stab at the lung with his bloody beak.

Bil claimed the liver and kidneys, grasping the bloody morsels in his dexterous hands before stuffing them into his pointy-toothed muzzle. The crows watched scornfully from their perches.

After that, it was a free-for-all. Woltr removed all of the remaining innards and tossed them into the air in the general direction of the crows. The Gang of Six descended on the steaming viscera like starving wolves on carrion. Most of it fell to the ground in a heap, causing raucous squabbles that teetered on the point of violence.

With his crows mostly sated, Woltr deftly skinned the porcupine and cut what little meat there was from the bones. These he saved for Bil. The rest of the carcass he tossed far into the woods before returning to the house with the heart and the strips of bloody meat in his broad palm.

The open door bothered him. Forgetting to close it properly would be like forgetting to button his fly. But he'd done that before, too.

Still, his instincts told him to pause, and so he did, knowing that his instincts had kept him alive in these woods even more than his ears, nose, or eyes.

Then he reminded himself that he was long since old enough to die, and walked through the door on legs that creaked like the rusty door hinges.

The little cabin was dark even in the bright of day, but in the early morning sunlight it was downright sepulchral.

He set the meat on the counter by the cast iron sink and found a box of matches on the table to light the alcohol lamp resting in its center. His eyes scanned the room in the feeble light, exposing nothing but a pine bed that sagged in the middle, a rocking chair that creaked worse than the door, and a few hides tacked to the walls. A loaded rifle and a shotgun hung above the door.

Nothing out of place.

His eyes followed the steep stair leading to the loft. He slept there in the winter, when the heat of the fireplace drifted up and kept his ailing joints warm, but in the summer and early fall he slept downstairs. He'd last crawled down from the loft sometime in May and hadn't been back since. And he wasn't about the climb back up until Ma Nature gave him one hell of a good reason.

So far, she hadn't.

Satisfied, he ambled back out as the rising sun crested the tall trees to the east. Most of the soil around his cabin was sandy and depleted, as mountain soils usually were, but down by the creek was an old alluvial bench filled with silt left by a flood that had come through a few years back. The turbulent waters had kissed the stones on the cabin's foundation before receding back within their banks to join up with Old Scratch downstream, but not before leaving several tons of fine topsoil just upstream from the cabin. To prevent erosion, Woltr had enclosed the perimeter with large stones and made a garden out of it.

It was a perfect little plot for potatoes, onions, garlic, carrots and radishes. And, of course, spinach. He'd even tried tomatoes this year. Picked up the seeds the last time he'd gone to town. Had that been February? Must have been; it was cold and foggy. January was cold and clear. March might be anything, but the wind blew, no matter what. February was the foggy month.

The season was about over for tomatoes, but some were still firm and plump, so he picked three to spice up his stew. It'd be a good one, and that was as good a reason as he could think of to live another day.

Grasping his walking stick in both hands, he carefully lowered himself to his knees and plucked out four carrots, two potatoes and a fat onion. He brushed off the dirt and smiled. He didn't have much, but he had all he needed. Not like most folks who spent more time wanting than giving thanks for what they had. He shook his head. A half century had passed since he'd moved here, and he wondered where common sense had gone, or if there'd ever been any to begin with. He was just thankful for being able to stay out of the world for all these years.

The three years of that Turning thing had been the worst. Couldn't find seeds to plant at any price, and the game got dangerously scarce. He'd taken to trapping birds—jays, mostly—just to stay alive. Gawd, but they were stringy old things. Once in a while he'd get lucky and bag a sage hen or even a wild turkey. Then there were the trees. Young bark and tender new pine needles worked in tea and stew alike, and the seeds were good, if a little hard to gather in abundance.

He'd gotten through it better than most, he reckoned. He just didn't understand why he still couldn't buy kerosene to burn in his lamps; the moonshine he cooked in the shack behind the shitter just didn't light up the same way.

He struggled to his feet with bounty in hand, and noticed his walking stick still lying in the garden. How had he gotten up without it? And how was he going to retrieve it without falling over? Were his joints improving at the cost of his mind? Gingerly, he bent down and snatched it up. Pain, his constant companion, was off visiting someone else. Perhaps the old mountain cat, he mused, though he hoped not. Give it to one of the bears. They didn't need to move with the same haste as the lion. Besides, a sore bear might not shit messy piles in the middle of his trails as often as a limber one.

He felt the hint of a spring in his step as he ambled back into the cabin, but thought no more about it as he washed and sliced the vegetables. They went into the iron pot that hung from a tripod in the fireplace, along with a couple cups of water, the porcupine meat, a pinch of salt and a few cloves of garlic.

He built a stack of tinder and small split logs beneath the pot, and watched as the flame caught from last night's embers. As yellow darts of flame engulfed the pot, Woltr eased back in his rocker, lighting his pipe with a long skinny twig he kept by the fireplace for just that purpose. The toils of the morning shed off of him like heat in a gentle rain, as he drew the soft smoke into his mouth and let it slowly find its way back out. Most of life was habit. And what little of it that wasn't almost seemed out of place.

The thought struck him as morbid, somehow.

But no less true, for being so.

Coughing. It was slight at first, maybe no more than the scratching of pine boughs against the cabin roof. Then louder, from the loft. Ten years ago, Woltr would have cursed himself for not looking earlier. Twenty years ago he might have flown into a rage at the intrusion. And before that? Perhaps a fearful dash to the shotgun above the door.

But not today.

Woltr smiled drew on his pipe. For one day, at least, he wasn't alone. Whoever the intruder was, he meant no harm; of that Woltr was certain. A fugitive from justice, whatever in the hell that meant? A lost traveler? There was only one way to tell.

"Water?" Woltr said softly, knowing his voice would carry easily to the loft, even over the crackling fire.

"Water," a voice croaked in affirmation.

Woltr dipped his cup in the basin by the sink, then thought better. He fumbled through the small cupboard for a clean cup and filled it with water. He dreaded climbing the steep stairs, but it turned out to be far easier than he remembered.

The man lay in Woltr's bed. Though he was turned away from Woltr and covered to the shoulders with a blanket, it was apparent that he was a young man; he could tell by the white smooth skin on the back of his neck where his long brown hair parted to flow over his shoulders.

That Woltr felt no fear of this intruder was surprising even to him. Maybe he had run out of things to fear. Or maybe there was nothing that he *should* fear. It hardly mattered. The young man needed help and Woltr was happy to offer it. "Here you go, young fellah. This ought to help some."

The man turned to face Woltr, then propped himself up on one elbow as he took the cup from Woltr's hands and greedily drank it down. His eyes were soft and gentle, and of the deepest blue. "Thank you. You're very kind," he said, handing the empty cup back to Woltr.

"More?" Woltr asked.

"Please," the man replied.

The second trip up and down the stairs was even easier than the first, which made no sense at all. Woltr put it out mind. The young man drank more slowly this time, carefully placing the half-empty cup on the floor beside the bed, before being seized by a coughing fit. His face was sallow and drained of all vigor. "I think you might be needing more help than I can give you, son."

The man rolled on his side and took another swallow of water. Woltr noticed his hands for the first time. Though they were soiled and scratched, the skin was smooth and devoid of scars, and his long, slender fingers were graceful and fluid, like an artist's hands, or perhaps a musician's. A bandage covered his left wrist. "I just need some rest," he replied.

Woltr pulled a chair out of the shadows and sat facing him. "What I mean is, you look like you just had all the energy wrung right out of you." he said, honing a little finer point on his earlier observation.

The man met his eyes, and a strange feeling washed over Woltr. This was not a normal man accompanied by easily explicable circumstances. It was as though the man were observing Woltr from across a great expanse of time and space. Curiously, it was not an uncomfortable feeling.

He said, "Rest. All I need is rest."

Woltr took him for his word.

21

Love and Mystery

I never thought it conceivable that I could do anything in this life that would have consequences for the fate of humanity. At least until I met Dobry Robak in the fall of 2012. It took me five years to realize who he was really working for, and by then it was too late.

Just the same, history may yet declare that the last irony was mine...

FROM THE UNPUBLISHED MEMOIRS OF CARLOS HERRERA

Jack was up before first light. He thought surely Jennifer would be making an early appearance and he'd rather not be trapped in bed when she did. Call it petty, but it was as awkward as it was embarrassing to be woken up by a woman who'd never seen him naked. Especially if said woman had a big, meaty bone to pick.

If Silas were true to his word, he was already gone; a troubling development that Jennifer would soon discover if she hadn't already. And then she would be casting all the logic of the situation to the wind, for Jennifer, with all her wondrous talents, was not a logical being.

She was deeper than that.

Deeper than me, at any rate, Jack thought wryly. *Probably because she hasn't spent her adult life structuring every thought to fit into a mold that's inherently flawed.*

And so for the last hour he'd been trying to tease out the meaning of the cryptic little mathematical statement in the postscript of his father's letter...

PS: $6 \subset 79 + (14 + (8 \times 2))$ *Memorize it, and destroy this letter.*

...with no luck at all. In that time he'd found in the cupboard a ceramic jar half filled with coffee, and an old electric Mr. Coffee on the top shelf of the pantry. In the refrigerator he discovered a partial loaf of raisin bread and a small bowl of butter he was certain hadn't been there yesterday. She was obviously looking after him on the sly and it made him want so badly to see her that he didn't care if she was angry or not.

He was sitting at the table drinking coffee, eating buttered raisin bread and trying to crack the code when the door opened (why lock it?) and she stepped lightly through the opening with the aura of the rising sun behind her head, as it had been yesterday.

Does she time it that way or is that just how it works out with this woman?

Jazzman had noted her approach with puppy-like anticipation, and let loose a high-pitched whine long before the door opened. And when the dog saw Sasha on the stoop he bolted through the doorway to begin a day of unending adventure.

Dogs had it so damned easy. They mated like minks for a solid week every six months, then somehow managed to remain the best of friends the rest of the time. People, on the other hand...

He never finished the thought.

"I guess you know he's gone," she said. She sounded reasonable, and when she stepped into the room he saw no anger on her face. But what he did see made him long for the fiery outburst he'd been expecting. Her eyes, customarily so clear and bright, were ringed with red and downcast, and the sadness expressed in her face was difficult to observe. When she tried to summon up a wan little smile it only made her visage more pitiable.

In her hand she held a small piece of paper that could only have been a note from Silas.

For a moment he hesitated, then crossed the room to hold her.

At first his embrace was one-sided; so much so that he felt small and useless against her sorrow. But then she wrapped her arms around him and buried her face in his chest. He expected her to cry, perhaps even to wail, but she must have cried herself out before coming. Instead she tightened her embrace, breathing gushes of warm air against his chest, sniffling after every few breaths. He felt her heart beating furiously and he lay his face against the top of her head for several moments before kissing her head and forehead, neither expecting it go any further nor wanting it to.

Nevertheless, she snuggled tighter against him.

Finally, when the embrace had lingered to the near point of awkwardness, she said, "God, but life can really suck sometimes." She gave a forced chuckle, and sniffled, then pulled away from Jack. She was done feeling sorry for herself, though Jack had yet to run through his sorrow for her.

He said, "Jennifer, I...I'm so sorry. Maybe I should have told you, but—"

"He made you promise not to?" Her voice was disarming, maybe even a little wry. But he felt a barb snag his heart, just the same.

"Something like that," he affirmed with a sigh.

"I tried being mad at you, Jack. I knew something was up last night when you blew me off for dinner. But in my wildest dreams I never thought Silas would...fly the coop."

"He was counting on that, Jennifer. Had you suspected, you might have—"

"Might have what? Tied him to a chair? Held a gun to his head until he came to his senses?" The emotional storm he anticipated earlier was starting to build. He welcomed it.

"...Might have found a way to dissuade him from doing what he knew he had to do," Jack answered reasonably. "Or worse."

"And what could be worse?"

Jack said, "Getting him to reveal information that could get you killed, maybe? C'mon, Jennifer; he's looking out for you. He's looking out for all of us."

"Thanks for not using my brother's name in the past tense," she said, holding the note out to him. "Here. He left this."

Jack unfolded it and read:

Sorry, dear Jennifer, that all you find of me today is this note. I really hated to skip out the way I did; I would much rather have spent the day drinking Luke's dandelion wine and catching up on all that I'd missed the last 17 years. Unfortunately, our benefactor Carlos planted some things in my head before he died and I can't get them out. So I'll have to take my head someplace where she can't find it.

I think you know who I mean.

Stay close to Jack, and to Tay. It's me she wants. There is nothing for her to gain by harming you. With Carlos gone, I am her last hope. She knows I can destroy the one thing she wants. Anytime. And if I did? Better not to think about that.

It's just a guess, but I doubt she'll risk it.

Please don't look for me. I'll find you when the time comes.
I Love You, Jennifer,
Silas
P.S. I owe you 17 years of love and care, and it's not a debt I intend to welsh on.

Jack handed the note back to Jennifer. "Like I said, he's looking out for us."

"But, Jack, he was so frail...certainly in no condition to go running off into the wilderness!"

Jack recalled how much strength and mobility Silas had regained in the short time he was with him yesterday. It bordered on miraculous. He said, "We have to trust that Silas knows exactly what he's doing, Jennifer. No one makes that kind of recovery after so many years just to throw their life away the next day. Your brother knows what he's about; he's certainly not some pissed-off eight-year-old running away from home. He has a plan; he just couldn't share it, that's all. Can you blame him?"

"No," she said, "but what could Carlos have told him that *she* would want so badly?"

"I don't know."

"I'm worried," she said.

Jack placed his hands on the side of her head and kissed her forehead. Her soft blonde hair was fine as a baby's. He thought she might pull away but instead she warmed to his touch. He looked in her eyes (now beginning to brighten) and said, "So am I. But I don't think he had any choice." He drew her to him, and again she embraced him. It felt good to hold her, and this time the feeling persisted.

After a long moment she gently pulled away. She was scanning the room as if she might find something that would lend meaning to the situation.

"Found the coffee and raisin bread, I see."

"Yes. Thank you. It was a nice surprise. I thought I might have to settle for water and granola bars. Where'd the butter come from?"

"Catalyn's cow," she said absently as her eyes fell on Jack's letter from Carlos. She snatched it up without asking and quickly scanned the contents. When her eyes came to rest on the postscript she set it gently down as if it might be explosive.

"Just can't leave it alone, can you?" It was an accusation.

"Considering the situation, I can't see that it matters," he answered in self-defense. "Whatever Silas is onto, it goes way beyond *this*." He stabbed at the postscript with an index finger.

Without comment, she asked, "And have you figured it out?"

"No."

She seemed pleased to hear this.

"It would help if I had some context," he suggested.

"Context?"

"Yeah, as in 'what the hell are we looking for?' Gold? Silver? Howard Hughes' *real* last will and testament? If I knew, the numbers might begin to make sense."

She gave him an appraising look, then shrugged. "Diamonds," she said.

"*Diamonds?*"

"Like I said." She fished around in the cupboard and found a mug, then poured herself some coffee and sat down at the table. Jack took his seat across from her. He said, "Do I want to know where they came from?"

She cocked her head and rolled her eyes—*who cares? I'm going to tell you.* And she did. It was a short tale from which Carlos had withheld most of the details. Still, it was enough to make Jack lean back in his chair and let out a long, dry whistle.

He asked, "So no one ever suspected that my grandfather left Spain with millions of dollars in diamonds in the linings of his suitcases?"

"Apparently not. I don't believe anyone ever figured it out. Your grand-father seems to have been a sly old devil."

"Like father, like son." Jack said.

Jennifer nodded. "Carlos *was* his father's son, to be sure. But to his credit I don't think he stole the diamonds from Juan Ramon. The way he told it to me, when your grandmother died the old man kept what he needed, which wasn't much really, considering how well he'd invested. The rest he gave to Carlos. And, of course, Marissa. I guess you could call it a wedding present."

"Deborah and I got a wok and a matching set of satin sheets and pillowcases."

"Sounds nice, actually," Jennifer said, and he knew she meant it. It made him pity her in a whole new way, though he knew she would resent his pity. Yet for all the love she held in her heart, at the age of thirty-four she'd still never opened a wedding present. He reached across the table and wove his fingers into hers. She smiled warmly at the unexpected affection, and he knew in that moment that he had to kiss her.

She knew it too.

Just one kiss.

*   *   *   *

Afterward they lay together in the narrow bed, she on her back with her head against his shoulder, Jack reclining into the single pillow propped against the headboard. His arms lay across her body, just below her breasts. As before, their hands and fingers were entwined.

The scent of their lovemaking lingered in the air like a sweet incense.

In the day and a half since they first met, Jack had made love to her in his mind many times over. Sometimes he fumbled; sometimes she did. Sometimes it was so perfect the cherubs played their flutes in the background. When it came right down to it there was simply a man and woman. No drums rolled, no trumpets sounded.

It was far better than that.

It was the most natural thing he'd ever done in his life; gazing upon her, not as an object of sexual desire, but the woman he was meant to be with. His natural mate. The feeling was foreign; he'd never felt that way before. But he warmed to it quickly.

And when the looking was done and the time was nigh *(put up or shut up, Vara)* there was on Jennifer's part none of the nervous vacillating that had always been her trademark. She kissed him softly, then lay in his bed and held her arms open in a wide welcome, her face radiant and her bare breasts the color of cream.

Never had he wanted a woman more.

Even so, in the seconds before he gently lay down on top of her, he tried in his mind to make a case for self-delusion. This could *never* be as good as he wanted it to be; the cynic inside him would not allow it.

Jennifer knew otherwise. He saw it in the desire revealed in her face— lips gently parted, eyes closed in anticipation—as she slowly guided him into her.

And when he felt himself join with her in a shared plunge into ecstasy, he remembered what he had tried to forget, because he didn't believe it could be so. That he had fallen in love with Jennifer the first moment he saw her.

Their lovemaking began slowly, then hastened imperceptibly until they were together seized by a shared passion that sped them to the apogee of their desires.

They collapsed beside each other and trembled in one another's arms. For several moments not a word passed between them. They lay together and reveled in the primal rhythm of one heart beating beside another. After a long silence Jennifer said, "Tell me something. Tell me anything, just so long as you mean it."

At the risk of appearing out of character and exposing his soft underside, he said, "There's something I knew...knew the first moment I saw you."

"And that was...?"

He kissed the side of her mouth and whispered, "That you were the only one I would ever want to be with again." It was true.

A smile. "Um...I like that," she said.

They made love again.

When at last they dressed, Jack said, "I think a horseback ride is in order."

Curious, she said, "Toward what end, fair knight?"

Picking up on her cue, he answered, "A quest, my lady. A quest of discovery."

Hand in hand, they made their way to the barn.

22

Diamond Quest

*By the end of the Turning, those of us left in Purgatory had developed
a healthy mistrust of technology. We had always been told our success
or failure depended on how much technology we could bring to bear on
a particular problem. After the Turning we had no choice but to trust
our instincts and the ways of Nature; knowledge arising from beyond
the five senses. This rediscovered way of experiencing the world spilled
over into every aspect of our lives, even into matters formerly left to
chance and providence ...*

FROM THE UNPUBLISHED MEMOIRS OF CARLOS HERRERA

The sun beamed bright above an azure sky, and the day was warming
nicely by the time the horses were saddled. With a pleasant breeze from
the west it was about as nice a day as nature could serve up; a day made for
lovers. But Jennifer, who after so many years could happily include herself
among them, felt only the weight of her misgivings.

"This really is a bad idea, Jack," she said, once they were under way. It
wasn't the first time she'd thought this since hearing Jack's plans, but it was
the first time she'd voiced it. And hearing it from her own mouth made it
seem even worse. *I have every right to be jumpy,* she told herself as if to justify
her concern, which was at the moment neither immediate nor well formed.
*Riding in front of me is the third man I've ever made love to. The first two are dead
and the man who killed them could be anywhere.* But for now her alarm was
more logical than intuitive and for that reason she had reluctantly agreed
to go with him.

"Possibly," Jack answered confidently from over his shoulder, "but sometimes following up on a bad idea is better than doing nothing at all."

She laughed in spite of an effort not to. "Did you study the subject of bullshit, my dear, or do you just have a natural aptitude for it?"

Jack drew gently back on the reins until the gelding stopped in the trail and waited for Jennifer to ride up beside him. Sasha and Jazzman trailed behind. Though it was a stretch, he managed to lean over and kiss her by hooking a hand behind her head and pulling her halfway out of the saddle. It was a long slow kiss, a bedroom kiss, and certainly not what she was expecting. "It's in my genes," he whispered in her ear.

"Hmph!" She righted herself in the saddle and said, "Really, Jack. I think we ought to leave the diamonds where they are."

"And we will. Just as soon as we *know* where they are."

They rode on across the barren terrain just east of the forest. The trail was wide enough here that it could accommodate both horses abreast. Jennifer kept her mount beside Jack's so she didn't have to talk to his back. "You might as well tell me where we're going, you know. That way, maybe I can find the diamonds on my own after Primm shoots you off your horse." It was a perfectly wicked thing to say but worth it to see his cocksureness falter, if only for a few seconds.

"Tell me you're kidding." His voice carried just enough urgency to make her believe she might be getting through to him.

"Just pointing out one of the many possibilities that lead to an unsatisfactory conclusion."

The horse grunted as Jack stood up in the stirrups and scanned the terrain. The landscape could easily conceal a lone gunman; badlands and ravines to their right, forested hills to their left. Both within the range of a high-powered rifle.

Suddenly Jennifer regretted what she'd just said. She felt exposed. Worse, she felt Primm. *He's out there, somewhere, hiding and brooding. And watching.* Gooseflesh began to rise on the back of her neck. Jack must have felt it too. "What say we keep moving?" he said.

"To the trees," she said urgently, slapping her mount with the reins as the words left her mouth. The horse responded to Jennifer's stinging imperative by bursting into a gallop. Jack followed off to one side to avoid riding blindly into the dust she was kicking up. Sasha and Jazzman laid back their ears and struggled to keep pace, bounding over the barren ground with wolfish strides.

The tree line was no more than a couple hundred yards ahead and they closed the distance quickly. After riding far enough into cover that they could not possibly be seen from any vantage point more than a few yards distant they pulled up their winded mounts and turned to face each other.

Although he wasn't dripping with sweat and blowing globs of snot through flared nostrils, he *was* panting as hard as his horse and she wasn't doing any better. "Were...we...being silly?" he said.

"Yeah...sure. Must'a been," she coughed a hollow laugh that Jack matched with one more substantial. It got them both to leaning over their saddles, laughing until they had tears in their eyes.

But it wasn't funny; no more funny than surviving a plane crash. *Here we sit, laughing like a pair of fools. Fools who just got lucky.* Then the spiders once again started crawling up her neck, and she knew, *This is wrong. We shouldn't be here.*

She rode up beside him until they were face to face. The humor was gone from his eyes. She took his hand and pressed it to her lips. "Primm is out there, Jack. I don't know what he's up to, but he's out there."

Alarm briefly registered in his handsome face, only to be replaced with a gritty smile. He leaned back in the saddle and pulled Carlos' bolt-action 25.06 out of its scabbard, hefting it to his shoulder and sighting through the scope at nothing in particular. "Let him come." He dropped the well-oiled Remington back in the scabbard.

She saw in him a coldness she'd not sensed before, and she felt it pass into her. It gave her comfort.

"We're in good cover now. He can't get close enough for a clean shot without the dogs hearing him so we might as well do what we came here to do."

They rode on through pines and aspens while billowy clouds passed overhead, and soon they reached the tailing pile at the base of the mine tunnel Jennifer had showed him two days before. They both dismounted. Jack slung the rifle over his shoulder with a leather strap while they climbed up the mound of loose, angular rock. Sasha and Jazzman met them at the top.

"Here we are," he announced.

She smiled wryly. "So, are you offering any more explanation, or is this the part where we play twenty questions?"

"Oh, right. Sorry," he said, removing the letter from his shirt pocket and pointing to the postscript:

$$6 \subset 79 + (14 + (8 \times 2))$$

"When you told me we were looking for diamonds, it hit me. The numbers represent atomic elements. Six is the atomic number of carbon, the only element found in diamond. Seventy-nine is gold, fourteen is silicon, and eight is oxygen. The odd-looking symbol between them means 'contained in,' if you recall."

He looked at her as if he expected her to shout *Eureka!* She hated to disappoint him. "I still don't get it," she said, planting a small kiss on his cheek. "Chemistry wasn't exactly my strong subject."

Jack gave her a sly smile. "But you've got so much *of* it."

"You would know."

"I'd really like to know better."

"So would I. Let's make sure you're around to make it happen, shall we?"

He took her hand and led her into the dark tunnel. Like a pair of sentries, Jazzman and Sasha sat on either side of the entrance. She heard the rustling of fabric, then, *click!* The beam of a flashlight played along the jagged walls of the crudely cut tunnel, then across the ceiling which was barely high enough for Jennifer to stand. Jack had to hunch over. The walls were wet, and she could hear water dripping in places. Puddles filled the low spots in the uneven floor and the dank air smelled of mold. "I don't think I'd ever make a miner," she said offhandedly. "What are we looking for, anyway?"

"A quartz vein," Jack replied. "That's how gold comes to the surface, you see—always in quartz which, chemically, is silicon dioxide. Two atoms of oxygen for each atom of silicon. Silicon, plus oxygen times two. That was the riddle. Basically, Carlos was saying 'the diamonds are hidden in a gold-bearing quartz vein.'"

"Clever."

Jennifer kept her arm wrapped tightly around Jack's as he shuffled farther back into the mine. A few yards before the end, the flashlight illuminated a wide streak of translucent white rock imbedded within the granite. "There it is," he told her, handing her the small light. "Here; hold this up to the wall."

She shined the light on the vein of milky quartz as Jack slowly scoured it from end to end, digging his fingernails into every minute crack and crevice in hopes of dislodging the loose chunk that would reveal the diamonds. One, two, three passes over the vein. Nothing gave but a few small fragments. Prying with the blade of his pocketknife produced only more frustration and a bent blade. "It's got to be here," he huffed in exasperation. "It's simply *got* to be! We'll have to go back and get a pick. Maybe it's just lodged in there too tight; maybe it's—"

"The wrong mine?" Jennifer suggested.

He quickly spun his head toward her. "There's another?"

His surprise was comical, and she couldn't keep the bemusement out of her voice. "I might have told you, had you bothered to tell me what we were looking for."

"Well...shit."

"It's the only other one I know of, so the diamonds must be there."

"Yeah...okay. Where is it?" He was impatiently gathering pebbles with his feet like a downcast little boy who'd been told he had to do his homework before he could go play.

"It's just—"

Two gunshots rang out in quick succession from beyond the mine, followed by three more fired from a different weapon.

*   *   *   *

Prygor heard the shots issuing from within the trees off to the south. Big-bore handguns, he thought; maybe a 9mm or a .38 for the first two shots, a .44 or .357 magnum for the last three.

He himself was crouched behind a rock, northwest of the entrance to *Vientos de los Dioses*. From this vantage point he had a good view of Carlos and Jennifer's houses and all the land to the west. He'd been hiding here since before sunrise, having been assigned by Baker to keep an eye on the place until Jack Vara made a move for the diamonds. *Or until Tay finds me and cuts my throat.*

The plan seemed unimaginative, even to Primm. It was like trying to kill a goose by throwing a bullet into the air and hoping the goose flew into it. "Let me arrest him," Prygor had suggested. "I'll get it out of him." But Baker didn't like the idea; too many loose ends, he said. The truth was he was squeamish; despite his foul mouth and larcenous nature he had no stomach for inflicting pain.

So Prygor sat lurking behind his rock in a terrible mood. To avoid detection, he'd left his mare hobbled in an aspen grove by the creek a good two miles back, completing his way on foot. Not a difficult walk for a man with two good feet. But Prygor only had one. The other was red and swollen all around the wound, which was badly infected, and it burned like the fires of Hades every time he took a step.

To make matters worse, he hadn't thought to bring any food or water. His belly groaned and his throat burned. And since he'd reluctantly left his Stetson with his horse to keep from being easily identified in case he was spotted, his head was quickly getting sunburned beneath his thinning hair.

But these were all small complaints. Pain, thirst and hunger were bodily discomforts and Prygor could bear them better than anyone. He'd learned early in life that all the things that bedeviled the body either passed in time or killed it.

It was the pain that tore at his heart that was eating him up inside. And it would neither pass nor kill him; it would simply bore a little deeper every day, until...

How could she do it? the voice inside his head bubbled over. *How could she kiss a man she'd known for only two days?* He'd seen *him* pull her close and cover her mouth with his, just like he would do if he was about to conjugate with one of Baker's harlots. And she had kissed him back! Good God! Didn't she know how fine and perfect and delicate she was? Didn't she know she wasn't made to be loved...so coarsely?

I know, the voice said, as if whispering in his ear.

It was the same voice he'd heard last night. The voice that told him to kill...her. He'd wondered about it off and on ever since; both the nature of voice—*could it be divine, or am I drifting into psychosis?*—and the identity of the woman he was being asked to kill. But this he thought he knew already.

"Who's there?" he asked the voice.

Come to me.

"Go away." He rested his back against the rock, wishing he were dead, for the pain was beginning to get to him, no matter how insistently he told himself he could ignore it.

I can take the pain away. All of it.

"How?" *I must be losing my mind,* he thought. But he refused to believe it, and his refusal gave him hope.

Come to me.

The voice was insistent…and seductive.

Again he asked, "How?"

Just close your eyes.

After a brief hesitation, he did. And in a moment his pain was gone, from his foot to his head to his heart. Just like the voice promised.

* * * *

From inside the mine it was impossible to tell from how far away the shots were fired, or even which direction they'd come from. Jack glanced quickly at the entrance. Both dogs were gone. Grasping Jennifer's hand, he scurried quickly to the mine entrance.

Great fucking idea you had, Jackie boy. Go off looking for riches and end up trapped like a rat in a hole.

He motioned for Jennifer to stay back, then poked his head out with a hand behind one ear. No barking dogs, no voices, no snapping of twigs. Just a light breeze soughing through the treetops

He unshouldered his rifle and chambered a shell with an authoritative slap of metal against metal, then stepped out of the mine far enough to peer over the eastern edge of the entrance. Nothing. Then… something—multiple somethings—running toward him through the underbrush. He eased the rifle to his shoulder and peered over the top of the scope. Heart hammering, he flicked off the safety and waited.

"Careful, Jack," Jennifer cautioned from inside the mine.

He grunted "Yeah," but didn't look her way.

Quick movement in the trees, closer now. He let his finger slip inside the trigger guard and pulled the rifle tight against his shoulder, but quickly lowered it when Jazzman and Sasha broke into the clear. Tay was close behind and bleeding badly.

23

Saving Tay

Once things start down the road to hell, it never takes them long to get there...

FROM THE UNPUBLISHED MEMOIRS OF CARLOS HERRERA

Catalyn was pacing nervously at the edge of the bridge when Jennifer and Jack pulled up their mounts before crossing. Jack held the reins with one hand while keeping Tay balanced in front of him with the other. His horse was heavily lathered and sweat dripped down over its hooves. Catalyn ran to examine Tay; Luke grabbed the headstall to prevent the excited horse from tossing his head.

The tourniquet Jack had applied around Tay's thigh was slowing the bleeding from the ragged slash in his leg, but not nearly enough. He needed medical attention, and fast.

"We heard the shots," Catalyn cried urgently. "Where is he—? Oh, shit Tay! You really went and got into it this time." Tay slumped in the saddle, not seeming to notice her.

Her eyes were intense and her face all business as she examined the wound—a large, gaping hole a few inches above the knee. Blood ran in rivulets and dripped to the ground.

She reached up and slapped Tay lightly on the face. "Doin' all right there, Tay?"

"*No problema,*" he croaked. Jack thought he sounded gravely weak.

She turned to Cassie and said, "Do you think maybe you can do something to help with the bleeding, honey?"

"*No problema,*" the girl replied.

"Dammit Cassie, this is serious!" Catalyn scolded.

"I know!" Cassie shot back. "So quit yelling and let's get a move on!"

Shaking her head, Catalyn quickly gave Cassie a leg up into the saddle, where she slid in behind Jennifer. To Jack she barked, "Get him to his house, fast! I need to get my surgical kit. We'll be right behind you. Lie him down on the bed and elevate the leg. Release the tourniquet for one minute before tightening it again. A minute off, five minutes on; We'll be there by then. And get his damn pants off. Got it?"

"Got it," he affirmed, and dug his heels hard into the gelding's flanks. Tay fell into him like a heavy rag doll when the horse bolted. Jack struggled to keep from tumbling off the back but managed to right himself. Tay's house was about a quarter mile from the bridge. It was small and built of stone, with a steep roof and rounded dormers. A compact sorrel horse paced nervously in a pole enclosure east of the house, just south of where a well-worn trail disappeared into the trees along the creek. Jack pulled up by the door, using the left stirrup to break his hasty dismount while balancing Tay with both hands.

Jennifer's horse slid to a stop beside him. She grabbed Cassie's hand while the girl threw her leg over the cantle and dropped to the ground. Before Jennifer could run around the horse to assist him, Jack had pulled Tay from the saddle. He carried him to the house; Cassie ran ahead to open the door. It groaned plaintively on heavy iron hinges, and if not for the urgency of the situation it would have been comical to watch this small girl struggle to open such a large, stubborn door. Seeing the girl's difficulty, Jennifer sprinted a couple of steps ahead of Jack, who was beginning to feel the strain of holding a grown man in his arms. The door was open wide by the time he reached it.

"In there!" Jennifer directed, pointing to a small room off the main room. An unmade single bed sat in the middle of room. Jack quickly laid Tay on top of the tangle of sheets while Cassie and Jennifer worked the laces of his boots. Jack released the tourniquet per Catalyn's instructions, and blood began to gush from the wide, jagged wound. Together Jennifer and Jack pulled off Tay's trousers, outer shirt and shoulder holster while Cassie ran to the bathroom for a towel. The left pant leg was soaked with blood all the way the hem, as was his boot and sock. A steady trail of blood led to the doorway of the room and out onto the porch. When Cassie returned with the towel Jack slapped it against the wound and applied pressure while counting to sixty in his head.

Jesus, Jack thought, upon seeing that Tay's legs were a patchwork of scars from what must have been knife slashes, stab wounds, bullet holes and God knows what else. *This guy's been to hell and back. And now he's got himself a return ticket.*

The towel was mostly red by the time Jack reckoned a minute had passed, and he hurriedly reapplied the tourniquet—his leather belt—to Tay's bare leg and yanked it tight to stem the copious flow. Cassie willingly took over the task of holding the towel against the wound, although Jack thought the chore might end up being more than the girl would be able to stomach. He was wrong. Cassie appeared unaffected by the grisly scene before her. Indeed, she seemed almost to be studying the morbid setting with a clinical fascination. She pushed on the towel with her left hand while holding the fingers of Tay's left hand with her right. While she did, Jennifer found a couple of pillows to place behind Tay's head and rolled up a small throw rug which she placed under his knees to raise his legs as best she could. Tay was deathly pale except for the old scar on the side of his face, which glowed hideously pink.

Jack barely registered Jennifer's efforts; all of his concentration was on the girl. Cassie spoke rapidly to Tay in a voice so soft he could scarcely hear it. Jack wasn't even sure she was speaking English. After a moment Tay opened his eyes to slits and smiled at her. Then he squeezed her tiny hand so hard Jack thought certain she would pull it away in pain. Instead, she returned the smile and squeezed back. Then more words, almost like chanting and soft as a sparrow's breathing.

Whatever sorcery the girl was performing, it was purely instinctual. And it was working.

The muffled trill of an ATV grew loud out the open doorway, then stopped abruptly. By the time Catalyn and Luke ran through the doorway— Catalyn gravely serious, Luke wide-eyed and anxious to help in any way possible—Tay's eyes were mostly open and he was mumbling something in Cassie's ear the girl thought amusing.

Catalyn was clearly in charge. She hurried into the small bedroom to assess Tay's condition while Luke unloaded a large backpack and disappeared with it into the kitchen with Jennifer. She thanked her daughter and gently nudging her aside, then touched the back of Jack's hand and told him to remove the tourniquet. She pulled the towel away from Tay's wound and bent over for a closer look. The bleeding had mostly stopped, making it possible to examine the damage in detail for the first time. To Jack's eyes it looked like a pack of rats had eaten their way from the front of Tay's thigh to the back. There was a deep gash on the side of his leg with a fearfully large amount of meat either shredded or missing.

Catalyn examined the bloody towel, and the pool of blood that had formed on the sheets. "No arterial blood, here, Tay. You got lucky. Again."

He tried to laugh, but coughed instead. "Not feeling so lucky," he managed to say with a crooked grin. Jack saw that some color had returned to his face, and he attributed it to Cassie's inexplicable ministrations.

Presently, Jennifer appeared with a large tray filled with instruments, syringes and other surgical materiel, packed around a basin of steaming, soapy water. Obviously they'd been through this sort of thing before. Luke cleared a lamp and small clock off the nightstand and repositioned it next to his wife's right arm. She washed quickly in the basin and dried her hands on the small towel beside it. When she was finished Jennifer ran back into the kitchen for more hot water and another towel.

"We're going to have to do a local, Tay. It'll hurt, but I don't feel good about giving you a general with so much loss of blood. Same with the morphine. I don't want to sully your blood with drugs if I don't have to. And since it's my blood you'll be getting, I'd rather not give you a transfusion until I'm through sewing you up."

"You talk too much," Tay murmured weakly.

Catalyn smiled approvingly and prepared to go to work. First she motioned for Jack and Luke to hold his feet. When Jennifer returned with more soapy water, she was assigned the chore of holding his head. Cassie stood opposite her mother, holding Tay's right hand in both of hers. She continued her sub-audible incantation while the wound remained obediently quiescent.

Catalyn opened a green foil packet with the U. S. Marine Corp logo on the side and removed a gauze pad with a hemostat. Then she dipped it in the soapy water and scoured the wound inside and out. Tay jumped reflexively, but Jack and Luke held his legs firm.

After filling a small syringe from a frosty bottle labeled "Lidocaine," she made a series of small injections, first outside the wound, then inside. While waiting for the drug to numb the traumatized tissue, she patted Tay's head with a wet towel. "Who did this to you Tay?" she asked.

"An old friend," he whispered.

"Tharp?" Jack asked.

Tay nodded.

"*Hadrian* Tharp?" Jennifer said sharply.

"Yeah," Jack answered. "Ran into him last night in The Blue Fox. A nasty piece of work."

"*That's* putting it mildly. Shit! Why'd *he* have to show up?"

Not figuring her question needed an answer, Jack asked Tay, "What'd you do to *him*?"

"Didn't exactly stop to compare wounds...."

"But you did wound him?"

"Sounded like it...yes...must have..."

Jack asked, "How did you end up on his trail?" but Catalyn cut the conversation short.

"You can unravel this later," she said with gentle finality. "I'd like to keep him quiet while I close the wound."

"You're no fun," Tay told her.

"No, but I'm good."

"*De veras,*" Tay said. *This is true.*

Using scissors Catalyn cut away all the ragged skin and flesh from inside and outside the wound. It caused more bleeding from the fresh cuts but she made quick work of it. She applied the sutures from the inside out. Beneath the skin she pulled the muscle together with several large dissolvable sutures which caused the wound to bleed so intensely that Catalyn's emotions finally bubbled to the surface.

"Damn it, Tay, quit bleeding!" she pleaded, slapping a large wad of gauze into the wound. "You don't have that much blood left and we can't afford to lose you!"

Catalyn's alarm sobered all of them. And Jack saw that it was true—he couldn't lose any more blood; he was going into shock. His brown skin had become nearly gray and his body shook violently.

"Cassie? Get over here. NOW!"

Cassie quickly scurried to her mother's side and placed her hands on the skin around the bloody slash. Blood ran like a river around Catalyn's ineffectual wad of gauze. Jack held his breath while Cassie worked. Catalyn scavenged around on the sterile tray until she found a rubber tube with a hypodermic needle in each end. She soaked a gauze pad in alcohol and rubbed it first on Tay's arm then her own before inserting the needle in her forearm below the elbow. Once a droplet of blood appeared at the tip of the needle on other end, she placed her thumb over the vein in Tay's arm and expertly inserted the needle. She squeezed her upper arm and made a fist while pumping rhythmically to speed the flow of blood into Tay's veins. The tube pulsed with Catalyn's heartbeat.

After a minute or two Tay's bleeding slowed to a trickle. Blood dripped all down the front of Cassie, where it pooled on the floor on top of previously spilled blood that had already congealed. The room looked and smelled like an abattoir. But Cassie either didn't notice or didn't mind.

"Nice trick," Jack said to no one in particular.

Catalyn made quick work of it after that, working around Cassie who refused to leave Tay's side. Her numerous sutures were deep and strong and destined to hold. They would leave an ugly scar, but Jack doubted Tay would mind. Before tying the last knot, she filled a large syringe with antibiotic and emptied it into the red angry hole. Then she plopped down on a chair where she sat pumping her blood into Tay until his color was better than hers.

For emergencies, Tay had made certain everyone knew who could give blood to whom. Catalyn was O-positive so she could give blood to Luke and Tay (who were, respectively, B-positive and A-positive) while Jennifer, Silas and Cassie—O-negative, O-negative and A-negative—could only share each other's blood. Jack realized he did not know his own blood type.

Luke tapped Catalyn gently on the shoulder. She nodded, pulling the needle first from her arm, then Tay's. She was exhausted, and shaking as if half frozen. Luke threw a blanket over her shoulders and helped her into the main room. After Jennifer bandaged Tay's leg, Luke and Jack held him up momentarily while Jennifer replaced the blood-soaked sheets and covered him with a blanket. He immediately nodded off the sleep.

When he saw that she was shaking, Jack wrapped his arm around Jennifer's shoulder. The arm had been bathed in blood from the elbow down, but there was so much blood everywhere it hardly mattered. He kissed her lightly on the cheek before they shuffled outside. The sun was past the midpoint in the sky when they stepped onto the porch for a breath of air.

"Jesus Christ!" Catalyn railed with all the fury as she could muster in her weakened state. "What in God's name could cause a wound like *that?*"

Whether she wanted an answer or not, Luke provided one. "A hollow point with an 'X' scored in the head, most likely. Or a drop of quicksilver sealed with lead in a cavity just behind the tip. Either way, it causes the bullet to decompose into shrapnel on impact. If it'd him square in the leg we'd have lost him."

It was probably more than she wanted to hear; she pulled the blanket tight around her shoulders and shivered. Cassie wrapped her arms around her mother's waist and said, "It'll be all right, Mom. Tay's gonna be all right."

That wasn't really the point and they all knew it, but Catalyn graced her daughter with a weary smile and kissed the top of her head. "Because of you, honey. Only because of you."

"And you," Luke said proudly. "The best damned horse vet this side of the Missouri."

"Horse vet?" Jack said, curious.

"Catalyn said, "Yeah. My dad was a vet…at least until the Turning. Then by default he became a battlefield surgeon. A good one. And whenever he needed a third and fourth hand, well…" She held up her strong, feminine hands for emphasis. "I've been stitching up horses, dogs, cats, goats and people since I was eight years old. It's a skill that comes in handy; especially when you've got a guy like Tay around.

"But we'd have lost him for sure if not for Tay's large inventory of Marine-issue surgical supplies." She put a hand on Cassie's head, adding, "And one very special little girl."

"It was easy, Mom," Cassie said. "It's easy to help someone when you love them."

What if you hated them? What could you do to them then? Jack wondered. As did they all.

By early evening Tay was awake and in good humor, even more so after Catalyn administered a standard field dose of Marine-issue morphine. Blood had seeped into the bandages, but not enough to worry her. Finding little of nutritional value in Tay's ancient refrigerator, Luke and Cassie rode the ATV to their house for food and a change of clothes. Jennifer, Jack and Catalyn washed up as best they could in the kitchen sink.

They ate—Tay a little, the others ravenously—sitting around Tay's bed in squeaky wooden chairs, drinking tea and beer and enjoying a well-earned peace among themselves. Tay seemed revitalized by the camaraderie, especially after Catalyn allowed him a sip or two of whiskey. His color was returning and the skin on his face had begun to draw tighter.

Jack finally asked the question everyone wanted the answer to. "So what happened? How was Tharp able to get the drop on you?"

The room grew silent as Tay explained. "I was coming home from... should we say...my night in town. Since I had gone in with Jack—but then been delayed—I rode Carmen's horse home along the creek trail early this morning. Two miles back, I found the mare belonging to the sheriff. She was hobbled in a clearing, eating grass."

Jennifer quickly bristled. "That *bastard!* I knew it!"

"I don't think he came to hurt anyone. My guess is that he was only watching. Perhaps he has gotten wind of what Carlos has hidden away," he suggested, glancing first at Jennifer then at Jack, who said nothing. "Anyway, I tracked him for a short distance. Across the creek, the road...he had gone up into the badlands and I knew if I followed he would see me before I could see him. So I tried instead to shadow him. Me in the forest, him in the desert. Maybe I could catch a glimpse of the sneaky *pendejo*, moving from rock to rock.

"I knew it was a good plan when I caught the reflection of the sun on his binoculars. He was watching the two of you from behind a rock before you galloped into the trees." He smiled at Jennifer. "I am guessing he was not happy to see the two of you kissing."

Jack shrugged; Jennifer flushed bright red.

Tay continued without comment. "I was busy watching the sheriff, not paying much attention. Foolish, but also quiet. I was close where he was hiding before he heard me."

"Tharp?" Jennifer murmured. The fear etched on her face made Jack feel like a complete fool for putting her—and by circuitous extension, Tay—into such danger. *And all for the intellectual satisfaction of proving I had solved a riddle.*

"*Si*, it was *Hadriano*," Tay confirmed. "He was following you, and much closer that the sheriff was. He was no more than a hundred yards from you when I flushed him out."

"And then?" Luke asked, hanging on every word.

Tay shrugged. "He turned and fired. Bang, bang. The first shot went wide, but not the second."

"We heard five shots," Jack said.

Tay grinned. It was good to see. "I fired twice while jumping out of the way, once more as he ran away. My guess is that *Hadriano* is not feeling so well, himself."

He speaks of him almost affectionately, Jack thought. *Would he be sad to discover he had killed him? Good enemies are hard to find, after all.* He said, "It's lucky that you found us so fast."

"*Los perros, amigo.* They found me after *Hadriano* ran away. They led me to you." He narrowed his dark eyes and directed them at Jennifer. It caused her to flush brightly. He said, "It leads me to wonder: what were you doing at that old mine, *muchacha*?"

Jennifer looked first to Jack, then back to Tay. "It seems that Jack has, uh, solved Carlos's riddle. We know where the diamonds are...well, at least we think we do." With Jack's help she explained the rest of the story. Three things became perfectly clear as she did: One, that Luke, Catalyn and Tay were all aware of Carlos's cryptic code; two, that they all knew it referred to Carlos' stolen diamonds; and three, that none of them seemed in the least bit interested in finding his cache of precious stones.

When Jack wondered why, Catalyn said, "I think that's obvious, Jack. As long as no one knows where they are, no one can steal them..."

Tay added, "So, if we do not need them—and for now we do not—they are better left unfound, *amigo*." He took a tiny sip from the half-jigger of whiskey Catalyn had allowed him, and chased it down with a long swallow of water from the night stand.

"And it would appear," he went on, "that *Hadriano* and the *pendejo* sheriff know about the diamonds, though not where they are hidden."

"Uh, yeah...of course," Jack said, feeling more than a little foolish, "but if it's any consolation, they weren't where we thought they would be. But they might—"

"Say no more, *amigo*."

Jack held his tongue.

Just before dark Luke, Catalyn and Cassie made their way home. Jennifer agreed to spend the night in case Tay needed something. Jack stayed to watch over Jennifer. There was a larger bed in the loft and nothing or no one to disturb them.

2♱

Prygor In-Between

Salia's talents grow more frightful by the day. I am now convinced she is able to affect the present by changing events in the past.

FROM THE DIARY OF ISAIAH WARCHEZ, SEPTEMBER 21, 2016

"Where am I?" Prygor asked the darkness. He heard his own voice with such clarity it frightened him. There was nothing or no one to dampen it, not even the beating of his heart or the sound of his breathing. Nor was there any pain to distract him.

Just the bare essence of Prygor Primm; formerly Pryus Gordon Primm, known in those forgotten days as Gordy.

At the moment, he was a seed. A seed that had sprouted in nearly barren soil and nurtured by two conflicting hands: one that loved him too much, one that loved him too little.

It was all there in the tone and timbre of his voice, like a roadmap marking the way to the unfortunate confusion of events that had conspired to make him the empty loveless shell of a human that he had become. This much he knew. He didn't like being stripped of his humanness—all the distractions he hid behind to avoid facing the cold fact of who he really was—yet in his own unimaginative way he found it all uninteresting.

After all he was who he was, was he not?

Again he asked the darkness, "Where am I?"

In-between, came the reply. The voice was feminine, though not anything like Jennifer's voice (hers being the perfect feminine voice against which he judged all others). Nor was it the voice of one of Baker's harlots or any other woman of Prygor's acquaintance. It was a calm voice, though not calming, and self-assured to the point of being domineering; a trait he despised in women.

"In-between what?" he queried.

In-between what is, and what might have been.

No help at all.

In-between who you are and who you wish you could be, the voice answered, as if sensing his desire for clarification.

Better, but still pointless. "I am who I am," he said.

So you have always thought.

He had just begun to ponder this when he smelled the homey aroma of chocolate-chip cookies fresh out of the oven, wafting into the void he now occupied. The unmistakable smell of cinnamon and that little pinch of ginger. He knew these cookies were the ones his mother (well, his step-mother) would sometimes make when she wanted something from little Gordy.

The smell alone was enough to transport him back to *that* day, that one fateful day, but this disturbingly vivid daydream was just getting started. His imagination drifted on a temporal cloud, filling in the recollections of his senses one by one until he was there in that moment. With the cookies.

Gordy was eleven years old on this particular day in the spring of 2010; a good-looking boy—looking at himself as he was then—though something of a brooder even at that tender age. Thick dark-brown hair, long, though with none of the feminine affectations boys in the large cities gave in to, and a thin face that made up with seriousness what it lacked in imagination. His eyes were small and unusually dark for someone so young. But then, it wasn't easy being him.

Especially after this day was over.

He watched as the boy caught a whiff of the cookies several paces from the house and stiffened, for a conflict arose inside the boy that had no satisfactory resolution. And so he pulled open the squeaky screen door that hung slightly ajar on its hinges and saw her waiting by the kitchen counter as she always waited on cookie days, with a wholesome motherly smile, just like on the old black & white reruns of *Leave it to Beaver*. Except Gordy wasn't The Beav, and Rachel Primm was a far cry from June Cleaver.

"Hello, Gordy," she said, with that silky voice and that electric smile that had transported Arnold Primm from the depths of mourning to the altar in four short months. That was back when Gordy was only six, and he had to admit that back then both he and his older brother thought that if they had to have a step-mom (to replace their *real* mom, who had died of some disease they could barely pronounce), Rachael wasn't half-bad. She was younger than his dad (a *lot* younger, his brother Abel had said, but to little Gordy, old-enough-to-be-his-mother was old and didn't need any more quantification), but that was okay because she was terribly pretty, something that remained for Gordy's father a fount of unending pride.

Until today.

Today was the day Cookie-Day and Arnold-Primm-Gets-Fired-for-Drinking-on-the-Job-Day collided head on.

With little Gordy in the middle.

"Hi, Rachael," Gordy says, as if he doesn't know what's going on. He sets his school books on the red Formica counter in the white kitchen with the pink sheer curtains on the windows. Then Gordy eats two cookies and washes them down with a glass of milk. What the heck? What happens next is inevitable so he might as well go into it with a few cookies in his belly. She'd let him eat the whole plate if he wanted to, but he stops at two; it was just too distracting to try to eat when Rachael was running her hands over him.

Hands with long, soft, talented fingers. This he knows, even though he can remember no other fingers ever touching him in this way. But they have their own magic; oh yes, they have that. Even as a boy of eleven (just barely eleven) who has not yet crossed that sacred threshold from childhood into manhood, those fingers can make him think of things of which experience has taught him nothing.

Except for what Rachael has taught him.

She leads him into his bedroom. Gordy knows he should say no; knows that for once in his life he should stand up to an adult and do what he knows is right. Do it for his father, who worships Rachael almost as much as he worships Jesus. (Gordy thinks this is why his father drinks so much. He doubts Jesus and Rachael were created by the same god and suspects that might be the root of the problem.)

Instead, he does what she tells him to do. He undresses. Then she undresses while he watches. He can't help watching; Rachael is slender and beautiful, even if she is almost twenty-five. As he sees her nakedness unveiled, he feels his tallywhacker rise and harden, even though he wishes it wouldn't. (If it would just stay limp like I want it to, she'd leave me alone, wouldn't she?) He thinks it's embarrassing and he covers it with his hands, pinching it, hoping to make it go small again. But Rachael thinks it's marvelous, and she moves his hands aside for a better look and a long caress. Gordy does not resist…

The in-between Prygor begins to panic, because he knows what's about to happen even if little Gordy doesn't. In about five minutes Arnold Primm is going to pull open the squeaky screen door. They will not hear his car pull into the drive because Arnold ran out of gas on Juniper Street between Third and Fourth Avenues and had to walk the remaining six blocks home. Had he stopped to get gas on the way to work this morning, he would still have gotten fired from his job fixing tractors and hay balers at the John Deere dealer, but at least he would've gotten home a good twenty minutes sooner. And on this day twenty minutes would have meant a lifetime.

Gordy see his father the minute he grabs the handle on the screen door. This is because he is standing up, looking through the crack in the bedroom door Rachael has, in her haste, forgotten to close. Rachael is on her knees with her back to the door, so she doesn't see Arnold's red face and wild eyes, but Gordy does...

"STOP IT!" the in-between Prygor screams. Those eyes have haunted him every day of his life since *that* day and he can't bear to look into them one minute longer. In his mind he sees those crazy eyes aglow with rage as his father tears into Rachael, pummeling her with closed fists until she scurries away on her hands and knees and collapses in the corner, shaking and bawling, and bleeding from her nose and mouth. Then he sees those eyes boring into little Gordy, and remembers how close he came to dying that day.

And when he looked away (as he had to look away) the sadness overwhelmed him, for he remembered the loneliness that day had wrought. For all of them. Rachael was gone before sundown; Gordy never set eyes on her again. Arnold was left a broken man who never again looked his youngest son in the eyes, or graced him with a kind word. ("The Lord may forgive you someday, Pryus, but I won't.") And Abel hated Gordy for what he had done to their father; hated him until the day he died, side by side with Arnold during the final assault on Purgatory in the War of the Turning.

The in-between Prygor remembered the satisfaction he felt seeing them die, from his hiding place in the loft of a nearby barn, and the memory sickened him...

Then he heard the voice, again.

Change it, the voice prompted.

"I can't," he replied angrily. "It's done."

You can if you want to.

"No—"

Yes. Look...

Reluctantly, he did; he looked back into the bedroom, seeing Gordy and Rachael face to face, Gordy's swollen pre-pubescent organ hard as an axe handle, and suddenly Prygor Primm is in-between no more. No longer does he watch what he cannot change, for he *is* Gordy, a boy of eleven—a good boy; a timid boy, perhaps, but a good boy, nonetheless—who finds himself in an untenable situation that is wrong by any ruler he chooses to measure it by (and most certainly by his father's strict biblical interpretation of just about everything).

A good boy who does not and cannot know the in-between Prygor...

He stands with his hands over his penis, asking God to give him the courage to stop her unwelcome advances. She smiles and reaches for his hands, but he grabs himself and will not let go. "C'mon, Gordy," she coos, and Gordy almost relents, but then he looks into her eyes for the first time and he sees the devil lurking in the depths behind them.

It frightens him and he barks, "No way! Get away from me, you slut!"

Her face transforms into an angry mask and she slaps him across the cheek. Then she pulls his head to her soft full bosom and whispers, "Sorry, Gordy. You must know I didn't mean that."

But Gordy knows nothing of the sort. He pushes her away, catching her off balance. She falls to the floor and glares up at him as he picks up his clothes and runs naked into the kitchen. That's when he see his dad, half a block away and quickly closing the distance with a purposeful stride. He hollers, "Dad's coming!"

He sees only her face appear from around the side of the doorway. "Oh shit!" she exclaims, glancing through the window at her husband on the sidewalk, now just two doors down. "Gordy? Honey? You wouldn't..."

"Say a word?" he answers, knowing what she's going to ask. He ponders his reply as he quickly stabs his legs back into his trousers. The old Gordy, he knows, would be accommodating; he'd say, "Are you kidding? No way José. Not a word." But the old Gordy is gone and the new Gordy bids good-riddance to the little wuss.

"That depends," he announces calmly, as he bends down to tie his sneakers.

"On what?" he hears her pleading amidst frantic shuffling sounds behind the now-closed bedroom door.

"On whether or not you ever try to touch me again."

"I won't, Gordy. I promise!"

But he wants to make sure. "Never?" he says.

She emerges from the bedroom, clearly distressed but otherwise looking fresh as a daisy. "Never," she affirms. "Never again. Honest."

"I'm thinking," he says. But he's not thinking, he's testing her and he expects her to fail. And then he's going to tell his dad everything.

But she surprises him. As if praying she holds her hands beneath her chin and says, "Please, Gordy? Pretty Please?"

When Arnold storms through the screen door, red-faced and red-eyed, he is greeted by his dutiful son and his adoring young wife, sitting across the kitchen counter from one another, enjoying milk and cookies. Despite his troubles he looks skyward and counts his blessings.

"Hey there, Dad," Gordy says.

"Hi honey," Rachael chimes in. "Welcome home."

The elder Primm stands at the end of the counter and pulls them both into his arms. "How I have missed you both today," he tells them with tears in his eyes and whiskey on his breath. Together, Rachael and the new Gordy embrace Arnold in his hour of need.

Suddenly Prygor is in-between again. But he no longer feels like Prygor. He feels different, somehow. Lighter. Bolder. A man among men. He feels like... Pryus. "What happens to them?" he asks.

Don't you remember? the voice asks.

To his astonishment, he *does* remember. A year later his father catches Rachael with a strapping young stud from the high school football team and throws her out of their house and out of their life. In her rage, she tells Arnold of all the times she "fucked your precious little boy in his own bedroom." Most of it was lies, but not all of it, so Gordy can't really deny it. In the end, he's still ostracized and treated with open contempt for months, if not years. Arnold never remarries and neither his father nor Abel ever forgive him.

"Nothing really changes," he observed bitterly.

You did.

It was true. *This* time they hated him even though he'd done the right thing when he could just as easily not have. *This* time he was justified to hate them back.

"But nothing else changed."

It was her destiny to tear your family apart, the voice said.

"Maybe if I had stopped her earlier, before the first time, maybe then—"

It was her destiny, the voice repeated, and this time Pryus knew it to be true. Rachael would have found a way to ruin his family, no matter what. It was her nature, perhaps even her life's purpose.

He asked, "What now? What do you want from me?"

Kill her.

Pryus recoiled from the words. "Kill Rachael? I don't even know where she is. She may already be dead for all—"

NO! Not Rachael. Jennifer. Jennifer Teague, the voice hissed.

"Never. Don't even ask," he said with finality.

You must.

"I can't."

You will…

He shook his head and opened his eyes. He thought perhaps he might have nodded off to sleep for a few minutes, though it would have been a peculiar thing to do, considering his pains (which now felt greatly diminished) and the apparent gunfight that had just taken place in the trees to the southwest. *What did I miss?* he wondered.

His question was soon answered, for just then he saw Jennifer Teague and Jack Vara galloping nearly abreast out of the trees with the two big dogs struggling to keep pace behind them. A man rode in front of Vara; a man who was either dead or badly injured, Pryus concluded, by the way the head and arms rocked back and forth with the motion of the horse. His hand closed around Baker's field glasses and he quickly trained them on Vara. He was pleased to discover the man in peril was none other than his perennial enemy, Tay Villa. "I hope he dies," Pryus whispered to the wind, but realized this wasn't true. Pryus wanted Villa to *live*; wanted him to grow healthy and strong again.

So *he* could be the one to kill him.

He spied Jennifer. Her golden hair flowed behind her in the wind and her lithe body moved in perfect rhythm with the horse. The urgency etched into her delicate face only made her more desirable. God, but he'd like to roll in the hay with that woman. But she never would, would she? At least not with him. After all his kindnesses and gentle gestures, his continuing attempts to look out for her best interests, she pays him back by getting all romantic with a guy she's known for two days. *Probably already sleeping with him*, he thinks as a postscript.

At bottom, Jennifer Teague was no better than his old nympho step-mom, Rachael. *Rachael? How funny I should think of Rachael after all these years*, he thought. Why, he'd nearly succeeded in erasing her from his memory. The image of Rachael made him smile. If only he'd been a couple of years older he'd have given her the hard fucking she deserved for all the pitiful lies she told about him.

The mere thought of her caused a pronounced bulge in his pants. He couldn't ever remember being so horny.

"To hell with Baker and his stupid little candy-assed assignment," Pryus announced to sky above him. There were more efficient ways to get his hands on Herrera's diamonds. He headed back to town to find himself a proper whore. He'd been a virgin far too long.

25

The Hunt for COTO Begins

Dobry Robak. It always came back to that mysterious little man. Every quarter he would send me glowing reports detailing how well his company was performing. The truth of the matter (and perhaps the irony of it) was that I actually was making good money on the products developed by Robak Renewable Resources. But he was doing better than I could ever have known, and much of what he earned with my money was being neither returned to me as dividends nor funneled back into R&D. Robak, it seems, had applied my wealth to a far more sinister purpose...

FROM THE UNPUBLISHED MEMOIRS OF CARLOS HERRERA

"You sure do heal up fast, boy. Can't say as I've ever seen anything quite like it before. Hell, I thought for sure you were goin' down for the long count." Woltr was mumbling through the side of his mouth while trying to light his clay pipe, but Silas got the gist of it.

They sat outside his small cabin in what Woltr referred to with a wink and a grin as his patio, which was nothing more than a small leveled off area east of the cabin where the old man had laid down a few flat stones and a crude pine table on top of them. But the old weathered table didn't teeter, having settled over the same fraction of geologic time as the stones on which it rested, and the three-legged stools they sat on were likewise constrained from wobbling by the tenets of geometry.

They sat side by side, facing each other only obliquely, so they could both enjoy the warmth of the morning sun on their faces. Tendrils of steam rose from large mugs of Woltr's own special blend of tea. It tasted of pine and citrus and honey, and other flavors Silas couldn't make out.

"Must be the tea," Silas answered, not caring to take the subject any further. Yes, he had healed up fast; his terrible cough—which he concluded must have resulted from his body's efforts to expel seventeen years-worth of mucus from his marginally exercised lungs—had all but disappeared, and the weakness and soreness in his legs was beginning to diminish as well, though walking was still painful and he could feel a slight trembling in his legs from the overexertion of two nights before.

Woltr thought his answer funny enough to laugh at. "I may be ignorant, boy, but I ain't stupid. There's somethin' about you; somethin'...different. 'Course, if you don't care to talk about it, that's all right too. A man's got a right to his privacy." Smoke drifted from his mouth and nostrils as he talked, and mixed with the steam rising from their mugs. Warm intelligent eyes hid in a face framed in long white hair that fell to his shoulders and a white beard extending to his chest. Silas thought Woltr looked like Father Time.

"It's a gift," Silas offered, after a moment's thought.

"And a fine gift it is," Woltr replied, satisfied with this answer.

They sat in silence for a few moments. It was an easy silence; the kind shared between old friends who didn't feel the need to prattle endlessly to fill an awkward void. Woltr puffed on his pipe; Silas enjoyed the sunshine on his pale skin and the fresh cool air in his lungs. Reaching for his tea, he noticed for the first time that there was crude lettering carved into the tabletop, probably with a pocketknife. It read:

WOLTR AN BILS PATEO
WELCUM 1 an al

Seeing his interest, Woltr said, "Learned my letters once, but damned if I can remember the proper way to string 'em together."

Silas rubbed the words reverently with his fingertips. He said, "You did fine Woltr, just fine. The meaning couldn't be clearer if it were in neon lights."

Woltr seemed pleased with his critique. "Thanks for that, son," he said.

"You saved my life, Woltr. It's important to me you know that."

"Fiddlesticks!" he guffawed. "T'was Bil did that. The little critter led you right to me. Not for him you'd been food for the beasties, if you know what I mean." Hearing his name, the curious coon ambled out of the cabin and sat on his haunches at Woltr's side. Woltr reached in his pocket and produced a chunk of jerky he kept there for just that purpose. He broke off a small piece and offered it to Bil. The coon grabbed it up in his cunning little hands and chewed on it greedily.

The old man was right. Without Bil leading the way, Silas would never have found Woltr's little cabin tucked away, as it was, in a small valley with an entrance that could be easily overlooked. He'd trailed behind his unseen companion until just before dawn, when he finally caught a glimpse of him. Bil fell back then and walked just ahead of Silas. Figuring that the coon had the better notion of where they were going, Silas followed him to Woltr's.

"Isn't it a bit unusual for Bil to wander so far from home?" Silas asked.

"Never has before, that's for sure." He ruminated for a moment and drew on his pipe, then said, "But I ain't one to question a critter's motives. Bil knew what he was doin', even if he's keepin' mum about it."

Silas reached down to pet his masked savior. The coon inched close enough for Silas to run his hand all the way down his back. Woltr said, "Like I was sayin', there's somethin' different about you."

Silas scratched Bil behind the ears for a moment before the appreciative coon wandered off. He said, "I have to go, Woltr. I'm putting you in danger by being here."

A knowing smile appeared through tobacco-stained whiskers. "I thought as much," he said. "The law, is it?"

"Worse. It's someone who doesn't play by the rules."

"That'd have to be a woman, then," Woltr concluded.

Silas couldn't help but chuckle. "That's not really the first word people use to describe her, but yes, a woman."

"But there's more to it than that?"

"Only that she's quite probably the most dangerous person on the planet."

Without expression, Woltr said, "Sure know how to pick your enemies, don'tcha, boy?"

"This one was picked for me. I didn't have a whole lot to say about it."

"An arranged rivalry, huh? Can't imagine that would work out much better than an arranged marriage," Woltr speculated, "except that everyone'd know where they stood from the get-go."

"Very true," Silas agreed.

Woltr narrowed his clear green eyes and leaned close enough that Silas could smell the pipe smoke lingering in his beard. "What'd you do to get this woman on your tail, anyhow? If you don't mind my asking."

Yes, he did mind. It was the not-insignificant matter of Woltr's welfare. The more he knew, the more problematic it could be—for both of them. He said, "I have knowledge of a document that could...that *would*, change the future of the world. She wants it."

"To work her evil, I imagine?"

Silas shook his head. "You could argue that the knowledge itself is evil. That it might even need to be destroyed."

Woltr let go a long whistle, leaning back so far on his stool he almost fell over. He quickly righted himself and said, "Last time I heard someone talk about evil knowledge it was in relation to the H-bomb. How'd you come across it?" he asked.

"Carlos Herrera whispered it in my ear while I was in no position not to listen," Silas said matter-of-factly.

Woltr blew out a long, smoky breath. "Sounds like somethin' that wily old cuss would do, all right. How'd you get mixed up with him, anyway?"

"He was the closest thing to a father my sister and I ever knew."

Woltr flushed with embarrassment. "Waltzed right into that one, didn't I?" he said. Then his eyes lit up with recognition, and he said, "Hold on a minute...that would mean you're a Teague? Silas Teague...and Jennifer is your sister?"

"That's us," he admitted, amazed that a man who probably didn't set foot in town more than once or twice a year knew who he was.

Indelicately, Woltr said, "Weren't you wounded? I thought you were brain dead. Or somethin'."

"Not quite. Anyway, I snapped out it."

"Like I was sayin,' you're different."

Silas stayed with Woltr and Bil until the following morning. Both the man and the astute little coon were thankful for the company, as Silas was for the chance to recuperate before continuing on his journey. Woltr gave him a bag of dried food items, including a generous cache of jerky and hardtack, a small but functional compass, and an old machete in a scabbard he could wear on his belt. Woltr spent an hour on his treadle-driven honing wheel, and another half-hour with a small whetstone, working as fine an edge on the rusty metal as it could hold. When Silas told him he really didn't think he'd need it, Woltr raised a wooly eyebrow and pushed the machete into his hands, saying, "Then think again, boy. Those plains you'll be going over ain't exactly the peaceful prairies they used to be, back when the world was over-run with people. Far from it. There're wolves and cougars aplenty, feeding on antelope and deer. But they're nature's critters and the least of your troubles on account of they don't reckon you to be a link in their food chain. It's the mixed bloods you gotta be wary of. No fear, and no sense. The scent of blood drives 'em wild, even blood of their own kind. It's because they don't know how to hunt like God's creatures, so they're all the time starvin'. So you keep an eye out, will you?"

"Sure thing, Woltr."

"If you were to tell me where you're headed," Woltr suggested then, "it might be that I could steer you around some things you'll want to avoid. And maybe toward a thing or two you'd do well to fix in your sights." Probably so, but Silas saw by the sly gleam in his eye that the old man's curiosity had begun to get the better of him.

"Sorry, Woltr; can't do that," Silas told him. "I'm sure you know why."

Woltr said, "Figured as much. Don't s'pose I would either, were I in your shoes. But just so you know, you won't always be as lucky as you were the other night. Travel only by day and be wary of anyone you meet. There's good folks and bad ones out there, with precious little in between. As a rule, those on horseback are more trustworthy than those with machines. But not always. The world's become a haven for murderers and thieves, Silas Teague. You'd do well to avoid them both."

Silas again thanked Woltr for his kindness, then dropped to his knees to bid farewell to Bil. The plump little coon sat up on his haunches and grasped Silas's hand with both of his. "And thank you, little guy, for leading me here. Look after Woltr now, won't you Bil?" A slight squeeze of his finger signaled Bil's affirmation.

Silas rose and Woltr offered his own hand, saying, "Hate to see you go, son. Truth is, my old knees have felt better these last two days than they have in years. Can't but figure it's your doing, somehow."

Despite his simple ways and his homey phrases, there was a depth to Woltr lacking in most men; a gentle wisdom unfettered by the influences of a violent world. Silas would miss him. "Take care of yourself, Woltr. And keep Bil in your shadow."

26

Rumors of Pryus

So this is the way the story's always been told: Intelligence, indeed con-
sciousness itself, arises from inanimate matter that has self-assembled
into a small number of optimal biological configurations after billions
of years of trial and error. Thus has sight arisen from blindness, due to
the stimulation of light, and sound from deafness because of the per-
sistent presence of sonic waves. And likewise it is implied that think-
ing and self-awareness spontaneously came into being under the same
processes of biochemical entities responding to their environment.
From blind ignorance cometh intelligence, then? Yes, I believe that's
our creed, is it not?

And if I were to turn this thinking on its head and say that con-
sciousness precedes all that is thought to come before it, would you think
me insane? Even so, that is precisely what I'm saying...

EXCERPT FROM A SPEECH DELIVERED BY DR. JACK VARA
TO THE RANDALL RESEARCH INSTITUTE, JULY 14, 2037

The late morning silence was broken by the thundering of hooves echoing
from the rock wall along the creek trail. Fearing the worst, Jack raced
to see who it might be.

It was getting close to noon and he and Jennifer had been out of bed
since the sun had peeked over the small ridge to the east. Against his better
judgment, Jack had used the time to fashion Tay a crude set of crutches from
forked tree limbs, since he was determined to walk with or without them.

Reasonably certain that Catalyn would be more than a little peeved
to see her patient out of bed so soon, Jack had waited until Catalyn and

Cassie headed back home after an early-morning checkup and food delivery before he set out into the forest with knife and saw. The finished product looked like something out of a Dickens novel: crooked sticks of ash with cut-branch handles, bound with old sheets at the forks for padding. They were hardly a matched pair, but serviceable just the same. In any case, Tay seemed impressed.

"Primm or Tharp?" Tay asked from the bedroom, just before the horse slid to a stop in front of the covered porch. His Ruger rested in his lap like a sleeping snake.

"Neither," Jack answered. "It's your girlfriend."

"*Maldito.* That might be worse," Tay muttered.

Carmen dismounted quickly and headed for the door, her long locks swishing wildly over her shoulders and face. She wore tight-fitting clothes that drew ample attention to her waist and breasts, and if not for the scowl etched on her face it would appear she was here on a mission of seduction. As it was, Jack worried that she might try to break the door down before trying the handle so he opened it just in time for her to stomp across the threshold.

When her eyes locked first onto Jack and then Jennifer, who held both dogs by their collars, her determination gave way to an angry sort of confusion. Point blank, she rattled off, "*Por qué estan aqui, ustedes?*" in staccato-like Spanish. *Why are you here?*

Before Jack could explain their presence in any language, Tay's voice erupted from the other room. "Damn it, *mujer*, speak English! You are being impolite, and you are doing it on purpose!"

Her eyes darted into the side bedroom and softened in a motherly way when she saw Tay in a T-shirt and skivvies with his back propped against the headboard. The makeshift crutches leaning against the nightstand and bloodstained bandage on his leg helped to clarify any doubts as to why he was not alone.

"Tay?" she said, as if stunned from a hard slap. "*Que pasó?*"

"Just a little gunfight," Tay answered casually. "It got a little messy."

"Someone *shoot* you?"

Tay said, "Only once."

"Oh shit! *Pobre Tayito!*" She ran into the bedroom and fell to her knees beside the bed. Tay offered his hand and she took it in both of hers, first kissing it and then pressing it to her face as gently and as lovingly as a small puppy.

"What took you so long?" Tay asked, "Didn't you miss your mare?"

In Jennifer's ear Jack whispered, "Wouldn't that have been a circus, if she'd come storming through the door a minute before Catalyn's transfusion?"

She said, "I did miss her, *Tayito*, and I was angry. But it took me until today to borrow another horse to come looking for you," Before falling back into Spanish at which point the conversation became a personal one.

Jack and Jennifer stepped outside. It was a small house made even smaller by Carmen's large presence.

Jack asked, "How long have they been...?"

"Going steady? More or less for the last ten years. I think it drives her nuts that Tay won't ask her to marry him."

"Can you blame him?"

Jennifer shrugged. "Not really. She loves him to death and that's her problem. She seems to have been born with an extra helping of hot Latin blood. Tay's wise to take her in small doses."

"Can we leave them alone?"

She rubbed a hand against Jack's chest and looked up at him with a gleam he'd missed seeing in a woman's eye since he was a much younger man. "I think they'd appreciate it," she said in that innocent way of hers he found seductive more for what it wasn't than what it was. Like the scent of desire, caught quickly then lost, leaving him searching.

From the house, Tay spoke out with a raised voice: Hey, *amigos!* Come here, quickly."

"He *pinched* you?" Jennifer asked, incredulously.

"*Si. Mi culo. Aqui.*" Carmen touched a spot low on her nicely rounded buttock. "So I slap him in the face. He think this is funny."

"And he was in the bar? Drinking beer?"

She nodded. "*Si*. Him, and that *puta*, Rosa Lupino."

Jennifer turned to Jack. "Something is wrong here, Jack. More wrong than I can begin to tell you."

"Maybe he's finally letting his hair down after all these years," he suggested, perhaps too lightly.

Jennifer shook her head vehemently as Tay and Carmen looked on in silence. "No. I know this man. He doesn't drink alcohol and he's scared to death of women. Something is all out of kilter; it just makes no sense."

Tay said, "It gets even better. Carmen says that *Hadriano* was also there."

"I thought you said you shot him," Jack replied.

Tay shrugged, then answered, "I heard what I heard. A bullet hitting flesh is not a sound to be confused with another." Jack believed him.

To Carmen, Jack said, "Was he hurt? Sore? Limping? Slow in any way?"

Yes," she said. "Mostly he sit in the corner by himself, watching. But he had pain, like here." She hiked up her tank top to where it exposed the bottom of her breast and drew a four-inch circle on her ribcage with a graceful index finger.

"Was he having trouble breathing?" Jack asked.

She shrugged, "I do not know. He was very quiet, like he wait for someone. Maybe you, *Tayito?* But he keeps his arm to his side and he drinks his *cervesa* with his left hand. And then he make a face, like he is in pain."

"Sounds like broken ribs," Jack speculated. "Could he have been wearing a bulletproof vest?"

"I would put nothing past him," Tay said, as if only a child-molesting welfare cheat would be low enough to hide behind a vest, "but I'm guessing the bullet simply did not hit him squarely."

To Jennifer, he said, "We really ought to look into this. Buy you lunch in town? I know a place that serves a half-decent rabbit sandwich."

"I could never bring myself to eat a rabbit," she answered.

"Chicken, then?"

"Better, I suppose."

Catching the gist of their plans, Carmen said, "*Cuidado, amigos.* These are bad men. *Muy malo.*"

"I just want to take a look, that's all. What could either one of them do in the middle of town in broad daylight?"

"Probably nothing, but it is always wise to expect the unexpected," Tay said, dropping his eyes to his leg to drive home his point.

"I'll keep that in mind."

*　　*　　*　　*

Not long after Jack and Jennifer drove off, Carmen, who was finally beginning to cool down from the initial excitement of seeing her man incapacitated, said, "*Tayito?* I do not know if this is important, but twice last night I saw the sheriff sit down to talk with that *asesino, Hadriano.* And whatever it was those two talk about, they were not laughing. I think they are maybe planning something, but I could not hear what they say."

After a moment's consideration, Tay calmly told her, "Listen to me, Carmen; hurry and find Luke. He's probably in the shop, alone. Tell him to get his ass over here pronto. Whatever you do, steer clear of Catalyn and Cassie. Can you do that?"

"*Si, mi vida,* that I can do."

*   *   *   *

"We can't just sit at *Vientos de los Dioses* and wait for something to happen," he told Jennifer, a little defensively, she thought. She remembered that this was almost word for word what he'd said before setting out on yesterday's ill-fated venture. He went on saying, "Silas is gone, Tay is laid up for God knows how long, and we have no one else on our side. It's worrisome."

Yes, it was. Especially the fact that Silas was gone. And not just gone, but out of touch. Incommunicado. Try as she might, she could not feel Silas's presence, except perhaps to know that he was alive. And even that might be wishful thinking. Whatever doorway lay between her soul and his, Silas had found a way to shut it. *But of course he has,* she told herself in her most reasonable voice. *If I can find a way to him, so can she. She must know by now that Silas is awake and gone into hiding, even if no one else does. And she's just sitting and waiting for that small, insignificant door to open one tiny crack. I can feel it; I can feel her, crawling around the outside of my soul like a tick looking for an easy spot to burrow in...* She shivered reflexively.

"Cold?" Jack asked, catching her shudder out the corner of his eye.

She shook her head and mumbled, "No."

A blast of sand-laden wind scoured the back window of the pickup, causing the dogs to lie down with their ears flat. They'd traversed the wasteland of the high plateau and were now entering the narrows where, millions of years ago, the creek had cut through the last remaining granite ridge between the high mountains and Purgatory before flattening out into a peaceful meandering stream that joined up with the South Platte River many miles to the southeast. Depending on the direction of the wind, the narrows could either magnify the energetic air cascading down from the Continental Divide or subdue it.

"Jack, are you glad the oil is gone?" she asked offhandedly, hoping a change of subject would calm her frayed nerves.

The road was narrow at this point, and badly washboarded, causing the old pickup to shake and rattle. He eased off the accelerator when the truck began to fishtail. It had the effect of quieting the errant noises issuing from a thousand different places, and enabled him to divert his focus away from the road. "Yes, I suppose I am, now that it's all said and done. Are you?"

She looked wistfully out the side window. "Yes. And no. The death and suffering during the Turning were almost beyond comprehension. Certainly worse than anyone could ever have imagined. I pity the billions who starved, or were killed, or lost those they loved. At the time, I thought it was the most monstrous act against humanity ever conceived." She glanced at Jack. "But looking back on it now it seems inevitable, even necessary. I can't begin to fathom where we'd be today if Tar Baby hadn't happened."

"The same as always," Jack speculated. "Rationalizing our actions under the illusion that we were somehow in control, while reproducing ourselves without restraint in a polluted world with quickly diminishing resources. I can't help but think that Tar Baby may actually have saved us from an even worse fate."

"Even when I was a teenager before the Turning," Jennifer reflected, "I couldn't understand why everyone considered economic growth to be such a good thing when the world itself stayed the same size. It was insane. What were we supposed to do when there was no more *room* for growth?"

"Pretty much what we did; starve and die. In the end, nature corrects all failures. And we were bound to fail utterly, drunk on our own excesses."

Jennifer said, "Tar Baby sobered us up in a hurry."

"Cold turkey," Jack agreed. "I imagine in a hundred years from now, after everyone who lived through the Turning has long since died of old age, historians will judge the unleashing of Tar Baby as an act of compassion."

Jennifer considered this, then said, "It may take longer than that, I think. Generations have their own memories. But I agree. Sooner or later cold logic will judge the past in the same detached way we examined the French Revolution in school."

"And will it be concluded that the Turning was brutal but necessary?" Jack asked.

"Something like that, I suppose. I doubt anyone will try very hard to argue that we were in control of our own destiny in 2017."

"Or even in touch with reality, for that matter," Jack suggested.

"But it wasn't, was it? An act of compassion, I mean."

"No," he said, after a moment's hesitation. "More than likely it was a power play that went awry."

"How so?"

He shrugged. "Maybe someone wanted to destroy someone else's oil, but not their own. If you consider that Tar Baby first struck in Iran it doesn't take a lot of imagination to tease out a motive."

"But if that's really what happened," Jennifer reasoned, "whoever engineered Tar Baby grossly underestimated it virulence."

Jack said, "Yeah. It's got to be a real bummer if you're a germ designer."

Jennifer couldn't let it go at that. "But what if the inventors *knew* how virulent it would be—and it seems they would, wouldn't they?—*then* where is your power-play motive?"

"Out the window," Jack said, without further comment.

"You're not being at all helpful, my dear."

"I simply don't have any answers," he replied.

"Who would?"

"That depends on if we allow that my old man might be involved, somehow."

"Carlos? Are you kidding? Do you really think he—"

He cut her off. "I think nothing. I was simply hypothesizing. It's what we scientists do, you know."

"I thought you gave that up."

"Old habits die hard. After so many years, the brain becomes hardwired."

"Okay, do your thing. Hypothesize."

"It's something your brother told me."

"*Silas?*"

"Yeah. When I suggested that perhaps something went terribly wrong for the planners of the Turning, he said 'but was it an act of God, or did the devil have his thumb on the scale?'"

"So?"

"So I'm wondering," Jack ventured, "If the devil in question wasn't dear old Dad."

They entered the part of the narrows where the tops of the trees met high overhead in a natural archway. Since she was a girl, Jennifer had considered this part of the road to be the gateway between Purgatory and *Vientos de los Dioses*; that if God were to drive a wedge into the earth to cleave one from the other, this would be the spot where it would happen. It was a silly notion, she knew; a product of a child's imagination that somehow persisted into adulthood.

She raised her knee onto the seat of the pickup and turned sideways so she could face Jack while he drove. She liked watching him; liked trying to imagine what was going on inside his head without actually exploring, which would be cheating in the worst way. Everything about him was understated. He was kinder than she first thought, and smarter.

Yet for all of her suppositions, what did she really know of Jack Vara, beyond the standard agglomeration of biographical tidbits? What made him the unique man she found him to be? She reached across the seat and gently rubbed his neck with her fingertips. He smiled softly and placed his free hand on her leg. A touch, to paraphrase an old saying, was worth a thousand words. A million. A touch could not deceive with the same facility as words. Its intent was implicit in the feeling it evoked. No one was ever betrayed by a caress who did not wish to be betrayed. We might say things we don't mean and gaze upon things we'd rather not see, but rarely do we let our fingers or our lips touch things we don't truly wish to touch.

Perhaps what she liked about Jack most of all was the way he touched her.

As if picking up a thread of the fanciful weave-work she was preparing in her imagination, Jack asked, "What are you thinking?"

"About you."

"Hmmm. And what have you concluded?"

"Nothing just yet," she teased.

"Smart girl," he said playfully. "I may not be who you think I am."

"Like I said: I haven't reached a conclusion," she replied primly. He turned and faced her and she quickly leaned toward him and stole a kiss. "But I'm working on one."

They drove out of the narrows past the partially dismantled wind farm and turned right onto the far north end of Main Street. From this direction Purgatory looked like a town in transition from the twenty-first century to the nineteenth. The streets were mostly dirt, but islands of old cracked pavement remained in places. Horses and mules stood tethered next to dinged-up flatbed trucks and cobbled-together carts, buggies and bikes. The sun shone directly down on the street.

Under the shade of a giant cottonwood Sheriff Prygor Primm sat motionless on his mare, watching without expression as Jack and Jennifer cruised slowly by.

27

Pryus Sees the Light

The Universe is a vast place. Even with the aid of mathematics it leaves us stupefied, for what we discover is that there is room in the universe not only for what has been and will be, but also for what might have been but wasn't. Indeed, so enormous is the universe that the only logical conclusion we can draw is that everything that possibly could happen will happen, somewhere.

All that remains for us to resolve, then, is the manner in which different but similar events which we presume to take place in regions of the universe impossibly remote from one another, are causally connected, despite the obvious—but quite possibly illusory—constraints of time and space...

EXCERPT FROM A SPEECH DELIVERED BY DR. JACK VARA
TO THE RANDALL RESEARCH INSTITUTE, JULY 14, 2037

"We can still turn around," Jack suggested. His comment left Jennifer wondering if his earlier feelings of bravado had begun to succumb to introspection.

"I'm not afraid of him anymore, if that's what you're thinking." It was true. Her fear had turned to contempt.

"Being afraid is not the same thing as wanting to avoid a potentially dangerous situation," he pointed out.

"I know," she said.

"From what Carmen said, it sounds like the sheriff's train's gone off the track. Driving past a psychopath with a gun, a badge, and a bone to pick doesn't seem like the most auspicious way to start a pleasant day in town."

"Just drive, will you, please?"

He drove.

Jack paid Primm no more attention than he might pay to a familiar statue as they rolled silently by, but Jennifer studied him intently. He seemed not to move, but his eyes, dark and brooding, followed hers. She did not avert her gaze. *Do you see me Prygor? Do you see that you no longer hold power over me?*

Then they were past and she turned away. But not before she saw him smile. It curled his thin lips only slightly but was made menacing by the steely glint in his narrowed eyes; the cold hard eyes of an enemy.

Suddenly the warmth fled from her body and for a fleeting moment she wanted to tell Jack to turn around and drive back to the safety of *Vientos de los Dioses.* But she couldn't allow herself to do it. She'd played cat and mouse with Prygor Primm for too many years. It was time for it all to end. Now. Today.

Jack pulled in front of the Daisy Mae. Three blocks away, Primm still sat unmoving on his horse. Only when they stepped inside did Jennifer glance over her shoulder and see that he had begun to move in their direction.

As it was the noon hour, the place was almost half-full, mostly with farmers and woodcutters and other men with worn clothing and rough hands. Turney and his crew sat at a table in back. Jack nodded politely as he and Jennifer took the table by the window. She sat facing north so she could watch Primm.

Sue Delaney waited their table. When she saw Jack, she smiled. "Welcome back, infinity man."

Jack flushed and said only, "Thanks."

She took their order and disappeared back into the kitchen.

Jennifer allowed a curious smile, despite the tension she felt in the air. "Infinity man?"

"Long story," Jack said.

"I doubt *that,*" Jennifer retorted.

Then he told her what he had told Sue the day he arrived. "The thing is," he concluded, "It's not fanciful speculation. You could say that it's mandated by the immensity of the universe. If the universe truly is as big as it appears to be, there is no conclusion to be drawn other than to admit that anything that could happen *has* happened, and will continue to happen forever. All your memories are still real. As are your dreams and your hopes. And every dream you *didn't* pursue, another 'you' *did*. Somewhere, sometime."

"Interesting," she said.

"That's just the classical version. Once you allow quantum forces into the mix it gets *really* interesting."

"How so?" Jennifer asked, now curious.

Jack answered, "Well, the classical version is basically a demonstration of the brute force of large numbers. But once you allow that it might be a quantum process, you also allow some conscious control over things."

"Conscious control?"

"Right. Let's say, for instance, that you're walking through a forest and you come to a fork in the path. Since both paths look pretty much the same, you pick one at random and continue on your way. End of story, right?"

"So we are all led to believe."

"True. But suppose that in reality the universe splits in two and you take them both."

"You mean a different 'me' takes the other path, right?"

Jack shook his head. "No! That's the beauty of it. You remain you, either way. It's only because of the limitations of human consciousness that you can only focus on one probable you at a time."

"This is getting deep," she replied. Primm was halfway up the street now; little more than two blocks away, slowly walking his horse up the center of the road.

"It gets deeper," Jack went on, having clearly forgotten about Primm. "Once you allow time into the mix, or should I say, the absence of time. Rather than the world changing around us and splitting into alternate copies of itself every time someone makes a decision, suppose that every possible instant in time exists simultaneously, and what you perceive as time is really your remarkably fluid consciousness moving seamlessly from instant to instant, world to world."

"Sounds bizarre, but somehow pleasing," she said, gazing pensively at Jack. "It makes consciousness the primary player in the universe, rather than random physical processes. It gives everything..."

"Meaning?"

"Yes; meaning," she said approvingly. "As if thought and feeling and perception were at the heart of existence. I like it."

"I thought you might. "

"Still, it's a little, I don't know, simplified. And too structured," she said, after comparing the processes of Jack's theoretical world to her own implicit perceptions. "The feeling I have is that reality is far more fluid and complex... in a very, well...a very astonishing sort of way."

"Astonishing?"

"Yes, astonishing; as if the meaning behind existence is so wonderful it's beyond description. And if you could ever discover just *why* existence is so wonderful, you would have the answer to life, the universe and everything."

"You amaze me," he told her, reaching across the table, taking her small hands into his.

"Really? I bet it's hard to amaze a scientist," she mused.

"Practically impossible, jaded creatures that we are."

She said, "Maybe we should discuss this in more detail—a little bit later. Food's here." *And Primm will be in about two minutes.*

Sue set their food on the table—a grilled rabbit sandwich with fries for Jack, chicken pasta salad for Jennifer—and poured them both glasses of cold tea. "Anything else I can get you?" she asked. Sue gave Jack a wink and Jennifer felt little needles under her skin. Was she jealous? She couldn't help but smile to herself.

"No, thanks. We're fine," Jack said. Jennifer watched to see if Jack's eyes would follow Sue's backside as she sauntered back to the kitchen and was pleased when they didn't.

She was jolted back into the moment when she looked up and saw Primm sitting astride his horse in the middle of the street. He was watching them through the window.

His boldness angered Jennifer while at the same time making her stomach churn into knots. She said, "Don't look now, but someone has taken an interest in our dining habits." She shuddered. "The nerve of that man!"

Jack froze with his sandwich halfway to his mouth and slowly turned his head toward the street. "Asshole," he opined. Outside, Sasha and Jazzman sat up side by side to study the black-clad man on the dapple gray mare. Jazzman's head was lowered and the hair on the nape of his neck was standing at attention.

Jack found the turn-handle for the blinds and twisted it until Primm was barely visible through the upturned slats. The bright room dimmed considerably, eliciting shouts of "Hey!" and "Who turned out the lights?" from the other diners.

Jack ignored them. All except for Turney, who was preparing to leave with his two comrades. He nodded politely to Jennifer before turning to Jack. "Developed a sudden aversion to sunlight, have you there, Jack?"

Jack nodded toward the window. "It's getting hard to have a private meal around this town," he said.

Pardoning himself, Turney leaned across the table and spread the blind to give him a better view. "Rude sonofabitch. He's been acting funny all damn day."

"Funny?" Jennifer asked. "Like how?"

Turney scratched his stubbled cheek and glanced at his two friends who were inching their way closer now that it was apparent they wouldn't be leaving right away. He said, "Well, for all his shortcomings, our good sheriff is usually polite. You could almost say proper, in a standoffish sort of way. I think he must figure that by being both polite and aloof, it makes most people want to keep their distance—mostly because it's impossible to read a man who acts that way. With Primm, you never really know what's going on behind those eyes.

"Who'd *want* to?" Jennifer asked rhetorically.

Turney smiled quickly and went on, "But today he doesn't much give a damn about hiding his thoughts. He's not polite and he's not aloof. He's just plain mean."

"Mean? Prygor?"

The younger of Turney's friends stepped forward and joined in the conversation. "He rides up out of nowhere and says we're all lazy, that we couldn't put in a day's work if we had to. I told him what we did or didn't do wasn't any of his damned business. Which it isn't. We're just doing civil service for the town, to pay off new property; it's got nothing to do with him and Desa. But he gets off his horse and gives me a shove; tells me to watch my mouth. That's when Leo steps in." The young man nodded to his broad-chested companion, who picked up the story from there.

"Right," Leo said, "So I go and stand between Sam here and old tall, dark and scary, and he laughs and says 'Ooh, aren't I shaking in my boots now?' except he wasn't. He was itching for a fight and I was ready to give it to him."

Turney said, "When I saw the look in Primm's eyes, I knew he wouldn't be backing down, so I get Sam and Leo here to back away and give the man his space. He sneers at the three of us like we were spoiling his fun. After a minute he gets back on his horse and spits on the ground in front of us. Then he rides away."

Jennifer felt the blood drain from her face. "Great God in heaven," she said in a loud whisper. "Something is really, really wrong here. I've never met the man you're talking about."

"Neither have we," said Turney, with Leo and Sam nodding agreement. "It's like he suddenly grew hair on his chest and a big pair of balls. Pardon my French, Jennifer."

Jennifer waved away his trifling vulgarity. She'd hardly heard it, in any case. She thought, *What in heaven or hell could cause such an abrupt change in the man?* But she knew the answer the instant she thought it.

Her.

Suddenly she felt very foolish for her earlier brashness.

"Were any of you guys at the Blue Fox last night?" Jack asked.

They all three shook their heads. Turney said, "But I hear the good sheriff was kicking up his heels a bit."

"What else did you hear?" Jennifer wondered.

"Only that he left with Rosa Lupino," Turney said.

A coarse laugh erupted from Leo's deep chest. "Maybe he'll die of the clap and save the rest of us the trouble of dealing with him."

Jack peeked through the blinds just as a dark-brown jeep pulled up beside Primm. Jack opened the blinds for all to see. After a short conversation, the jeep headed north. Primm spun his horse around and planted his boot heels in her flanks. She broke into a gallop behind the jeep. "*That's* interesting," he said.

"Didn't know the old nag could run that fast," Turney offered.

"But where is he *going*?" Jennifer asked.

"To hell for all I care. Let's eat."

"Jack, that was Hadrian Tharp in the jeep."

"Who cares?" he said defiantly. "Whatever's going to happen is going to happen whether we eat or not. Personally, I'd rather not be scared away from a good meal."

They ate.

Turney, Leo and Sam made their way back out into the warm afternoon.

Through the window Jennifer absently noted that heavy clouds were building in the west.

Main street was empty as they drove out of town. Jack stopped to ask Turney's crew if they had seen any more of Primm. They hadn't. Jack and Jennifer continued north.

It almost seemed they were going to make it home without incident.

Still, Jennifer didn't like it. She wanted to see him by the side of the road on his rundown old mare, staring a hole through the two of them as they drove by, but Primm was nowhere to be seen.

Left off of Main. Past the wind farm. So far so good. Jack leaned back in the seat and drove casually with his wrist on top of the steering wheel. Jennifer let out a breath and it tasted stale; she'd been holding it for too long.

When they entered the narrows she allowed herself to relax a little. *The arch,* she told herself, *when we reach the arch we're home free.*

But they didn't get that far. Not quite.

As they rounded the last sharp turn before her imagined dividing line between Purgatory and *Vientos de los Dioses,* they saw the jeep parked sideways in the road, just ahead of Primm's lathered-up mare. Primm stood on the left with a booted foot hiked up on the back bumper, his black Stetson riding low on his forehead. Tharp leaned across the hood, smiling a devilish smile made all the more so by the way his white teeth contrasted with his tanned face. Primm with his service revolver, Tharp with something bigger and more complex.

Jennifer saw Jack's jaw harden, and she knew he was going to try to run around them. "Stop," she told him, almost gently. "We'll have to see what they want."

Tharp, she imagined, was just after the diamonds. But Primm was another matter. Diamonds, yes, but he was also after Jack; she could feel it in her bones.

"Please?" she said, knowing if they tried anything desperate Primm would surely shoot Jack, maybe both of them, in the back. That was his way.

Though Jack didn't know it, at the moment Hadrian Tharp was his best friend.

Jack slows the truck and looks at her. He is almost calm, she thinks, though it's clear he's pleading with his eyes. This is the only way, she tells him without words.

He skids to a stop in the road, five feet in front of the jeep. While Jack assesses the situation Jennifer jumps out to put herself between Jack and Primm.

"Lay a finger on him and I'll see you dead," she hisses at the sheriff.

Primm looks at Tharp and they both start to laugh. The laughing causes Tharp to bend over and hold his ribs. Then Jack steps out and speaks softly to the dogs. Neither dog likes being told to stay in the truck—she can tell this by the jagged chorus rumbling deep in both their throats—but they obey, for now.

Then Jack turns to face Primm and she instantly knows it's about to get bloody. Her heart starts to race, but she wills it to be calm. Primm's jaw flexes as Jack looks him up and down. He says, "So, if it isn't the long, lost son of the great Carlos Herrera. In the flesh."

A trace of a smile curls the corners of Jack's mouth and he replies, "He sent you packing with your tail between your legs a time or two. Or so everyone says." He scans Primm from head to toe and adds, "But that couldn't have been too hard." Primm stabs them both with a vicious stare; first Jennifer, then Jack, all the while slipping his finger inside the trigger guard. Tharp sees this; Jack doesn't.

"Hold it, Primm!" he says, firmly. "We're here for the diamonds, remember? It's bad business to shoot the only man who knows where they are."

Diamonds. Just as they thought. She can't imagine how they even know about Carlos's diamonds, but they do.

"She can find them," Primm counters. His voice is icy. It's the voice of a complete stranger. He waves his gun in Jennifer's direction in a way that makes her nervous.

Cautiously, she says, "I don't know about any diamonds...Prygor. That's between Carlos and Jack."

"Pryus," he bristles. "The name is Pryus."

"As you wish," she answers, knowing it will do no good to provoke him, "but the fact remains: I don't know anything about any damned diamonds." She sounds convincing, even to herself.

Tharp believes her. He backs away from the jeep and turns his big gun in Primm's direction. "No one dies until I say they die. Got it, Primm?"

Somehow she knows this isn't true. She feels her heart beating against the sides of her chest like an enraged animal in a small cage, and she wonders how much longer she can pretend to be calm.

From the opposite side of the Jeep, Tharp says reasonably, "How about it, Vara? Your diamonds for your life?"

Jack doesn't look at Tharp. He's having a stare-down with Primm. He says, "Sure thing, Tharp. We can split 'em 50:50. But you have to shoot this skinny prick to get your share."

Oh no, Jack! No! Why did you have to say that?

She quickly jumps in front of Jack, but he pushes her aside when Primm sticks his gun in her face. Is he threatening me? she wonders. Primm's indecision shows in his gun hand, which begins to tremble. Tharp sees this and says, "Don't even think about it, Primm; not him and not her. You're not that fast." Primm

REX A. EWING

looks over his shoulder at Tharp, then back to Jack. His eyes grow as nervous as his hand, but he points his gun at Jack's chest.

Watching Primm, Jennifer's concern escalates to alarm. Confusion is etched in his face. He's fighting a battle, and losing it. Something inside of him is about to break loose. Whatever it is, Jack tries to rip it free. He sneers at Primm and says, "What's the matter, lizard lips? Losing your nerve?"

Before Jennifer can even consider how foolish of a thing that was to say, Primm steps forward and slaps Jack across the face with his pistol.

As Jack goes down, Jazzman launches himself at Primm from over the top of the pickup. Primm doesn't aim; he just points his gun and fires. The dog's head spins in the air and he falls to the ground in a spray of blood. Sasha follows right on Jazzman's heels. This time Primm does aim, and the sound of the second shot explodes in Jennifer's ears. But even in the confusion she knows it was fired from a different, more powerful gun. Primm crumples as Sasha crashes onto his chest. A quick glance at Tharp tells her he's as confused as she is. Then another shot, this one in the dirt at Tharp's feet.

Without aiming, Tharp turns and sprays the slope north of the road with a quick burst of automatic fire, then flees into the trees holding his arm tight to his ribs. He disappears into a gulley dense with vines and thickets of bushes. Jennifer falls to her knees to untangle the carnage.

Sasha was the first off the pile, and the only one unhurt. Primm wasn't nearly so lucky. A bloody tangle of intestines pushed out from a fist-sized hole on his right side. He tried to lift himself up to rest on his elbow, but fell onto his back when the effort proved to be too much. She left him to suffer alone.

When she tried to pull Jazzman's body off of Jack, the dog began to stir. Shortly he jumped up and shook his head, sending droplets of blood in all directions. A wet red crease along the left side of his head pointed to a small hole through his left ear. The coy dog held his head low while Sasha licked the wound.

"Is it over?" she heard Jack say. Blood dripped from a gash on his cheek below the right eye. Before she could answer, they heard the sound of someone crashing through the foliage on the slope to the right of the road. She looked up to see Luke jump onto the road. A hunting rifle was slung over his shoulder.

"Oh, Jesus," he groaned, looking at Primm. "Is he dead?"

"It's just a matter of time," Jennifer told him.

As Jack struggled to his feet, Luke dropped to one knee beside the man he'd just shot. "Hey, Sheriff?" he pleaded, "I didn't want to shoot you, really I didn't, but I couldn't let you shoot Sasha; I just couldn't."

It was a perfectly stupid thing to say: to tell a man you killed him because he was about to shoot a dog, but coming from Luke's lips it sounded almost reasonable. Luke jumped when Primm opened his eyes and said, "It... was a...fair...trade." He smiled as he spoke and Jennifer thought it had to be the most magnanimous thing Pryus Gordon Primm had ever said in his life.

They heard the sound of a fast-moving vehicle from up the road. "It's Tay," Luke said, never looking up. Jack and Jennifer watched as a vintage black Cadillac hearse rounded the corner and came to a sliding stop a few inches shy of hitting Tharp's jeep.

Carmen's eyes grew large with surprise from behind the wheel. The two opposing side doors came flying open and she could see Tay struggling to pull himself out and onto his crutches.

"I think he's going," Luke said, still at the sheriff's side. "He's asking for you, Jennifer."

"Tell him I have nothing to say to him."

"Please?" Luke moaned, "for me?"

When she saw the woeful expression on his face, she relented. "Sure, Luke. For you."

Blood bubbled from Pryus' mouth as Jennifer knelt down beside him, and his eyes were growing hazy. His voice was weak but she understood him when he said, "I couldn't...do it...Jen. She...told me to...kill...you...but I...I couldn't."

"Who, Pryus? Who told you to kill me?"

"The voice...her."

"Salia? Salia Warchez?"

He half nodded. "Yeah...her. I have to...get her...out of...my...head." He coughed, spraying bright arterial blood; it wouldn't be long. He said, "But...I owe...her...I guess... She...made me...a man."

"A man? What do you mean, Pryus?"

"She made me...the man...I might...have been...if only..."

"If only what?"

He coughed more blood and shook with spasms of pain. It was difficult to watch. "If only...I'd...been...stronger."

"That's good, Pryus; that's real good," she said, even though she had no idea what he was talking about.

From far away, he murmured, "I couldn't...kill you...Jen."

"I know."

"So...are we...square...now?"

She took a blood-soaked hand in both of hers and bent over close to him. "Yes, Pryus," she whispered, "we're finally square."

He forced a smile, then exhaled the words "Thank you...Jennifer," with his final breath.

Jennifer felt a single tear form in the corner of one eye as she gently laid his lifeless hand across his chest. She quickly wiped it away with her sleeve.

Tay shuffled up from behind the jeep, crunching gravel with each labored step. "That's one," he said without emotion.

"Yes," she answered, looking up at him. She was so completely devoid of feeling it frightened her. "One."

It began to rain.

28

Silas Goes Afield

Imagine, if you will, a house—perhaps your own house—with many rooms connected by halls and doorways and stairs. To travel from the master bedroom to the guest bedroom you might open a door and go down a hallway to a stair which will lead you to a lower level and another hallway which finally takes you to the door of the room in question. We all move from room to room in this way without ever stopping to think that the rooms are only separated by a few inches; a few inches of wall or ceiling, through which move things we never see or even stop to ponder...

EXCERPT FROM A SPEECH DELIVERED BY DR. JACK VARA
TO THE RANDALL RESEARCH INSTITUTE, JULY 14, 2037

When the rain began, Silas realized just how scant and naïve his preparations had been. The pleasant Indian summer he'd experienced up until now had serenaded him into believing that his only difficulties would come from impassable terrain, wild animals, or maleficent humans. The thought that he might freeze to death never occurred to him.

The storm came in from the northwest with no more warning than a slow thickening of billowy clouds passing overhead like fleet messengers from a faraway place, and when the first few drops of rain fell on his exposed skin, he welcomed them. It was the first rain he'd felt in years. But the novelty soon wore thin, replaced by goose flesh and shivers and chattering teeth, as he was exposed in open terrain with only a light jacket. It quickly became apparent that he would have to find shelter soon or face the unwelcome prospect of hypothermia.

After setting out from Woltr's early the previous morning, he had kept the foothills close to his right while making his way south over a fairly easy blend of prairie and brush where the inclines were neither so rocky nor so severe that Silas could not climb them with legs that were sore through every layer of skin, muscle and tendon from his heels to his waist.

As Woltr had cautioned him, he ceased his travels at dusk, taking shelter beneath a spreading juniper tenaciously rooted above a sandstone outcropping. It offered him satisfactory protection from the cool breezes whistling down the mountain valleys from the north and west. There he remained until dawn, warmed only by a light blanket. Long into the night he gazed into a starlit sky, deeply awed by the immensity of it all. For a man who'd spent half his life in an existential landscape where time and space were abstract oddities, the experience was breathtaking.

Only after the gibbous moon had diluted the sky's inky depths with its bright, diffuse light, did he at last fall into a deep and restful sleep.

Upon waking, he ate a meager meal of jerky and hardtack, and a few slices of the dried fruit from Jennifer's pantry. In the austerity of his surroundings it seemed a banquet.

He changed course early in the morning; not because of any prior knowledge of where he was or even where he hoped to end up, but because of the nature of the landscape. To the south lay row upon row of uplifted strata, sloping gently along the brushy east faces but dropping steep and jagged on the west faces, where exposed layers of red, tan, white and black sandstone alternated in no perceptible pattern. Beautiful, certainly, but also impassable should he happen to wander into a box canyon with no route of escape.

So he'd angled east, toward a gentler terrain. By midday as the sun was just beginning to give way to burgeoning clouds, his path intersected with the remains of a road. This seemed a milestone in his journey, even though the pavement existed only as patches from which sprouted a steely, prickly sort of weed particularly well suited to the depleted earth in which it had taken root.

Following the road, he soon came to the remains of a long-abandoned home. By all appearances the house had succumbed not to fire or vandalism, but simply to the ravages of weather. Although its brick walls remained mostly erect, the roof and interior walls had collapsed all the way through the floor and into the basement, creating an excellent breeding ground for rats, snakes and other vermin.

East of the house, in a fenced-in area that might have been a garden at one time, three wooden grave markers poked up from the ground. The lettering on the graying wood was carved with great care.

The first in the row was Ashley Munro, born May 16, 2012, died October 12, 2018. She had been six; six and a half, as children that age so proudly parse their years. The epitaph read: *There was none more innocent than she.*

The second marked the grave of another daughter:

Mary Jane Munro

Born: June 23, 2014

Died: October 23, 2018

TOO YOUNG

AND GOD DAMN WELL KNOWS IT!

This was inscribed harshly, but in a slighter female hand. The last marker provided the explanation:

Helen Lee Munro

Born: September 12, 1987

Died: November 30, 2019

May she find in death the peace

denied her in Madness

Silas continued on his way under a darkening sky with a gusty wind at his back. An hour later it began to rain.

He had matches; Woltr had made sure of that (*You'd best take 'em, boy,* the old hermit had insisted, *what with embers all the time in the fireplace, can't really say that I use 'em much anyway*). But with no place of shelter and no dry tinder with which to start a fire they were useless. He thought of running back to the ill-fated house, but knew that his legs could not yet be used for running. Nor did he relish the prospect of spending a cold night in the dank darkness beneath the small section of collapsed roof still supported by the brick wall. So he pressed on, keeping his heading in a general southeast direction, as best he could figure using the ever more distant Rockies as his guide.

The rain grew steadily worse, falling now from a bruised and angry sky in silvery ribbons that lashed his face and hands like freezing whips. He shivered uncontrollably and held his arms tight around his body to preserve what little warmth there was to be had. He would need to find shelter before nightfall, or perish. His frail body engine was not capable of generating enough heat to keep the body core above the critical temperature needed to sustain life. With his clothing soaked through to the skin, the rain and wind were pulling heat out of his body faster than he could produce it internally.

He had to find someplace dry, and soon.

Motivated by the prospect of dying, he trudged on over former fields now thick with thistle and ragweed, past abandoned homesteads that had either been razed or torn to the ground by survivors hoping to recycle the boards and beams and bricks into more efficient dwellings.

His legs burned with an icy fire as the firm topsoil beneath his feet turned to mud that clung to his boots in ever thickening layers, and he feared he did not have enough strength left in him to continue much farther. *A road,* he thought, *if only I could find the remains of road, I might have a chance.* He knew the farmland in northern Colorado had, when geology allowed, been divided into sections—squares of land a mile on a side—and that he should soon intersect with the remnants of a road composed of rocks and gravel rather than fine, gummy soil.

But it was not a road that fate led him to.

As his pace slackened and each foot he pulled from the mud grew heavier than the last, his mind sought refuge from the cold and pain in the old familiar places; the places he'd considered home until a few days ago. He fought the urge, likening it to the deadly lure of sleep that signaled the final stages of hypothermia. But he hadn't yet reached that point and if he could find some measure of relief by pulling his focus inward, at least until he reached shelter, what was the risk?

Plenty, and he knew it. There was always the chance of bumping into someone or something he'd be better off avoiding, particularly if the person or thing in question was intent on forging a link to you. *Bad idea,* he thought reasonably, *a surefire way to bring this quest to a short and calamitous conclusion.* It was much safer to stay focused on the cold and the pain that wracked his body, using only the five corporeal senses to find his way. Yes; oh yes. Much safer indeed, to not allow himself to duck under the curtain of physicality for even a moment. For if that were to happen…if…

If *what* were to happen?…

In his weariness, and for but a sliver of time shorter than a single footstep, he felt himself pulled into a familiar refuge beyond the cold and pain; where his spirit could soar free of encumbrances in the bright light of...

My God, what am I doing? No sooner had he realized what he'd done than he was back in the driving rain. It slashed obliquely across an alien sky; a sky alight with brilliant webs of lightning, heralding cacophonous peals of thunder that struck his eardrums like iron hammers.

But he was no longer in the endless field. He had instead begun to follow the contours of the ground beneath his feet as it led ever downward, and only now could he see that he had unwittingly wandered into a deep, narrow ravine carved out by erosion on a scale he could scarcely imagine.

Whatever forces had conspired to gouge the earth here so severely, they seemed not to be at work today, for only a trickle of water ran along the center of the unnatural gully, where porous sand had replaced the gummy topsoil that rimmed the edge.

Beyond the rim he saw the tops of buildings, some intact but most in varying states of ruin. And along and across the gully there protruded a network of pipes, large and small, PVC, steel and concrete, most bent or broken, or completely rusted through.

He had wandered into the remains of a town where he could at least get out of the rain. But how? The sides of the gully were nearly vertical, and even if he could have climbed monkeylike onto a protruding plumbing pipe, there was nothing on the rim above to grab onto. Then he saw it...a place where a small building had fallen into the ravine and crumpled in a heap; a heap providing a wealth of angular surfaces suitable for climbing.

He made his way for it, unaware that he was being watched by predatory eyes.

29

Salia Hits Pay Dirt

Anna's profound compassion could only have been gifted by God. She brought out everything wonderful in my daughter and Salia delighted in pleasing her. Why did Anna die? I can only think it was because she took Salia's darkness inside herself, hoping to swallow my daughter's demons. With Anna gone Salia is lost and so very angry.

FROM THE DIARY OF ISAIAH WARCHEZ, SEPTEMBER 21, 2012

I make no excuses. I am who I am...

FROM THE AKASHIC JOURNAL OF SALIA WARCHEZ

"**O**h, Hadrian, you meddling IMBECILE!!!" Salia fumed, her voice booming against the walls of the rundown farmhouse. "How could you be so incredibly fucking STUPID??!!"

Not only had he gone and gotten Primm killed—a man who had unwittingly become her eyes and ears in Purgatory, due in no small part to his dutiful, malleable mind and the utter barrenness of his life—he had done it in such a way that the Teague woman and all of her cohorts now knew that she, Salia, had been using the sheriff as the means to destroy the sister of Silas.

Of all the things that could have gone wrong, she lamented, *why this?*

It had been a perfect plan and a simple one: kill the sister to get to the brother. But the brother could only be gotten to if the killing were done by someone who might reasonably be *expected* to do it—like an unbalanced man with a known history of homicide. A man who'd carried a torch for Jennifer Teague his entire adult life.

Of course the motive would be questioned—*Why did he kill her when he never even laid a finger on her before?*—but there would be a ready answer: *He snapped; thinking back, we could all see it coming. It was only a matter of time.*

And then Silas Teague's noble monkey business would seem small indeed compared to the tragic loss of his forever-doting twin sister at the hands of a psychopath. And in Silas's inconsolable grief she would have found him.

And, oh, how she would have made him talk.

But if Silas suspected Salia's involvement it might crystallize his resolve, prodding him to find and destroy what she wanted more than anything on this Earth. Just to spite her.

God, how she hated these complications.

And it was all Tharp's fault, goddamn him! She should have seen it coming when he showed up yesterday afternoon, panting like a wounded jackal with a jagged hole in the right side of his ribcage and blood running all the way down to his boots; should've known then that Tharp had picked up a scent he wasn't going to let fade into the blue yonder.

"Help me!" he demanded through short, quick breaths, after stumbling into the house, interrupting her meditations and doing nothing to improve her mood.

"I heal the spirit, not the body," she told him dismissively. "If you want to mend your strained relationship with the Lord, take a seat. Otherwise go find a doctor."

"Damn it, Salia, this isn't funny. It fucking hurts!"

"I'm sure it does, but that still doesn't make it my problem," she retorted. "Who shot you, anyway? And more importantly, *why* did they shoot you? Don't lie to me, Hadrian; not unless you want hungry black maggots crawling in and out of those holes in your side."

"If I tell you, will you fix it?" he asked, holding a blood-soaked rag to his side and grimacing.

He tried not to sound like he was pleading, but he was. He was in terrible pain and she enjoyed seeing him squirm. It was one of the few true pleasures of her utilitarian relationship with the man. "I'll stop the bleeding and keep it from infection. You'll have to suffer the broken ribs on your own."

With great effort, he grabbed her arm near the shoulder and pulled her face to his. Anger boiled behind his cinnamon eyes. "The ribs too, Salia. I know you can do it."

"Of course I can, but that's not the point," she hissed, jerking her arm away. The sudden motion caused him to gasp. "Besides, the pain will remind you of how dangerous you can be to yourself."

"Bitch."

"Maybe," she answered evenly, "but I'm also the only friend you've got right now."

He gave her a jagged smile, saying, "That's a sad commentary in and of itself."

"True," she agreed. "You deserve worse."

He removed his blood-sodden shirt while she poured water into a large bowl. Indelicately, she sponged the wound clean. The bullet had passed all the way through without shattering any bone, but careful palpitation revealed that four ribs had fractured from the force of the impact. Blood flowed from both ends of the hole as quickly as she sponged it away. Seeing this, Tharp said, "Make it stop."

"Who shot you?"

"Tay Villa."

"Hmmm, let's see. Isn't he Herrera's mercenary?" she said. "An old enemy, as I recall."

He reexamined the wound and said, "Will you please stop the bleeding?"

She ran a hand over the wound and the flow slowed, if only a little. "*Why* did he shoot you, Hadrian?"

"I was in his way," he answered evasively.

She raked the wound roughly with her open hand and blood began to gush as if from a faucet. "Too bad," she replied.

"Damn it, Salia, make it stop!"

"Truth?" she asked. Sweat ran down his broad forehead. He took a clipped breath and nodded. His muscular chest trembled involuntarily from the pain. She pinched the holes gently with her thumb and middle finger and the bleeding stopped. Tharp let out a gasp.

"I can drain you of blood if I want to, Hadrian. It's something you should keep in mind."

As if he didn't know.

"I was following the Teague woman," he began, bearing up to the pain. "She was with Herrera's whelp, Jack Vara. They were looking for old Herrera's hidden diamonds. At least I think that's what they were doing. I didn't really take the time to ask, if you know what I mean." She shot him an impatient glance and he finished, saying, "Anyway, Villa somehow got onto my trail. I shot him, he shot me. End of story."

"Did you kill him?" she asked, although she already knew the answer, having watched Villa's rescue through Primm's eyes.

He shrugged. "He was alive the last time I saw him."

"And how was it that you heard about this so-called stash of diamonds?"

He said, "I overheard Primm talking with Baker. I thought it might be worth looking into."

"Like a dog sniffing after meat scraps, Hadrian?"

"It's business," he said defensively.

"Did you ever stop to consider that your business might interfere with mine?"

Tharp shrugged. "Since you never tell me your business, I just figured I'd go about mine."

"Figure again, Hadrian. The Herrera place *is* my business. We'll make it our own, soon enough. Until then, stay away from it or face the consequences. Got it?"

He clenched his jaw, then let it relax. "Yeah, I got it."

"Good. I've got things to do. Bandages are in the cabinet. Clean up the mess before you go."

And then she'd gone back to work on her current project: the reinvention of Prygor, aka Pryus Gordon, Primm. She'd whispered in his head all afternoon, sometimes her words caressed, sometimes they snagged his tender spots. It was amusing to feel his surprise—and, of course, to hear his objections—whenever she commanded him to kill the Teague woman. She'd been inside his mind until early evening, when he'd gone to the Blue Fox in search of alcohol and, she was amused to see, a woman to rut with. She allowed him to fumble through the messy act of losing his virginity without her assistance. Instead, she sat in a trance and searched for Silas Teague, hoping to catch him reaching for his sister. But he hadn't.

Had she stayed with Primm a little longer she would have learned of the unimaginative plot the sheriff had hatched with Hadrian to ascertain the location of Herrera's diamonds. As it was, she discovered what was afoot only moments before the ill-fated roadblock, and by then it was too late to stop it.

Even then she saw a chance that things just might work out in her favor. Primm had every chance to put a bullet in the female Teague's brain (*and oh, what a surprise that would have been for prissy little Jennifer)* and accomplish his single purpose in the new life she had granted him. And he *would* have, if not for Tharp and his mandate that no one was to die until *he* gave the order.

That one needless command was enough to cause her entire plan to come unraveled. Primm was born to take orders and Hadrian's imperative muddled the sheriff's thinking just long enough to stay his hand.

And *then* the fool goes and gets himself killed. But not before spilling his guts. She could still hear his words ringing in her ears; still feel the exquisite depth of his pain as he murmured

I couldn't do it, Jen. She told me to kill you but I couldn't.

Of all the pitiable, sentimental things to say!

She threw up her hands in exasperation and drew a deep breath. *If I could undo it I would, but it's gone beyond me now and there is nothing to be gained from lamenting what might have been. Just let it pass.*

So she did.

And was quickly rewarded.

For a sliver of time so slight that it might have driven through a lesser viator's senses unnoticed from entry to exit, Silas had allowed himself the comfort of the inner planes to ease a pain that better men are honor-bound to suffer as an icy torrent sucked the warmth and vitality from his frail body.

Good! Oh, how I want him to suffer!

And then he was gone; drawn back into himself like a drop of spittle not quite cast from the lips. It was maddening. Still, she had a sense of where he was. A gulley; a deep, unnatural gulley, leading...where? As much as she hated to admit it, she needed Hadrian.

30

Silas Goes Underground

Survival becomes a more salient enterprise when its success or failure depends entirely on one's own actions...

FROM THE UNPUBLISHED MEMOIRS OF CARLOS HERRERA

Silas didn't see the hideous creature emerge from a thick snarl of sagebrush until he'd worked his way up out of the gulley, and then he had trouble believing what he saw. It must have been waiting for him since before he set foot onto the road that had been the town's main street, and now after his hard climb he had little left in him to fight the monster.

The creature's ancestors were certainly dogs of some kind, back when primal instincts were subdued by breeding, but very little of that earlier blood showed through. What stood before him now was an abomination of crossbreeding and severe inbreeding between...what? God only knew. Its feet were enormous and each appeared to possess two or three extra toes. But it wasn't made fearsome by its feet (which under different circumstances might have seemed comical) or even the two fully functional dewclaws that flexed menacingly on the inside of each foreleg as the animal crept slowly forward.

The mouth was what commanded Silas's attention. It was not a mouth that nature would have ever devised on her own. It contained far too many teeth which, like trees seeking light in a forest, seemed to be competing with one another for dominance. The winners of the competition—sharp fangs top and bottom that glided closely past one another as the beast opened and closed its mouth—were each as long as Silas's little finger and glistened with the steady rain that dripped onto them from the creature's wickedly up-turned lips. Like Silas imagined his blood would drip in less than a minute.

Even crouched low with its ears laid back against its broad head, it was at least as tall as Silas's belly and would have stood as high as his chest in the unlikely event they were ever to stand side by side.

In the mutant's eyes—large, yellow, and locked on target—Silas was no more than a few days' worth of red meat, And yet the beast was wary, as if it'd had painful experiences with humans in the past. But not painful enough, apparently.

He thought of the machete Woltr had given him and prayed he had the strength to wield it. The creature watched with growing agitation as Silas lowered his hand to his side and slowly wrapped his fingers around the machete's smooth black handle. When Silas slid the weapon from its scabbard he thought surely the dog-thing would close the fifteen-foot gap between them with a single pounce before he could raise the blade for action, but it only watched him with narrowed eyes.

If he was lucky he would have time for a single blow, and likely not fatal since it would be delivered with rubbery arms that burned and trembled. So he held the blade straight out, hoping the dog-thing would impale itself as it leapt for Silas's throat.

Lightning flashed in the monster's eyes and thunder cracked behind Silas as the mutant moved sideways to avoid the tip of the blade aimed at its broad heaving chest. Silas matched the beast step for step, hoping he wouldn't trip over his own feet and become easy prey for a creature that knew a whole lot more about killing than he did.

The rain worsened, driven now by a sharp biting wind that drove the droplets into his skin like icy darts, and thunder boomed in quick succession to the bright streaks of lightning that sparked across a brooding sky. The beast traced a large circle as Silas kept his rotation tight and small, never taking his eyes off the thing as he shuffled over uneven ground on feet he could barely lift.

It ended quickly. The creature ventured a step forward; Silas instinctively stepped back. As he did his right foot dropped into a small hole, causing him to falter. The beast rushed him the instant he stumbled, but not before taking a quick sideways dash to avoid the menacing blade Silas held before him. He tried in the confusion to correct the angle of the machete but the attempt was futile. The dog thing was too fast and Silas too weak. His back hit the ground, knocking loose the machete and forcing the breath from his lungs. He shot one fearful glance at the lunging monster and prayed death would be quick.

It was. When the mutant was airborne and so close it blocked out what little light the roiling dark clouds offered, he heard a loud *whish!* from his left side, followed by a flesh-rending *whack!* Silas saw the dog-thing's murderous eye register total surprise as the arrow entered its right ear and exited through its left eye socket, jerking its head sideways as it did. The beast fell dead beside Silas, a yellow eye skewered on the shaft of the razor-tipped arrow.

He heard an excited cry. "Ha! Finally got you, you wily old sonofabitch!"

Noting only that the voice was feminine, he used his arm to shield his eyes from the driving rain as he felt the vibration of his savior's footfalls through the sodden gravel beneath him.

Presently he felt a hand tug on his arm. "Hey mister. C'mon, get up off the ground. You'll freeze if you lie here too long." Accepting her help, Silas sat up and gazed into the eyes of the young woman who had just saved his life.

It was the first time he'd smiled all day.

Her name was Keetna, though she wasn't sure where the name had come from and wasn't likely to ever find out, since her mother, who had named her, had bled to death shortly after giving her birth in an abandoned barn where she'd received neither medical nor practical assistance. An old man in the town who knew her family claimed Keetna was the name of a sleek palomino mare once owned by her paternal grandfather. It was a story she liked, and she hoped it was true. She was born during the first year of the War of the Turning, she told Silas while they dried themselves in front of a crackling fire. She was nineteen or twenty, though not sure which, and she was the sole remaining resident of the tiny town of Endow.

Silas sat on an old wooden crate, warming himself by the fire burning on the concrete floor of an old shop building behind the burned-out remains of a Conoco station (regular $6.14^9 the crooked sign still read). Smoke swirled wildly around the high ceiling of the airy building before exiting through a hole in the corner where wind had torn back the metal roofing. The smell of death in the place was overwhelming to Silas's pampered olfactory. She dressed all her game here; it was the only building still standing that had an old-style hand winch, which she called a chain fall.

The carcass of the dog-thing hung by a chain wrapped around its hind legs. It looked better than seven feet from foot to outstretched foot. Its tongue lolled lifelessly out of its misbegotten mouth and the remaining eye seemed not to mind one bit that its viscera lay in a pile on the floor, or that its shaggy coat was being expertly removed by a woman half the creature's size.

"I've been after this bad boy for better than a month now," she told Silas without taking her eyes off her work, "but he was a sly old bastard. Always slinking around, feeding on bones and innards, and running off just when he was about to get shot. So I guess it was a good thing you happened along. You took his mind off of me." She gave Silas a quick economical smile then returned to the chore of peeling back the hide around the creature's shoulders.

"You saved my life," Silas said, hoping his gratitude showed through his weariness.

"That I did," she answered matter-of-factly.

"Your shot was amazing," he said, this time with a little more emotion. She had given him an apple from a large wooden bin after dragging the dead beast through the door of the shop, and he'd eaten it greedily while she built a fire from sage brush and old two-by-fours scavenged from the rubble that was Endow's second defining feature. Then she'd heated him a cup of coffee—twenty-year-old Taster's Choice instant that wasn't half bad. Finally he was beginning to feel the sweet natural sugars from apple working in tandem with the caffeine to revive his spirits.

"I don't normally aim for the head," she went on. "With a bow it's just too risky. Either you miss your prey altogether, or the arrow glances off the skull and the animal takes off running until he's drained of blood. But if I'd hit him in the heart, chances are he'd have opened up your throat before I could've finished him off. That's the way these big muties are: they're too goddamn mean and vicious to know when they've been killed."

Keetna was clearly tougher than she looked. No more than five-six and just over a hundred pounds, she was even smaller than Jennifer. She dressed in warm ill-fitting garments made from synthetic fabrics; the type one would likely find in the boy's section of an old department store after the summer clothes had been replaced with the latest winter fashions. She wore a black beret, slightly cocked to one side of her head, much like a French mademoiselle, and her short blonde hair stuck out from underneath it in all directions. It had the effect making her look like a pre-Christian

Celtic warrior ready for battle. Certainly her eyes lent to the warrior mystique; they appeared carved from clear blue ice with symmetrical fracture lines running through the irises in fascinating patterns. Silas imagined they missed very little.

He said, "Why do you live here by yourself, Keetna? Wouldn't you be better off someplace with...people?"

She had the hide laid out on the floor and was sprinkling it with salt from an old Morton Salt container. She looked up at Silas. "I'm better off than most, the way I see it."

"That's not what I—"

"I know what you meant. But the truth is, I've got all I need, right here. When the big storm cut the town in half a few years ago everyone took it as some kind of omen from God or something. They all moved on to the islands or other towns less cursed than this one, but I couldn't see the point in leaving. It may sound funny, but killing is what I do best. I don't know why that is, but I can't pretend it isn't so. And around Endow there's lots of killing to be done."

She rolled up the heavy salted hide and hefted in onto a steel workbench. Then she sliced some meat off the shoulder of the dog-thing and dumped it in a bucket, along with the liver. Finally she shoveled the remaining viscera into a wheelbarrow. "I'll set it out tomorrow for bait," she told him.

One chore remained in the long sequence from killing to skinning: she needed to protect her kill. Grabbing the looped chain dangling from the chain fall, she pulled it round and round several times to hoist the creature's naked carcass high into the ceiling of the shop building, above the jump of any animal that might be thinking about a free meal. Satisfied, she picked up the bucket and made for the door. "Let's go to my place and see what this mutie tastes like," she suggested. Silas followed on tired legs.

Keetna's "place" was more a warren than a structure. They entered from a root cellar entrance beside a burned out house. Using an animal-fat lamp for light, they followed a narrow winding tunnel that led gradually downhill until it opened into a large room. Like the tunnel, the room was heavily braced with top-grade railroad ties.

Keetna set her bow and quiver beside the entrance and lit several more lamps mounted on the timbers. Soon the place was aglow with soft, yellow light. As his eyes adjusted, Silas let them roam free on a journey of discovery.

Perhaps twenty feet square, the room was a small cavern cut out of hard red clay. The floor was gravelly in the places not covered by rugs or animal skins, and smooth throughout. The walls and ceiling, by contrast, had been crudely hacked out with pickaxes and shovels. Macramé plant hangers hung from the timbers, holding pots filled with silk flowers. A velvet Elvis hung on the far wall above a crude wooden bookshelf with a couple dozen dog-eared volumes.

A kitchen area against a near wall consisted of a stainless steel counter-top with shelves above, the latter attached to cross braces spanning two timbers. A crockery water dispenser sat beside the single sink, which drained into a PVC pipe that disappeared into the floor.

Despite the cool dampness of the place and the closed-in feeling brought on by the lack of natural light, Keetna's small home was comfortable and cozy.

"How long have you lived here alone?" he asked.

She was at the kitchen counter, slicing meat with a carving knife that had lost a good portion of its blade to the whetstone over the years. "A year, I think. Maybe more," she answered without turning around. "When the flood came through a few years ago everyone left but me and old Abner Darby. There were maybe twelve or thirteen of us before that."

"Abner Darby?"

"Yeah. He was an old packrat sort of guy," she said almost wistfully. "Knew a little about practically everything, or seemed to at any rate. I kept him in meat and he supplied me with things from his garden and his 'stores,' as he called them. It was a good arrangement."

"Sounds like it," Silas interjected, just to keep the conversation going.

She turned to face him, casually holding the bloody knife in her equally bloody right hand. "We'd talk for hours in the evenings and he'd tell me about the stars and planets and rivers and oceans and all the places he'd been that I'll never have a chance to see. He was the only teacher I ever had, but teaching's what he was born to."

She lifted her eyes into the distance and a small smile appeared on her face. It possessed a warmth her usual tight smile did not, and Silas thought it a pleasing metamorphosis. She said, "I can still remember the way his eyes would sparkle whenever he knew he'd captured my interest. Then he'd string out his tale just to keep me hanging. God, but I miss that old coot."

"What happened to him?" Silas asked, half afraid to hear the answer.

"Died," she said flatly, fixing her eyes now on Silas. "Killed."

He waited for more, but when it wasn't forthcoming he said, "Do you get lonely?"

"For a man?" she asked. A tone of suspicion hung on the last word.

"For anyone," he clarified. "For Abner."

"Sure. Sometimes," she said, "but then I get busy with the business of staying alive and the feeling mostly goes away."

"Do you get many people passing through?"

She shook her head. "It's dangerous out here. Folks on foot usually don't make it this far. As for those with cars or horses, they can find a lot better places than here to wander into. Interlanders used to come around, but not so much anymore. There's nothing left worth stealing. Besides, they know they're not welcome."

Without asking what she meant, he said, "Ever have to kill any interlanders?"

"Of course," she answered, as if it were a stupid question, "but I don't eat them."

"So you bury them?" he asked, hoping to hear her answer in the affirmative, but somehow knowing she wouldn't.

"No," she said evenly, "I stake them out for bait."

Silas felt his skin crawl. "Does it work?"

She shook her head. "Not as well as you might think. Nothing but strays, muties and buzzards will eat a man. Respectable animals won't go near 'em."

"Pity," Silas said, absently.

"It makes me wonder," she said, "just what in the hell you're doing out here all alone."

"It's a long story," he told her.

"It's a long night," she answered.

*   *   *   *

"Could be Endow," Tharp said, scratching the prickly stubble on the side of his face. "A heavy rain cut a gulley right down the middle of town a few years ago after an old rusted drainage culvert collapsed."

"Yes, that's where he is," Salia concluded. It felt right. Although the impression she'd picked up from Silas was so vague it was almost devoid of useful information, the feeling that it was Endow had grown so strong that she could no longer entertain any other possibilities. "Go find him and bring him here to me."

Tharp laughed, then grimaced at the pain it caused him. "I'll need to know what's in it for me. There's a scrappy little hellion burrowed in out there, and she doesn't exactly roll out the welcome mat when she sees me coming."

"Poor Hadrian. And I'm sure you never did anything to provoke her."

"I didn't say that. But you'll need to make it worth my while."

"I'll make the pain go away," she offered.

"Damn right you will," he told her, "but I'll need more incentive than that."

She looked into his deep-set eyes and said, "Don't forget the sheriff is dead because of your meddling, Hadrian. I had plans for him and you went and got him killed. You owe me."

He returned the hard stare. "Maybe. But the fact remains: you need me. That's got to be worth something."

"How about your precious diamonds, then?"

"I can find those on my own," he replied.

"Yes, I can see that," she answered sarcastically. It brought a brooding scowl to his face she thought delicious. "One of the few things I love about you, Hadrian, is your complete inability to see the big picture. With you it's always tactics, never strategy. It makes you predictable."

"Fuck off," he barked.

She wrapped her arms around his big, square head and pressed her cheek to his forehead. "Oh, Hadrian; that's why you need me. Don't you see? Can you deny that I look after you?"

No reply.

"Locked inside of Silas Teague's formerly scrambled brain is knowledge that will make your diamonds seem like rhinestones," she cooed softly, "petty baubles of no more significance than a handful of small brass coins." When Hadrian neither moved nor answered, she unwrapped her arms and said, "So bring him to me, will you?"

"The ribs," he said mechanically. "If I'm going to chase this guy down for you, I'll be doing it without an anvil banging on my chest."

"As you wish." As casually as brushing a piece of lint off his shirt, she ran her hand gently down his right side, feeling the bones knit back together as she did. His features softened and he let out a breath; the pain was gone.

"Happy?" she asked.

"Overjoyed."

"Good. Now get going." When he turned toward the door she grabbed his arm and said, "And take someone with you, will you please? This is too important to be taking chances."

The hard muscles in his arm softened to her touch and he smiled. It was the trademark Hadrian Tharp smile that he saved for the moments he was in complete control. He said, "Don't worry, *Salia*. I'll have him gift wrapped and delivered by this time tomorrow. Provided, of course, he's really in Endow."

She let go his arm and said, "Oh, he's there. Just make sure you find him. I'd hate to think what might happen to our little arrangement if you screw this up."

With the speed of a viper a large hand clasped her jaw and pulled her face toward his. His dark eyes burned into hers and the strong manly scent emanating from his pores was a sanguine reminder of his raw power. He said, "Don't worry, you'll have him. And then I'll expect some real gratitude."

She pulled his hand away and thought, *Perhaps, Hadrian, but whether or not you get your fleeting pleasures, it will finally be time to prepare for a new order of things.*

31

Dark Passages

When I heard for the first time that my money had been used to bring about the end of civilization as we knew it, I was not as horrified as you might think. In fact, the whole idea held a certain appeal. But it doesn't mean I didn't want Dobry Robak's head on a pike...

FROM THE UNPUBLISHED MEMOIRS OF CARLOS HERRERA

Silas had to admit that severely inbred mutie wasn't as bad as he thought it would be. According to Keetna, the more extra toes or teeth an animal had, the better the eating. "It's because they've also got an extra set of muscles, which means they use each muscle less; it makes the meat tender."

Still, it was greasy (mutie grease makes good lamp fuel, so sayeth Keetna), and as gamey as venison though in a less palatable way, and so he ate only as much as he needed to sate his immediate hunger, even though his body told him he should take as much nourishment as he could for what might prove to be lean days ahead.

"So you're headed to Denver to fetch some sort of document? A document this Herrera guy told you about when you were in no state to argue?" Keetna asked. After a meal of mutie and apples they sat around a small woodstove, sharing a pot of genuine Lipton tea sweetened with little packets of Sweet'n Low.

"That's about it," he affirmed. Unlike Woltr, whose ignorance might keep them both alive, Silas saw no reason not to tell Keetna the truth. She lived as a warrior and when her time came she would die as one. Besides, he had a hunch.

" Old Denver, or the Denver island?"

He replied, " Old Denver. Right into the heart of downtown."

She looked up at him with eyes that flashed experience beyond their years. "You'd better have more than an old machete and a heart full of good intentions," she suggested.

"At the moment, it's all I've got."

"Then take some good advice: don't go."

She was right, of course. Old Denver was no place for anyone who looked forward to a long and happy life. To hear her say it only confirmed what he already knew. Suddenly his weariness returned; it settled into his bones like a condition of life itself. How could he ever hope to get in and out of a shithole like Denver?

He stretched out on the soft animal hide and said, "Have you ever heard someone say, more than likely in a disparaging way, that a person seems to be acting 'as if the whole world depends on it'?"

"Maybe once or twice."

"Well, in this case it's true."

She leaned toward him and said, "Because of this document?"

Keetna really was quite pretty, despite the wild hair, the paucity of expression and the economy of her features which, he realized in that moment, were harmoniously offset by her large, almond-shaped eyes. Why should he expect to find softness or joy accentuating that naturally pretty face? She lived life day by day, always one errant move away from death. For Keetna, even concern was a stretch and he appreciated seeing it now, etched across her visage as if his troubles had somehow become hers. "Yes," he replied.

"Well, first things first. Are you warm, now? And dry?" she asked.

Silas nodded, suddenly feeling a heaviness in his eyelids. "Yes. Thanks to you. I just want you to know...if I hadn't run into you..."

"Hush," she told him softly.

He lay his head down on the soft pelt and closed his eyes. Just before sleep claimed him for the night he felt Keetna gently spread a blanket over the top of him.

*   *   *   *

The sun was just cresting the eastern horizon as Tharp and his two confederates spied the remains of the hard-luck town of Endow. It was still a few miles to the west and hard to make out against the backdrop of the Rockies, and he knew it to be such an inconsequential place he had trouble believing that the one thing Salia wanted most in this world would be found there.

He'd driven most of the night to locate the only men under his control living close to Endow. Even then he'd had to drive all the way to an outpost within a few miles of the Denver island at a time when the military patrols were the most active. He'd found them at a respectable-looking farmhouse surrounded by a working farm, where the two men, under contract to Tharp, received, inventoried and distributed black-market contraband from a storage area located beneath the barn.

They were thieves and scavengers by trade. With no combat experience beyond whatever undisciplined skills they may have picked up in the War, they had been reluctant to come. And not just because Tharp wanted them for a job outside the range of their contractual duties; they were also badly hung over, having gotten but two hours of sleep before Tharp rousted them from their moonshine dreams.

So he promised them handsome bonuses for their trouble and they piled in the jeep unwashed, bleary eyed and stinking of homemade corn whiskey, cracking banal jokes Tharp would not have thought funny if he were driving to a wild orgy with a bottle between his legs.

It wasn't an auspicious beginning to an operation that promised more wealth even than diamonds (a *lot* more, he kept telling himself in a vain attempt to kindle some degree of enthusiasm for the task at hand), but Tharp was a professional who knew luck in his business was the result of making the right split-second choices in the midst of the action.

Still, he would trade these two, body and soul, for a man like Tay Villa with one arm in a sling.

"Quiet," he said, as the jeep rolled to a stop on the northern edge of town. "We wouldn't want to wake anyone so early in the morning."

Jimbo, the big one riding shotgun, smirked and turned to Bobby with an index finger across his lips. "*Shhhh,*" he whispered. Tharp glanced in the rearview mirror at the younger, smaller man in the backseat and was encouraged to see concern wash across Bobby's pockmarked face.

Tharp pulled an Uzi out from under the seat and ejected the clip. Out of the corner of his eye he saw Jimbo's eyes grow large and he smiled to himself. Satisfied the clip was full, he slapped it back into the handle and said, "Let's go. Quietly. Harm a hair on this man's head and I'll have your balls for target practice. And by the way—keep your eyes out for a blonde-headed minx with a real mean streak."

And a compound bow, he neglected to add.

"Don't we get weapons?" Jimbo complained as Tharp stepped out the driver's side door.

"Won't need them," Tharp lied.

* * * *

Keetna felt their footfalls as minute vibrations traveling through the walls of the cave. Men coming from the north. With no time to wake Silas, she grabbed her bow and slung the quiver over her shoulder before exiting the dark tunnel. Avoiding the entrance she'd taken with Silas—a large, squeaky overhead door that would expose her location, she ran through a branch tunnel that came up through the floor of the women's restroom in the burned-out Conoco station.

She slid aside the scrap of wall section that hid the hole and cautiously looked around. No one in sight. Quiet as a mouse, she pulled herself up through the hole and crouched in the corner, listening. Movement to the north, east and west; they'd split up, looking for something. Or someone.

Too bad. They'd come to the wrong place. Nothing here but pain.

The Conoco station stood on a street corner along Paradise Avenue, the town's main drag. The remains of the burned roof had long since blown away, leaving nothing but a few blackened wall sections ranging in height from two to eight feet. The women's restroom had high walls to her back and to her left. The south wall to her front had been all but obliterated, and little more remained of the west wall to her right. It was a bad place to hide. With careful maneuvering through the wreckage she might be able to avoid detection by one person or even a tight group, but not three men coming from different directions.

She thought about ducking back down the hole, but feared she would give her position away. Instead, she nocked an arrow and leaned back against the north wall.

She didn't have to wait long.

* * * *

"What are we looking for?" Bobby whispered after they were out of the jeep.

"A man in his thirties; frail, most likely," Tharp replied, as quietly as his rough voice would allow, "but keep your eyes peeled for anything.

Movement. Smoke from a chimney. An open door. Anything that might indicate someone's been here recently."

Bobby nodded, then spit brown tobacco juice out the corner of his mouth. Suddenly attentive, he was beginning to take this business seriously. Jimbo wandered to the backside of the jeep to relieve himself, farting then laughing as he strained to squeeze the last few drops from his bladder. When he rejoined them, Tharp said, "Okay, here's how it's going to work. Jimbo, you take point. If you see anything, anything at all, just look at me or Bobby and point. Bobby? You're the left flank, I'm the right. All information comes directly to me, and it comes without a sound. Got it?"

Bobby clearly did. Jimbo still seemed to regard the operation with the casualness of a farm boy looking to corner a rabbit. Which was precisely why Tharp had put the clumsy oaf on point. It was a position that in combat required stealth and perceptiveness. Jimbo had neither, but he made good bait.

*   *   *   *

Keetna watched the big man plod ten paces past her before he finally turned in her direction. He smiled at her; smiled in a lustful, unclean way that made her skin crawl. His belly sagged, as did the skin on his face, and his teeth were tinted brown around the edges; a man like that had no right to look at her in that way.

His smile quickly faded. As if suddenly remembering the task he'd been put to, he began making frantic hand signals that were almost comical for their lack of clarity. Instinctively, she drew the bowstring to her chin and held it effortlessly. Then she graced him with a cold smile. The gesture utterly confused the man, who hollered, "Hey, Tharp! Help me! I fou—"

Tharp!? Here? The name had a jagged edge to it. If there were ten reasons for the death of Endow, Tharp and his people were nine of them. Whenever the townspeople started seeing daylight, Tharp's men brought down the rain. Had this man been one of the raiders? He didn't look familiar, and yet...

...she wasn't taking chances.

Keetna let go the arrow and trailed it with her eyes right into the big man's heart. His bloodshot eyes grew big and round as his hands closed around the fletching, the only portion of the arrow remaining on the front side of his torso. Blood erupted from his mouth as he struggled for a last breath.

She had another arrow nocked before the dead man hit the ground.

She was hoping for a clean shot at Hadrian Tharp, the Holy Grail of ruthless sons of bitches.

She wouldn't get it. Tharp took one step into her line of sight but stepped quickly back as she loosed her arrow. It sped harmlessly across the gulley. No time for another. Keetna pulled her bow tight to her chest and stepped over the hole, dropping out of sight as quickly as gravity would allow. The last thing she saw before disappearing into the tunnel was Hadrian Tharp, spinning toward her with a machine pistol held in military fashion. Five quick rounds slammed into the concrete wall behind her as her feet hit the bottom of the tunnel.

Silas was just sitting up when Keetna ran into the room. He'd been startled awake by gunfire. The cavern was well lit by a quartet of light tubes that had escaped his attention the night before, and it was easy to see the agitation on her face.

"Time to move!" she ordered.

Silas pulled on his boots and jumped to his feet. He searched around for his backpack and machete, finding them at the same time Keetna pulled an extra quiver of arrows and a backpack of her own from under the kitchen counter. "For emergencies," she said in a much softer tone, arranging the pack and the two quivers so quickly and effortlessly it was clear she had done this before. "Ready?" she whispered.

Silas nodded. She jumped into the passageway and let an arrow fly toward the entrance. Silas heard the whooshing of the arrow magnified in the passageway, then it's ripping impact.

"Ow! Oh, shit! You little *bitch*! I'm bleeding!"

"Who's *that?*" Silas asked.

"Never mind," she answered. Her mouth was slightly upturned at the corners in a smile that might have been wicked and vengeful if not for the caution that constrained it. "Take my hand and follow my lead. If I run, you run. If I stop, you stop. Got it?"

He nodded. "Yeah, I got it."

At that moment the wounded man stumbled into the cavern. Short, gaunt, and not yet thirty, his thinning hair was slicked smoothly back, contrasting the unruly whisker stubble that sprouted from his acne-scarred face, which was contorted with pain and anger. The razor-tipped arrow had sliced through the fleshy part of his right shoulder, creating a clean wound that bled copiously but did not appear to be life threatening.

"You don't belong here," Keetna told him calmly. "Get out, while you still can."

"Fuck that, you little bitch!" the man growled, lurching toward her with outstretched hands.

Keetna jumped low to one side and raked her leg behind the man's ankles. He let out a squeal and went down on his back so quickly he was unable to break his fall.

"Then catch us if you can, you whimpering little pussy."

Whimpering little pussy? Silas fought to restrain a chuckle.

Grabbing Silas's hand again, Keetna ran into the tunnel, away from the entrance. After a few steps she paused to make certain they were being chased. For a moment the man stood in the light emanating from Keetna's cavern, not sure if he should continue his pursuit. Keetna hollered, "Hey! What's the holdup, you whiny little chickenshit? No *cojones*?"

They heard "Bitch!" then feet slapping dirt.

Hand in hand with Keetna in the lead, they ran in total darkness just fast enough to keep ahead of their unarmed pursuer. In contrast to Keetna's lair, which was kept warm and dry by sunlight and the heat of her cooking stove, the tunnel was cold and damp. Groundwater from yesterday's rain had begun to accumulate in low spots along the floor of the tunnel, making it easy to gauge just how far back the man was by his splashy footfalls. Every time he slowed Keetna taunted him with another verbal assault on his manhood.

Silas was amazed; she maneuvered in the dark tunnel like it was bathed in sunlight. But then, she'd probably spent her whole life running up and down these dank passages.

After covering a considerable distance, Keetna stopped abruptly and kneeled down. In his ear, she whispered, "Feel this. Very gently." She guided his hand to a rope stretched tight across the bottom of the passage, six or eight inches from the floor. "Can you step over it?"

He listened for sounds behind them. The man had slowed, but was still moving their way. "Yes," Silas answered, carefully stepping across the trip rope on hands and knees, then paused on the other side. The man must have heard whispers; he stopped, anticipating a trap. Quickly Keetna exclaimed in a mournful whisper meant to be heard, "It's not good, Silas. It feels like it's sprained."

Picking up her cue, Silas replied, "C'mon. It's not far to the end, now.

Let me help you." Of course he had no idea how far it was to the end, but he grabbed Keetna's wrist and helped her hop on one foot to complete the ruse.

Behind them, footsteps. Slow at first, then faster. After a few more steps the wounded man stumbled and hollered, "Oh shit!" just before the tunnel reverberated with the ominous *clank!* of an iron door dropping down behind him.

"Ha! No turning back now, you gullible asshole!" Keetna taunted.

"ARRRGGG!" The sound made Keetna chuckle with vengeful delight. *She's actually enjoying this,* Silas realized.

Over the next hundred paces the tunnel split twice, and Keetna slowed each time to make sure their pursuer took the same fork they did. After the second junction she stopped and whispered so quietly Silas could barely hear her, "We're going to run ten paces, then jump as far as you can."

How can she remember all this with such precision?

In a flash she was off. Silas struggled to keep up and count at the same time. Eight, nine, ten...jump! The toes of his leading foot landed on solid ground while his heel dangled off the edge of a precipice. Keetna pulled hard on his arm; Silas fell on top of her in a heap.

From back in the tunnel, they heard, "Hey...what...what's going on up there?"

"Why don't you come and find out?" Keetna suggested.

"C'mon now. There's another trap, isn't there? Look, lady, I didn't want to do this; Tharp made me. I'm not even getting paid that much for it."

"Why are you here?" Silas asked.

A pause, then, "We're looking for a guy named Silas. That's you, right?"

"Why do you want him?"

"I don't know, honest." the disembodied voice drummed through the corridor. "Tharp woke me and Jimbo up and made us come with him. He's not the kind of guy you want to say 'no' to, if you get my meaning."

"Was Jimbo the one I killed?" Keetna asked dispassionately.

A pause. "Yeah...that was him."

"Are there others?"

"No. Just Tharp."

Silas asked, "And where is Tharp now?"

A long silence. "He'll kill me."

Keetna laughed. "Like you're going to get out of this tunnel alive if you *don't* tell us?"

Another silence. Then, "Yeah, I...I see what you mean." His voice was beginning to crack at the edges. "Okay..." A deep breath and a cold chuckle. "What the fuck... it's only life, right? He's waiting at the exit."

"Not the entrance?"

"No. He said to run the two of you out the exit."

Silas said, "He's played you for a fool, friend. He never expected you to get out alive. He just wanted you to drive us in the right direction."

"Bobby. The name's Bobby. And, yeah, you're right; I can see that now."

"How's the arm, Bobby?" Keetna asked him.

"Still bleeding pretty bad," he answered, with no real emotion.

The sound of a zipper. Keetna riffling through her pack. Then she throws something across the void. "Here," she said, with a kindness Silas found reassuring. "It's a package of gauze. Wrap it tight, but not too tight. There's a drop-off a little ways in front of you. If you fall in, you'll never get out. You'll have to jump to make it across. Then take the next two left forks, and a right after that. Take your time. If I ever see you in Endow again you're a dead man."

"I believe you," Bobby said.

"Good. You're smarter than you look." She took Silas's hand and left Bobby to his fate.

They moved quickly again, one left fork, then another. At the final junction they took another left. Silas protested. "What are you leading him into?" he asked sharply.

"Only Tharp," she replied.

"Well, then where—"

"The people of the town dug these tunnels years ago, during the War. After everyone left, Abner and I filled in the ones cut off by ravine, then added a few improvements. The point is, most of the tunnels lead to dead ends or booby traps, or both. Others meet up again. There are two ways in and out. Our friend Tharp has only seen one—the one Bobby is headed to. We're taking the other one."

"You're smarter than the average bear," Silas quipped.

"What the hell is *that* supposed to mean?"

"Cartoons? Reruns? Yogi Bear and Boo Boo? Oh hell, never mind; you're too young and it'd take too long to explain," he told her.

"I'm sure."

After another fifty paces she stopped and put a finger over Silas's lips. He nodded that he understood. She let go of his hand and cautiously climbed a short ladder. A shaft of daylight assaulted his eyes as she pushed open a small hatch just far enough to have a look around. A moment later she closed it and climbed back down.

"This won't be easy," she said.

"Tharp?"

"Yeah, crouched behind an old car, waiting."

Silas said, "I have an idea..."

Five minutes later, Keetna watched cautiously as Silas pushed aside the rusted iron covering of the hatch where Tharp lay in wait. In a flash, he was on his feet roughly pulling Silas out of the shaft. "Where's the she-devil?" He demanded, holding him tight by the collar.

"Dead, along with your friend," she heard Silas lie.

Tharp looked down the shaft as if he didn't believe him. "How?" he asked.

"Your buddy caught up with us. He and Keetna stumbled into a pit while they were wrestling around in the dark. I never heard a sound from either one of them after that."

Tharp stood at arm's length from Silas, looking him up and down with his hand tightly grasping his shoulder. "You Teague?"

He hesitated, then slowly said, "Yeah...what do you want with me?"

"A certain lady wants to talk to you."

"Is her name Salia?"

"Give that man a star," Tharp said.

"I'd rather you shot me," Silas told him.

Tharp laughed. "Yeah, me too, but that won't pay the rent."

Silas took a clumsy step backward and fell to the ground; it was the break Keetna had been waiting for. When Tharp turned to hoist him to his feet Keetna slid the hatch aside and bounded to the surface, bow at the ready. But before she could let fly an arrow Tharp spun and aimed his machine pistol in a single swift motion. She rolled quickly away from the *rat! tat! tat!* of a trio of bullets, ending up with a pile of concrete rubble between herself and Tharp. *Jesus,* she thought, with newfound respect for her old adversary. *No wonder this bastard is still alive.*

It occurred to her then that she might need Silas's help to get to Tharp, who would surely be more wary now that he knew Silas had lied to him. Chancing a peek, she saw they had both disappeared. Had they gone into the tunnel? No way. Where then? She slowly poked her head above the rubble and looked around. They were heading back north, Silas's collar in one hand, the machine pistol in the other. Every few paces he spun Silas around like a rag doll, surveying the landscape with eyes that missed nothing.

He was leaving without trying to flush her out and kill her? This was not at all like Tharp; he was a born predator who craved the smell of freshly spilt blood. He had to want Silas badly to walk away from a good hunt. Perhaps she could use this to her advantage.

Keetna scurried back down into the tunnel.

*   *   *   *

Even in its heyday, Endow couldn't have been much of a town, Silas figured. Five blocks long and four blocks wide with a few dilapidated houses at the outskirts. The gulley running down the center of Paradise Avenue effectively divided the town in half. It was fifteen feet deep in places, leaving water and sewer mains dangling in midair like the dead limbs of a half-buried tree.

It wasn't much to fight for.

Silas did what he could to slow down Tharp, though it wasn't much. A couple of times he tried dragging his feet but Tharp quickly pulled him up-right and growled for him to keep walking. And when he tried to stop and talk reasonably to his captor, Tharp lifted him off the ground with one meaty arm until Silas's wind was cut off.

Still, he could see that Keetna worried Tharp. It was obvious from the way he moved: turning frequently but not rhythmically, and always keeping Silas between himself and the place he was looking. It would be practically impossible for Keetna to get off a shot without hitting him. Small wonder Keetna found this guy such a threat.

Where was she now? He had no idea and neither did Tharp. There were a thousand places to hide in the ruins of Endow but a lot of open ground in between where she could be spotted. She must have ducked back down into the tunnel system, hopefully to reappear where Tharp least expected her to. But why should she risk her life to help Silas to escape? Tharp was on his way out of town with someone who meant nothing to her. Why not just let them both go?

Because of the hunt, he told himself, *because Tharp would be a trophy kill.* Besides, she'd promised to free him from Tharp and she meant it.

In the middle of town most buildings had either been razed to their foundations or stripped of their useful building materials. Here and there a sign lay in the rubble, still legible. Hank's Feeds. Pork Belly Restaurant. Schmidt's ACE Hardware. It was depressing to see how completely the hopes of a community could be undone.

Silas saw the dead man lying near the old Conoco station. His dull eyes stared sightlessly into a crisp blue sky. He looked peaceful except for the congealed blood drying in sticky globs around the corners of his mouth. His hands still clutched the arrow that had ended his life. He waited for Tharp to say something, anything, but he walked by without comment.

"Aren't you going to do something with him?" Silas asked.

Tharp said, "He's not my problem. You are."

Silas tried not the look at the dead man, but couldn't help himself. The body should've looked out of place, but somehow it didn't. Not in Endow.

When the dead man was well behind them, Silas said, "The other one is still alive, you know. The man named Bobby."

Tharp didn't miss a stride or even look Silas's way. He tugged hard on Silas's collar and said, "Then I imagine he can find his own way home."

Silas struggled against Tharp's iron grip without success. Finally he planted his heels and said, "I'll walk with you. You don't have to drag me."

Tharp stopped in the road, slowing their progress for a few more precious seconds that Keetna could use to their mutual advantage, if indeed that was her plan. Tharp released his grip and said, "I won't kill you, Teague, but I can make you hurt." He was grinning, exposing large white teeth suited for tearing raw meat from the bone.

Silas had never met a man like Tharp. There was a toughness to him only Tay Villa, with his lean, spring-steel strength, could match. His eyes were as cold and hard as his face, which almost seemed frozen in its intensity. "I have no doubt," Silas answered.

On the north side of the Conoco station the jeep came into view. Although it was still a good distance away, it was obvious from its unnatural angle that both tires on the driver's side were flat. Seeing this, Tharp growled, "That meddling little bitch just signed her death certificate!" Turning quickly to Silas he hissed, "If you try to run away, Teague, I'll make you hurt in ways you can't imagine."

"I'm not going anywhere," Silas said, sounding far calmer than he felt.

Tharp gave him one last hard stare, then raised his automatic and ran toward the ruins of the Conoco station, spinning and weaving and scanning the area for signs of a brash young guerilla fighter in a black beret.

He had just reached the north wall when Keetna appeared on the south side of the shop building where she had gutted and skinned the mutie. Her bow was slung over her shoulder and she held a gracefully bent piece of wood in her hand. When she looked inquiringly at Silas, he gave his head a quick nod toward Tharp, who thankfully was looking the other way. She responded with a thumbs up. Then she disappeared around the backside of the shop.

A moment later Silas heard a peculiar fluttering, akin to the sound made by the wings of a large bird. A boomerang. It whirled around the northeast corner of the shop building, tracing a high arc before plunging toward Tharp on a sharp trajectory. If he saw it at all he saw it only after it was too late for him to react. It struck him squarely across the face just as he turned toward it. He went down in a heap.

Keetna emerged again from side of the shop, looking inquiringly at Silas. "You got him!" he hollered.

Tharp lay like a rag doll with his arms and legs all akimbo. Blood percolated from an oblique slash that began beneath his right eye and ended near his left temple. Silas plucked the boomerang off the ground and examined it. It was fashioned from a dark, dense wood. The leading edge was draped with shiny steel, creased to give it a deadly sharpness. As he examined the ancient weapon with awe, Keetna dropped to her knees and drew a knife from the outside of her boot. "This is for Abner, you bastard."

Seeing that she intended to slit the man's throat like a wounded game animal, Silas pushed her roughly aside. "No!" he commanded, "I won't allow it!"

"Listen, Silas," she fumed. "This is the man who killed Abner and God knows how many others in this town. We can't just—"

"No. Just no," he said again, this time shaking his head and speaking softly, "you simply can't kill a man like that."

She looked up at him with her crystalline blue eyes and said, "You know if we let him live I won't be able to stay here. Not after this."

"I know. I'm sorry. I really am."

She stood and faced him, raking her eyes across his face as if she expected to find a visible flaw of some sort that would explain his nettlesome humanity. When at last her eyes locked onto his she smiled and said, "What the hell. I was getting tired of living in a hole."

"You mean...?"

"Yeah. Let's go to Old Denver."

32

Last Rites for Pryus

The final incarnation of the Tar Baby bacterium was called COTO 2.82. For five years Robak's team worked to perfect it, then realized they could not control it. Just the same, they were delighted to see their baby carry out the civilization-destroying instructions encrypted in its cobbled-together DNA. Robak, however, did not share the team's enthusiasm...

FROM THE UNPUBLISHED MEMOIRS OF CARLOS HERRERA

The land around the lacuna embodied some of the most peculiar geology Jack had ever seen. In the hundreds of feet of smooth vertical granite between the creek and the summit, there was but a single ledge, formed when the upper part of a large slab had broken off a couple hundred feet above the creek bed on the northernmost monolith.

It was the ledge that struck Jack as being so out of place. It could not have been more perfectly flat and agreeable if it had been cut into the side of the cliff by a legion of engineers.

Accommodating though it was, the ledge was just wide enough for a horse or two people walking abreast. No more than five feet at its widest point, it narrowed in places where the outer edge dipped away in a gradual curve of weathered rock too smooth to be trod upon; a single errant foot-step would result in certain death on the rocks in the creek far below. Pryus Gordon Primm's body, therefore, was borne on a travois pulled by a single riderless horse, a large muscular steed of draft-horse ancestry Luke used for logging, and for plowing Catalyn's small field. Old Joe's inherent docility made him the natural choice to bear the body.

Catalyn and Cassie walked behind the travois; Jack and Jennifer trailed behind them, with Jazzman and Sasha close to their masters' heels. Jazzman's wound was now no more than a wide scab from his left eye to his ear. Even the hole in his ear had begun the fill back in with new tissue. Catalyn assured Jack it would heal up on its own without further complications, just as soon as Jazzman lost interest in rubbing off the scab.

Tay and Carmen concluded the small group. Tay had allowed himself to be strapped into an electric ATV, which Carmen drove as far as the ledge. From there he insisted he could make it alone with the aid of a cane.

Carmen had refused to leave his side since the morning she'd rode onto *Vientos de los Dioses*, except for the two hours it took her deliver Primm's mare back to the corral beside his house, where she left it fed, watered, and still saddled. The idea was to further confound anyone wondering what fate might have befallen the missing sheriff of Purgatory.

The lack of concern for the sheriff's whereabouts was comforting, if not sad. According to Turney, who Jack cautiously regarded as his eyes and ears in town, the rumor mill had been turning briskly for the last two days, grinding out scenarios ranging from improbable to absurd. The fact that Primm had gone missing without his horse proved a real challenge for the local theorists, whose conjectures leaned toward abduction, possibly by Pox operatives hoping to move into Purgatory unchallenged. Others thought he might have run off with a former girlfriend, now that there had been such an abrupt change in his attitude toward the fairer sex, but no one could ever remember the man having a relationship with anyone, other than the brief affair he'd had with Rosa Lupino the night before he went missing. Rosa denied with indignation any complicity in the man's disappearance. Nor did it make much sense that he would simply head out of town alone and on foot, although it was becoming generally accepted that he had been creeping ever closer to the precipice of psychosis. Had he finally plunged into madness? Would his body one day be found on the outskirts of town, ravaged by predators? It seemed unlikely.

The possibility that he might actually have been killed had not yet been widely or loudly voiced, nor did anyone who puzzled over Primm's fate seem particularly worried about the man himself.

He lived a shadow; he died an enigma. Thus would Pryus Gordon Primm be remembered.

Jack peered cautiously over the edge toward the creek below. From this height it appeared no bigger than a rivulet of water running down a line scratched in the dirt. Not a great lover of heights, he silently thanked the powers that be for giving them such a warm sunny day, and an unusually calm one at that. He could think of nothing he'd like less than to find himself clinging to this ledge in the wind or the rain. To Jennifer he said, "Tell me again why we're doing this?" hoping he didn't sound as flippant to her as he did to himself. With the persistent *clop, clop, clop* of shod feet against the stone ledge echoing across the canyon, he felt as if he were speaking to the cadence of a giant metronome.

"It's a matter of honor," she answered, staring now at the wrapped body jostling back and forth as the poles of the travois moved rhythmically up and down and side to side with the horse's lumbering strides.

"Honor? The man had no honor."

"Not his. Mine. He couldn't kill me, Jack, even though *she* wormed her way inside his head and ordered him to. It was important for him to know he'd evened the score...that *I* knew he'd evened the score...for the other things he'd done. I told him he had. And now I'm giving him a proper burial to show my forgiveness."

They walked on in silence.

Soon the procession reached the backside of the monolith and Jack breathed a little easier, seeing that the ledge widened considerably on the western edge of the lacuna, where it continued around the backside as a gently sloping trail leading down to the creek.

The backside of the monolith was peppered with caves that had been cut into the granite by the steady pounding of waves in the enormous lake that had once resided here. Some caves could be accessed from the ledge, but most were above it, having been cut at different times in Earth's geologic history as the level of the lake dropped in response to the gradual wearing away of the rock that had at one time joined the twin monoliths.

The valley below was richly verdant with tall fir and ponderosa on the facing slopes and groves of aspen near the creek, their spade-shaped leaves quaking ceaselessly in the gentle breeze blowing down the winding canyon. Jack thought it perhaps the most peaceful place he'd ever seen.

The grave was in the alluvium of a narrow winding watershed that emptied into Old Scratch. The small meadow was surrounded by aspen and cottonwood, and the morning sun shone brightly through the foliage in bold darts of light.

Refusing help in the grave's preparation, Luke had carefully removed the sod on top of the three-by-seven-foot rectangle before shoveling the dirt from the hole onto a large canvas tarp. In a week or two, the only evidence of Primm's final resting place would be an engraved stainless-steel marker placed beneath a large chunk of jagged granite that would serve as the head-stone. The marker read:

Here lies Pryus Gordon Primm
9/11/2000 - 10/14/2037
A life lived alone
May the gods receive him
Better than Purgatory
And never send him back

Jack helped Luke lower the tightly wrapped body into the grave while the others looked on. Tay rested only casually on his cane and Jack was en-couraged by how much weight he was able to put on his injured leg. He wore a plain white shirt, open at the neck, with leather laces loosely threaded through the placket. His hair was tied back with a leather thong from which dangled three simple gray feathers and an assortment of beads. If he car-ried a gun, it was not anywhere Jack could see it. Carmen stood beside him, dressed, as always, in tight jeans, a loose top that left her narrow waist ex-posed, and a heavy long-sleeved shirt open in front. Her hair hung freely down her back and across her shoulders. She and Tay looked a pair, if an odd one.

Jennifer was clad in a long black dress that fell below her ankles. She stepped forward and read an oft-quoted passage from the Book of Ecclesiastes, beginning: *To every thing there is a season, and a time to every purpose under the heaven...*

And ending with: *a time to rend, and a time to sew; a time to keep silence, and a time to speak; a time to love, and a time to hate; a time of war, and a time of peace.*

She added, "Your time of peace is at hand, Pryus. Make the best of it." She remained dry-eyed throughout, although her voice cracked slightly when Cassie stepped beside her and took her hand.

Then it was over. No one else had a word to add, not even Luke, who must have felt he'd done all the apologizing he could do.

As they turned and walked away, Jennifer said to no one in particular,

"It's going to end here, in this place. I can feel it." Jack looked at Tay, who merely nodded.

"*What's* going to end here?" Jack asked.

"The things your father set in motion, Jack. They will all end here."

Catalyn approached them, saying, "The wind is coming; we should go."

Jack stayed behind to help Luke fill in the grave and repack the sod. He wondered about Catalyn's prediction, as there was only a hint of a breeze.

"You gonna be okay, Luke?" Jack asked, after the others disappeared around the corner of the monolith. The pain etched in his face the day of Primm's death was still evident.

"Yeah, sure," Luke said without meeting his eyes.

Jack said, "You didn't see his eyes, Luke. I did. Primm was fighting for control, but believe me: he was losing the battle. If you hadn't shot him when you did, well…"

"I know, Jack. It just doesn't make it any easier; to kill a man, I mean."

Jack thought to tell him that most men alive today who had been of age at the time of the Turning were alive because *they* had killed other men, that he himself had killed other men in that insane conflict; that he had seen men stabbed or bludgeoned to death over things as trifling as a can of peas, but he doubted it would help. In the end, killing was a personal thing, and Luke would have to deal with it on his own terms. He grasped the younger man's shoulder and said, "Thanks, Luke, for having the guts to do what had to be done. You saved my life."

Luke gave a strained laugh. "Yeah, I know. But I shot him to save the goddamn dog."

"Would you rather Primm were alive, and Sasha dead?" he asked. "You made your choice. Would you choose differently if you had another chance?"

Luke gave him a pained look and smiled mirthlessly. "No," he said, "and that's what's so fucking hard to live with."

They rolled the headstone on top of the marker and began the journey home.

As Jack feared, Catalyn was right about the wind. Errant gusts teased them on their ascent up the winding trail on the west face of the monolith, as if daring them to continue onto the south face where instant death awaited the ill-fated or the ill-prepared. Jack suggested that perhaps they could place a few large stones in the travois to hold it down for the three or four minutes it would take them to traverse the ledge that spanned the breadth of the monolith, but Luke insisted on leaving it.

Thinking Luke a bit too cautious, he said, "How bad can the wind get, anyway?"

"Don't ask," Luke replied, his shaggy locks sticking straight out from his head as he shouted to be heard above the roar of air rushing through the lacuna.

They unhooked the travois and bound it to a tree. Even then the journey was an ordeal. Jack had never felt wind so strong; he could easily imagine the stone-laden travois flying over the gelding's head like the arm of a trebuchet. As it was, they clung to the rigging on the horse's left side, but not so tightly they would be unable to pull their hands free if Old Joe lost his footing or was otherwise cast over the cliff by a wind determined to sweep the intruders into the creek below.

Talking was an impossibility, walking nearly so. The scouring wind whipped his clothing so hard it stung as it slapped against his skin. He dared not lift his feet more than a few inches for fear of having his legs whisked out from beneath him. To their good fortune, the stout gelding was steady as a glacier and perfectly content to plod steadily along in defiance of the mounting gale whipping his broad backside.

When at last the ledge gave way to open ground on the lee side of the monolith, Luke led the horse out of the wind where they plopped down with their backs to the stone wall.

"Jesus Harold Christ," Jack gasped, "that was like being downwind of a jet engine!"

"It gets worse," Luke told him.

"That's impossible."

Luke shook his head. His shaggy hair fell right back into place. "This wind's maybe ninety miles per; a hundred, tops. Sometimes it screams through here at over a hundred and seventy."

Jack was still doing the calculations in his head when Luke said, "That's nearly seven times worse than what we just experienced. Nothing could stay on that ledge in that kind of wind, not even Joe."

Jack shivered.

When Jack came into view, striding jauntily beside Luke with Old Joe plodding along behind, Jennifer couldn't stop herself from running to greet him. Jazzman got there first. In an uncharacteristic display of adoration, the big coy dog jumped up on his hind legs and threw his front paws over Jack's shoulders, nearly knocking him to the ground.

"Whoa, there, big guy! Glad to see me, huh?" Jack hugged the dog, eyeing Jennifer as he did.

She said, "Beat it, mutt," then threw her arms around Jack the instant Jazzman dropped back down on all fours. In his ear she whispered, "Tell me you were off the ledge before the wind started,"

He said, "Okay. We were off the ledge when the wind started."

Although there was barely a breeze where they stood, the wind turbines at the power plant were furling against the powerful blasts of air coming out of the lacuna, and the treetops swayed violently back and forth high overhead. It was enough to make anyone jittery. "You're a damn liar, Jack Vara."

Jack absently reached down and patted Jazzman and Sasha, one with each hand. "Truth was not a condition of your request," he reminded her.

"Okay...damn scientist, then."

"Ex-scientist," he amended.

"Whatever. Just don't get yourself killed."

He began walking up the road and Jennifer fell in beside him. "How's it going?" he asked, nodding in the direction of the Malloys', still hidden from view by the thick foliage along the creek.

She looped her arm around Jack's and rested her head against his shoulder, saying, "Better, I think. Or maybe Catalyn just figures Carmen will tear her hair out by the roots if she says anything more to Tay. Either way, tensions are easing up a bit. I think she's finally beginning to accept the fact that Luke did the right thing."

Jack replied, "That's the truth of it, but she's still left with the fact that Luke isn't taking it too well. And she'll always blame Tay for that; at least until Luke comes around." Jack kissed the top of her head and she reveled in his easy affection. It made her wonder how she had endured for so many years without the simple pleasure of a man's touch. Or a man's strength.

She said, "It's nothing new. Catalyn and Tay have never really seen eye to eye. Tay is a dangerous man who gravitates toward dangerous situations. Catalyn would rather pretend the danger doesn't exist. She thinks Tay is trigger happy, Tay thinks Catalyn is blind to reality. It's an old story."

"So it is," Jack agreed. "It's ironic they share the same blood."

Jennifer tried and failed to stifle a chuckle. "Business first. That's Catalyn."

"And how are you doing?" he asked.

As horrible as the whole affair had been, she was glad Primm was dead, despite his last words to her. Because they were exactly that: last words. Words that he would never have spoken if he'd thought he would live to see another day. The man's entire existence up to that moment had been a lie told to himself.

"Right as rain," she answered truthfully. "Particularly since I know he's six feet under. Dreadful affairs that they are, there's still a comforting finality to a funeral. It will help Luke; Catalyn too. They're both strong people. They just need time, that's all."

An especially strong gust of wind tossed the treetops overhead and caused the turbines to shudder violently. "By the way," Jack said, glancing up at the noisy turbines, "how did Catalyn know the wind was going to pick up? I never thought she was a viator...at least not like you and Cassie."

Jennifer nuzzled closer and chided, "You still don't have it figured out, do you?"

"Apparently not."

She smiled sweetly, if a bit condescendingly. "Okay, imagine time as a river; a river that contains everything that can ever be known about the past, present and future. And imagine that it flows through all of us. You. Me. Everyone. Constantly and eternally..."

"I like the analogy." He imagined a rush of knowledge-laden ether passing swiftly through his body. This led him to thoughts of neutrinos; ghostly subatomic particles that pass by the trillions through everyone and everything every second of every day without ever arousing a single physical sensation. A cosmic river, certainly. And if each tiny particle held even a modicum of knowledge? But she wasn't talking about particles. She had something far more wonderful and mysterious in mind.

"Whether you dive in head first or just test the waters with your pinkies is up to you," she continued. "Ability has nothing to do with it. It's more a matter of will or desire; of what you choose to tune in and what you tune out. With a lot of people—*scientists* in particular," she emphasized, elbowing him in the ribs hard enough to cause a spike of pain to run along his side, "the innate knowledge that the future really is knowable is buried too deep. Like an artery you're scared to tap into. As far as Catalyn goes, well, she'll pause long enough at the riverbank to sense changes in the weather, or the workings of nature in general, really. She can tell you if it's going to be a bad year for grasshoppers or if the mule deer will drop their fawns earlier or later than last year. But when it comes to the energies surrounding people, she just tunes them out."

"Curious."

"Of course, the deeper you step into the river, the more you change it."

"Change it?"

"Oh yes, Jack," she whispered, as if the conversation were wandering into forbidden viators-only territory. "The future. And the past."

"The *past?* It's possible to change the past?"

"Oh yeah."

"Curiouser and curiouser."

"Beyond logic. Thank God."

"Perhaps," he answered, thinking, hoping, that it was just beyond the present scope of logic. He recalled that the mathematician, Kurt Gödel, had proven over eighty years ago that Einstein's relativity field equations confirmed that time was an impossibility and the cause-and-effect relationships we perceive as time were but a convenient illusion. Then, as now, Gödel's stark logic had been too much for his colleagues to digest. But if Gödel was right, the past existed eternally and should, in theory, be no less accessible than the present or future.

Someday, he imagined, when science finally tires of its smug exclusivity and decides to earnestly examine the extraordinary phenomena it habitually turns a blind eye to, scientists really will tap into that forbidden artery Jennifer rightly said they were afraid of. But as a former member of that dogmatic brotherhood, Jack wasn't going to hold his breath.

Besides, what would the world be without a little mystery?

Another blast of wind shook the wall of trees along the pathway and sent bits of foliage swirling around them in a tight funnel. Jack pulled Jennifer close and murmured in her ear, "Maybe someday you can explain it to me. The world according to Jennifer. We may discover we're looking at different ends of the same elephant."

"Maybe," she replied smugly, her face pressed against his, "But I like my end better."

"It's still only half the elephant."

Her womanly essence swirled about him in the unstill air and mingled with his own musky scent. He took it as her reply.

The unofficial funeral reception was centered around the large table in the shaded yard, as were all gatherings of the *malagente* when the weather permitted. Today the weather's permissiveness was marginal. The wind howling through the trees overhead occasionally dropped leaves and pine needles on the gathering and crept in around the corners to make its presence known.

Tay sat quietly in a backed chair, his injured leg elevated on a footrest. A small glass of sipping whiskey rested on the table near his left hand. Carmen sat on the edge of the bench seat beside him, an arm around his shoulder that he seemed neither to mind nor appreciate. She glanced intermittently at Catalyn who seemed not to notice.

Cassie pulled up a small chair beside Tay. Catalyn had plaited the girl's long blonde hair into a French braid and sprites of yellow sunlight danced lively upon it. If the girl was bothered by the sheriff's death it was not evident on her face, which glowed with a vibrancy only a child could possess.

The fare was minimal; finger food, really. Dried fruit, celery and carrots, apples sweetened with cinnamon, and squares of coarse bread beside slices of smoked elk sausage. A pitcher of Luke's custom brew attracted more attention than usual.

Jack took a seat beside Carmen while Jennifer slid onto the bench next to him. Carmen turned and offered them both a forced smile, then turned back to Tay to continue her singular pursuit of his affections. Jennifer thought her fascinating, maddening, and completely out of place in this gathering. Judging by Jack's muted congeniality, he and Jennifer were of the same mind.

It surprised Jennifer to see Catalyn drinking Luke's stout beer. When her mug was half drained Luke refilled it without a murmur of protest from his wife. Jack poured a mug for himself and drank a good fraction of it while Jennifer prepared a mug of tea.

Catalyn spoke first. "Things are starting to come unraveled," she said with customary solemnity. "Primm is dead and people are beginning to wonder what happened to him. It's time we figured out what we're going to do about it."

She cast an eye to Carmen in hopes that she might take the hint and go away for the remainder of the discussion. No one missed her intent, least of all Carmen. Tay turned to say something to her, but it was unnecessary. She shot a sharp glance at Catalyn, then kissed Tay on the cheek before leaving the gathering without a word. Her long locks swished wildly from side to side in response to her exaggerated footsteps as she stomped toward Tay's house.

After a moment Tay said casually, "You worry too much. We all knew someone would eventually get around to killing the sheriff. It was only a matter of time. I would have done it myself years ago if only Jennifer had told me about him."

"But now people are looking for him," Catalyn insisted gloomily. "Whether or not his job was a sham, he did work for Desa. And Sturm Baker will be wondering what happened to his eyes and ears in Purgatory."

Tay sipped his whiskey and said calmly, "What is that to us? No one will ever find him."

"Someone could *talk*, dammit! Tharp could talk."

Tay shook his head. "*Hadriano* will speak to no one."

"How can you be so sure?" Catalyn asked doubtfully.

Tay answered, "Because there is nothing to be gained by talking. It is the diamonds he wants. Once he talks, he can no longer *threaten* to talk. And the threat is the only thing *Hadriano* possesses that is of value to him. It is a useful currency and he will not spend it foolishly. When the time comes we will deal with him, in whatever way works best to our advantage."

"By giving him the *diamonds?*" Jack said.

Tay laughed. "Maybe we will give him one or two. Or maybe we will give him nothing. We will see."

Jennifer thought Tay's confidence reassuring, particularly because he held fewer illusions than most. He usually accomplished whatever he set out to accomplish and didn't burden himself with the impossible. He was a pragmatist grounded in his deeds which, she suspected, were more covert and numerous than she would care to know. Still, she had to ask: "And how will you two negotiate without killing each other?"

Again Tay laughed, as if Tharp were an amusing subject. "As one professional to another," he replied.

At last becoming animate, Luke leaned over the table and asked, "Have you seen the diamonds, Tay? Do you know where they're hidden?"

Tay eyed Catalyn, then Luke. "*Como no.*" he answered. *Of course.*

Determined to cast as dark a shadow as possible on Primm's death, Catalyn said, "Forget the damned diamonds, will you? At the moment they're a luxury we can't afford to think about. We have other problems, such as what to do when Baker comes snooping around."

Tay shrugged as if the question had no meaning. He answered, "He will come and he will look, but he will find nothing. Then he will go away."

At this point Jennifer said, "Aren't you all forgetting about my brother? Silas is out in the wilderness somewhere—God only knows where—on some secret quest Carlos put him onto that no one else in the world seems to know anything about, and—"

"*I* know," Tay interjected.

Jennifer was stunned. She said, "You *know* what Silas is out there looking for?" All eyes fell on Tay. Luke drew his focus out from the netherworld he'd begun to drift back into and gazed curiously at his friend.

Tay smiled at them and stroked Cassie's head. It was the smile of a man who'd just laid four aces on the table. He took a slow sip of his whiskey to savor the moment, then said, "Of course, *muchacha*. I am the one who stole it for Carlos."

33

Truth of the Turning

One thing became immediately obvious at the time of the Turning: the more ancient a man's skills, the more liable he was to live through the war. Thus did more tradesmen live than office workers, and more farmers than tradesmen. Warriors, of course, endured in the greatest numbers, since killing is the oldest skill of all...

FROM THE UNPUBLISHED MEMOIRS OF CARLOS HERRERA

The whiskey burns his throat in a way Tay finds pleasing. He remembers the day clearly; over the years his mind has repaired the broken images and made them somehow more real than they were at the time. This might be, he thinks, because now he knows what was at stake on that day; not like then, when it was only a job he was doing for Carlos with no idea how much the fate of civilization turned on how the events of the day unfolded.

Tay begins, and everyone's eyes lock onto him. "Carlos told me only this: that a man named Dobry Robak was developing something called COTO 2.82. He was working for, or perhaps with, the preacher man, Isaiah Warchez." Recognition flares in Catalyn's eyes. Jack leans forward with his elbows on the table while Jennifer stares at Tay with her chin resting on Jack's shoulder. Luke drinks hastily from his mug before sidling up close to Catalyn. Tay looks into Cassie's wise, adoring eyes and strokes her shoulder. It feels warm and small beneath his big hand, like a bird basking in human affection.

"Warchez..." Catalyn repeats the name. She makes it sound like an accusation.

Tay continues. "How Carlos knew this, I cannot say. But he did. It was my job to learn what COTO 2.82 was all about. It was for me to decide how to find out what Carlos wanted to know, but it would be better, certainly, if I was not seen by anyone.

"Robak had a laboratory in the Nevada desert, a few miles outside Tonopah. It was where he developed COTO—what everyone calls the Tar Baby bacterium—although at the time I did not know this, either.

"It was a large one-story building with many small rooms, all filled with equipment I could not begin to understand. Seven people were there: Robak, who I recognized from a photograph, his bodyguard, and five others. Three men and two women, I think, though I cannot say for certain since they all died so quickly..."

A growing uneasiness spreads across Catalyn's face and she tells Cassie to go and play with the dogs. Cassie protests, "Ah, Mom, he was just getting to the good part," but it does her no good and she gets up and runs across the yard with Sasha and Jazzman in tow.

Tay recalls entering the building from the north, through a small service door with an easily disabled alarm system. Every room is built with large windows to the adjoining rooms and Tay quickly finds all the building's occupants in a conference room near the front. A celebration is in progress, as evidenced by a champagne bottle on the table. Everyone is standing and all have clear plastic cups in their hands; all except for Robak's bodyguard who stands in the corner with his arms crossed. A big man with a shaved head above a tree-trunk neck, he looks on with the kind of disinterest that can only come from years on a job that requires him to be disinterested.

Robak, by contrast, is a small man with a disarming manner; the sort of man, Tay thinks, who is easily liked but not so easily trusted. As Tay watches from the shadows in a laboratory next to the conference room, Robak makes a toast: "To a job well done!" he exclaims. He speaks with a subdued Slavic accent that is noticeable but not distracting. He appears to drink from the cup in his hand, but he doesn't. The five look at each other cautiously, but they all drink. "As we speak," Robak continues, "cultures of COTO are being set free in every wellhead in Iran."

As one, the five stare at him and smile. They clearly know something Robak doesn't, though Robak is too full of himself to notice. A large heavyset man with a neatly trimmed salt-and-pepper beard, steps forward and says, "Congratulations, Mr. Robak. You have done the world a great service."

"The world?" Robak asks, confused. "I presume you mean because we have taken the lifeblood away from a terrorist nation?"

"Oh, not just one nation, Mr. Robak; the entire world." Robak is utterly confused and the man continues. "You see, COTO is far more virulent than you think. With the airborne capabilities we gave it, it will spread like mold spores from oilfield to oilfield. It will travel on the wind as easily as it will travel on the boots, hands and clothing of petroleum engineers and oilfield workers. Any oil deposit with a casing to the surface will be vulnerable— COTO won't stop until the last drop of oil has been infected."

Robak glares at him in disbelief, then says, "What the hell are you talking about? What have you done?"

Tay sees that the big man who just delivered the bombshell shattering Robak's perfectly structured little world is suddenly not feeling well. Sweat begins to bead up on his forehead and he plops down in a chair, appearing more bewildered than alarmed by the rapid deterioration of his health. Two of the others take notice of his condition. One is a young man with short brown hair, the other a middle-aged woman with thick glasses. Both go to comfort him, speaking in hushed tones while glancing furtively at Robak. A second woman steps forward as the older, balding man behind her drops into a chair, breathing heavily. She is maybe forty and pretty beyond her professionalism. Reasonably, she says, "We only did as Isaiah instructed."

"Isaiah? Isaiah Warchez? But you work for me!" he barks. He is agitated in a way that even Tay, thirty-one years old and ignorant of most of what is being said, finds worrisome. He begins to suspect that Robak is a short man with a shorter fuse.

As if suddenly coming into possession of a wonderful idea, he holds up one finger and exclaims, "Wait a minute! You told me it could be...what were your words?... genetically disabled! You said there was...what did you call it? An anterium...a backdoor to shut down COTO."

Reasonably, she says, "And there is; theoretically, at least. But you see, Dobry, even with the anterium it's too late. Nothing can stop the spread of COTO to every working oilfield. Nothing. We're making sure of that."

"What do you mean '*making sure*?'" Robak roars with the desperation of a man who has just seen the wings fall off his airplane.

"It wasn't just Iran, Dobry. Our people have taken it everywhere: Alaska, Venezuela, Russia...there's no stopping it now." She holds her hands in front of her and uses them for emphasis. Tay sees that her fingers are long and graceful, and he thinks it a shame she is about to die. Like the big man who is now nearly unconscious behind her, she begins to sweat. Tay pities her. "Face it, Dobry: we've just unloosed Armageddon." Her eyes wander past Robak to a counter behind him Tay cannot see. She says, "You didn't send... the anterium along...with COTO, did...you?" She gives a quick, vengeful smile and murmurs, "Too bad." Then she begins to falter. The big man is slumped in his chair and her other colleagues are getting woozy.

Robak runs to her. It is not for love, or pity, or even remorse. It is because he wants information. He grabs her by the collar and shakes her, screaming, "HOW DO I TURN IT OFF?"

She doesn't tell him. She says, almost in a lover's whisper, "You...killed us...didn't you?"

"JUDITH!" Robak bellows, with more vehemence than Tay would've expected from such a small man, and he shakes her violently, as if a sufficient degree of agitation might counteract the effects of the poison he's administered.

Her eyes grow glassy and she laughs. "You'll have a...tough time... recouping...your investment...you...pathetic...little...man." She dies with a rueful smile etched on her handsome face and Robak lets her drop to the floor. In a rage, he stomps through the room pushing the others, dead or dying, out of their chairs.

Then he throws a real tantrum.

From a countertop that Tay cannot see from his vantage point, Robak seizes a box of vials and looks at them as if they were filled with an elixir from a distant planet. He looks up when he sees the young man with the neat brown hair struggle to his feet. "Jeffrey!" he says, almost as if this were a chance meeting between old friends, "tell me how to use this...this anterium." Dobry's accent grows thicker as he talks, like his tongue suddenly perceives the English language as a viscous fluid.

But Jeffrey clearly doesn't care about his accent or the anterium, or anything else on this Earth. He only wants to see Robak in eternity. His face is bright red and cast in a primal rage. He lunges drunkenly toward his former employer, catching not Robak but the edge of the Styrofoam box Robak holds in his hand.

From the far corner, the bodyguard rushes to help Robak, who fights to hold onto the box Jeffrey has in a death grip. The bodyguard grabs Jeffery from behind as Robak begins to kick him, much like one girl would kick another in a schoolyard fight, but Jeffrey's hands remains locked onto the side of the box.

Jeffrey is beyond the point where pain is an effective deterrent. "His fingers!" Robak shouts at his bodyguard. "Pry his fucking fingers off the box!" But before the bodyguard can do as instructed, the box is rent in two with an earsplitting *POP!* All the vials spill to the floor as the two halves of the box fall from Robak's hands.

"You clumsy oaf!" Robak screams, and pushes the guard aside. As he does he slips on the snarl of debris beneath his feet and falls to the floor in a cacophony of breaking glass.

Robak rises quickly to his feet, stunned at what has just happened. Shards of broken glass cling to his hands and blood drips from the tips of his fingers, but he seems not to notice as he looks down at the mess on the floor and exclaims, "They're broken, Thomas! They're all broken!!"

Maybe they are and maybe they aren't, but Robak then erases any doubt as he proceeds to crush the shards into powder in a violent tirade. Spittle spins from his mouth in slithery globs, and his eyes burn with anger. He begins to shake all over, a sign that he is nearly spent. To the bodyguard he turns and says, "They *lied* to me! Do you *believe* it? They *fucking lied* to me!"

He then throws his bloody, glass-studded hands to his face and moans, "Oh sweet Jesus, what just happened? Oh God! Warchez has just destroyed us all."

At this point, Tay suspects that he, himself, will be the only one in this building still breathing when it's all over. But maybe not. He waits. He senses there is more here, something for Carlos. He is right.

Completely helpless, the bodyguard makes an astonishingly puerile observation. "I think you just smashed all the vials, Mr. Robak," he says.

Robak turns on him like a small vicious dog. "No shit, I smashed them, you overgrown moron! Do you think I did it on purpose?" He throws up his hands, saying more to himself than to Thomas, "Oh what fucking good would it do now, anyway? Am I supposed to sneak it through airport security on a non-existent flight to Iran? And Venezuela? And the Caucasus?" He shakes his head. "It's too late, goddamn it, it's too fucking LATE!"

Then, inexplicably, Robak smiles and says, "Or *is* it too late?" He gathers himself together and wipes the spittle from the side of his mouth with a bloody hand, then straightens his tie. Seeing his hands for the first time, he bends down and wipes the blood off on Jeffrey's white lab coat. This makes him feel better, even though blood continues to drip from his hands and fingers. He says, "There is still this. Perhaps there is time. Yes! Perhaps they were wrong!" He picks up a glossy blue satchel held closed with a white string wrapped around two buttons. Tay is not sure what is in the satchel, but he knows he wants it.

He just doesn't know yet how to get it.

But an idea begins to form in his mind when Robak, now collected, says, "Thomas, go back the van up to the door. We have to dispose of this...mess."

Thomas nods obediently, as if being told to sweep up a pile of sawdust off the floor. He leaves the building through a side door, providing Tay with the opportunity he's been looking for. Silently he scurries out from under the desk and creeps to the door of the conference room. He slides his .357 out of its holster and steals a quick glance through the window. Robak is pacing the floor, holding the satchel to his chest with one hand, rubbing his chin with the other, unaware that he's smearing blood all over his face. When his back is turned, Tay pushes through the door, steps into a wide assault stance, and points his gun at Robak. It's an overdone posture for the situation, calculated to induce fear.

Robak freezes, his back still turned. "Who are *you?*" he asks.

"A thief," Tay tells him, calmly.

"Ah, a thief. And you are working for...?"

Robak sounds almost amused, and Tay realizes there is a cold calculating side to this little man he has not anticipated. He's already made up his mind to kill Robak, so he answers, "Carlos Herrera."

"Oh, yes...Carlos Herrera. I might've known. Carlos is smarter than the other...investors. He was always suspicious, as if he couldn't quite believe the reports everyone else found so convincing." He takes his hand from his chin and slides it inside his jacket.

"I would not do that, *amigo*," Tay says calmly. "Turn around."

As commanded, Robak turns slowly to face Tay. His right hand is covered by the satchel, but Tay knows that Robak is now clutching a gun. "Don't try it, my friend."

Robak smiles, not just with his mouth, which is expressive for its smallness, but also with his eyes which shine with a steely glint beneath their friendly warmth. "There has been enough death already, don't you agree?" He turns slowly sideways as if to gaze upon the death his poison has wrought. He turns in such a way that his hidden gun will point directly at

Tay from inside his jacket...as if he's betting that Tay will hesitate just long enough—

Tay merely touches the hair trigger and the impact of the slug passing through Robak's torso knocks the small man two feet sideways before sending him to the floor.

Dead.

It's Tay's first civilian kill and he hopes it's the only one today. But he knows it won't be. He looks up from Robak just as the outside window shatters, and he feels the bullet slam into his left side with the force of a sledge hammer. The impact spins him around and out of the path of a second round that rips a hole through the gypsum-board wall behind him. Before he goes down he fires a quick round in the direction of the bodyguard, hoping he was too big of a target to miss.

He's a big man, Tay thinks through the pain, *but he's not a shooter.* Then he realizes he has to deal with this man now, before he has a chance to gather what few wits he might possess. Tay struggles to his feet and runs to the outside window in a crouch. So far, so good. He pokes his arm through the broken window and fires off two quick shots before chancing a look. No one. Just a parking lot with one large van and a half dozen compact cars against a backdrop of endless rolling desert. The single maple tree in the small grassy area between the parking lot and the building looks entirely out of place.

Then he sees a man's shadow cast upon the concrete walkway by the afternoon sun; sees it an instant before Thomas bursts through the door behind him. Instinctively, Tay spins and catches the man in the chin with a boot heel. The blow causes Thomas to drop his pistol but doesn't render him unconscious. It only pisses him off.

Snarling, he lunges at his assailant. Tay counters by grabbing the big man's wrists and pulling him into a roll. All of Thomas's considerable momentum is sent rippling back through his body in an audible shockwave as he slams against the floor. The maneuver gives Tay time to spin to his knees and wrap an arm around the big man's throat.

"Give it up, *grande*. I have you now," Tay tells him.

But Thomas doesn't agree that he's been had. He roars with rage and reaches behind his head with groping hands, grabbing for any part of Tay he can. *If he gets hold of me,* Tay realizes, *I may never get loose again.* Quickly, Tay tightens his grip and surges against the back of Thomas's head with his chest in an attempt snap the bodyguard's muscular neck, but the neck is too strong and Tay's wound has made him weak.

He lets go and scurries away before Thomas can find a handle. As he does, his hand pushes against the big man's gun. It's a snub-nose .32-caliber revolver; not a lot of stopping power, but his own gun is buried beneath Thomas's considerable mass. A mass, Tay notes with grave concern, that is now rising from the floor holding his .357 magnum, a kick-ass, knock-down, organ-rending weapon if ever there was one.

No time for contemplation. Tay aims the .32 at Thomas's forehead and pulls on the trigger, only to discover to his mounting consternation that it's a single-action revolver, a weapon that fires only after the hammer's been cocked.

What kind of bodyguard carries a gun like this? he asks himself. The answer? *A big dumb one, amigo, just like the one holding your gun.* Tay pulls back on the trigger again, this time fanning the hammer, and gets off two quick shots while rolling out of the way of any bullets that might be coming from his own gun. He hears the flat *thud!* of a .32 round connecting solidly with flesh but he fans the hammer once more for good measure.

He looks up in time see Thomas fire two rounds into the ceiling tiles before falling onto his back, clutching his neck. Blood streams through his fingers; bright arterial blood. It is a flow that no surgeon could possibly stem in time to save the man's life.

Tay stands and looks down at the dying man. The fear in his eyes is absolute and hard to watch, but Tay doesn't turn away. He says, "*Lo siento, grande,* but you should have listened when you had the chance."

Hearing Tay's glib assessment on the termination of his life, Thomas's rage overrides fear. He grabs for Tay's leg, but Tay steps easily out of the way, watching blood spurt from a pair of holes midway between the big man's head and shoulders.

Thomas clutches once more for his neck, but he is finished. Having failed to catch his assailant, he falls onto his back again into a thick pool of his own blood, expelling the last breath from his lungs in a crimson eruption. His face softens and his eyes grow lifeless. Tay weaves his way through the bodies to fetch the satchel from Robak's dead fingers.

*   *   *   *

"Holy shit!" Luke exclaimed, sounding like a little boy who'd just been read a scary bedtime story, "where did he shoot you?"

It drew a barbed look from Catalyn, who didn't appear to have appreciated Tay's graphic recollection, but Tay ignored her and hiked up his shirt, pointing to a pair of scars—two of many on his chest and abdomen, pink and prominent against his brown skin—forming web-like circles on the front and back of his pectoral muscles.

While Luke was still examining the combat record etched, gouged and slashed on Tay's body, Catalyn said, "So the satchel contained the secret to turning off this COTO thing...the Tar Baby bacterium?"

Tay lowered his shirt and took another sip of whiskey. "So it was said," Tay answered with an amused smile meant to let Catalyn know her attitude was becoming onerous.

"Why didn't Carlos turn it over to the government," Jennifer asked. "I mean, if there was still time to do something about it...?"

"No time, *muchacha*. No time at all. The damage was already done, as the scientists believed."

Scowling pensively, Catalyn said, "'It doesn't matter. What's done is done. The real question is: what good is this anterium to us, or to anyone, at this point?"

Jack answered. "Tar Baby—COTO—was found to be virulent beyond anyone's imagination, so Tay is right: there was no time to do anything. Once Warchez's people set it loose, the Turning was inevitable. COTO went on a feeding frenzy and when it finished there was nothing left but energy-depleted sludge. Hell, it even found its way into all the above-ground storage reserves. It was relentless."

"So what damn good—"

"New fields. Untapped reserves," Jack answered. "The anterium could be used to prevent COTO infections there."

"How?" Jennifer asked. She was truly in awe that destiny had delivered such a powerful instrument of Good—or Evil—into Carlos's hands. And how Carlos and Tay had sat on it for all these years with the fate of the world hanging in the balance.

"Without seeing what was in the satchel, I can only guess," Jack answered. "You see, COTO is not just a single organism; it's a symbiont, made up of a virus and a bacterium genetically compelled to cover each other's back, so to speak. Tamper with either's DNA—even a little—and it induces an intense defensive reaction that quickly spreads to the surrounding COTO population. It's why all attempts at introducing a genetically altered Trojan horse into COTO cultures have failed. But if there were a key, like a specific string of proteins that could be triggered internally without actually tampering with either organism's DNA, then COTO might have a self-destruct feature. And if Robak's team managed to install such a trigger...craftily disguised, considering no one has ever found it...then the so-called anterium virus could use it to instruct COTO to disable itself. And all the while COTO would just think it was reacting to 'environmental pressures'." He shook his head and added, "If that's what it is—and I really think I'm right about this—then the contents of the satchel is worth billions."

"Oh, my God," Catalyn gasped. "And the one who possesses it could..."

"Name his price. Or hers, which I think is more to the point," Jack interjects, "be it money or power. Or both."

"But why has Carlos held onto it for all this time?" Luke wondered.

"This is only a guess, but he must have figured that once the Turning was set in motion it would've been too little too late. The remaining untainted reserves wouldn't have been enough to quench the world's thirst for oil. And if it fell into the wrong hands? Well, it's a tool custom made for world conquest. Personally, I think he was wise to sit on it."

"But for *twenty years?*" Catalyn said incredulously.

Jack shrugged and replied, "Maybe he thought the world was better off without oil. I mean, really: after going cold turkey for three perfectly hellish years to break our addiction to the stuff, what's the point in going back to it? On the other hand, maybe he simply liked having something Salia Warchez would crawl to the ends of the earth to possess." He paused to let that take effect, before adding, "The important thing is, we have it—well, sort of have it, anyway—and she doesn't."

Tay finished his whiskey and asked Luke for another two fingers. To Catalyn, Tay calmly said, "It is a good thing you are such a good doctor, don't you agree?"

She shook her head, saying, "Oh shit! Tay—Jesus!" She jumped up from the bench and bent over him. "What were you thinking? Why didn't you tell someone? If you had died...?" Words escaped her at that point as her mind processed the implications of what Tay had just told them. She turned away.

Jennifer asked Tay, "Do you know where the satchel is?"

"Not anymore," he replied.

"But we have to assume that my brother does. I mean, why else would he be wandering around out in the wilderness like some new-era prophet on a pilgrimage to the Holy Land."

Luke brought Tay's whiskey and set it on the table. The death of the sheriff was the furthest thing from his mind, lost in the mists of a world far simpler than the one now emerging.

Tay nodded to Luke and took a small sip before answering, "So it would seem."

"But *where?*" Jennifer pleaded.

Tay shrugged. His dark eyes emanated sympathy. "Only Carlos would know that. And your brother."

Silence fell across the group. Catalyn paced back and forth between Luke and Tay as if deducing the best way to diffuse a bomb. Luke sat with his elbows on the table, supporting his head in his palms when he wasn't tossing beer down his throat. Jennifer hugged Jack in a clumsy sideways embrace, and though it felt awkward she couldn't let go because Jack was all she had. Jack responded by wrapping an arm around her and pulling her close, but he still sat with mug in hand, running permutations through his mind like a player in a chess competition. After considerable contemplation, he asked, "Why is Warchez suddenly after the blueprint...the anterium... after all these years?"

"Maybe she thought it was destroyed or lost," Catalyn suggested, "and just recently found out different. After all, she was only a teenager when the Turning began."

Jack shook his head. "I don't buy it. When Isaiah kicked the bucket she fell into his shoes running. Teenager or not, Salia knew what was going on."

Tay sat up and shifted in his seat to get comfortable before saying to Catalyn, "I think you are right about her believing the document was destroyed."

"Why do you say that?"

"Because I set fire to the laboratory as I was leaving." He shrugged. "It seemed like a good idea at the time."

"You're just full of surprises today."

"*Si, señora,*" Tay answered with a grin, "eet ees my beesness to surprise peeple." When he saw Catalyn smile he winked and blew her a kiss.

It was the straw that broke the camel's back. Laughter burst from Catalyn like water through a floodgate and it quickly got everyone going, even Luke. Jack sprayed a mouthful of beer all over himself and Jennifer, adding to the levity. Jennifer laughed mostly to keep Catalyn laughing, because she had been carrying the burden of Luke's guilt like a yoke around her neck these past two days and she needed the laughter even more than Jennifer.

The merriment was short lived. From the corner of her eye Jennifer spied Cassie walking slowly toward them from the backside of the house. Sasha and Jazzman were padding behind her, bewildered that their playmate was no longer playful, but not nearly as bewildered as Cassie, herself. The girl's normally bright eyes had a distinctly faraway look, as if Cassie were somewhere else and her physical self were functioning without the luxury of awareness.

When Catalyn caught the perplexed look on Jennifer's face she abruptly broke off her laughter and followed her gaze to Cassie. "Cassie?" she said. "Sweetheart? What's the matter?" The warm laughter was replaced by frozen silence, and for a long moment nothing could be heard but the sound of the distant wind rushing through the lacuna.

Catalyn ran to her just as the girl looked up and smiled; smiled as if everything was fine, had been fine all day, and why in the world was everyone looking at her? It was enough to stop Catalyn in her tracks before approaching the girl slowly, as if her daughter were a small, dangerous beast.

Cassie said, "Mom? Who is Salia?"

An icy chill ran up Jennifer's spine, depriving her skin of all warmth. A haunted look crept across Catalyn's face as she repeated, "Salia?"

"Yes. Salia," the girl said. "She's been talking to me. What a bitch."

34

Race to Old Denver

History will judge me for withholding from the world the means to keep the COTO bacterium at bay, and I suspect that it will judge me harshly for the first fifty years. But when it finally becomes clear even to the academics (who are always the last to read the writing on the wall) that the survivors of the Turning were better human beings without access to oil, they will acknowledge that we were forced to think creatively; to reassess what we truly need in this world, and what we are better off without...

FROM THE UNPUBLISHED MEMOIRS OF CARLOS HERRERA

The route to Old Denver was neither straight nor easy but it did afford them, in Keetna's estimation, the safest way into the belly of the beast. The plan was to continue southeast from Endow across prairie and farmland until they met up with the St. Vrain River. The trees and thick foliage along the river would provide cover as they followed it downstream to the point where it emptied into the larger South Platte River, a broad, meandering waterway with even more forest cover along its banks. Following the Platte back upstream would take them right into the heart of the old city.

It was a good plan and Silas readily agreed to it. He would have agreed to any plan Keetna came up with, of course, even if it meant marching down the broken and buckled remains of old I-25. The girl knew how to stay alive. Without her he would've been dead two days ago; as it was, he might actually live long enough to see his sister again.

He was recuperating nicely, thanks the assistance he was getting from the aery realms. It was only because of the interplay of energy between what is seen by the eye and what is known to the soul that he could continue.

And yet he couldn't allow his consciousness to drift beyond his immediate surroundings; could not even ponder too deeply what may lay ahead,
for fear that he might slip into that oh-so-familiar plane of consciousness
where *she* could find him—find him and follow him back to the point in
space and time where his physical self was presently engaged in a quest that
was beginning to resemble a journey to the far corners of an alien planet.

He was, by his own will, a fish out water. Because the water was poisoned.

*But is it really? Why should I suppose that her craft is greater than mine?
Before my physical brain regenerated itself, I traveled freely, knowing that she
could neither follow me nor take from me anything that I wished to keep as my
own. Why should things be any different now?*

Perhaps they weren't. He didn't know. But Hadrian Tharp had not arrived in Endow by chance; Salia Warchez had learned exactly where Silas
was during that one fleeting instant when he'd allowed his consciousness
to wander back to its old familiar haunts. Because she'd been watching the
world through his eyes.

It was a sobering thought. But with each step his focus in the heavy
world grew more acute, drawing his energies away from anything that did
not serve the outrageous needs of the physical Silas. He was stronger and
more in control of himself. Perhaps now he would be able to redirect his
energies quickly enough to avoid Salia's scrutiny. But could he afford to experiment when so much was at stake?

Could he afford *not* to?

How long would he be able to stay out of touch with Jennifer, knowing
the ravenous needs that were driving Salia and the dreadful acts she was
capable of? It would be a cruel irony to retrieve the anterium protocol, only
to discover he'd lost everything of meaning in his life in the process.

"The river is just up ahead," he heard Keetna say.

Silas looked up from the sparse prairie before them and saw the leafy
branches of countless cottonwoods in an east-west band a mile or two to
the south. Between them and the river he spied two burned out homesteads and a foundation for a house and barn that had been methodically
deconstructed. They soon reached an old road with broken-down barbed-
wire fences on either side, and easily stepped across them both into a fallow
field overgrown with unfriendly weeds. After twenty years respite from the
workings of a plow, the field was as hard-packed as the prairie, even after
yesterday's rain, yet it was a simple matter to tell one from the other by

the spectrum of plants that grew in each: The prairie was a symphony of mutually symbiotic species, all sharing the available nutrients as a single organism, while in the abandoned field there raged a war between equally hostile hybrid weeds, pillaging the earth of its natural wealth as their shoots and roots fought a bitter battle for dominance.

Keetna used Silas's machete to cut a swath through the worst of them. It made the going easier and Keetna took pleasure in hacking through organisms she perceived as abominations of nature. They reached the banks of the St. Vrain in less than a half hour and stopped to rest on a deadfall beside the water. The river was swift and laden with silt from the previous day's storm.

With a seriousness of expression Silas had grown accustomed to, Keetna said, "How're those legs holding up?"

"Fine. Better than I feared," he answered.

Against the backdrop of the deciduous forest that lined the riverbank, he imagined her a female Robin Hood, a fantasy inspired by the beret she wore on her head, the two quivers of arrows crisscrossing her slender torso, and the bow she kept always by her side. That Robin Hood's clothing was probably tighter fitting and his bow several degrees less complex stole from the illusion only slightly. As did Keetna's natural lack of a merry disposition.

She said, "Good. I'd like to reach the Platte by nightfall, if you're up to it. It's a broader floodplain that will make it easier to avoid detection." She bit off a piece of hard jerky and chewed it before adding, "It's also a more likely place to scare up some fresh meat."

They rested only until Silas felt the strength flow back into his travel-weary body.

The thin strip of forest along the St. Vrain varied in width on either side from no more than fifty yards to well over two hundred, and was laced throughout by trails; some narrow and visible only to a practiced eye like Keetna's, others heavily trod and wide enough to negotiate without snagging their clothing. These were the trails made by humans and Keetna avoided them whenever possible.

"Do you think he's following us?" Silas asked when they stopped for another breather.

"Tharp?" she said. Silas detected a trace of smile that suggested she would be disappointed if he weren't on their trail. "Probably not me. But you? I guess it depends on how bad he wants you."

"Pretty bad, I imagine, considering who he's working for."

"And that would be...?"

"Salia Warchez," he answered flatly.

Keetna glanced around in all directions, as she habitually did, with eyes that sliced right through the dense foliage. Satisfied they were alone, she said, "That bitch, huh? This document we're after must be pretty valuable."

Silas nodded and said, "Whoever possesses it possesses the means to resume the pumping of crude oil."

"Then we should burn it," she concluded quickly and with finality.

"Perhaps we will," Silas answered, his voice trailing off in thought.

*   *   *   *

Tharp awoke with his hands bound, his face and neck covered in sticky drying blood, and a headache so intense it redefined his notion of pain. And his left eye was partially closed from the swelling induced by...the boomerang? *Squirrelly bitch*, he thought. Then he laughed, despite his pain and his predicament. *Squirrelly* resourceful *bitch*, he amended, and laughed again. Victims were a dime a dozen; a good enemy made life worth living. He could hardly wait to even the score.

"What'cha laughin' at, boss?" The voice came from behind him.

"Bobby?" he said. He turned his head toward the sound, right into the midday sun. It added a new layer of pain on top of the old.

"Yeah, it's me," Bobby answered, embarrassed to have to admit the fact of his identity.

Hadrian turned a little farther and saw him. In exactly the same predicament as he was: propped against a steel support post in a broken-down gas station, his hands tied behind his back with narrow cord. One sleeve had been torn off Bobby's shirt and a seeping wound on his shoulder had been bandaged.

"How long have I been out?" Hadrian asked gruffly, his mind now focused on the immediacy of their situation and the unrelenting pain in his skull.

"A couple hours, I'd say," Bobby calculated, "that is, since we've been tied up."

The knowledge did nothing to improve Tharp's mood. Nor did it help matters when Bobby said, "You look like shit, boss."

"At least I'll get over it," Tharp grumbled. He fumbled with his restraints to find a knot he might untie or a loose loop he might work over the side of his hand. But there was nothing. The rope was expertly tied, as he knew it would be.

"I've just about got mine loose," Bobby said, almost proudly.

"And how did you manage that?" Tharp asked derisively.

"With my thumbnails. It was the girl who gave me the idea; it's hemp rope and it's old. She said I ought to be able to scratch through the rope in a couple hours," Bobby answered.

"How nice. What else did she tell you?"

"Only that I would end up just like Jimbo if she ever set eyes on me again."

"Then I guess you've got problems, Bobby Boy."

"I knew you was gonna say that."

Twenty minutes later they were headed southeast out of Endow, on foot and traveling light.

*   *   *   *

Silas and Keetna reached the confluence of the Platte and St. Vrain rivers just before nightfall and found a small clearing in the midst of a thicket of dwarf willows where they could make a small camp. Silas cleared the area of rocks and twigs while Keetna strung trip lines across the most likely pathways leading into it. "The biggest problem camping next to a river is the sound," she told him in the same matter-of-fact way she'd shared a dozen other survival tips. "You can't hear anyone coming in the night over the sound of the water, even this time of year when rivers are at their lowest."

She also forbade Silas to make a fire; it was an invitation to all the wrong sorts of people. So they huddled in blankets in the dark, nibbling on dried fruit, jerky and hardtack, listening to the sounds of the night. When their eyelids were slapping shut and it came time for sleeping, Keetna slipped in beside him and offered to share the wolf pelt that served as her mattress.

The ground was cold and a light blanket was little comfort. So they clung to each other on the small soft hide, light from the moon and stars overhead diffused and filtered by the verdant growth along the broad riverbank.

Having been deprived of a woman's touch for all his adult life, Silas found the feel of her... sensuous. She was far softer to the touch than he would ever have thought. And when she kissed him lightly on the cheek and fell asleep in his arms he felt like a man for the first time in his life. He held her through the night, reveling in her female scent and wishing the sun would never rise.

It rose, just the same, although Silas slept far beyond sunrise, finally rolling out of his blanket when he caught the smell of meat roasting over a fire.

"You've been busy," he observed, eyeing the rabbit Keetna was twirling on a forked stick.

She looked up and said, "Jerky's fine to stave off hunger, but it's short on energy. This will last us through the day." Her eyes were bright and clear and Silas felt drawn to them. It was a new sensation; like hunger, though not as urgent.

The rabbit smelled delicious. Keetna salted and peppered the meat with little paper packages, each with a big, rounded M printed on the side. Silas tried to recall the taste of McDonald's French fries, hot and greasy and grainy with salt, but it had been too long.

"Abner?" he asked bemused.

"Yep. Abner," she said, never taking her eyes of the roasting rabbit. "He had mounds of little giveaway things from before the Turning; salt, pepper, sugar, tea, coffee, powdered milk...anything dry that would be expected to keep for a long, long time. He kept his stash in a little room dug out under his house. Said I could have it all when he was gone." She pulled a piece of meat off the rabbit and sampled it, then went back to roasting. "As it worked out, that was the next day. One of Tharp's men shot him in the back before he could crawl down in his room to hide. Or make it into the tunnels where they knew better than to follow. He died for a handful of silverware and a couple of gold rings." She eyed the sizzling meat appraisingly, then tore off a leg and handed it to him.

"That's why you killed that guy?"

She looked at him in a way that told him he should have held his tongue. "Armed or not, he was twice my size," she said pointedly. "Then I hear him call out to the one son of a bitch who has caused me more misery than everyone else in the world put together. He had to be stopped, that's all. I'm not happy about it, but I'm not unhappy, either. If he'd lived, I might not have. And you'd be having breakfast with your friend Salia."

Silas suddenly felt very naïve. And a little ashamed. Who was he to judge her? She did what she had to do. It was why she'd outlived everyone else in the doomed town of Endow: survival was her stock and trade and she was exceedingly good at it. He said, "I'm sorry, Keetna. I didn't mean—"

She waved off his apology. "Forget it. For you, the war ended seventeen years ago. For me it's an occupation."

They finished their meal in silence then packed up their belongings and headed upriver.

By late afternoon the silhouette of Old Denver was in sight through an opening in the foliage provided by the river, which now ran smooth and clear and shallow across its broad expanse. Ever-shifting sandbars rose between the winding channels that wove their way slowly downstream, providing places for flotsam to collect; mostly limbs and branches that had fallen into the river from dead and dying trees, but there were other items; remnants of a bygone age when energy was cheap and manic materialism was a societal addiction. Bottles and jars, and chairs made of plastic and aluminum were trapped within the organic debris, the natural decay of the old city proving an endless source for new refuse as the old refuse worked its way downstream to the Missouri, the Mississippi, and eventually the Gulf of Mexico.

On the leading edge of one large sandbar Silas noticed a plastic frame trapped in a snarl of driftwood. Tatters of fabric still clung to the sides, and a harness, mostly intact, still restrained the bones of an infant. The setting sun reflected off the sun-bleached skull. It was then Silas realized he was looking at a child seat; the kind mothers used to strap to the seats of their cars, SUVs and minivans to protect their toddlers as they drove to and from the market or the soccer field.

He thought that he should be sad, if not for the child then for the decay that had embraced civilization since the abrupt and unforeseen end of oil. But he wasn't. The past had already extracted every last vestige of sadness the new race of humans had to give to the old.

Whatever sorrow remained in his soul he saved for this world.

Perhaps Keetna was right; the anterium protocol *should* be destroyed. He could see no good that could come from the reintroduction of oil back into the world of man. But it was not a decision he alone could make. He had to believe he was fated to his task for a reason; he doubted it was because he possessed a heretofore undeveloped inclination toward impetuousness. He would have to return it to *Vientos de los Dioses* where he could discuss its disposition with the rest of the *malagente*. He hoped Keetna would understand.

Where *was* she, anyway? She'd trotted ahead as she frequently did, to scout for obstacles in the trail—living, dead, or otherwise. This time she'd been gone for nearly a half hour, which was unusual. Most of the time she was back within five minutes, ten minutes tops. Suddenly Silas was worried. If anything were to happen to her...

Better not to think about that. No good could come from dwelling on what he wished least to happen. Of course she was all right. Maybe she found something in their way and was trying to figure out what they should do about. Maybe there were friendly people up ahead, people who were giving her directions and warning her of pitfalls they should avoid.

Yeah, right, a voice inside taunted. He believed it, even though he knew it was the voice of fear and not the canny voice that had guided him through all the years of his infirmity. But that voice had been silenced by the immediacy of his situation and his fear made gooseflesh spider-step up his backbone.

She was in trouble and he would have to find her; find her and figure out a way to help her. But how? If she'd walked into a trap, how could he avoid it himself? An unwelcome door opened inside his mind and from it escaped every wicked thing he had ever encountered in this world and all the worlds beyond. Things conjured by children when left alone in the dark for the first time in their lives, when grownups tell them there is a monster lurking right underneath the bed and if their foot should happen to touch the floor in the night...?

"Hey, there!"

His head snapped up from the well of doom he'd been drowning himself in, and he saw Keetna ambling toward him. She carried a wild turkey by its scaly feet, the bird's head dangling side to side and its wings drooping away from its body. He saw that she was smiling and he thought in that instant it was the most radiant smile he'd ever been graced with and he wanted to throw his arms around her and tell her exactly that. But he couldn't.

The embarrassment alone might kill me, he thought wryly.

Instead, he felt something unexpected well up inside of him; a hard, gritty resolve to become a part of the world he now found himself in. Perhaps he wasn't made of the same stuff as Keetna *(who the hell was?),* but he was living in her domain under her rules and the more of his own weight he could carry the more effective Keetna would be at keeping them both alive.

"Hey there, yourself," he said, as nonchalantly as he could without sounding like a caricature of himself, "you were sure gone a long time."

She handed him the turkey and said, "I climbed a tree for a look around. I got lucky. Tharp and his buddy are making their way toward us in the open ground beyond the greenbelt. Must've given up tracking, betting that we're headed upstream, which makes sense, since the only thing downstream is the Denver island and a whole lot of people Tharp would rather not run into."

"How long before he gets here?"

"We're safe. He won't make it before dark." She handed him the knife that almost slit Tharp's throat. "Cut off the breast and legs, then make a fire and cook the meat. And do it fast. Once the meat's done, we're moving on."

Silas looked first at the turkey, then the knife. "Where are you going?"

She offered up another rare smile, but wickedness tinged the edges of this one. "To give my old friend Hadrian something to remember us by," she said.

35

Murmurs of Gambits

I have often wondered how much of what happened at the beginning of the Turning was in accordance with Isaiah's original plan and how much was engineered by his daughter. For a man preaching the end of the world, COTO was a dream come true. But I can't help but think Isaiah got cold feet when he saw the suffering he created. Did his change of heart cost him his life? We'll probably never know...

FROM THE UNPUBLISHED MEMOIRS OF CARLOS HERRERA

"Do you think it's true that when two people make love their souls become entwined," Jack wondered aloud, "and the more they make love the more entwined their souls become?" He lay naked in his small bed propped up on one elbow. She pondered the question as Jack idly used his fingertip to trace circles around her breasts and her naval. She still shone with the soft glow of their lovemaking and her radiance drew him close like a fire draws man from the cold.

"Is this something your ex-wife told you?" Her furrowed brow contrasted sharply with the smile on her lips.

Jack chuckled. "Not hardly. I'm sure the idea of her soul being in any way bound with mine would not have been at all to her liking."

"Glad to hear it."

A few delicate strands of hair fell across her face and Jack gently brushed them aside before asking, "Are you jealous?"

"Do you want me to be?"

"Yes," he replied, softly running his fingers between her supple breasts, down her smooth flat belly, across to the curve of her hip and down her leg as far as the knee. As his explorations reversed course and headed back upstream, he paused to savor the soft flesh on the inside of her milky-white thighs. "Savagely so," he whispered.

"Savagely?" she echoed, responding to his touch. "Intensely wouldn't do?"

He shook his head and scooted closer. "No. It's got to be savage jealousy or nothing."

"Well, then...yes, my love. I am savagely jealous at the thought of your soul being entwined with hers."

He smiled and gazed deeply into her warm blue eyes. In the soft light of the gas lamps it seemed he was able to see all the way to very core of her, to where her spirit waited join with his. "Don't worry," he assured her. "It isn't. It's way too tangled up with yours."

She pulled him to her and kissed him hard. Then she wrapped her leg over his and said, "Let's tangle them a little more, shall we?"

Jack's hand crept an inch or two higher, until he felt Jennifer tremble against his touch. He whispered, "Yes...let's find out just how entangled they can get."

Later they made their way downstairs for tea and whatever morsels could be scavenged from the barren cupboards and a refrigerator that contained little more than cold air and a jar of blackberry jam. Added to slices of Catalyn's oat bread, toasted lightly in Carlos's pre-Turning Black & Decker toaster, it was a feast; a feast shared measuredly with the dogs, who possessed a practiced talent for making Jack feel as though the frozen meat scraps they'd been given earlier were just an appetizer.

As twilight gave way to full darkness, Jennifer kept the lamps turned low to revel in the soft shadows the muted light provided.

"Did you have any idea what Carlos was mixed up in?" Jack asked between a bite of toast and a sip of tea.

Jennifer answered, "No...I just knew he was wealthy. Everyone knew that. And we've all known about the diamonds for years. I think it might've been his way of testing us...to see if anyone would take the bait." She sipped her tea and let her eyes drift across the room. "No one did, of course, and I'm sure Carlos would've been more surprised than anyone if one of us had.

"But he never confided in us about his investments. Why would he, after all? And this business with COTO and the...the anterium protocol? It's not the sort of thing you'd want too many people to know about."

"Not if you want to live a long life," Jack said, reaching across the table and knitting his fingers with hers.

"No," she whispered under her breath, as if reflecting on the ramifications of what Tay had told them. After a moment she looked up and said, "We're in lot of trouble aren't we? I mean, if we give her what she wants, she'll kill us just to keep us quiet. And if we don't, she'll kill us out of spite. The only reason we're still alive is because we know something she doesn't. It's not the sort of stalemate she's going to accept forever."

"No," Jack agreed.

"What then?" she said, an edge of anxiety sharpening her words. "She's evil in every sense of the word, Jack, and yet for reasons I can't comprehend, there are thousands willing to die for her because they think she's Christ incarnate. Worst of all, she has a frightening ability to control people. I mean, Jesus! From out of nowhere she latches onto poor little Cassie like a tick on a dog."

Jack chuckled. "Didn't get very far, did she?"

"No, thank God, but the fact that she even found the poor girl is unnerving. If she wanted to, she could summon an army to rip us to pieces and raze *Vientos de los Dioses* to the ground. How do you defend against *that*?"

"By killing her first," Jack said reasonably.

"Just like that?" Jennifer replied. "What's the plan here? Should we have Luke pop her off, or would you rather the honors go to Cassie this time?"

"You're being a smartass, Miss Teague. You know who."

"Yes, I do. But I don't think it would be that easy, even for Tay. I'm sure others have already tried, with results all too apparent. God knows she's broken up her share of marriages, yours included, and that means there are hundreds or maybe even thousands of spurned husbands and wives out there, all of whom would sacrifice body parts to see her dead. And yet she remains alive, and vindictive as ever."

Jennifer paused and looked away. "She knows what's going to happen. At least to some degree. As a viator, she would have to. But how far can she see?"

Jack answered, "Far enough, apparently. She's skinny dipping in that river of time you were talking about; sensing danger before it becomes life threatening."

"Yes..." she said thoughtfully. Then she spun her head toward him and said, "But do you have any idea how much energy it takes to be so intensely vigilant? I mean, really, Jack, it's not an easy thing to do."

"No. Probably not."

"Which means she would be *really* hard to kill."

Jack held a finger to her lips and said softly, "If she breathes she can be made to stop breathing."

She kissed the finger and pushed his hand back across the table. "I think that can be said of us all, and some far easier than others."

"True. But that doesn't mean—"

Jennifer gave her head a shake, then pulled away several strands of hair away from her face. "Sorry. I just don't feel comfortable sitting here plotting a murder. Even if it's hers."

"Then I'll go plot with someone else."

"Oh, really?" she jeered, "Go ahead. But before you pick up your marbles and stomp over to Tay's house, you might want to hear me out."

"Boy, you can really get mean after great sex, can't you?"

"You would be the only one to know, love."

"Well *that's* good news," he said. "What's on your mind?"

"Well, it all goes back to something Prygor told me just before he died. He said, 'She made me the man I might have been, if only I'd been stronger.' What do you suppose that means?"

After discarding a half dozen overly witty answers, Jack replied, "Judging by the fun he had the night before he died, she must have found a way to, uh…"

Pull the cob out of his ass, he started to say.

"Remove Prygor's inhibitions?" she said.

"Uh, yeah. Exactly," he replied.

"And how would she do that?"

"Maybe it goes back to what you said yesterday," Jack said, following a sudden inspiration. "Changing the present by monkeying around with the past. If we assume that Primm wasn't *born* a psychological basket case, then it probably means he had a traumatic childhood; there might even have been a single defining moment when he stood on the knife's edge and slipped off on the wrong side. Then along comes good 'ol Salia, saying 'That's not the real you, Pryus dear,' and to prove it she leads him down the road he never took and lets him develop a fondness for the scenery."

"And gets herself a grateful new lapdog in the process."

Jack nodded. "So what are you thinking?" he asked.

"I'll let you know when I get it figured out."

He reached across the table and gently brushed his finger across her face. He said, "Personally, my love, I think it would be a whole lot easier just to shoot her."

* * * *

She was prying open stubborn doors and finding little of value behind them. Tharp was off somewhere, but she could get no clear sense of where he was, where he was going, or what circumstances compelled him to go there. Had he found Silas? She couldn't tell. The detritus of thought and feelings filtering through to her were fragmentary; all she knew for certain was that he was injured, and he was angry. And that he was dangerous to be around when he got that way.

As for Silas Teague, it would be easier to see through a mountain of lead than to locate the man when he did not wish to be found. The best she could hope for would be to catch him in another moment of weakness, perhaps brought on by Hadrian himself.

And then there was the girl, Cassie. She was the biggest disappointment of all.

(Call it what it was, my dear: a slap in the face.)

Salia had found her trolling for Silas Teague as she herself had been. The girl had formed an unusually strong attachment to Silas, considering they were not related by blood, and she thought certainly the child would be a malleable subject; she was sweet and naïve, and seemingly unprepared for meeting another wayfarer on the ever-changing pathways between worlds. Such places can appear dangerously nebulous to an innocent mind, and Salia pretended to offer assistance, as a concerned adult might lend aid to a lost child. Oh, but *this* child was not lost by any accounting, and once the girl discovered that Salia was also seeking Silas—seeking him with urgency, the girl sensed with a precociousness Salia found unnerving—she struck at Salia with extraordinary fierceness for one so young. Anger welled up inside her then, and she wanted nothing more than to strike out at the girl, but...

(It may not have been that easy)

...too quickly she was gone.

It was just as well. The girl would never become an ally, witting or unwitting. And if she were to ascertain that Salia was on the outskirts of Purgatory? Alone. The thought made her shiver.

But then it gave her an idea.

36

Old Denver

Does anyone possess the wisdom to use the anterium protocol? I fear not. A tenuous new balance has finally been established and the re-sumed pumping of oil would only upset it. At worst, the oil could be used to mobilize an army. But this would be the most fearsome army the world has ever seen, considering the war-making disparity that would exist between those with oil and those without it...

FROM THE UNPUBLISHED MEMOIRS OF CARLOS HERRERA

Keetna didn't like what she saw. The old rusted girders holding up the 20th Street viaduct leading into the heart of downtown Denver looked strong enough, but the tarmac on the surface was cracked, broken or altogether missing and the concrete beams below showed areas where huge chunks had fallen out, leaving a web work of exposed rebar. Abandoned automobiles canted obtusely where the surface had given way beneath one or two wheels; wheels that poked out through frayed rubber like bone through skin. The bridge would probably hold their weight well enough if they were careful where they stepped, but a misstep would mean a death fall to the deserted train yard a hundred feet below, a haunting place where decrepit box cars and rusting locomotives sat foreboding and motionless like iron ghosts frozen in time. That place she *really* didn't like.

"Where is it we're going, again?" It was the second time she'd asked, but she wanted to be sure. There was no point in taking one unneeded step in this ill-favored place. Death hung in the air, more as a condition than an odor, a disturbing corollary to the gnawing feeling that they were no more than small parasitic insects invading the surface of a large rotting corpse.

But the corpse wasn't yet dead, and that was the rub. There was movement all around them; a scurrying of creatures large and small, some on two legs, but most on four. The rats in the decaying metropolis had grown large and bold—larger even than Endow's jack rabbits, it seemed—and were clearly unafraid of Silas and her. Which was more than could be said of the few humans they had thus far encountered. Shabbier, more malnourished specimens of humanity she had never seen. No sooner would they spot another human than he or she would run and hide. It was unnatural to live in such fear; unless, of course, there was something very definite to be afraid of. If there was (and Keetna would've bet her stash of salt that there was), it was something they had yet to encounter.

She looked again to Silas and he answered, "The old State Capitol building. There's a large bronze statue on the grounds in front of it. The document I'm looking for is supposed to be beneath it."

"How could something be beneath a statue?" she asked reasonably.

Silas shrugged. "That's what we're about to find out."

"And where is this State Capitol building?" she asked.

"It's...let's see...we go a few blocks past this bridge, hang a right, then two or three more blocks to Lincoln, if by any chance there's still a sign."

"Or a statue," she muttered.

"Anyway," he went on, "the Capitol should be easy to spot. The roof is a big gold dome."

"If it was really gold, it won't be there anymore," Keetna pointed out.

"Whatever," he retorted, tiring of her commentary. "It's the biggest goddamn dome in town, okay?"

The words shot out of his mouth like an expelled cherry pit. Keetna laughed. His impatience was amusing. She said, "Sometimes Silas, I actually think you might be a little bit human."

"What's *that* supposed to mean?" he asked. The Silas that stood before her now bore only slight resemblance to the feeble, floundering being she had rescued from the rain and the mud and the mutie just a couple of days ago. His clothes seemed tighter, as though the muscles they enshrouded had toned up and grown larger in the span of three days; a foolish thought, perhaps, but hardly impossible, considering the other changes that had come over Silas, making her understand he was a special kind of man with extraordinary resilience. Color now suffused his formerly ghostly white face and hands, and the raw stubble on his face had grown into a short, downy beard, dark brown in color, streaked throughout with strands of golden blonde. It made him handsome, she thought, for it framed his strong jaw and full expressive lips and drew attention to his deep blue eyes; eyes that had gone from the confused and vacuous orbs of a lost child to the keen and focused instruments of discernment that now peered at her with such intensity.

She said only, "You did a good job last night, Silas. I thank you for that."

"With the turkey, you mean? And the fire?"

Like his beard, shocks of blonde shot through the long, shiny locks that grew from his head. Keetna had parted his hair for him and tied it in back with a soft buckskin string, but the breeze had blown loose a few strands that now fluttered about his head, giving him an untamed ruggedness that she found entirely agreeable. But mostly she liked his newfound resolve; he had finally decided to become an equal partner in the joint matter of their continued survival. They just might make it yet. She smiled and kissed him high on a cheek made rosy by the sun and the blood that surged hotly now through his veins. "Yes, Silas. The fire, and the turkey. And the companionship." Though they hadn't made love as they lay close together sharing warmth, she realized for the first time in her life she wanted to. As long as it was with Silas.

"Yes; the companionship," he answered, smiling now, as if he could read her like an open book. The gesture bunched the slight wrinkles in the tanned skin around his eyes, adding to the attraction she now felt for him.

Later, she told herself. Providing they lived that long. For the moment and the immediate future all of their energies needed to be directed toward staying alive from one minute to the next.

They slowly made their way across the overpass, Keetna leading the way. They clung to the remnants of the high railing on the side, testing the surface gently with each step before committing their full weight to it. They crouched low to make themselves as inconspicuous as possible, but the sprawling expanse of the disabled city was so great, and the sight of movement within it so unexpected, they would surely be noticed by even a casual observer. Providing there were such a thing in this place of death and decay.

At the high point of the overpass a large section of road had crumbled and fallen to the train yard below, and they had to straddle the heavy steel railing—bent and jagged in places—and scoot across the fifty-foot span in greater profile than either of them would've liked. But no shots rang out and no one appeared on the bridge to challenge them. As they inched across the void the wind became playful almost in the way a large dog becomes playful; becoming dangerous by its own strength, despite its benign intentions. Nor did Keetna enjoy the perspective of a hundred feet of sky between her toes and the rusting tracks below. She was a creature of the earth, a ground dweller both by habit and inclination, and in her entire life she had never been more than ten feet above the ground without the comforting embrace of tree limbs to provide her with a much-appreciated sense of security. This was madness. And when the railing creaked and wove at a place where the concrete had shattered beneath the supports, she knew for certain she could not continue. But then she felt Silas's strong hand grip her backpack to keep her from swooning, and she pulled herself forward another few feet until the railing was once again solid, if only slightly more inviting for its rigidity.

Inch by inch they spanned the void and were on their way toward the heart of Old Denver, one gingerly step at a time. To their right they saw the remains of the Elitch Gardens, an amusement park, as Silas had called it, though Keetna found nothing amusing about it. More like the skeletal remains of a large iron beast which had died decades ago in the throes of a violent convulsion.

And to their left, Silas explained, lay the baseball stadium—Coors Field, he told her—where men once played a game whose object was to hit a small ball with heavy sticks into places where other men couldn't catch it with large leather gloves. Thousands of people each night belayed their quests for survival to watch this peculiar event. She could hardly imagine why. And when he told her that they all came from distances of several miles, collectively burning tens of thousands of gallons of highly concentrated fuel, it made even less sense.

Better they stay close to their homes and hunt. Lean was the reward for the fat ones who did not think ahead.

In any case, the place was a hulk, stripped of its bricks below a narrow canopy that was caving in against its own weight and the forces of nature, and the sooner it crumbled to the good earth and people forgot the folly that had drawn them to the place the better.

Silas argued that people needed diversions, but she knew better. What they needed was focus.

A frail man awaited them at the far end of the bridge. Keetna nocked an arrow and watched guardedly as Silas spoke to the waif-like creature. He was not much more than a shadow living on rats and mice and an occasional dog, coyote, or mutie if he was lucky, but by his slight build and the infirmity that seemed to have settled into his bones, it was doubtful that he could secure more than a day's worth of meat at a time, if that. But as she was soon to discover, she was wrong.

"Hello, there," Silas greeted him in a friendly tone

"And greetings to you," the small man said with a gruff voice and a raucous cough. His eyes were too small for Keetna's liking, and his smile, showing several places where teeth were missing, too large. She suspected he wanted more than he was in any position to give.

"Let me kill him," Keetna whispered insistently. "He's trouble."

But the man, clad in an old topcoat that nearly dragged the ground, held up hands that wore fingerless gloves, and Silas shook his head. "Not yet. I have a feeling we're going to need him."

When they drew closer and Keetna saw how desperately unhealthy he was—his wrists were spindles and his neck no more than a thin post for support of his head—she almost pitied him. But her misgivings remained. "I have never seen the likes of you two before," he said. He held a hand to his face and coughed, before adding, "Not many interlanders ever venture here, especially by way the bridge; it is far too treacherous and you would have done well to choose another route."

"Is that a threat?" Keetna asked, pointedly.

Again he held up his hands and gave a smile, saying, "Only a fact, young miss, I assure you. For the place you have just passed through is a place only for killers and thieves, and those unfortunates who have nowhere else to go."

"And *this* side is different?"

"Oh, indeed it is, my dear girl, most different; like night and day, you might say."

He spoke almost melodically through the mucous that rumbled in the back of his throat, as if he were a man of erudition. By the deep creases that lined his face and the stringy strands of gray hair that stuck out wildly from beneath a tattered knit cap, he appeared to be well along in life.

Silas asked, "Who are you, anyway?"

"A good question, sir," he responded politely, "and one that deserves an honest answer, to be sure. But you shouldn't feel threatened. No, not by me, for I am what you would call a diplomat, charged with the task of settling disputes between the ruling factions of the outlying territories here, before they escalate into all-out war. It is a thorny vocation I have chosen, but one for which I am nonetheless suited, for I was a mediator of legal disputes before the world changed, and I must say that it was a most natural calling." He coughed long and hard at the end of his soliloquy.

"You sure talk a lot," Keetna observed.

"Yes, it's true," he agreed, "and every word I speak is one word closer to my last. But professing is my profession, after all, so may I be so meddlesome as to inquire what your business here may be?"

"You may not," Keetna told him flatly.

He gave her a deferential bow and said, "As you wish, young miss. But it might be that I could offer a degree of assistance and perhaps even protection that you would not otherwise enjoy during your visit here, providing of course that it is short and of a benign nature."

"Short as possible," Silas affirmed, "and we mean no harm to anyone."

He found this answer agreeable, but studied them with narrowed eyes before asking, "And you are going where...?"

"To the Capitol," Silas answered.

"And do you have names?" he asked, as if it were important.

Sharply, Keetna said, "None of your fu—"

"I'm Silas and this is Keetna," Silas interrupted, drawing a scornful stare from Keetna.

"Very well then, Silas and Keetna. You may call me Erasmus. Please follow."

Keetna refused to move a muscle until Silas grabbed her hand and pulled her along, and then she followed only grudgingly. "I don't trust him," she protested.

"You don't trust anyone," Silas reminded her.

"Please stay close," Erasmus said over his shoulder, "and for pity's sake, young miss, remove the arrow from your bow. You are unlikely to reach your destination if it appears you are holding me hostage."

She did. They followed.

Without explanation, Erasmus took a zigzag route to the Capitol. Possibly to avoid trespassing across unseen territorial boundaries, or because it was the route offering the least resistance. The streets were littered with rubble and automobile carcasses but there was an order to it somehow, as if the rubble had been purposely placed, perhaps for defense or to demarcate property boundaries. Or maybe it was just landscaping. Down each street there was a meandering pathway wide enough for two to walk abreast pulling a wagon or a cart, and everywhere there were side paths leading to building entrances or basement accesses. Around some entrances they were surprised to see planters with flowers and even small gardens where the tarmac had been chipped away to expose the soil beneath.

Silas clearly felt eyes upon him, but few actually showed themselves. The ones who did venture into the light all knew Erasmus and returned his greetings with a wave or a nod.

The presence of young children was surprising to Silas, until he reminded himself that reproduction is the way of the world, regardless of the conditions under which people lived. Sex was a guaranteed pleasure and from sex cometh children.

But still he wondered, how can they smile so, and play together in such a destitute place? Because seeking joy was what children did best. Silas smiled at every child he saw; most smiled back.

When the Capitol building came into view, Silas noted that the dome above the colonnade had indeed been stripped of its gold. Keetna dropped back out of Erasmus's earshot and said, "I've been doing some thinking, Silas."

"About what?"

"The document you're after."

"And…?"

"Well, I've been wondering: did you ever stop to consider that it might not be the real thing."

"Why *wouldn't* it be?" he asked. As much as he appreciated Keetna's cunning mind, he wondered if she might be looking a little too hard for ulterior motives. Cunning went hand in hand with deception. It was a useful trait, but why was she trying to find deception in Carlos's motives?

Had he overlooked something?

Keetna furtively scanned their surroundings before saying, "Think about this, Silas. You were…sick…when that old man told you of its whereabouts, right?"

"I guess you could say that," he said.

"And you weren't ever supposed to get any better, were you?"

"The prognosis certainly wasn't favorable," he agreed, curious now to hear her out.

"So the old man never really expected you to act on the information he gave you, right? You were only supposed to keep it in your head…like maybe for someone else to find."

For someone else to find? Something clicked right into a place it didn't belong.

"Look at it this way," she went on, "if you were in as bad of shape as you said you were, why would the old man ever think you might ever end up here?"

"Then why tell me in first place?"

"Perhaps the whole thing was a blind...a dodge..."

"A ruse?"

"Yes, that's the word," she said, "a ruse...to lead someone other than you in exactly the wrong direction."

Silas stopped in his tracks as everything suddenly meshed with steely precision. That was *exactly* what Carlos had in mind. Had to be. The information in his head was meant for someone else...

He grabbed Keetna by the arm and spun her toward him. "*Salia*," he whispered in a low hiss, his voice electrified by the implications of her words. A chill washed through him. If, as it had seemed, Silas was destined to live out his life in a semi-vegetative state, then the knowledge Carlos had forced upon him could only be recovered by someone with special abilities possessed by very few. And when those few were counted, Salia Warchez would be at the top of the list.

Keetna said, "It's a good bet that she, or maybe Tharp, is supposed to be here instead of you. If so, we're on a fool's errand to retrieve a forgery other fools are meant to find."

Laughter erupted in Silas's throat. *Of course* Salia was supposed to find the protocol! Why else would he hide it in such an inaccessible place? Certainly Carlos never expected Silas to one day jump out of his recliner and run into the heart of Old Denver to retrieve it.

Hacking with an open fist over his mouth, Erasmus said, "Did I miss something funny? Tell me, please. There is so little to laugh at here, after all."

Silas quickly composed himself; he may have been laughing at events destined to bring about his own death, after all. He said, "Sorry...it's a long story. But tell me; do you recall seeing an elderly gentleman come this way, at least a year ago, maybe much longer? Tall, slender—"

"With intense blue eyes? Name of Carlos? How could I not remember him? He's not the sort you could easily forget. He came in through what we like to call the trade corridor, a route that conveys a certain degree of immunity to outlanders wishing to do business here. It was one summer ago. I recall it was summer because—"

"Never mind," Keetna growled, "just tell us what he brought with him."

"And if he was alone," Silas added.

Unruffled, Erasmus said, "Well, yes, he was quite alone and unarmed, but hardly worried for his own safety despite his considerable age. He carried himself in a way that was both fearsome and disarming, as if to convey that he had neither the time to threaten nor to suffer threats. As for what he brought with him, that is a difficult matter" —he paused for a brief fit of coughing— "excuse me; a difficult matter to determine. He used our facilities to store something he felt to be of great value, that much is clear. But what it was, I do not know."

Silas asked, "How is it even possible to store something valuable in a place...like...?"

"Like this one?" Erasmus said, more amused than offended. "Because, young man, contrary to what you might have been taught, there is indeed honor among the downtrodden dregs that inhabit this place. Besides, with hard currency all things are possible, I assure you. And your friend Carlos had enough of that to pay for several years of protection for his...parcel."

"But why here?" Silas pressed. "Why not a bank vault inside the Denver island?"

"Because, in his wisdom, your friend knew that nothing can be truly hidden inside the islands. The rights of property and privacy are not so strongly embraced there as they are here."

"And so you're storing it...his 'parcel'...for him?" Keetna asked.

Erasmus looked Keetna up and down, as if he were seeing her for the first time. Whether or not he approved of what he saw was impossible to tell. Politely he said, "Not me alone, you understand, for I could not even protect a rat from a flea, but my compatriots can and do provide such a service." He paused to cough and turned away to spit a glob of gray phlegm onto the street. When he turned back to them he wiped his lips with a dirty coat sleeve and said with a rather pleasant smile, "And I imagine you have come to retrieve the parcel put on deposit by your elderly friend?"

Silas glanced quickly at Keetna, then said, "That is correct, Erasmus."

"And tell me, master Silas: how is the old gentleman?"

"Dead, I'm afraid."

"Oh, how unfortunate. But I assume he told you which vault the parcel was in...before his passing. And the box code?"

Vault? Keetna silently mouthed. Silas said, "The one beneath the Bronco

Buster statue. And yes, I have the code." He spoke in the polite tone of a bank customer requesting to view the contents of his safe deposit box. Which is what he was.

"Very well. Follow me." Erasmus turned and again they followed.

Though hardly what they were in the heydays before the Turning, the Capitol grounds had been remarkably well kept. The formerly lush, well-watered bluegrass lawns were now reduced to tenuous patches of native grasses, and once colorful flower gardens had been taken over by dandelions, larkspur and wild roses, but some attempt had been made to keep the grasses and flowers separate from one another and to keep the weeds at bay without actually pulling, poisoning, or otherwise declaring all-out war on them. Compared to the parts of Old Denver they'd seen so far, the Capitol grounds seemed an oasis and the well-maintained colonnade in front of the Capitol building an entrance to a palace.

The Bronco Buster statue sat alone on a separate lawn south of the Capitol building, but it was clear by the groomed grass and pruned trees that it too fell under the auspices of the same authority that maintained the rest of the grounds. The large bronze sculpture depicted a hardened cowboy atop a horse whose head was tucked and its back legs thrown out in an attempt to unseat its rider. As they approached, two large men appeared from the direction of the Capitol building to block their path. Clad in military-like garb and holding assault weapons across their chests, both giants had smooth skin so dark as to be nearly black, and long dreadlocks tied in the back. Obviously they subsisted on more than rats and roots. Silas found them both dangerous and fearsome, but also professional and unlikely to step beyond the bounds of their mandate, whatever that mandate might be.

Between them stood a large creature Keetna would call a mutie. It was wolfish in stature, and stood nearly four feet at the shoulders. The top halves of its ears lopped to the side, resembling horns. Although presently as passive as its two masters, there was a deadly gleam in the creature's eye, made all the more menacing by the dual sets of canine teeth extending beyond its closed mouth.

Standing between them and the guards, Erasmus turned to Silas and said, "As you can see, we take our business here seriously. We have brought order from what was once chaos and we have earned a reputation for discretion. That is why your friend Carlos entrusted us with his parcel."

Actually, it's beginning to look like Carlos expected his parcel to be taken by raw force. He said, "So I see."

Erasmus approached the guards and they parted to allow him through. The big mutie also stepped to the side, shadowing the movement of the guard on the right. Keetna fell behind Silas, who cautiously stepped between them and followed Erasmus to the east side of the statue, where the tail of the bronze horse curved gracefully back between its legs. There they saw a heavy steel door, as if from a large safe, with a smaller steel box attached to the top.

Erasmus worked a small padlock and opened the lid of the smaller box. This exposed a larger combination lock beside a heavy wheeled handle in a door taken from either a small bank vault or a large corporate one. "Everyone turn your heads please," he said, "and I trust there will be no peeking." He tried to laugh but coughed instead.

Silas wondered how anyone could justify the time and expense involved in building a vault beneath a statue, and then providing fulltime security for it. What the hell was in there? Erasmus worked the combination and spun the handle; the two guards strained to lift the massive door from its nearly horizontal repose. It looked as if it must weigh a thousand pounds or better.

He peered into the dark maw that had just opened up beneath the statue. Steps led down into a large, dimly lit concrete room. Hundreds of drawers were built into the walls and as a rush of stale air escaped from vault Silas felt a strong sense of the drawers' contents; Family heirlooms. Necklaces, earrings and rings of gold, silver and platinum, diamonds, sapphires and emeralds. Coins, ingots and medallions. But also old photos, precious books, and fragile memorabilia from a bygone age; wealth less tangible but no less precious. Wealthy or poor, everyone possessed something of great value to them and he imagined they would gladly pay to keep it secure in a world where security was in such short supply.

"Hold on! What in the hell do you think you're doing, Erasmus?"

Silas turned to see a small black man trotting toward them with two unarmed guards in tow. Compared to the two beefy specimens beside the vault, these guards were lightweights, and the small buzzing man now approaching someone of little consequence. But it quickly became clear that this was the man who ran the show.

Erasmus hurried to meet him before he and his guards reached the vault, and said in a raspy whisper that carried much farther than it was calculated to, "I was simply assisting in a legitimate withdrawal, Your Honor, and I didn't see a need to trouble you with—"

"No, no, no, NO!" the little man barked at Erasmus. "You cannot remove anything from the vault without my authorization!"

The ruffled little man looked up then, and smiled pleasantly at Silas and Keetna. Silas thought he recognized him; older and grayer but... "Excuse me, sir, but aren't you Arty Checker, the former Mayor of Denver?"

"Former, my ass! What do I look like to you now, son, a bus driver?"

"No," Silas answered, unable to suppress a smile, "but, well...everyone thought you were dead, and since..."

"Since what?" he bristled. "Since 'officially' Denver picked up its roots and moved east? Let me tell you something, young man: I went into hiding with my own people when the military came rolling in here all high and mighty with their howitzers and their goddamn tear gas. I didn't *get* any lacey invitation to that fancy new island they built out there in the scrotum of nowhere, and I didn't *want* one. This is where I belong because *this* is the Denver that needs me!"

His etiquette had slipped a notch or two from the days when Silas used to watch news clips of the irrepressible Arty Checker, but his rhetoric was still in top form. Silas stepped forward and extended his hand, saying, "It's a pleasure, sir."

Arty's toothy smile quickly reappeared. "And you are...? And please don't tell me you're from that squeaky-clean, holier-than-thou Denver island or I'll have you both strung up on the spot."

Not entirely sure he was kidding, he answered, "Silas Teague, sir, from Purgatory. And this is my companion, Keetna, the sole survivor of Endow." Hamstrung though she was by a retarded sense of decorum, Keetna nonetheless stepped forward to be properly greeted.

"That's good news for both of us," the mayor answered. He first shook Silas's hand then Keetna's, remarking, "That's a deadly-looking contraption you've got there, young lady," nodding at her compound bow with its confounding assortment of strings and pulleys. "Know how to use it?"

"Yes...sir," Keetna murmured haltingly.

"Show me," he instructed. "That elm tree, over there. There's a knot about six feet up from the ground. See if you can—"

Before he finished his sentence, Keetna loosed an arrow that sped forty yards and struck with a resonant *thwack!* into the center of the four-inch knot.

Goliaths one and two exchanged glances, then looked on Keetna with newfound respect.

"Impressive," a wide-eyed Arty Checker exclaimed. "Would you like a job?"

Keetna laughed and grabbed Silas's arm. "Got one, already," she replied.

"Could be I pay better," he chided.

"Don't think so," she said.

"Fringe benefits? Pension plan?"

Keetna shook her head resolutely while Arty laughed and cupped them both on the shoulder. "Fair enough," he conceded. "What is your business in my town, anyway?

Erasmus stepped around Silas and said, "Caught up with them coming in off the 20th-street bridge, Your Honor. They've come to retrieve a parcel left in our safe by an elderly man of their acquaintance the summer before last. I was just about to ask them the code for the box when you—"

"When I showed up to remind you of your breach in procedure?" Arty finished, casting a sharp but benevolent eye to his resident diplomat.

"Just so," Erasmus agreed with due deference.

Arty switched his attention back to Silas and Keetna, regarding them as he might two small children who'd gone walking alone in the forest at night. "It's a dangerous way to come," he admonished them, his bushy gray eyebrows dipping into the furrow that formed in his forehead. "There's no protection for anyone coming in from that direction. We have only a limited territory here where you can enjoy relative safety. Once you're beyond that you might as well be back in the Dark Ages."

"Why?" Silas asked.

"It's a matter of economics, young man; economics and the hard realities of existence. It's because of fossil fuels and federal aid, the two things that used to keep cities from collapsing into chaos. Now we've got neither, which means that all rule here is local. And I do mean local."

"Local?" Silas asked.

Arty looked up at Silas as if his meaning should be obvious. "Let me put it into simple terms for you. Suppose you're an honest citizen who's staked out a claim here, and you're hoping to eke out a peaceful existence. Right out of the gate you realize you're going to need a certain degree of protection just to stay alive, which means you'll have to form an allegiance with someone more powerful than you are. Get it?"

"Like a feudal lord, you mean?"

"Exactly," Arty beamed, "But who are you going to form an allegiance with? The self-proclaimed warlord ten blocks away, or the bad-ass boss five blocks away? You're going to go with the bad-ass boss because you're living on his turf and that makes you *ipso facto* one his subjects.

"The point is, everything's divided up just as it was in medieval times. There are dozens of little fiefdoms throughout the city and moving from one to another is as dangerous as crossing a national border without a passport; maybe more so." He looked at Silas and said, "And that's why you were lucky to have made it as far as you did without running into trouble."

Silas said, "So what you're saying is that you just control a small part of the city?"

Arty shrugged and looked at his shoes. "As much as I hate to admit it, yes. Mine is just one of many fiefdoms." Then he looked up and smiled, saying, "But you can rest assured that mine is the biggest and the most enlightened."

"Indeed it is, Your Honor," Erasmus interjected in a way that came off without sounding patronizing. "Without you we'd all be living on rodents and insects."

"How *do* you live?" Keetna asked, perusing the surroundings.

"Trade, dear girl," Arty replied, proudly, "trade with interlanders. We trade anything you can imagine: plastics, building materials, machines and machine parts, and metals like copper and aluminum, just to name a few. We trade for fresh produce, seeds, and also for medicines, which have to be smuggled out of the islands."

"Smuggled? Why?"

"Because we don't officially exist, no more than the city itself. Oh, they know we're here, but they pretend we're not. That way they don't have to share anything with those of us who didn't have the skills or the pedigrees they're looking for. All we had to offer the 'new world' were strong backs and common sense; two things islanders don't seem to hold in much esteem." Arty held up the white palms of his brown hands and added, "But that's okay. You could even say there's reciprocity on that count, because we don't let their kind do business in *our* city, either."

"Ever do business with a man named Hadrian Tharp?" Silas asked.

Arty and Erasmus exchanged surprised glances before Erasmus turned and said, "Yes. Often. Why? Is he a friend of yours?"

"An acquaintance," Silas replied. It was time to go. However 'enlightened' Arty Checker's little fiefdom might be, food would always be a stronger currency than flattery. To Arty he said, "You've been very kind, but we've taken up enough of your time, Mayor. Perhaps we should get our parcel and be on our way."

"As you wish," the mayor replied, sensing a chill in the warm autumn air. He looked to Erasmus, saying, "Check their code and give them their parcel," then to Silas and Keetna. "Good day, and safe travels," he told them. Then he turned and walked back toward the steps of the Capitol building with his brightly clad bodyguards mirroring his movements.

"And what is the code, young man?" Erasmus asked, concluding with a muffled cough. Silas repeated the seven digits as Carlos had whispered them to him. Erasmus said, "Wait here, please," and disappeared down the stone steps into the large vault. A moment later he labored back up holding a plastic button & string envelope. There was no lettering on the outside. After a brief coughing fit, he handed it to Silas. Silas thanked him.

Keetna was stuffing the bright blue envelope into Silas's backpack when she spied Hadrian Tharp rounding the southwest corner of the Capitol grounds.

37

River Rogues

There has always been a nefarious element living on the fringes of society, an element steeped in violence that resists all attempts to bring it into the fold of civilization. The Turning increased their numbers several fold...

FROM THE UNPUBLISHED MEMOIRS OF CARLOS HERRERA

Keetna quickly assessed their situation. Tharp was better than two hundred yards away and it was doubtful anyone here had been instructed to take orders from him. As long as they acted quickly they still had options. Keetna stepped behind Erasmus and whispered in a hairy ear, "How do we get out of here? Tell me quick or I'll kill you first."

Erasmus stiffened and whispered back low enough that the guards could not hear, "You needn't threaten. Go northeast to the trade corridor. Follow the path of the fire. I'll do what I can to stall him."

"You *will?*"

"Heavens yes!" Erasmus answered resolutely. "The man is a menace; a menace who, unfortunately, has access to highly valued trade goods. Hurry now, young miss, and Godspeed!"

She patted Erasmus on the shoulder, saying, "Thanks, Erasmus; I was wrong about you," then she grasped Silas by the hand and pulled him into the tree cover to the east. Silas at first seemed either confused or unwilling, but he quickly picked up his pace. They ran as fast and as far as their feet would carry them, leaving the Capitol grounds as Erasmus instructed, not even taking time to look behind them until they were both so out of breath they needed to rest, if only for a few moments.

Thus far they hadn't heard anything to suggest that they were being pursued or even that Tharp had recognized them. But how could he not? She and Silas hardly looked like a pair of typical inner-city denizens out for a casual jog across the Capitol grounds.

"What...are we...doing?" Silas asked, gasping for air.

"Doing?" Keetna asked, bent over holding her sides.

"Yeah...why are we...running?"

She stood and faced him, still breathing hard. "That was Hadrian Tharp, Silas! What do you want to do, stand there and have a friendly little chat with the man? Maybe go have tea and cookies with the Mayor?"

"In a manner of speaking, yes," he answered.

She shook her head in disbelief. "Have you gone loco?"

He put his hands on her shoulders and said, "Look at it this way: he wasn't going to gun us down in front of Erasmus and those two guards, and he's not going to bind us and drag us off, either. Not if he wants to keep doing business here. All he really wants is what's in my backpack. We give it to him and he goes away. Simple."

"No it's *not* simple!" she shrieked, finally losing her temper. "Tharp doesn't operate that way, Silas! He takes what he wants and he kills you *anyway*, just because it's the efficient way to do things! *You* don't know this man. *I do*!" She paused for a breath, then said, "Erasmus knew it, and your hotshot little friend Arty what's-his-face knew it too! Why can't *you* see it?"

Silas suddenly looked like he'd been mugged by reality. The blood drained from his face and he appeared dazed. "Oh, my God, you're right! How could I be so stupid? These people aren't going to sacrifice a solid trade relationship for the likes of us; they may protest a little, but in the end it'll be business as usual, no matter what Tharp does."

Keetna put an arm around him and pulled him close. "You've just been away too long, that's all. That other world of yours wasn't filled with pain and death like this one." She lifted his head and met his eyes. "That's why you need me; however good or bad it may be, this is my world and I know how to stay alive in it."

He gave her a half-hearted little smile, then, quite by surprise, he kissed her. It was short and not especially wet or sensuous, but a kiss just the same, and she realized it was the first time she'd ever been kissed in the way a man kisses a woman. She gazed at him with wonder (for it truly was a wonderful kiss) and took his hand. "We've got to get out of here, Silas, okay? Erasmus said to look for the 'path of the fire.' We'll find it, alright? We'll find it and we'll get back to the river where things make sense. Then later, when everything calms down, we can maybe try this again."

*   *   *   *

Such a base and forceful man, Erasmus thought. Who does he think he is to wander in here and demand privileged information about one of the City's paying clients? The answer came easily enough: He's Hadrian Tharp, of course—Arty Checker's foremost supplier of pilfered potatoes, contraband medicines and bootlegged syn-fuels.

It made Erasmus's position several degrees more difficult than it ordinarily would've been.

"If you won't tell me what they took, then at least tell me where they're going. How hard can that be, old man?" Tharp was trying to be reasonable but there was a dangerous edge to his voice Erasmus found worrisome. Even the two barrel-chested giants guarding the vault looked on dubiously. Only the mutie seemed more curious than concerned about the short, powerful man with the wide slash across his face. But that was only because it wasn't as well acquainted with Tharp as the rest of them.

Fearing for his life—what little remained of it, at any rate—Erasmus was nonetheless about to deny Tharp's request for information yet again when he saw His Honor rushing toward them with his personal guards struggling to keep pace.

It was now out of Erasmus's hands.

"Hadrian Tharp?" the Mayor said, eyeing with amusement the crusty scab that cut across the sullen man's face. "You look like you just had a mauling contest with a grizzly and ended up with the red ribbon."

"More like a wildcat, Checker," Tharp corrected, showing blatant disrespect for the Mayor's position. "And Erasmus here refuses to tell me where she's going."

"You mean Keetna? Black beret and a deadly bow?"

Tharp nodded. "And Silas Teague."

The Mayor looked around in mock confusion, then replied measuredly, "No one knows where they're going, Hadrian. And even if we did, you can't expect us to betray a paying client."

A young man with a bandaged shoulder and injured foot limped into their midst as Tharp pushed his nose to within an inch of the Mayor's face.

Erasmus expected his devilish machine pistol to come out of its holster as Arty Checker's guards moved to either side of their liege, but Tharp kept his hands at his side. Still, there was a desperation in his voice that didn't go unnoticed. In a raspy whisper he said, "I expect to get what I came here for, Checker. And unless you want me to take my business to the other side of town, I will."

Commerce was the Mayor's Achilles heel. A profitable exchange of goods was what made his section of the old city the enlightened sanctuary it was, and Hadrian Tharp was responsible for much of it. Just the same, the Mayor attempted to save face. He said, "Hadrian, you have to understand my position. Business is trust and trust is business. If I tell you what I shouldn't, then what good is my word?" Hadrian shifted impatiently on his feet. "But unlike knowledge, which comes with a price, reason is free, is it not?"

Oh, how I wish I'd said that! Erasmus lamented with silent admiration.

"The fact is, Hadrian, it doesn't matter in the least where they went, as long as you can reasonably predict where they'll come *out*. And I don't have to remind you that this is hardly the open city it used to be. There's more than geography at work here, if you catch my meaning."

Apparently he did. Tharp said, "One more thing, Checker. I'll need a little help. And don't make the mistake of thinking I'm asking..."

*   *   *   *

They ran through a maze of streets, looking for Erasmus's "path of the fire." Quickly the commercial district evaporated, replaced by the ruins of former neighborhoods. Perhaps one in five houses remained standing in some form or another; of those another one in five appeared livable. Fires had destroyed some of them, vandals or nature the others. But a path of fire? She didn't see it. Were they still in Arty Checker's docile little fiefdom or had they wandered into the domain of a more ruthless lord? They ran north.

"There!" Silas exclaimed after another hundred yards. "The 'path of the fire'!" They'd overshot it by a block, but the corridor Silas pointed to was unquestionably what Erasmus had told them to look for. It was a burned out strip two blocks wide where every house, shed, tree and bush had been burned. Nature had washed away the ash, leaving only a few cinders protruding from foundation walls. Hordes of weeds had reclaimed the yards around them, but the street running through the middle of the destruction was intact and unencumbered by debris of any kind. At the near end of it a

warehouse of sorts had been constructed from reclaimed building materials—no two windows matched, and the siding alternated between tin and
wood and vinyl—and an odd assortment of piecemeal vehicles waited at or
near the two large doors, one for loading and one for offloading.

It was clearly the trade corridor but was it as safe as Erasmus claimed?
Keetna didn't like it, and she told Silas why. "It's too open; too easy to be
seen. Tharp could travel parallel to the road using buildings for cover and
spot us easily among the traders. We could be killed without even setting
eyes on the man."

"I don't think he wants us dead," Silas said, as the men in the vicinity of
the warehouse began to take notice of the strange pair. "I have the feeling
he wants to take us back to Salia."

"A feeling?"

"Yeah. A strong one."

"Maybe you," she said, "but not me. I'm of no value to him. We'll follow
the corridor from behind the houses."

They kept moving, traveling between the ruins of houses and down
pathways winding through patches of trees, bushes and dense overgrowth,
careful always to avoid any pockets of human habitation while keeping the
trade corridor in sight, hoping to get a glimpse of Tharp and Bobby and end
this chase in the only way Keetna knew how.

"You'll kill him, won't you?" Silas asked during a brief rest between
houses.

"In a heartbeat," she replied. "I should have slit the bastard's throat
when I had the chance."

They moved on.

The path of the fire was neither straight nor confined to a two-block
breadth. It had been a wind-driven fire and it burned a wild swath north-
ward; sometimes two blocks wide, sometime eight or more. They stayed
within sight of a road that was remarkable in the diversity of traffic it supported. Horse carts with produce going in. Open-bed trucks with metals,
plastics, or reclaimed building materials going out. Old men with handcarts
and young women with backpacks. A hodge-podge of motorized conveyances coming and going with cargo that could eventually be turned into
food, or warmth, or a small, fleeting bit of security. The sight saddened
Keetna. Life needn't be this difficult.

As Erasmus had said, no one who traveled the corridor was threatened.
Yet all around them, as they cautiously wound their way through the tangled

depths of razed, deconstructed and rebuilt neighborhoods, they encountered small pockets of humanity; ragtag tribes of men and women any wise traveler would do well to avoid. And yet they seemed to know that if the lifeline that moved before them were broken by lust or hunger or greed, then what little taste of civilization they enjoyed would crumble.

Arty Checker had given them hope; she couldn't deny it.

After two or three miles they reached a broad expanse where I-25 met up with the Platte River. It was there that their luck ran out.

They quickly crossed the trade corridor that had turned sharply eastward, and scurried down a sandy embankment making for the safety of the river which lay better than a half mile distant on the far side of the old highway. After blindly following a trail through the tall snarled brush that grew in abundance on the broad floodplain, they emerged into a clearing beneath the elevated highway. Instantly and without warning they were besieged from all sides by a band of brigands; the kind Keetna had feared they might encounter along the river. It was the first time in her short and violent life Keetna wished she had Hadrian Tharp fighting at her side.

Eight in all, their common identity was made evident by the dark red headbands they wore. Beyond that, any thread of similarity ended. Seven men whose skin colors ranged from white to brown to black, and a single fair-skinned woman; a tall, blue-eyed beauty lightly clad in denim shorts and a crude leather top cut low enough to expose the redness above her nipples. Two wild turkey feathers stuck up from the back of her headband. Long locks of matted red hair swished back and forth across her shoulders and breasts as they swarmed toward Silas and Keetna from behind the stout concrete pillars supporting the road above.

Their camp must have been close by. They'd heard Silas and Keetna crashing through the brush and quickly set up an ambush, hoping for some easy booty. But however they'd come upon these unfortunate circumstances, Silas realized, their fate now depended on what they did in the next few seconds.

Keetna nocked an arrow and drew it to her chin; Silas withdrew his sharpened machete. Without a word they stood back to back, turning together in a slow circle. The male warriors, some serious and focused, others leering like hungry hyenas, flowed into a bigger circle around them. All but one of the men were armed with edged weapons: three with knives, one with a scimitar-like sword that Silas might've thought funny under different circumstances, one with a steel-tipped spear, and another, the smallest of the lot, stood with a crossbow resting against his belly. The last one carried a roughly woven net that dragged the ground behind him. He looked like trouble.

This was obviously not the band's first such encounter. They moved like individual cells in a single fluid organism, maintaining a safe distance from Silas and Keetna while awaiting orders from the Amazon, who stood apart from the men with her arms crossed over her bosom. A large hunting knife gleamed in her belt. A bemused smile curved her lips as the standoff developed. Silas could feel Keetna's hatred for this woman flow from her like heat from a raging bonfire. Will she try to kill her first, or will she go for one of the others? Hopefully neither. Over his shoulder he whispered, "Maybe we can talk our way out of this."

"Don't think so," came the reply.

"We won't know till we try. Maybe if we—"

"What do you have to trade for your lives?" the Amazon asked. Her voice was strong and authoritative, but also sensuous. Small wonder she had so much control over these desperate men.

"Nothing *your* kind would find of value," Keetna growled defiantly. She and Silas continued their slow back-to-back dance in the sand.

Cruel laughter erupted in the Amazon's throat. "My, you are a pissy little thing, aren't you?"

"Yeah, that's me," Keetna agreed. "Pissy. But at least I don't need the services of seven foul-smelling girly men to keep me satisfied."

Good one, Keetna, Silas thought. *You've managed to insult all eight of them at once. That's got to be helpful.*

Hoping frantically to work some sort of deal, Silas said, "Listen; I've got something in my pack; a document. A very valuable document. You could trade it for anything you ever—"

"Document?" she barked. "I have no use for paper!"

No, probably not, Silas realized, *but it was worth a shot.*

"Kill him," commanded the Amazon. Then she laughed. "And capture her. She'll make a nice plaything for you foul-smelling girly men."

When the men's faces lit up with lewd grins Keetna sent her arrow into the mouth of the small man with the crossbow. He dropped like a stone with the arrow's fletching sticking from his mouth like the backside of a small bird. The crossbow discharged as it hit the ground. The bolt sped past Silas on a low trajectory and, with a loud rending of cartilage and bone, lodged in the kneecap of the hairy man wielding the spear. He squealed like a pig as he fell over on his side.

With considerable urgency Keetna said," Its crunch time, Silas." He was still staring in disbelief at the man Keetna had killed, but quickly put it out of his mind and swung his machete at the man with scimitar, opening up a deep gash in the man's arm from the top of the wrist to the elbow. Blood ran through his fingers as the dark-skinned man dropped his weapon and grasped his arm.

That was the good news. The bad news was that the Amazon and net thrower had Keetna pinned to ground. It left Silas all alone to deal with three knife-wielding men focused on the task of covering his body with holes and gashes.

No time to lament. He plunged through them, spinning and swinging his machete wildly before emerging on the other side. The butterflies in his stomach had departed, carrying away his fear. He felt strangely calm and luminous now, and his adversaries sensed it. As he advanced they retreated. He laughed vengefully and charged them again.

Silas The Warrior.

What irony. He had never been in a hand-to-hand fight, not even during the War of the Turning, and he was enjoying himself...

"Tharp!" Keetna screamed. She was still striking out at her captors like a netted leopard, but somehow she'd seen him.

Silas dared a quick glance along the line where the gnarly bushes gave way to the sand and saw Tharp and Erasmus's two goliaths running toward them from the west, perhaps a hundred and fifty yards away. Bobby hobbled painfully behind. In the far distance he saw a large dune buggy with a small cargo area in back, parked behind an impassable field of debris strewn across the broad floodplain.

The oversize mutie ran in front. It's ears were laid back flat against its massive head as it ran swiftly and silently in a sort of stalking crouch that belied its unnatural height. Silas tried and failed to swallow the dry lump in his throat.

"Run, Silas!" Keetna hollered, "You can't help me anymore!" Considering the odds, he was inclined to agree with her. But he couldn't bring himself to leave her. His opponents backed away and braced themselves for what they rightly perceived to be the fight of their lives. The Amazon and the net thrower did the same.

"Run, Silas! Please run," Keetna pleaded.

"But Keetna, I can't just—"

"Listen to me! He'll use me as bait to get to you!"

"But—"

"If he has you, he doesn't need me. So run, damn you, run!"

He ran.

*   *   *   *

The mutie reached them first. It went to work with cold efficiency, throwing itself on the Amazon as she tried to flee. It knocked her to the ground, raking its dual fangs down her face and arms as she struggled to defend herself.

"How's it feel, bitch?" Keetna said from under the net.

Unfortunately, the dog's assault was short-lived. A large shirtless man with bulging muscles threw himself on the beast and plunged his knife into the creature's shoulder. The only noticeable effect was to draw the monster's wrath away from the woman and toward himself. He screamed as the animal chewed and clawed past his outstretched arms to find his throat. The shrieks ended abruptly.

The beast rose, hobbled on three legs for a moment, then plopped down next to the body of its victim. There it sat, panting and lapping at the blood pooling in the sand. Peaceful as a tired hound back from the hunt.

Keetna struggled to free herself from the net as the first shots whizzed by overhead, but was pushed sharply back to the ground by the Amazon. Blood flowed from the gashes on her face and arms, but they weren't deep enough to bleed her out. She pushed her face next to Keetna's and hissed, "Your man is about to die."

"And you think you aren't?" Keetna retorted.

Shooting her a hard glance, the Amazon snatched up a spear off the ground and trotted swiftly away in the direction Silas had fled.

Keetna managed to untangle herself from the net only seconds before Tharp arrived on the scene. Seeing the firepower concentrated against her, she didn't even attempt to put up a fight. He yanked her roughly to her feet while the two goliaths ran after the four remaining men.

If they were hoping to reach the safety of the river, their plans were quickly thwarted. The vault guards quickly ran them down and dispatched them with automatic weapons. The man with the crossbow bolt in his knee tried to crawl unnoticed into the tall weeds but Tharp caught the motion from the corner of his eye and casually gave him a three-round burst in the back.

Keetna knew the type of ammo Hadrian used. The man died instantly without a whimper. When she objected to the executions, Tharp replied, "You shouldn't be getting sanctimonious, little girl. It doesn't fit you. They've been after this bunch for months; there's been a lot of bloodletting on this end of town."

"Not anymore," Keetna observed, thinking it would've been better if they'd died armed and facing their killers. "Glad we could be so helpful in bringing them to justice."

"Not everyone deserves a warrior's death," Tharp countered, not knowing how close Keetna had come to slitting his throat while he lay unconscious in the bloodstained dirt of Endow.

"No. I suppose not."

He grimaced as he smiled and droplets of blood seeped from the wound Keetna had given him. "Where's your boyfriend?" he asked, squeezing her arm with a vice-like grip. "He's carrying something I want."

"Long gone."

"Well, you'd better hope Corona doesn't catch up with him."

"That *thing* has a name?"

Amused, Tharp said, "Why? Are you jealous?"

Bobby finally closed the distance just as Tharp finished tying her hands behind her back. Concerned for Silas's welfare, she prompted, "Hurry it up, Tharp. Silas in trouble."

He finished quickly and whistled to the guards, pointing in the direction the Amazon had disappeared into the brush. Bobby bent over to catch his breath as the four others took off running.

*   *   *   *

Silas ran in the soft sand, weaving through the massive supports under the useless old highway until the unyielding foliage to his right gave way to tall grasses that swayed in the breeze and glinted sunlight in waves soft and inviting. He ran even faster when gunfire erupted at the scene of the battle, until his legs felt like rubber bands and his chest heaved.

Even then he only slowed, trusting that even the briefest respite would replenish his screaming muscles with enough energy to continue on. Because there was no other choice: it was run, or be captured. And then it would be the end of Keetna, a woman in whose debt he would forever remain. Carlos's game meant nothing to him now. All that mattered was Keetna. If it took his last breath, he would find her and set her free.

After a mile or more, when the flat terrain gave way to rolling hills and tall slender saplings shot up from the earth in ever-greater abundance, he heard the sound of footfalls behind him, louder and louder, soon to overtake him. Could it be Keetna? Was there any chance she'd gotten away? He quickened his pace before he dared to look behind him, and what he saw took his breath away.

It was the Amazon, tall and athletic running toward him with a litheness and speed he could never hope to match. Her natural beauty had been sundered with blood and her composure replaced with an animalistic rage that haunted her features with a hard indelicacy. And still she ran with the grace of a gazelle.

He admired her in a way that brought him great sorrow, because he knew he would have to kill her.

She clutched a spear in one hand, a knife the other. Silas carried his machete; its empty scabbard flapped wildly at his side. In a desperate gambit he slowed almost imperceptibly, allowing her to close the gap more quickly. He glanced back every few seconds to gauge her progress, taking the straightest route he could find through the forest of small trees. He intended to provide her with an unimpeded path to launch her spear at his back. He hoped she threw it quickly, before his legs and his lungs failed him.

He heard a low growl issuing from the back of her throat and turned in time to see a glimmer of sunlight reflecting off the double-barbed spearhead speeding toward him. He reflexively jumped to one side, stumbling slightly as he did, and felt the spear sizzle past his shoulder. It flew for another twenty yards where it plunged deeply into the grassy earth. The Amazon let loose a scream of frustration. Silas had hoped to grab the spear as he ran past but, she was too close and the spear's angle too slight for a quick and easy grab. He ran past it.

Thankfully, so did she, running now with only the knife in an overhand grasp, preparing to stab him in the back.

Silas slowed, listening to her ragged breathing (not easy to do over his own ragged breathing) and the rapidity of her footfalls, willing himself to trust his ears as the small gap between them narrowed.

When he thought she was but a few feet behind him he lifted the machete's handle to his chest, planted his feet, and spun to face her. Her eyes widened in fear and she instinctively threw her hands in front of her but it was too late; she could do nothing to slow her momentum in time to save herself. Her body met the tip of the blade with such force it knocked Silas over backward. She came down on top of him and they both rolled in the grass another half circle until they came to rest, Silas on top. The machete had pinned both her hands, palms out, tightly to her chest.

Her eyes still held life and her mouth moved as if to speak, but only a few crimson bubbles escaped. He watched quietly until all motion in her face and chest ceased and the dullness of death settled upon her once-striking eyes; he touched her fiery hair and felt the soft, sensuous skin of her fiercely beautiful face. He felt a great sorrow for this spirited woman, but before it could engulf him, he ran.

As fast and as far as he could.

*   *   *   *

Keetna gazed coldly into Corona's filmy dead eyes, but didn't feel the satisfaction she thought she would. Was Silas's maddening humanity rubbing off on her? The rusty machete remained buried in her chest, but Corona's knife was nowhere to be found. At least he had a weapon.

"Where's he headed?" Tharp asked as goliaths one and two dragged the fallen Corona off by the heels.

Drawing her attention away from the morose but anticlimactic scene, she said, "Nothing would please me more than to lie to you, Hadrian, but I honestly don't know."

She expected an outburst. Instead, he shrugged. "Doesn't matter. We both know where he'll end up."

"Where's that?" she asked with little interest.

"Purgatory. Just like you, little girl. It's time to meet the wicked witch of the west."

38

Silas Breaks Through

How was it that so many viators came into possession of their powers at the time of the Turning? Some suggest genetics is involved and perhaps they are right. But if so, it is something found in all human genes, something that has lain nearly dormant for centuries, if not millennia, and was awakened only in the first part of the twenty-first century. But why now? This is another question altogether, and a more difficult one. Human history is not a tale of steady progress. It is replete with long periods of stagnation accentuated by sudden leaps forward. The invention of farming. The domestication of animals. The discovery of light-concentrating optics and the realization that the Earth circles the sun. The full-scale utilization of fossil fuels. With each of these advances came a restructuring of our perceptions of the world and our place in it. Consciousness itself evolves to embrace each new paradigm.

What then can we say of the sudden appearance of viators? Only that it was time for consciousness to take the next bold step forward.

FROM THE UNPUBLISHED MEMOIRS OF CARLOS HERRERA

Silas drew his blanket round him as he sat cross-legged in the tall prairie grass. A cool wintry breeze blew down from the high country and he shivered against it, but the crickets still serenaded him and the stars overhead embraced him with twinkling light from a billion billion worlds.

He hadn't bothered to seek shelter, as there was none to be found. He was far out on the eastern plains, miles away from Purgatory and the tortured, crumpled, uplifted terrain that preceded the towering Rockies. There was not so much as a tree to sit under or knoll to back himself into. Nor was there any human habitation of any kind, and for that he was thankful. He'd had enough of humans for one day.

How do people live like this? he wondered. *How can they scratch the ground for food each day, as if the ability to obtain sustenance were an arcane art? And then kill one another over perceptions of wealth, or territory, or power, when the Earth is more than willing to look after all the needs of everyone who cares about it?*

He missed Keetna terribly. The thought of her as Tharp's captive churned sharply in his gut. She was too free a spirit to be bound or caged; it must be driving her crazy. But then he reminded himself that she was a warrior, willing to concede a battle or two as long as the war was eventually won.

The war.

The insidious covert little war between the heirs of Carlos Herrera and the woman who would presume to be the next Messiah, if only she could work one miracle. *The* miracle. The biggest, shiniest miracle the world had ever seen.

How would she do it, if she suddenly found herself with the power to stave off Tar Baby's virulence? Simply handing over the genetic blueprint for the anterium to the local energy company would hardly do. She would guard her secret jealously and reveal it only under a veil of mystery. It would require a demonstration with a theatrical flair—a theological flair—to make the masses believe her ability to re-enable the pumping of oil was given to her by God, rather than the same gang of scientists that had brought about the Turning in the first place.

It would be a hard sell, but if anyone could pull it off, she could. After all, she'd had twenty years to think about it. To obsess over it. To salivate at the prospect of finally finishing the job she was born to do.

In the envelope in his backpack there was indeed a thick, technically written document labeled "COTO 2.82 Anterium Protocol" that Silas hoped would spell ruination for all of Salia's carefully laid plans. Imagine the witch's embarrassment when her great miracle, the bombshell of the ages, turns out to be a hoax.

Boy, will she be pissed.

He tried to laugh coldly into the endless night sky, but his chest was as tender as an open wound and badly bruised where the machete's hilt had been driven against his breastbone.

This brought on a disturbing thought:

An act of divine benevolence is hardly what Salia has in mind, he realized.

She has no intention of giving oil back to the world as a shining token of her godliness and her goodwill toward men, women, small children and dogs. She's going to keep it for herself; herself and those foolish enough to follow her. It's not a miracle she's after, it's a theocracy.

Of course! How naïve could he be? All her preaching about the end days was not just fanciful biblical rhetoric, it was the literal truth. Why would she give anything back to the same people who had branded her an outlaw and proclaimed her ministry a cult? Salia was nothing if not vengeful and God help us all if she gets her hands on the means to make war. Suddenly the stakes rose exponentially.

Silas shivered.

He tried to put it out of his mind, succeeding only after giving in to the deep longing he felt to contact Jennifer. After so many days without hearing his sister's voice, intoned with the affection that had been the sustenance of his soul for seventeen long years, he could hardly wait.

Could he still access the same realms he'd become so familiar with during his infirmity? Things had changed so quickly. Before he could hardly stop his mind from wandering beyond the body. But now, after so many days of intense physical activity, he felt like he *was* the body. And, like a jealous mistress, the flesh had a way of drawing focus back to itself when it felt it was being ignored. From the body's point of view, it was folly to expend energy for non-body pursuits. Even now, Silas could feel the needs of the flesh tugging at him, demanding warmth and nutrients and making it clear that wherever the spirit wished to soar the body would try to pull it back.

But there were places he'd discovered during his long convalescence; portals through which energy could be drawn to replace the energy the ever-myopic body feared it might lose. These were dangerous places, certainly; not the kinds of places where you'd want to belly up to the bar and drink night after night, because in the end energy borrowed was energy owed. And if the debt turned out to be too large when the tab was called due?

Nature, it was rightly said, hates a vacuum. So the real trick was to make sure the energy ended up right back where it started from. If you take nothing, you're beholden to nothing. But that was always easier said than done because it was so damned difficult to be humble and remember where your power is *really* coming from when you feel like you've got the whole world by the short hairs. History was full of examples of uncannily powerful people suffering irreparable meltdowns for exactly that reason, and he was hoping to assist Salia Warchez in joining their ranks. *Sorry, old girl, but you've been puffed up just a little too long.*

Jennifer, however, was the first order of business. And, with a little luck, Cassie. Would Salia be eavesdropping? Most certainly; he was counting on it.

He breathed deep and cleared his mind, willing his body to believe it was sleeping, for it would be far less demanding while in a state of rest, and less likely to oversee his activities. And yet he wouldn't be dreaming. A dream, after all, was really just a short trip the body lets the soul take with a rope around its ankle. And for tonight's business a rope simply wouldn't do.

He sat straight-backed with his hands in his lap and stared beyond the backside of the infinite night sky. He stared as if trying to look beyond a veil designed by the gods to disguise the true nature of their creations. He looked on unblinking and unthinking until at last a hole opened in space and the sky and all that it contained gradually vanished as if all that his eyes formerly beheld was no more than a photograph; a photograph that had suddenly caught fire in the middle and burned to the edges until there was nothing left.

And then he called to his sister in a voice he feared he might've lost; a voice that was, he quickly discovered, stronger than at any time during his seventeen-year convalescence. Quickly he was transported on the harmonic of one soul seeking another. Like a magnet seeking iron with conscious intent.

The feeling built slowly, like the warmth of the winter sun, then:

"Silas? Is that you Silas?"

"Hello, Jennifer."

"Are you safe, Silas?"

"Yes. You needn't worry."

The greeting was said in an instant without the distraction of words. And then they found themselves together without the allurements of sight or sound. It was an exchange with neither precedent nor explanation in the science of the old world, but one that would have brought a knowing smile to the lips of a certain ex-scientist of the new world, now sleeping peacefully beside Jennifer. (*So she has finally found love*, he sighed.)

One by one, he sought those in his fleeting domain who he knew and loved and feared:

Tay...Primm...Jennifer...Jack...Luke...Cassie...Catalyn...Keetna

and in a turbulent sea of possibilities and probabilities there came swirling to the surface a certitude concerning them all, a knowing expressed as a passion, incapable of deceit. Sitting under a firmament that had disappeared, for a time, into the great totality of everything, he knew where each of these souls stood in the present incarnation of the world they shared.

Then, from the swirling void,

a darkness

(cloying)

a lust

(insatiable)

a hunger, red and raw, and savage with need.

Her.

"Hello, Salia," he sent to her, his casualness belying the intensity of his feelings.

The fiery breath of her soul surged past him like a hurricane of crimson embers. *Silas Teague!* the winds roared, *You have taken what is mine and I want it back!* These were words, distinct passionate words, sullying a realm where words were not meant to be heard. But how? He suddenly felt himself gripped with fear in a place where fear *(like words)* was not supposed to be. It was the voice of a tortured being who had drawn deeply from the darkness, and was drawing deeply still. When there should be nothing left to draw, but somehow was. It chilled his soul.

She feels this, he knew with an icy certainly. *She revels in her seizure of this peaceful plane.*

Confirming his fears, she cooed a soft susurration. *"So return it, will you please?"*

He hesitated. How was it pos—

"Because I am ME, you foolish little man. Who do you think you're dealing with, Dorothy from Kansas?"

This was going terribly, terribly wrong. The breadth of her remarkable talent was exceeded only by the vehemence with which she fed it. How could he ever hope prevail in the face of such overwhelming power?

From the void came an answer: *"We can beat her Silas, I know we can. Hurry home. I love you."* It was Cassie, ringing true and clear through the dense staticky fog of Salia Warchez's domineering presence.

"*And I love you, Cassie,*" Silas replied warmly. He braced himself for a vociferous barrage of venomous insults that never came.

Salia murmured only, *"Touching,"* before falling inexplicably silent. The witch had been rendered mute by the love of a child.

It made no sense.

But it was no less comforting for it.

And there appeared before him then a path that forked left and right, and just like in the old riddle pondered so often by schoolboys, he knew that one fork led to life, the other to death. And a great many things of importance depended on which fork he took.

His soul breathed deeply of the life-giving ether and he murmured, *"Go back to Hell, Salia. You bore me."*

"You'll see her die," Salia hissed like a serpent that had just been stepped on, *"you'll see them all die."* And then she was gone.

Silas awoke cold and trembling and completely exhausted. Had he chosen the wrong fork? Should he have tried instead to placate her? He refused to believe it.

But he quickly rose and resumed his eastward journey as fast as his weary legs would carry him. With a little luck, he could be back in Purgatory before the next sunset. Many lives depended on it.

39

Into the Denver Island

The so-called urban islands were created by the military for a single purpose: to preserve the pre-Turning "American way of life." Toward that end, artificial cities were created and populated with bright healthy men and women who possessed the knowledge and skills needed to re-establish the societal conditions under which, it was naively assumed, people were "meant" to live. But no one ever stopped to consider that a society of specialists is vulnerable to the same maladies that made the War of the Turning an unthinkable catastrophe, rather than a difficult but natural adjustment to a radically altered set of conditions ...

FROM THE UNPUBLISHED MEMOIRS OF CARLOS HERRERA

As the first rays of daylight stole across the eastern plains, Silas caught a glimpse of the outlying structures demarcating the perimeter of the Denver island. Houses, he thought, casting long shadows stretching far to the west as the solar panels mounted on roofs and porches awaited the energy they required to fulfill their purpose; some to gather heat for water, others to gather light to be converted into electricity in a process he didn't understand and was of no mind to ponder.

When he'd begun crossing the outermost fields surrounding the islands in the middle of the night he could see even in the scant starlight that the houses were all laid out in a concentric pattern, the same as all the island's structures.

Here and there were barns with small efficient dwellings beside them, and machinery from a bygone age, retooled, no doubt, to run on the synthetic fuels produced from vegetation grown in the very fields through which he walked; fields that had already given up this year's bounty to a meager population that was nonetheless hungry for food and ravenous for fuel.

In some fields the stubble had been plowed under, but in others—corn fields in particular—cattle grazed on the stubble and other detritus not gathered during harvest by the giant machines. The cattle, he presumed, were to be harvested later.

As the sun crept higher in the clear cool sky, he was able to make out more details of the island. A single highway bore straight through the middle of the urban center now looming before him. Train tracks paralleled the wide thoroughfare, and on either side of the civilian transportation corridor wide gravel side roads supported a variety of military conveyances.

Even from this distance—which he judged to be a mile or more to the closest gate—he discerned a degree of efficiency and tidiness unknown in the town of Purgatory. It seemed that the two places were separated by nearly two centuries, but even then it was a small disparity when compared to the feudal Dark Ages that defined Old Denver.

Of the three (and conceding that he had not yet ventured inside the island), he far preferred the friendly easy comfort of Purgatory, where both food and fuel were blessings to be consumed sparingly and reverently.

There was no actual wall around the island, just a wide swath of earth from which sprouted low narrow-bladed grasses. On the perimeter of this verdant demarcation ran an interwoven electric fence, tall enough that it could not be breached by even the most energetic deer or high-jumping human, yet light enough that it could be easily moved outward and expanded as the population of the island inevitably grew and new habitations were required.

Perhaps the absence of a wall meant that the Denver island was still growing, though there must be a point beyond which all islands would no longer be allowed to expand. He imagined that when that point was reached a new island would be formed some distance away at a scientifically predetermined location along one of the protected corridors that linked all the islands. It would be erected under the supervision of the military and with the expertise of pioneers—either volunteers or draftees—from this and other islands. Thus would all islands have a precise carrying capacity determined by the men and women who studied the patterns of commerce and human interactions with far more precision and tenacity than Silas cared to ponder.

He trundled onto a side road that ran at an angle to the main corridor and followed it up to a gate at the southwestern corner, one gate removed from the main gate where security appeared more active.

He was greeted by a tall well-built young man who appeared to have been born without a sense of humor. "State your name, your trade and your business," he instructed in a monotone he might have learned by studying the canned messages that used to drone through airport loudspeakers.

"My name is Silas Teague and I have no trade," Silas answered, "but my business is with Sturm Baker, the head of Desa, and I have traveled on foot all the way from Purgatory to speak with him." This last part was a lie, but the junior commando didn't need to know that.

The guard—Sergeant Heiner, according to the shiny brass nameplate pinned to his crisply pressed gray uniform—raised an eyebrow, creasing an otherwise smooth forehead beneath the brim of a carefully placed gray cap, and replied, "You have an appointment, I presume?"

Quickly losing his patience with Sergeant Heiner's mechanical adherence to a protocol hardwired into his brain from an early age, Silas said, "No, Sergeant *Heiner,* I don't have a fucking appointment. If I did have one I wouldn't have blisters all over my feet and I would probably have arrived by some mode of transportation that came into general use after the end of the Stone Age. As it is, I'm tired, hungry and thirsty and the matter I wish to discuss with Secretary Baker is orders of magnitude more important than you could possibly imagine in your limited capacity as border guard. *Comprende?*"

With a searing scowl, Sergeant Heiner stepped into his small booth and punched a few numbers into the handset of a cordless telephone while Silas paced back and forth. After a moment the young guard asked Silas again what his name was, then nodded curtly to no one after relaying the information to the person on the receiving end of the conversation.

With somewhat less emotion than a department store mannequin, Sergeant Heiner handed Silas a one-day pass and instructed him to wear it in plain sight at all times. He pinned the green plastic-laminated pass to his coat—there was no date printed on the pass, making Silas suspect that each day was a different color, a scheme that would allow the passes to be efficiently reused countless times—and asked how to get to the Desa offices.

"All government offices are at the center of town," Sergeant Heiner instructed, in a way calculated to make Silas feel like a fool for his outlander's ignorance. "I trust you can find your way?"

Silas looked him up and down, managing to hold back the comments rumbling in his throat. He signed the register (the first time he had signed his name in over seventeen years, he realized, after seeing how tenuous his signature appeared on the page) and walked away. Behind him Sergeant Heiner said, "Have a nice day, Mr. Teague," using a tone meant to let Silas know that, in his professional opinion, outlanders occupied a point in the food chain somewhere between slime mold and cockroaches.

Without turning around, Silas raised an arm and gave him the bird over his shoulder. Unlike his penmanship, his sign-language skills had not suffered.

He walked down a perfectly level sidewalk beside a wide paved street that led straight as an arrow into the heart of the town for a mile or more before terminating at a large block of buildings that must have been at least a half mile across. The side streets, in conformance to the general circularity of the place, were all curved, forming ever-smaller blocks of houses as he neared the town's center. Thus a side street on the outer edges of town might have twenty or more houses, while the number diminished to only four or five as he worked his way inward. Pedestrians walking with quick, efficient gates, helmeted bicyclists, and small electric cars were everywhere evident.

Most of the homes were of the Southwest style, of the kind formerly seen in the sprawling suburbs of Santa Fe or Albuquerque, the difference being that in these island homes adobe was used as an actual building material rather than a stylish façade for a wood-frame house. Judging by the breadth of the window sills, the walls of these houses were better than a foot thick, built to retain heat in winter and repel it summer, when large overhanging eaves kept the sun from directly falling on heavily-glazed south-facing walls. Solar-electric and solar hot-water panels were ubiquitous. As far as Silas could tell, allowing his limited knowledge of such things *(I've been away for a while, after all),* the panels were designed not to simply cover the roof, but to *be* the roof.

Variations in home architecture were mostly cosmetic, since the theme of a long and narrow east-west axis seemed to have been mandated by the city's planners. All houses were canted south for optimal exposure to the sun, leaving every house at a slightly greater or lesser angle to the street than its neighbors, a variability that was somehow eye-pleasing despite its predictability.

Another curious aspect of the island's residential district was the lack of lawns or tall trees around the houses. In their stead, exquisitely detailed rock gardens were built around low-lying shrubs, while trimmed hedges demarcated property lines. Yet spaced throughout were small parks with fish ponds where tall trees grew in abundance and soft grass could be felt underfoot, and these too were smartly landscaped.

At first blush, the place was idyllic. But it was also creepy. It resembled in most of its particulars the great utopian dream so often alluded to; an ideal the human mind couldn't seem to let go of, despite the fact that every utopian society ever attempted had failed utterly.

He had to remind himself that those who lived here did so voluntarily—just like the people in Old Denver. And Purgatory. At least until some day in the future when a well-meaning group of political and scientific elites met behind closed doors with an eager military to decree that everyone should be *made* to live in the islands.

For their own damn good, of course.

A shiver spread across his skin like ice water.

Perhaps it was the people themselves that made the island so disturbing. Everyone he saw regarded him—even without the laminated green pass on his torn coat, his ragged clothing, soiled face and uncombed hair marked him as an outlander—with the same curious but pervasive arrogance he'd first seen in Sergeant Heiner. As if anyone too stupid to not live in an island was certainly not worthy of respect.

It was as if life in the island had for these people become the alpha and omega of existence; the ultimate purpose of life, their smug expressions told him, was to live under the protective covenants of the island. Which, of course, was no purpose at all.

I'll bet they're all a riot at cocktail parties.

He was awakened from his ruminations when a vintage black Hummer coming from the direction of town pulled up to the curb and stopped beside him. Even though it had been a few years, he recognized the driver as Sturm Baker, a man whose merry-but-calculating expression could never be hidden by age. Sturm had always been a complex person hobbled by his own goodness, a quality that often got in the way of his clandestine pursuits.

It was hard to be a greedy bastard when, to your dismay, you discovered you actually cared about the people you were screwing. Still, it didn't stop him.

The electric window on the passenger side rolled down and Baker said, "Teague? Is that really you, Silas?" His smile was 24-karat and Silas couldn't help but smile back. They'd never really been close; Silas was only seven-teen the last time they saw each other—a kid, in other words—and Sturm a man well in his twenties. But these days heritage could be almost as thick as blood, and one Purgatory native finding another on the streets of the Denver island had to be a rare occasion.

"Hello, Sturm."

The leather of the extra-wide seat groaned in protest as Baker reached across and opened the door from the inside. Silas removed his backpack and dropped it on the plushly carpeted floorboard before stepping in to take his first good look at Baker in nearly two decades. He'd put on more weight, of course, and a little gray was beginning to sprout above his ears, but beyond that the years had treated him well. He was dressed casually in jeans and a heavy button-down shirt, and his proportionately small feet were clad in hiking boots of the style fashionable before the Turning. Sturm rolled the window back up and immediately the bass-like drumming of the biodies-el-fueled engine quieted to a soft, rhythmic beat. Sturm held out a beefy hand and Silas shook it. "Good to see you, boy! When did you...uh, well—"

"Snap out of it?"

Sturm laughed, and the capillaries on his nose and face glowed red. "Yeah. Snap out of it." Sturm had always been a lousy liar—probably because lying conflicted with his continually tested sense of right and wrong—and Silas knew in a flash that Baker had already been told, probably by Primm, that his mind had mended. Still, the subterfuge didn't offend him. Baker was who he was, and as long as Silas could sort the wheat from the chaff it was the same as talking to someone incapable of lying.

The front half of the Hummer was immaculate. Everything shined with a showroom brightness Silas thought amazing, considering that Hummers had been out of production since before the Turning. This was in sharp contrast to the backseat and cargo area, where sheaves of printed paper, discarded bags, and food wrappers lay haphazardly in a chaotic jumble.

Sinking down into the soft leather seat made him realize just how bone-tired he was. Wearily he answered, "A week ago, maybe. It's hard to say, Sturm. I've sort of lost track of time."

Baker looked him up and down and offered a sympathetic smile. He said, "I hate to be the one to tell you, Silas, but Jesus Christ, boy, you look like you've just walked out of a shit-slinging festival. If that bonehead Heiner hadn't gotten hold of me I doubt he'd have let you in."

Hearing this, Silas looked at himself as someone else might and he was aghast at what he saw. The blood on his hands and coat sleeves and jeans (probably from the Amazon, or the mutie Keetna had killed, or maybe even the turkey he'd dismembered) was bad enough, but every inch of exposed flesh was dark and gritty and covered with small cuts and scrapes. Worst of all, he suspected that he might have begun to smell more than a little ripe. "Yeah, I see what you mean," he said, almost by way of apology.

Baker made a U-turn in the nearly empty road and headed back into the heart of town, driving with his thick wrist laid casually over the top the steering wheel. Silas couldn't help but notice the expensive watch he wore. "What the fuck?" Baker shrugged with a who-gives-a-shit smile, "I'm sure there's a good story behind it."

"And it's a long one, I'm afraid," Silas confirmed. "Suffice it to say I have to get to Purgatory, and fast." He looked all around at the passing scenery as he talked, his curiosity about this place unaffected by the sense of urgency he felt.

Single-family homes had given way to row upon row of two-story apartment buildings, constructed with the same attention to solar exposure as the houses. Silas wondered if this was where the "newbies" ended up, wannabe islanders who were as yet unable—either by decree or personal finances—to move into their own personal dwelling.

"Good timing," Baker told him, shaking him out of his ruminations. "I was just getting ready to head up there myself. Another thirty minutes and you'd have missed me."

"Business or pleasure?" Silas asked.

"Business. Seems my sheriff has gone missing."

"Pity," Silas said, not feeling like it was his business to tell Sturm he'd heard through the ethereal grapevine his sheriff was dead.

Baker laughed in the deep, rumbling, jolly way fat people laugh. "Don't much care for him, do you? I don't either, to tell you the truth. The man's a prick, and a strange one at that, but, well..."

"He does his job?"

"Exactly," Baker replied, not caring to defend Prygor Primm any more than he had to. "But I don't suppose that's the reason you're in such a hurry to get home, is it?"

"Let's just say it's family business," he answered without elaborating, even though he felt a temptation to tell him that Salia Warchez was there waiting. It'd certainly light a fire under his ass. Hell, Sturm would do back flips at the prospect of nabbing the slippery sorceress, but he would call in the Army and the Marines to do it, an action that would end up making matters worse than they already were.

But Baker was no fool. He narrowed his eyes and peered across the seat at Silas, saying, "Does your family business have anything to do with my missing sheriff?"

"Possibly." When he looked back at Baker and saw that his brevity had begun to annoy the Desa chief, he added, "It's complicated, Sturm. More complicated than you could ever imagine."

Baker felt a rough edge and he seized it. He raised an eyebrow and drew his mouth into tight knot. It gave his face an officious cast that made Silas uneasy. "Maybe we should go talk it over with someone in enforcement," Baker suggested.

Silas sensed he was on a fishing expedition with no intention of carrying out his threat. But he wasn't willing to bet his life on it. Nor the lives of everyone he loved and cared about. "Look, Sturm; I'll tell you everything you want to know," he lied, "but not to enforcement, and not now. There are things that need to be taken care of as quietly as possible. And I can't do it without your help."

Still testing the waters, Sturm said, "Why not?"

"Why?" Silas bellowed, determined to get his point across. "Because I'm a hundred miles away from where I need to be in a day and age where hitchhiking is about as pointless as fishing in a fucking bathtub. I need a ride, pure and simple, because if I have to walk back it's going to be too goddamned late."

Baker was persistent. Calmly he replied, "Sounds like you're going to need more help than I can give you, Silas. Maybe if we could just talk with some—"

"No!" Silas insisted. He took a deep breath and used the time to gather his thoughts. Baker was angling for something, feeling Silas out to see just how desperate he was to get back to Purgatory. It was a game only one of them could afford to play, and they both knew it. Playing it cool didn't work, and neither did desperation. What was left? Stupid question. It was the one thing that always tempted Baker. "I quite honestly don't have the time, Sturm. I'm sure you understand. But if you could get me up there today I'm sure Jennifer and I could reward your timely assistance by making a sizeable contribution to Desa. To help fund the valuable work your office is doing, of course."

Keeping his eyes on the road, Baker's chubby face worked into a curious smile. He said, "Bullshit, but keep talking."

Though it pained him to do it, Silas leaned across the seat and whispered seductively, "Diamonds, Sturm. The hardest currency on earth."

Baker turned and the surprise Silas expected to see writ large upon his face simply wasn't there. It was more a look of relief. And joy. He slapped Silas on the thigh and said, "Well, hell! Why didn't you say so in the first place, boy? Let's get out of this hive of mindless conformity and head back to God's country."

"Glad we got *that* straight," Silas murmured under his breath.

"Yeah, me too," Baker agreed, apparently willing to let the particulars of their gentlemen's agreement hang in the wings for the time being. It gave Silas a chance to relax and think things through.

As they drove into the downtown area the geometry of the island changed abruptly. The straight boulevard that had been like a spoke on a wheel ran headlong into the hub—a wide circular loop that circumnavigated the tall, straight structures rising from the center of the Denver island. Baker turned left across light traffic, thus avoiding the busy business corridor that ran through the exact center of downtown.

Like the houses, there was a disturbing sameness to these buildings as well. They were uniformly ugly. But at least it was ugliness with a purpose, as each successive row of buildings was a few stories higher as they proceeded from south to north, so that all the buildings of fifteen or twenty stories were in the extreme north end of the downtown area. The purpose of this arrangement was made obvious by the photovoltaic cladding on the sides of every building, beginning, he would bet, on each one at the point where the light of the winter sun would fall above the shadow of the shorter building in front of it.

"Is sunlight the sole source of power here?" Silas asked, naively.

"Sure," Baker sneered, "along with the nuclear reactor outside of town."

"Sounds a bit excessive," Silas said. He took one last look over his shoulder as the Hummer cruised out of downtown and passed into the northern residential district. "Not that I know anything about it."

"Fuel is the biggest issue," Baker explained, as if he had some knowledge of these matters. "That and power for manufacturing. You can string together solar panels until the cows come ambling home, but you'll still be a long ways from any process that can melt steel by the ton or turn acres of weeds into pools of diesel fuel. For that you need heat, and a hell of a lot of it. And nothing creates heat like a nuclear reaction. That's why all the manufacturing and fuel processing facilities are set up around the nuke—it's the most efficient way to do it."

"The dark side of paradise," Silas commented without emotion.

"Yes, well, it's really not as bad as it sounds. This is a new-generation nuke, designed to run for centuries on nuclear wastes from the old nukes. Basically, the more energy they produce, the less radioactive mess there is left to deal with."

"You sound like a spokesman for the nuclear industry," Silas told him.

Baker laughed. It reminded Silas of why he liked the man, in spite of the subterfuge and double dealing he was famous for. Because Baker was a likeable guy. It was no more complicated than that.

They avoided the main cross-country corridor and left the island through the northwest gate. The guard there might have been Sergeant Heiner's twin brother, except that the neatly trimmed hair beneath his cap was brown instead of blonde. He smiled at Baker and waved him through, giving Silas a what-the-fuck-did-the-cat-drag-in look as they drove by.

Striving for consistency, Silas flipped him off too.

✦𝓓

Brother Lyman

In the War of the Turning it was often the case that the enemy would employ the tactic we least expected...

FROM THE UNPUBLISHED MEMOIRS OF CARLOS HERRERA

The rich soil rolled like a solitary wave on a sea of dirt against the sharp shin of Lyman Moran's wood-beam plow. Guided behind his sure-footed mule Henry, the single iron share sliced cleanly through the moist ground and turned the chaff and the stubble of this year's wheat crop back into the Good Earth. There were streaks of black in the brown freshly turned soil, and as always, they reminded Lyman of his mother's and father's ashes.

Mixed in with the ashes, he recalled, had been bits of bone. Ash and bone. No dust to speak of; not a single grain. It made him wonder what in the world the preacher had been talking about when he spoke of "ashes to ashes, dust to dust."

The dust was easy enough to savvy, since man was created from dust. It said so in Genesis: "for dust thou art, and unto dust shalt thou return." That was clear enough. And yet when it came time to scatter the remains of his good mother—and more recently his father—on this very field where they'd slaved and sweated and prayed and sworn at the weather as if it were a god unto itself (albeit one you could call names without being struck dead or cursed, though lately he was having his doubts about his fragile sense of impunity in that regard), there had been no dust. Only ashes. And those little pieces of burnt bone.

Reverend Warley, the lukewarm Presbyterian preacher who had presided over both his parents' small memorial services, had it all wrong: it should have been "dust to ashes, ashes to dust." That way it squared with what the Lord had said in the Great Book and what he knew to be true, and the rest of it wasn't worth a drop of piss in a tin cup, as his dad would say, though never when his mother was within earshot.

At least his father had seen fit to commit Lyman's younger brother's body to the ground one year after the end of the Turning, when poor Kip had drowned (or been drowned, as some had said). But then his father had decided his own body should be burned the same way Lyman's mother's body was burned back in '19 when the dead piled up so fast there'd been no time to bury them. Eight in ten of Purgatory's own had died in that horrific war, and most of those in the prime of their child-producing years. In the cities he'd heard it as high as nineteen in twenty. Or worse.

And now both of Lyman's parents were so much ash in the field and would have no bodies to rise up when they were called by the Lord Jesus when the *real* end days arrived. Only Kip, whose body lay intact and well preserved below ground, would be able to breathe air again and fight beside him when the forces of Light met head-on with the forces of Darkness in a pitched battle the likes of which the world had never seen. It would all take place on the plains of Armageddon—the place some called Megiddo—and once the dust settled, the devil would be banished from the Good Earth for all time to come. Praise Lord Jesus.

But that was a ways off. For now he'd bide his time and avoid dealings with unbelievers as much as possible. It was an often difficult proposition, now that the State—the great whore as was spoken of in the Great Book— had branded him and his brethren in the True Faith enemies of the New Republic.

He tugged on the reins and hollered "Whoa!" at Henry. The sweaty old mule didn't need to be told twice. He stopped in his tracks and gave a satisfied snort of hot snotty air as Lyman relaxed the reins. He removed his straw hat with a gloved hand and wiped the sweat off his brow with a dusty sleeve. As he did he caught movement out the corner of his eye and heard the distant bang of the screen door against the jamb.

It was Ellie, his wife of fifteen years (*thank you, Lord Jesus*) and the only woman Lyman had ever known, in the biblical sense. He felt a little tug at his heart, the one he always felt whenever he saw her in the distance. It was like the joyful rejoining of two kindred souls unaccustomed to long separation, though he'd woken up beside her just three hours ago.

Strapped over her shoulder was a gunny bag filled with water; in her hand she carried an apple. *Always the temptress*, he thought with gentle amusement.

"It's a warm one, Lyman," she said with a coy smile. "Might be you'd want a break from your toil? We could pack a little lunch and head down to the creek—maybe have ourselves a little respite under that big cotton-wood?" Her hazel eyes flashed conspiratorially, but Lyman wasn't ready to quit just yet.

He took the gunny bag and drank greedily, then exchanged it for the apple. "It's a good day for work, Ellie," he answered. "A day made for plowing." The apple was sweet and crisp. Fresh off the tree. Cool juice oozed from the corners of his mouth and mingled with the gritty sweat clinging to his face and neck.

Ellie's expression hardened in a playful way. She said, "That's fatuous, Lyman. The day's not made for anything except what you make of it. We had a good crop this year, and got it in early. And you're mostly done with setting the stubble back to the earth. Can't imagine the Lord would mind if you gave poor Henry the day off and enjoyed a little time in the shade with your dutiful wife. While she's still young and desirable."

Fatuous? Ellie loved her words, though she rarely flaunted them in his face like that. Only when she really wanted something. The woman didn't ask for much, but when her mind was set, arguing only postponed the inevitable. If Ellie wanted her time at the creek then, by the angels, she'd have it.

The clouds were plump and white, and the sky as clear blue as a young boy's daydream. The slight breeze across his bare skin was enough to cool him, despite the day's heat. And Ellie, standing before him behind a blanket, was as vibrant as a rose in spring. She smiled alluringly and let the blanket fall just enough to expose one soft, shapely breast. The sight of her filled Lyman with desire. He pulled her to the ground and cast the blanket aside. It was indeed a perfect day.

For a while, anyway.

"Greetings, brother," came the voice, as if carried on a breeze from the Promised Land. Then a disarming chuckle. "I see that you are naked in the wilderness."

They were at that. Having dozed off after their lovemaking, they hadn't thought to cover themselves. But quickly Ellie pulled the blanket up around herself while Lyman stood on his knees and stared in fascination, his manhood dangling between his stout, hairy legs.

"For Heaven's sake, Lyman! Cover yourself!" Ellie prodded in a whisper so loud it surely must have been heard from the far side of the creek where *she* stood.

Oh, and he knew it was *her*.

"Lyman!"

Ellie's cry was distant; removed from the moment in the same way a dream was removed from the mind of the waking. Lyman stood and stumbled into the creek, paying no heed to the slippery stones underfoot or the icy water that rose to just past his knees.

She was clad in white, a radiant gown draped modestly around her. Just as he dreamed *she* would be. And he knew the time had finally come.

She waded into the creek and moved effortlessly toward him as if her feet were gliding on smooth flat ground, and immediately his legs were no longer cold. Her smile was that of an angel and when she reached out and touched his forehead he shuddered in ecstasy at the feel of her flesh against his. He cried for more when she removed her hand and fixed her gaze upon the far shore.

"My God, Lyman!! What is she doing to you?" he heard a woman shriek from somewhere in the back of his mind. He wondered if it was Ellie.

"Cover yourself, Lyman," *she* commanded in a voice Lyman had heard calling his soul for many years, and one he prayed he would someday day hear with his own ears. "You're nakedness won't do."

Eager to obey, he turned quickly and splashed his way shoreward. Ellie grabbed him when he reached the sandy beach and held his head, forcing him to look at her. He did not understand the alarm on her face. He smiled and said, "She's here, Ellie! Really here! Isn't it wonderful?" But Ellie didn't think it was wonderful; didn't understand at all the momentousness of this occasion. He watched as her alarm quickly turned to scorn and for the first time in his life he saw how hellishly ugly his wife really was. How was it that he hadn't noticed before that her eyes held a demon's glow, or that her teeth were all yellow and chipped? How could he have ever married a woman like this? He could see now that Ellie had bewitched him all those years ago, and bewitched he'd remained until now. Until *she* arrived to free him from his wife's dark sorcery.

He pushed her away in revulsion and began dressing himself, unmindful of his wet skin or the sand that clung to his feet and ankles. The ugly Ellie glared hatefully at him from the place where she'd fallen, but rose quickly when *she* stepped onto the near shore. Rising on rickety legs showing a sickening network of varicose veins, Ellie attacked her with taloned hands.

In the midst of stepping into a pant leg, Lyman threw himself clumsily into Ellie's path and nearly fell over, but his gallantry was unnecessary. Ellie froze in her tracks far short of Lyman and fell back onto the beach, gasping for breath and clutching her bare bosom. Not wishing to gaze any more upon Ellie's frightful visage, Lyman turned his back to finish dressing.

It was then he felt a piece of his captive mind break free and reach desperately for Ellie. *She* caught it and pulled it back, saying, "Forget her, my dear. She was never the woman you thought she was."

She pierced him with her sea-blue eyes and he knew he was *hers*, body, mind and soul. He would never see his wife Ellie again, of that he was certain. And for the briefest moment a sadness washed over him too painful ponder.

But it quickly vanished.

"Ready?" *she* said tenderly.

He answered, "Yes, I'm ready."

Ready to die for Salia Warchez.

* * * *

"You spineless little worm!" Keetna screamed from a back room of the farmhouse where she lay on the rough wood floor with her wrists and feet bound. "I spared your miserable life, you gutless prick!"

The place was a first-class dump. Nails were popping up from the splintery floor and in places the joists below had given way, making the simple act of walking from room to room a dangerous proposition. Nor was the rest of the house any better. The old water-stained wallboard had fallen off the ceiling and walls in great chunks, exposing wood studs white with dry rot and gaps in the lap siding wide enough to peek through. The only room in the house that was livable was *her* room—the witch's room—and Bobby was scared half to death to even walk past it. It seemed to glow with its own light, warm and inviting, but the one time he'd tried to step inside he was repelled by a blast of air *(it wasn't air; it was something else altogether)* so cold he shuddered, even though the day was hot as Hades—way too hot for this time of year—and getting hotter.

And now he stood in the kitchen, wishing there was a cold beer or two in the empty old refrigerator, trying to ignore the wildcat in the back room. But it wasn't that easy. She was right. The girl would certainly be a more loyal ally than Tharp, and if it were only Tharp he had to deal with he might take his chances and turn her loose. But Tharp was teamed up with the black-haired witch-woman, and not for love or money would he cross *her*.

"Look, I'm sorry, all right?" Bobby moaned. "If I let you go she'll have my guts for garters." A pause. "And anyway, my shoulder's throbbing where you shot me and my leg still hurts from that snare you set in the trail along the river." The last part was added as further justification for not having the courage to do the right thing, and it did nothing to assuage his conscience.

A rueful little laugh. "Then you're screwed, *Bobby*, because whatever that witch can do to you, I can do worse."

Without daring to look at her, Bobby pleaded, "Jesus! Gimme a break, will you? I didn't ask for any of this, you know! All I've ever done is grow corn and potatoes and a little pot, and sometimes run contraband on the side. And for that everyone and his fucking pet ferret is threatening to kill me. Hell, maybe I should just kill myself and save you all a lot of trouble."

"Good idea," Keetna agreed. "Just make sure you untie me first."

"Piss off." Bobby slammed the door and stomped outside.

*   *   *   *

"I can feel it coming," Catalyn said with that eerie certainty that always presaged a powerful meteorological event. Luke looked up at her from across the kitchen table and wove his fingers into hers. He loved his wife with an intensity he couldn't comprehend, and he knew he would until the day he died. But sometimes she scared him shitless.

"What's coming, Cat?" he asked, not really wanting to hear the answer.

"A snowstorm," she said, "and it feels like a big one."

"In September? When it's ninety degrees?"

Catalyn shrugged and Luke replied, "How about you cancel it for a week or two? There's a lot of stuff going on, what with the world coming to an end and all, and I just don't know if we can fit a blizzard into our schedule."

Catalyn leaned across the table and gave him a peck on the lips. "I married a smartass," she said affectionately.

"It's not like you didn't know what you were getting into," Luke countered, giving his wife a smile and a wink.

"It's good to see you smile again, darling," she told him.

"Feels good, too."

"Gonna be all right, now?" she asked with gentle concern.

Luke nodded. "Oh, yeah. The more I replay the whole thing in my mind the more I'm sure if I'd waited two more seconds Primm would've killed Jack and maybe even Jennifer. So, if I *hadn't* shot the crazy bastard I'd surely be sitting here *wishing* I had."

Smiling, Catalyn extended both hands, palms up, and said, "Your logic is inescapable, my dear."

"So are my clutches," he said playfully, grabbing her outstretched hands tightly and pulling her across the table. It was an ill-conceived maneuver that sent the salt and pepper shakers rolling off the edge of the table and upset the vase of freshly cut marigolds, but she didn't seem to care and he dragged her into his arms and smothered her with kisses.

"My, my, my. You *are* feeling better." she cooed, melting into his embrace.

"Where's Cassie?"

"With Jack and Jennifer," she whispered in his ear. "I think they're all down at Tay's place."

"That's all I need to know." Luke picked her up easily in his strong arms and carried her through the arched doorway leading into the earthen bedroom, where the ceiling and walls were rounded and roughly plastered and it was easy to imagine they were in a magical grotto built by gnomes in an enchanted forest.

And for a time they completely forgot about Salia Warchez and the COTO 2.82 anterium protocol, and even the blizzard Catalyn felt whistling in her bones. They enjoyed each other with an intensity known only to lovers living on the gleaming edge of fate.

* * * *

"I cannot predict what this woman will do because I do not know how she thinks," Tay told them, pacing briskly back and forth in front of his house without the aid of a cane, "but I can tell you that whatever she does, *Hadriano* will precede her. It is the way he does things." He walked with only a trace of a limp. Every now and then he grabbed his boot and pulled his foot backward almost to the middle of his back, as if to assure himself he would be limber enough for the action they all knew was coming. His recovery had been nothing short of miraculous, a development for which Jennifer was thankful, since she knew that Tay's good health was directly connected to everyone else's.

"Do you think Tharp will try anything...before Silas gets here, I mean?" Jennifer asked, trying not to appear to be wringing her hands quite as intensely as she was. The only thing she hated more than violence was waiting for it to happen. The thought of it sent her heart into the pit of her stomach and brought a weakness to her knees that only made her feel more helpless than she already did. It was a nervous reaction she hoped would disappear once the inevitable confrontation got underway.

"I think we can count on it," Tay said matter-of-factly. "The more confusion he can create, the easier it will be for them." A breeze was kicking up, as usually happened on unseasonably hot days, and it brought down a rain of dried cottonwood leaves from the towering trees east of Tay's house. He seemed not to notice as he continued to pace, head lowered and fingers mindlessly caressing the hilt of his knife.

Jack rose from his seat beside Jennifer and leaned against a porch support, looking so perfectly nonchalant that Jennifer couldn't help but smile. Tay had provided him with a black-handled boot knife and a large revolver which he wore, like Tay, under his left arm in a leather shoulder holster. Wearing nothing but jeans and T-shirts, Jack and Tay looked like a pair of hit men on a country outing.

"Maybe we should take the battle to her, instead of waiting for her to come to us," Jack suggested.

Bad idea, Jennifer thought. She stood and stepped out beyond the porch overhang, squinting momentarily in the bright sunlight. The playful breeze tousled her hair about her face and she pulled a few strands away from her mouth before saying, "I don't think so, Jack. We don't even know where she is, who's with her, or what direction she plans to come from. All we know for sure"—*allowing that last night's get-together with Silas and Salia was not a colossal shared illusion*—"is that she believes Silas has the anterium protocol and that she intends to take it and kill us all. The question is: how? Without knowing that, we could walk right into a trap."

Tay considered this for a moment before saying with a cunning smile, "Then perhaps we should make a stand somewhere less confusing; a place more defensible than this one. There's no need to make things easy for them."

Jennifer started to object. "But Silas—"

Tay held up a large scarred hand and said, "Preparing to go is not the same thing as going, *muchacha*. We will wait for your brother, I promise. If you say he will be here today, I believe you. But he had better hurry. I am beginning to feel that we will soon be out of time."

* * * *

Sturm Baker knew several ways to get to Purgatory on the old unmaintained roads that crisscrossed the countryside beyond the protection of the military, which concentrated its presence close to the island. He could take the straight and rough route, which would put them in Purgatory in under two hours, or a roundabout and smooth one, which might add another hour to the journey. Or he could mix it up and split the difference.

Today he was choosing straight and rough, which meant potholes and eroded shoulders and deep ruts in places where drainage had been compromised over years of neglect. He didn't like stressing his Hummer—parts were getting harder and harder to come by—but he was feeling rushed by the thought of easy wealth.

Diamonds! My God, it's true! Even now he could see them glittering before his eyes.

He turned to Silas, and asked in that friendly tone that came so easy him, "I really hate to ask, Silas, but what the hell were you doing out there in the middle of nowhere?"

Silas had been dozing. He opened his eyes and looked around to get his bearings before saying, "Just taking a little vacation, Sturm, that's all."

His backpack rested loosely in his lap and something interesting caught Sturm's eye through the partially opened flap. Something in an important-looking button & string envelope. There was no writing that he could see, and he dared not gawk too long else Teague might notice, so he looked hard at Silas and laughed. "Must've had a hell of a good time."

"Yeah, it was a real riot," Silas answered flatly, his head beginning to bob.

"Kill anyone I know?" he couldn't resist asking.

His head snapped up and Silas said crossly, "Drop it, will you, Sturm? I wasn't breaking any laws, if that's what you're after."

"Sorry," he said disarmingly, "I didn't mean to pry."

Not yet, anyway.

Again Silas began to nod off and Baker reassessed his strategy. He'd take the smoother roundabout roads, at least for a while. Silas needed his rest, after all.

Every End Has a Beginning

In battle, harm comes quickly to the unprepared, quicker still to the unwilling...

FROM THE UNPUBLISHED MEMOIRS OF CARLOS HERRERA

Bobby sat on the steps of the old farmhouse, enjoying the radiant warmth of the midday sun and thinking he should put the gag back in the wild-cat's mouth. But he wasn't quite able to bring himself to do it. For one thing, it would be unbearable to listen to her insults for the short time it would take to force open her mouth and stuff a rag in it. And for another...well, he kind of liked her. Not that it would do him much good when he pleaded his case in hell.

Let her scream, he finally decided. *It's not like anyone is around to hear her. Maybe she'll wear herself out and go to sleep*, but he doubted he could get that lucky.

He was just biting off a piece of rope tobacco when he saw a cloud of dust arising in the south.

He stood and took a few steps away from the house to get a better look at the fast-moving vehicle, even though Tharp had specifically told him not to even stick his head outside, much less stand in plain sight and gawk at passing cars. It slowed down as it passed, causing Bobby to instinctively shrink back toward the house. But there was no time to get back inside so he stood there like a painted target and watched as a dusty black Hummer rumbled by, gravel crunching loudly under its truck-sized tires.

The driver didn't look familiar, but the passenger certainly did. It was that Silas guy, Silas Teague. Tharp would want to know about this. Then he laughed at himself. How the hell was he supposed to tell him? The jeep was still on the side of the road outside of Endow with two flat tires and Tharp was off in the dune buggy he'd borrowed from Arty Checker.

That left Bobby all alone with no way in hell of letting Tharp know Teague was back in town. And why should he, anyway? He wasn't even supposed to stick his nose outside.

He walked back up the crumbling concrete steps to the ratty old house. Maybe he could find a bottle of booze in the cupboard.

*   *   *   *

Baker saw Silas begin to stir just after they passed the broken-down farmhouse Tharp leased from him. Baker didn't recognize the low-life standing out in front of the place, but he had the unsavory look of someone working for Tharp. He suddenly sensed a conflict of interest. Not to mention the possibility of serious danger to life and limb.

He shook Silas awake and said, "Hey Teague, what do you know about a man named Hadrian Tharp?"

Silas opened one bleary eye and said, "He's a ruthless bastard."

"What else?" Baker pressed.

Silas sat up and looked around. "Jesus! Did I sleep the whole way?" he exclaimed.

"Yeah," Baker confirmed. "What of it? Tell me about Tharp."

"I need to get home."

"Yeah, yeah. You'll get there," Baker told him. He was quickly growing impatient. And maybe even a little worried. Again he asked, "You were going to tell me about Tharp?"

"Don't know shit about the man," Silas answered, "except that he's trouble."

"Nothing to do with the particular trouble you're in?"

"Who said I was in any trouble?" Silas answered defensively. "Just take me home, okay?"

Baker leaned over him. "Tharp?"

"What's the big deal, Sturm?" Silas asked. "Did we run over him while I was asleep or something?"

Why was the man so worried about Tharp all of a sudden? It made no sense. The mystery became acute when Baker said, "Was he the one chasing you?" An uncustomary nervousness had crept into his voice.

"What if he was?" Silas asked, for no other reason than to gauge Baker's reaction.

For an instant the big man's face blanched white, but quickly regained its natural ruddy hue. "No reason," he said. "Just curious, that's all."

"Bullshit," Silas countered.

"Let's talk about the diamonds, shall we?" Baker said, his meaty cheeks unnaturally bunched by the upturned corners of his mouth as he tried a smile that didn't quite work.

"Let's get me home first."

They drove through Purgatory in silence, Baker slowing the big rig down appreciably as the lonely old highway turned into Main Street. It was the first time Silas had seen his hometown in seventeen years and he looked quickly around to see what had changed while at the same time wishing Baker would kick it up a notch or two.

On cursory inspection, it looked peaceful; that was the biggest change. No barricades in the street. No defensive ramparts hastily thrown together from the rubble of collapsed buildings. No smoldering ruins. Purgatory was clean.

But maybe not quite as peaceful as it seemed. There were few people on the street, but those he saw stopped in their tracks and gawked as the big Hummer rolled by. Others watched furtively through cracks in drawn shades. Suspicion. Fear. Or both.

Baker didn't seem to notice. Something else had him spooked. Suddenly Silas's growing sense of urgency blossomed into full-blown apprehension. "Punch it, Sturm. I don't want to be late for lunch."

Baker punched it.

*   *   *   *

Lyman watched the Hummer drive by. Silently, he raised an arm, hailing to the brethren to let it pass, and the seven men lowered their weapons— varmint rifles mostly, along with small-bore handguns and a high-powered hunting rifle or two thrown in the mix. The one *she* sought was in the vehicle. Silas Teague. Lyman didn't know how he knew this, but he did. Most likely The Lord had seen fit to make things known to him as His hour of triumph grew near, but Lyman could see no reason to ponder it further. A gift was a gift, not a question or a riddle.

They trotted their steeds along the creek trail in single file, Lyman leading the way. He rode his plow mule Henry, a surefooted beast but a bit stubborn under saddle; it was a malady Lyman corrected from time to time with a willow switch. To remind the dimwitted beast of his rightful place.

He turned in the saddle and looked behind him. Formerly God's sheep, gentle in manner and soft in judgment, the brethren had become hard and ready to strike at their enemies without mercy. As *she* had commanded them, each in his turn.

God's wolves.

Suddenly

(*Ellie! Oh, poor Ellie! Dear God, what have I done!*)

The feeling tore through his soul like spinning shrapnel. Oh, God, the pain!

(*Lyman, my dear, she was a betrayer, a temptress scheming to keep us apart. It's better that you think of her no more.*)

As quickly as it had befallen him, the feeling faded into the depths of time. He heeled the mule in the flanks and proceeded down the narrow path along the creek named after the one who should not be named, and as he did he felt new strength flow back into him.

He was made strong by his pain, righteous by his loss, and noble by his dedication to—

"*Hijos de Putas!!*" came the shrill scream of the whore who galloped through their midst like a demon on fire. She rode tight to the saddle, her devil-black hair streaming behind her like the fluttering cape of a witch gone mad. She spit in Lyman's face as she stole past the brethren, finding an opening among them where none had been, and rode toward the conspirators' lair.

Lyman gave the order and a volley of shots rang out. The whore slumped in the saddle but did not slow.

* * * *

Sturm Baker's Hummer pulled into the drive just as Carmen's horse came galloping through the trees east of Tay's house.

Thick clots of lather clung to mare's breast and shoulders, and glistening beads of sweat dripped down its legs and over its hooves. Tay ran to Carmen and pulled her from the horse as the winded steed shook its head and blew phlegm from its nose in a hot sticky spray.

She was still alive but the look of death was upon her; she had only moments of life left in her. He laid her on her back, resting her head on his leg while he gently caressed her face. Blood gushed from several wounds from her shoulders to her buttocks, and dripped ominously from the corner of her mouth. "Carmen?" Tay ask gently, "who did this to you?"

"*Chacareros,*" she replied weakly. Farmers.

Car doors opened and shut behind him. Many voices talking quickly. Tay paid them no mind.

"Who, Carmen? Who was it? Give me a name."

She shivered. "*Lyman...Moran, y seis...o siete...mas.*"

Lyman Moran? The farmer? It made no sense, at least not to Tay. But he was certain it made perfect sense to Salia Warchez. It was a thought that troubled him deeply.

"*Tengo...mucho frio...Tayito. Y miedo.*" I am very cold and afraid.

"I know," he whispered softly, cradling her head against his body in hopes of giving her some small comfort in her last minute of life. "You are very brave, *mi vida,* and I love you."

She smiled adoringly and craned her head to look into his eyes, a move that caused her great pain. "*De veras?*" she whispered.

Have I never said that to her before? "Yes," he told her again, "*Yo te quiero, mi vida,* and I will always love you." The words were so simple. Why had he waited until now to say them?

He bit his lip to hold back the tears, then let out a ragged breath and kissed her one last time. Again she shivered; a short and violent convulsion as she blew her last breath into his lungs. She was dead. An inconsolable sadness fell over him as he closed her sightless eyes. He tasted her warm blood on his lips and knew it would take many lives to pay for this one.

Jennifer appeared behind him and gently touched his shoulder as he sat motionless, still holding Carmen's lifeless body next to his. "Is she...?"

"Yes," was all he could utter.

"Tay, I...I'm so sorry."

"Better that you pity the ones who did this," he answered coldly.

"Tay?" he heard Jennifer say, as if from far away, "you have to know that they are almost certainly not acting under their own volition. Sturm and Silas saw them from the road. They told us who they were and I know none of those men would 've done this were it not for Salia."

"In that case," he said, "you should pity them even more."

Tay carried Carmen's body into the house and lay her on the bed in the side bedroom. When he came back out, Jennifer saw a hardness in his eyes that sent waves of fear rippling through her body.

"Tay," she said, "we have to leave this place. We have to—"

"I know," he answered stonily. "You should go through the lacuna, to the other side, where they cannot easily follow. There are guns there, remember?" His hands and face were smeared with Carmen's blood, and huge splotches of it had soaked into his T-shirt and jeans.

"Yes, I know where the guns are. At least I think I do." They had hidden them there years ago when Desa began nosing around Purgatory, reasoning that a large cache of military armaments would certainly appear seditious, should they be discovered. "But guns aren't enough. We need *you*, Tay. Please come with us?"

He shook his head only slightly. "I have other things to do." He looked at her then, but it was not the Tay she had known all her life; he had become cold and fearsome. "There are vehicles in the shop. Take them and go quickly."

She grabbed his arm, hoping against hope to change his mind. "Please, Tay?" she pleaded. "Don't do this."

Tay gently removed her hand and turned away. Without another word, he pulled himself onto Carmen's horse and disappeared into the trees.

"Where the hell is he going?" Jack asked, running up behind her.

She said, "To his death, I would imagine," and felt a tear tumble down her cheek.

Jack spun her around and shook her lightly until she met his gaze. "Jennifer? Sweetheart? It's time to go. We have to trust that Tay can take care of himself."

She nodded and followed Jack when he took her hand and pulled her toward the Hummer where Sturm Baker stood by the open driver's-side door with one foot resting on the running board. He was clearly impatient to leave.

Silas stood on the other side of the oversized SUV. Cassie hugged him tight around the waist while the two men engaged in a brisk and heated conversation.

Hand in hand, Luke and Catalyn approached from the west. Even with the surprise at seeing Sturm Baker etched on their faces, they looked very much like two young lovers out for an afternoon stroll. They had just reached the corner of Tay's house when the shop building exploded behind them.

* * * *

Tay heard the explosion and saw the huge fireball erupt from the ridge above the creek trail where he waited for the men who had killed Carmen. *Hadriano*, he thought with no emotion.

Probably a bomb on a timer set during the night. He would be long gone by now so there was no point in looking for him. But what of the others? How would they get to the lacuna with all the vehicles on fire or in ruins?

He turned back west just as eight mounted men rounded the corner a hundred and fifty feet below him.

To the west he saw heavy clouds churning over the high mountains and in his mind he saw a more interesting fate for these men than the one he had been planning.

* * * *

The explosion threw debris more than a hundred feet in the air. Part of that debris came from Jack's pickup, which had been parked beside the shop with a power cord plugged into the battery bank. Sections of the metal building and its contents rained down around them and the shockwave knocked everyone off their feet; everyone but Baker who was protected by the Hummer and his considerable mass.

"Shit!" Jack screamed, seeing the burning the wreckage that had until five seconds ago been his only form of transportation. "That was the best damn truck I ever owned!"

In the midst of the chaos, Baker jumped quickly into his vehicle and slammed the door with every intention of making a quick getaway.

It was something Jack couldn't allow. He pulled himself to his feet, wobbled for just a moment, then drew his pistol and ran to the Hummer as Baker attempted to turn around and head back out. When he saw Jack his face lit brightly with fear but he didn't stop. Instead, he cranked the wheel and gunned the engine, sending gravel flying in Jack's face as he attempted to spin the unwieldy SUV into position to make a quick exit.

He only stopped when Jack fired two shots through the back window.

Baker hit the brakes and held his hands over his head as if he'd been nabbed in a Desa sting operation. Under different circumstances, it would've been comical. As it was, Jack was just thankful he'd stopped, because he doubted he could've killed the man and taken his vehicle if he'd hit the accelerator instead of the brakes.

"Put your hands down, you sniveling coward," Jack told him. "We just want a ride, that's all. Seems that you now have the only roadworthy vehicle in town."

Visibly shaken, Baker stepped out of the vehicle and said, "Sure. Just a second." He opened the back door on the driver's side and began throwing piles of papers and debris over the seat into the cargo area. All except for a half-inch-thick sheaf of papers he shoved under driver's seat.

"What the fuck are you doing?" Jack said tersely.

"Uh, just making room, that's all," came the nervous reply.

Jack barked, "Who gives a damn about your stupid trash? C'mon everybody, pile in."

They did, and quickly. Jack and Jazzman rode shotgun while the others, including Sasha, fit comfortably into the extra-wide backseat. Baker started to object when the big dog jumped in beside him, but held his tongue when Jazzman curled his lips. Once the doors were shut and Luke gave a thumbs-up from the backseat, Jack commanded, "To the lacuna, and step on it."

Baker stepped on it.

42

Salia's Orchestra

I struggle with the thought of the pain I may someday cause those I love, because I possess the COTO anterium protocol. When I worry about what will happen if they should be caught with it I can nearly resolve myself to destroying it. But then I wonder if it might not worse if they were caught without it...

FROM THE UNPUBLISHED MEMOIRS OF CARLOS HERRERA

It began as a tingle in the back of his head, so slight it was barely notice-able. He told himself it was a nerve zinger, the kind of errant synaptic impulse that plagues anyone whose neck is slightly out of place, as Jack's neck easily could've been after being knocked down by the shockwave from the explosion. So he forgot about it.

He stroked Jazzman's broad head and the dog repaid his attention with a wet tongue across his cheek. "Thanks, furball," he said, elbowing the big dog in the ribs. It earned a chuckle from Cassie, but no one else. Certainly not from Baker who stared straight ahead and mumbled nervously to him-self as his motorized anachronism lurched and bounded over the mile and a half of Martian terrain separating the lacuna from the old county road.

Jack flipped open the cylinder on the nine-millimeter revolver and pulled out the two spent casings which he replaced with live rounds. That left six in the gun and ten more in the leather pockets sewn into the front strap of the shoulder holster. More than enough to get them to the weapons cache, con-sidering all the bad guys were downstream and not even in sight yet.

"What are you so worried about?" he needled Baker. "No one's trying to kill *you*."

"Don't be so sure," he replied without expression. "You've gone and stirred up a hornets' nest and dragged me right into the middle of it."

"You'll be compensated," Silas said from the backseat, "just like we discussed."

"Diamonds aren't much use to a dead man," Baker replied.

"You worry too much," Jack told him, rubbing the back of his own neck as the subdural tingling crept slowly toward the front of his head.

*   *   *   *

"How's it feel, knowing you'll be dead by this time tomorrow?" Keetna asked Tharp. He was just finishing up the chore of tying her hands and feet to one of the two seats mounted over the engine in the back of the dune buggy.

Tharp grinned and the dried scab across his face released tiny droplets of fresh blood that clung to the wound. "You're pretty cocky for someone in your predicament," he told her.

"I'm just being inquisitive," Keetna replied. "Cocky is for pecker-bearing brutes like you, clinging to the lower limbs on the tree of life."

Bobby let out a chuckle but quickly stifled it when Tharp jumped in the driver's seat and growled, "Can it, shithead. And make sure your girlfriend keeps her mouth shut on the way through town."

Bobby slunk into the passenger seat and looked back at Keetna with dark pleading eyes.

She caught his gaze from over her shoulder and smiled pleasantly. What the hell; it was never too late to make a new friend.

*   *   *   *

Confusion. As any warlord will tell you, it's the best way to defeat an enemy. Make him react to every feigned attack and he will be in complete disarray when the real one comes from a completely different direction.

Salia loved creating confusion. It was one of her special talents.

What would Jack Vara think if he knew that he had doomed his friends and set Salia up to be the world's undisputed religious and political authority, just by innocently accompanying his wife to one of Salia's orations a year and a half ago? Oh, and he would know before the end. That much she could promise.

Deborah Vara had been such an easy mark. Salia knew right away she was not a woman happy living in her husband's shadow, always pretending to be the dutiful wife of the esteemed scientist, as if the mere act of sharing a bed with someone would impart to her the same meaning in her life that he found in his.

Whether she knew it or not, Deborah was looking when Salia sought her out; looking for something, anything, to give her her own identity, her own sense of self-worth. To be part of something truly important.

Deborah didn't have a clue who Salia was when they first met in the park. Had she, she would've been overwhelmed by an encounter with someone of Salia's notoriety. So Salia became what Deborah needed most that day: a friend; someone met on a serendipitous meeting between two attractive young women, both looking for an identity in the faceless, sterile environment of the East Bay island.

The point of the meeting—the only face to face meeting between the two under Salia's carefully crafted pretenses—wasn't to enlist or indoctrinate, but to gather information about Deborah and, more importantly, her husband—the long-lost son of Carlos Herrera.

And to plant a seed.

A seed that would grow inside Deborah's head, day by day, sleeping and waking, attuning her consciousness to Salia's guidance. And allowing Salia access to the things she needed to know about Jack Vara; things so private she would never knowingly share them with anyone.

After that, all that remained was to engage Jack Vara eye to eye, as she had that day when she manipulated the crowd to assure Jack and Deborah a front-row position at the gathering in the flowery meadow outside the island.

That was Salia Warchez's greatest gift as the world's preeminent viator: to be able to touch anyone's mind just by gazing into their eyes. But not just to touch, but to leave a small piece of herself behind. Nothing physical, of course, but a living, growing fragment nonetheless; a bit of Salia that would forever guarantee a person's loyalty and obedience.

How it all worked she couldn't say. She had learned long ago not to question the miraculous too much, lest the miraculous should begin to question her. All she knew was this: that she could "feel" a seed of her consciousness enter into another's mind and take root. It was a lot like a girl getting knocked up, without the wet sweaty pleasure of sex. The difference was that in this case the baby would never be born.

Lyman Moran and his compatriots were all men she had seen before, and she had left within each of them a seed. She'd done this many years ago, before the fascist military deemed her a threat and had begun their feeble attempts to hunt her down.

Her alluring melodies had been soughing through the heads of the men in Lyman's loyal band for a very long time. And like they say of a fine wine, the longer it's allowed to age, the more pleasing it is to the palate.

But what of Jack Vara? Had he "aged" sufficiently?

She felt certain he had.

This was going to be fun.

*   *   *   *

Once he saw from his high vantage point that no one had been killed or injured in the explosion, Tay breathed easier, if only a little. The oversight had been his mistake, just like it was his mistake to send Carmen to town when she had wanted to stay, and for no better reason than he wanted some time away from her.

Well, he had his time now—an eternity of it.

He felt like his soul had turned to ash. He was not fighting a normal foe and he should have realized that fact long before now. The Warchez woman was resourceful beyond any adversary he had ever faced, both in her cunning and in the weapons she held in her arsenal—weapons of the mind any military would wage all-out war to possess.

And he knew in the pit of his stomach that she was saving her best weapons for last. He swore to himself that when he got his chance to kill her, he would not tarry. It was little consolation, really, but it was something. Something to hold onto; something to live for.

As for the farm-boy warriors in Salia Warchez's little crusade, his thinking had softened. Jennifer was right: they were not in control of their own simple minds. He would watch them closely and kill them only as they needed killing. Not that it mattered in the long run. They were all doomed.

Dispassionately, he watched what was happening down below in the aftermath of the explosion:

Baker trying to drive away.

Jack firing two shots through the back window.

Baker stopping.

Everyone piling into the Hummer.

Baker driving off.

He was satisfied all was as well as it could be, for now. A few minutes later, the crusaders arrived at his house and rode on through toward the lacuna without even pausing to inspect the damage caused by the blast. As if it was of no interest to them. He thought it peculiar that they should be riding so slowly, considering that Carmen had ridden through their ranks with every intention of delivering a warning. What were they doing? Why didn't they follow quickly on her tail and catch them all unawares? Why plod along and waste the chance to end the battle before it even started?

Then it hit him. It was not their purpose to engage the enemy. These men weren't fighters, they were herders.

* * * *

"I don't know what you did to piss those guys off," Baker harangued from the perceived safety of the driver's seat, "but whatever the fuck's going on, it's not my problem." They all stood beside the Hummer near the ledge leading to the backside of the Lacuna. Baker's meaty face was flushed and his nervous eyes darted back and forth, looking for a sympathetic smile or nod and having no luck at all. Even Cassie crossed her arms and glared at him with her eyes narrowed and her lower lip stuck out.

He's hiding something. And he's afraid that if he doesn't leave quickly we'll find out what it is. Could Silas have told him about the anterium protocol? A quickly exchanged glance with her brother told Jennifer he was as confused as she was.

"C'mon, Baker, what do you suppose we did to make eight simple sodbusters dust off their deer rifles and take after us?" Jack asked, leaning against the top of the Hummer with his arm slightly crooked and his revolver dangling in Baker's face. "You think maybe last night we got all liquored up and cut a swath through rural Purgatory, burning crops, killing livestock, and raping women?" Jack leaned in to look Baker in the eye. "Man, you're crazy as a shithouse rat if you think that mindless band of hayseeds is going to let you cruise right on by."

Jack laid it down hard, and Baker stared at him for a long moment, unbelieving, until finally he said under his breath, "I'll take my chances."

Jack laughed. Jennifer thought it a cruel laugh. "Be my guest," he said, removing his arm and extending it in a mock gesture of capitulation.

A cloud of doubt had crept across Baker's face. For a moment he stammered, then looked in all their faces one last time. It was a look of pity. "Good luck," he murmured.

He veered north in hopes of avoiding Salia's posse. The tires squealed on the smooth rock as eight diesel pistons hammered out the dirge of his retreat.

Jennifer sucked in a breath as the brethren crested the ridge to the east, and she grasped Jack's arm in anticipation of what was to come. The arm was hard and cold, and a chill ran through her; a chill she credited to the clouds building overhead and the mounting breeze blowing from the west.

Although she knew better than to dally, she couldn't help but watch Baker's fate unfold. When he saw the brethren approaching he tried to cut an even wider path around them, but quickly found himself hemmed in by a deep ravine to the north. What he lacked in geography he tried to compensate for with speed, but the Hummer was too big of a target, even for a band of farmers. They formed themselves into a line and fired their weapons in unison. *Like a firing squad,* Jennifer thought in horror. Sounds of shattering glass and ripping steel filled the air, followed by an explosion that could only have come from one of the Hummer's huge tires. The big SUV veered sharply to the left into the narrow ravine, and crashed into the far side. A sickening cacophony of rending metal confirmed the force of the impact.

Only the back bumper was visible when the dust subsided, and nothing more could be heard but the eerie whistling of air rushing through the lacuna.

Having dispensed with Baker (though for what reason, Jennifer could not imagine), the brethren now turned their sights on the small group huddled on the northeastern edge of the giant stone wall. With Jack in the lead, they scurried along the ledge toward the safety of the backside where a cache of automatic weapons sufficient to arm a platoon begged to be put into use.

Salia's posse was fast gaining ground as Jennifer and the others bucked a strong headwind on the narrow ledge. The first shots pummeled the rocks in the cliff overhead about the time they reached the halfway point. Jack turned and fired three shots in quick succession. It did nothing to slow the brethren's progress.

*   *   *   *

The rifle felt good in his hands, like an old girlfriend who had come to visit from a great distance. It was a bolt-action M-40A3 Marine-issue sniper rifle, chambered for a 7.63 mm round. The A3 was a plain-looking weapon;

its lines were simple and its oddly shaped stock seemed almost unrefined. But it was deadly accurate and designed to be effective at a thousand yards. Having used this weapon in two different wars, Tay knew he could top that on a calm day, but this day was turning out to be anything but calm.

The rifle had been hidden under the mattress in the side bedroom—the bed where Carmen's lifeless body now lay—and retrieving it had not been pleasant. To gaze upon the ruined body that once held such a vibrant, fiery soul pained him greatly, and he tried not to look at her as he lifted the edge of the mattress to work the gun case out from under it. The action tossed her bullet-riddled body from side to side in a way that mimicked life, and Tay thought it a cruel irony that she lay above the instrument that would avenge her.

He slung the rifle across his body by the shoulder strap and bent down to kiss her now-cold cheek one last time. "*Adios, mi vida*. I pray that you will be watching me. Perhaps when you see me destroy the witch, you will find a way to forgive me."

He set out at a gallop along the creek trail, hoping that Carmen's mare shared her mistress's spirit, for time was of the essence and the climb that awaited him on the south side of the lacuna would not be an easy one. Especially if the clouds building overhead held as much misery in their billowing folds as it appeared.

The mare had more to give than Tay dared hope for. He reached the rise on the south side of the lacuna just as he heard the first volley of shots fired. Having killed Baker, they were riding hard, a hundred yards shy of the ledge, when they fired on the *malagente*. He saw Jack spin and point the revolver. A moment later he heard the blasts echoing through the canyon.

Jack and the others quickened their pace as the brethren slowed, unsure if they should ride their clumsy draft steeds across the narrow ledge in the building wind. Seven held back while one determined soul astride a short stout horse followed. Tay found him in the rifle's ten-power scope and squeezed off a warning round that slapped into the cliff just in front of the horse's nose. The horse was startled, as much by the supersonic blast of the high-speed shell as by the rock chips spraying its face, chest and legs. The beast reared and the overweight soil-tiller tumbled off the horse's back like a round rock rolling downhill, futilely trying to hold onto the reins as his legs landed on nothing but the thin air beyond the ledge. Fearful for its own life, the horse jerked his head up, pulling free the reins and dooming its rider.

It took the man less than three seconds to meet up with the rocks in the creek below, but his screams echoed off the cliff walls for several seconds more.

Unable to turn around on the precarious ledge, the riderless horse ran to the far side of the lacuna. It stopped, wide-eyed and shivering, when it found itself in the midst of so many strange people. Luke spoke to the frightened beast until he was able to take its reins and lead it to safety.

Tay watched the seven remaining brethren through the rifle scope. He took but small pleasure in their fear and confusion.

Satisfied the battle was at a standstill for the time being, he continued his climb up the rocky slope where great broken slabs of gray granite lay stacked in all manner of repose, none of which made the climb an easy one, especially with the stiffness that remained in his wounded leg.

When next he looked back, he saw Tharp and another man approaching from the east with a third person—a woman he thought, or a tall sinewy child, wearing a black beret—tied in the back of a dune buggy. Tharp had heard the shot and scanned the southern hillside for the shooter, but the distance was too great and Tay too well concealed to be seen by an unaided eye.

His knee-jerk reaction was to take Tharp out fast and hard—remove him from the conflict as quickly as possible. But as he played the powerful scope on his old nemesis seated in an open vehicle (as easy a shot as there could ever be), he decided instead to wait. When he killed Tharp he wanted to do it with a personal touch. Just so he knew he'd died at the hands of an old friend.

Call it professional courtesy.

Against the protest of his injured thigh, Tay climbed ever higher over the barren crags as a light rain began to fall.

*   *   *   *

Seeing no more than the back bumper and a little of one wheel and a fender, Tharp knew it was Baker's Hummer sitting nose first in the ravine. It didn't look like a crash anyone would've lived through and the thought that his single close associate inside the State government was dead didn't sit well with him.

On the other hand, if what Salia said was true, all of his little nickel and dime contracts with Baker wouldn't amount to a drop of spit in the wind.

But it didn't mean he was happy to lose Baker.

He pulled into the midst of the group of dismounted men and their steeds, all standing in the scree at the eastern edge of the ledge. They moved quickly out of his way then stared at him with distrust and confusion. "Well, hello, girls," Tharp said. "Nice day for a ride, huh?"

"Who would thee be? And what is thy business here?" asked a tall slender man wearing soiled suspenders and a wide-brimmed hat soaked with sweat.

Oh, brother, thought Tharp, *she's outdone herself this time.* He jumped out of the doorless vehicle and began untying Keetna's feet while Bobby loosened the straps holding her to the seat. Over his shoulder he said, "Well, Moses, or Abraham, or whatever the fuck you call yourself, me and the lady here are two of the stars of this little show. What's your story?"

When the answer was not immediately forthcoming, Tharp turned and said, "Okay, try this, farmer Bob: which of you bible-beating donkey fuckers ran my friend into the ravine?"

"We were told to let no one escape," answered a short, stocky man holding the reins of a tired-looking mule. "It is what Salia commanded."

"Hear that, Hadrian?" Keetna jeered. "These men are your new co-workers."

Ignoring her, Tharp growled at the man with open contempt, saying "New orders. Go home or face the consequences. You're not needed here anymore." He pulled Keetna roughly off the seat and held her tight by the collar as he pushed her through the bunch of them, her hands tightly bound behind her. Bobby hobbled along in the rear, thoroughly bewildered.

Tharp turned after a few paces. Seeing no one had moved, he snarled "Fine. Stay, then. But don't think for a minute I won't kill any plowboy who tries to follow."

No one did. Tharp's trio lowered their heads against the wind-driven rain as they pushed on toward the other side.

* * * *

Jennifer was the first to see them coming. Peering around the corner, she announced, "Two men on the ledge, Silas, and I think they've got your friend."

Silas ran up the hill for a look, holding his hand above his eyes to keep rainwater from dripping into them. "Keetna!" he shouted, unable to contain his relief at seeing her alive. He started to run to her but Jennifer grabbed him tight and said, "No, Silas. Let them come to us."

Reluctantly, he backed away from the ledge and hollered down the trail to Luke and the others, "Hey, everyone! Get ready! Tharp and Keetna are heading this way!" Luke, Catalyn and Cassie were searching from cave to cave, trying without success to find the cached weapons.

Jack, the only one among them who was armed, was nowhere in sight. *Must be in one of the caves*, she thought absently.

Jennifer asked Silas, "Did you manage to find what Tharp and Salia are looking for?"

After a brief hesitation, he answered, "Yes."

"So Carlos hid a copy of the anterium protocol, and you found it?"

"Yes. I've got it."

"Good. We just need to figure out how to trade it without getting killed in the process."

Silas cocked his head to one side and said, "You'd trade the protocol to save the life of a woman you've never met?"

"Wouldn't you?"

"Depends on the woman," he answered honestly.

"Her?"

"Of course, but—"

She put a cold wet finger across his lips. "Shhh...say no more. If we have to sacrifice someone you love to the save the world, then the world's not worth saving. Somehow, we'll find a way out of this."

*   *   *   *

The tingling in Jack's head had now lodged in his temples and was accompanied by a change in his outlook on things. At first it had seemed foreign but now it was beginning to settle in and make itself right at home.

He'd slipped away on the fallen brethren's horse while the others busied themselves looking for weapons; weapons that were buried under rocks and dirt in one of many caves that all looked the same. They would never find them in time. How he knew this, he couldn't say. Nor could he say how he knew there would be a horse available for this most important ride. All he knew was that in his mind he had seen the events of this day fall into place like the tumblers in a lock, and there was no event where the buried guns were put into use. On another day in another time the tumblers may have lined up differently, but not today.

Too bad for his new friends, but it was for the better.

He realized now just how selfish Carlos had been in keeping the COTO anterium from the world when so much good could be done with it. All the people living hand to mouth beyond the comfort of the islands could be included in a meaningful new social contract that would, with all the knowledge and wisdom gained in the past twenty years, meet the needs of everyone. With the human population now reduced to a sensible level, the new energy technologies would ensure that oil would only be used as a stopgap measure, to provide energy where energy was truly needed. There would never be a return to the old ways, when conspicuous waste and blatant disregard for nature had become cultural imperatives. In the new world, oil would be revered as the precious gift it had always been meant to be.

All of this was so clear to him he couldn't believe he'd ever thought otherwise.

He had seen other things too. All the confusion he formerly felt whenever he tried to speculate about future events had vanished. Jennifer had been right: the future could be seen by those who knew how to observe it. It was an open book and Jack read it zealously. To see who would make it through the day and who would fall by the wayside. And who would ultimately triumph.

It was all so simple, he felt like a fool for not seeing it sooner.

She wins.

With every roll of the dice, in every one of the multitudinous permutations allowed by an infinite universe, *she* comes out on top.

As *she* should.

He waited now in the side valley near the stone marking the spot where they'd buried the murdered sheriff. Jack was out of the worst of the wind but had been unable to avoid the rain which now stung his bare skin like miniature hail stones. He narrowed his eyes and shielded them with his hand in hopes of getting a glimpse of *her*, but—

"Hello, Jack Vara."

He spun quickly on his heels and found himself staring at the most strikingly beautiful woman he'd ever seen. "Salia," he whispered breathlessly.

With a voice like fine silk, she said, "I believe they are just about ready for us, dear. Shall we go?"

᛭ろ

Mind Games

What happens when two or more gifted viators combine their abilities?
No one knows.

FROM THE UNPUBLISHED MEMOIRS OF CARLOS HERRERA

Jack was with Salia. It was nothing Jennifer wanted to believe, but she knew it just the same. She knew it because this was Salia's moment in time and nothing in heaven or hell would keep her away from this place. But where was she? Not with Tharp. Not with the brethren. Not anywhere. And since *she* was nowhere else, *she* must be with the guy who went missing along with the dead farmer's horse.

Damn it, Jack! Why?

Take it in stride and keep your head, a calmer voice told her, *it's the only way you're going to live through this.* Jennifer had never before thought of herself as a rational sort of person, and she wasn't known for making decisions based on a neat collection of carefully weighted facts. She shot from the hip usually, for better or worse. But this was an occasion that called for a little more shooting than she could handle on her own.

So, as she stood shoulder to shoulder with Silas, Luke, Catalyn and Cassie in the wind and the icy rain that was quickly turning to snow on a day that had topped ninety degrees just a couple of hours before, she had to believe anything was possible.

Anything but what she now saw.

She was alerted to their imminent arrival by Hadrian Tharp, whom she thought the most dangerous looking man she had ever seen. He had the appearance of a large man who had been compacted into a smaller form without sacrificing anything, except, perhaps the slowness and lack of agility that often defined large men. From the heavy square jaw line to the intense cinnamon eyes, he emanated strength and nastiness in a concentration that was unsettling. Only the thick scab running across his face from his mouth to his temple hinted that he might by vulnerable. But, in truth, it only enhanced his fearsomeness.

Had Keetna done this to him? The brashness and temerity Jennifer saw etched on the young woman's sparsely efficient face told Jennifer she had. She had the countenance of one who feared nothing, even though she would likely be the first one sacrificed when it came time for killing.

Hadrian had them loosely assembled and ready for Jack and Salia's arrival. Everyone stood shivering against the rough cliff side, arms across their chests in a futile attempt to hold onto the precious body heat that was slowly being sucked out of them by an impossible meteorological phenomenon. Facing them from a few feet away, Keetna stood in front of Hadrian Tharp, her mouth curled defiantly at the corners. Tharp held her collar with his left hand and a knife to her throat with the right. A man called Bobby—out of shape, out of place, and looking very much like he was out of luck—held a gun to the rest of them, though he did it with such reluctance he hardly seemed threatening.

But that probably didn't matter. Should Bobby falter, Tharp, with his quick hands and his holstered automatic, would easily pick up the slack, more than likely over Keetna's dead body.

Tharp was the first to see their approach. Jennifer followed his eyes as they burned through the sleet and the foliage obscuring the lower part of the trail and wondered how a man could stare so keenly at a dark spot within a shadow.

They arrived on horseback, the plump steed slowly plodding up the steep grade, Jack seated behind the cantle while Salia rode regally sidesaddle in the seat. Through the driving snow—all pretense of rain had now vanished—it seemed more a surreal vision than an actual event. The scene lost its artistic qualities as Jack and Salia drew closer and their initial vagueness resolved into flesh and blood reality.

Jack helped her off the short horse and Salia carefully inspected her captives, much as a butcher might examine a row of carcasses before cleaving them into small portions. Curiously, she paid little heed to Cassie, who glared at Salia with unvarnished contempt while resting on her haunches, one arm wrapped around each of the dogs' necks. Jennifer had the feeling the omission was not incidental. Did she fear the girl? It was too much to hope for.

In contrast to Cassie's brazenness, Jazzman and Sasha looked on with vacuous stares, as if Jack and Jennifer were strangers and this woman were their new mistress. *A mistress of weak minds*, Jennifer mused emptily, knowing it didn't explain her power over Jack.

When she reached Silas standing on the end of the line next to Jennifer, she stopped and said, "So, the remarkable Silas Teague. Such miraculous healing powers, to pull your damaged mind back from the edge of oblivion." She scoured him with eyes that grew disturbingly intense before becoming even more disturbingly soft and warm. "We've known each other a long time, haven't we Silas?" She spoke as if to an old friend.

Salia was dressed warmly, the only one among them who was, in a fur coat *(wolf?)*, fur boots *(also wolf)*, and a long dress so black it seemed more a dark void in the space around her legs than a garment. By contrast, Silas wore bloodied jeans and a light jacket which was soaked through, exposing the seams of the shirt below.

"Have we?" Silas answered, "I really don't recall."

Salia laughed in a way that sent icy darts into Jennifer's stomach. She said, "I could never crack you, Silas. Not the way you were. Your brain was too muddled. So I had to help you along, help you heal, so I could learn what I needed to know.

"But you were resourceful. You surprised me, going after the protocol the way you did. Gutsy move, for someone in your delicate condition. I imagine it would even have surprised Carlos." She paused for effect, then said, "Did I tell you he had the bad taste to die while I was…discussing…the matter with him?"

"You *killed* him?" Jennifer blurted. Suddenly she felt nauseous.

Salia laughed. Under different circumstances it might almost have sounded pleasant. As it was, it only compounded the uneasiness in Jennifer's stomach. "Oh, no," Salia replied evenly, "he did that to himself. He put poison in his heart pills, a fact I discovered too late. But no matter; the old man had outlived his usefulness."

"No wonder we found him with a smile on his face," Catalyn said.

"Yes," she said, intense eyes fixed on Silas, "but as you can see, his death was for nothing. Thanks to you, Silas. Now, turn over the protocol, if you would be so kind."

"Why should he?" Jennifer asked reasonably.

"Jennifer Teague," Salia said slowly, as if noticing her for the first time. "You are an impudent little thing, aren't you? What a pity the sheriff couldn't bring himself to kill you."

"Yeah. Too bad," Jennifer said. "In the end he must've realized what a phony bitch you really are."

Salia's eyes flashed and Jennifer thought she would strike her, but instead she turned and ran a finger along Keetna's jawline in a movement that would have seemed a caress had it not opened a wound along its course. Keetna clenched her teeth and glared coldly at Salia, but betrayed no pain. Blood flowed instantly in a steady stream that ran down her neck and under her clothing. "Phony, you say?" Salia crooned.

Silas lunged for Salia at the same time Keetna thrust out her foot in an attempt to hook the sorceress behind the knees. With the grace of a ballerina, Salia spun clear. Keetna's heel caught Silas in the shin and knocked him to the ground.

"Don't be foolish," she snapped harshly as Tharp pulled Keetna roughly to his chest and Jennifer helped Silas back in line. "It will not have the result you are hoping for; I promise it won't." Her voice softened as she looked back toward Silas and said, "Give it to me, Silas Teague, and we will allow you to return to your petty little lives."

"You'll kill us all," he countered.

"Oh, but I don't have to," she said in comforting tone that was almost believable. "I can make you forget; all of you. It's much cleaner that way, don't you think?"

No one answered.

"NOW!! FOR THE SAKE OF YOUR VERY LIVES!!" she roared.

Without a word, Silas left the group and fetched his backpack from an erosion hole that had never developed into a full-blown cave. When he walked past Jack he hooked an arm around his neck and said, "How's it going there, old buddy?"

"Don't *touch* him," she barked sharply.

"Sorry," Silas replied. "Didn't know you were so sensitive about your... things."

Jack raised his head and gazed at Salia—gazed at everyone—and Jennifer thought *(prayed?)* she might have seen a glimmer of the old Jack before his eyes went dark again. She was not yet daring to hope, but neither had she abandoned it.

Silas opened his pack and extracted a blue plastic envelope, which Salia instantly snatched from his wet fingers. Jennifer looked on breathlessly as Salia quickly worked the button-&-string closure and pulled out the contents, holding them tight to her chest with her back to the driving snow.

With long delicate fingers she thumbed through the half-inch-thick sheaf of papers, her anger becoming progressively more evident. She extracted one sheet and threw the others into the icy wind where they fluttered out of sight. The remaining sheet she shook in Silas's face. "Is this your idea of a joke?" she turned and pressed a bare finger to Keetna's neck. It looked remarkably like a blade. "Talk fast," she said, "or I'll slit her throat."

Keetna drew a breath through flared nostrils and glared at Salia. Jennifer leaned to get a look at the paper Salia held in her hand. It was a requisition form from the Colorado Department of Seditious Activities. Desa.

"Please," Silas pleaded, "don't hurt her! It was in there; I saw—"

"Then where *is* it?"

Speaking for the first time, Jack said, "I know."

"Do you now?" she cooed sweetly, gliding in his direction to run her lovely hand along the side of Jack's whiskery face.

Am I seeing things, or did Jack recoil slightly at her touch?

"I saw Baker hide something under the seat of the Hummer when we were getting in. He must've stolen the protocol from Silas. I'll be glad to go get it."

"Would you, Jack? That would be very kind of you," she answered in a lover's tone, "but leave your gun. Just in case we need it...to quell an insurrection."

So, she doesn't trust him. I wonder why?

"What about the plowboys?"

"The brethren? You needn't concern yourself with them, Jack. They won't trouble you."

He glanced quickly at Jennifer (*Jack, or not-Jack? She couldn't tell without touching him*), then removed the revolver and handed it to Salia. She took it gingerly and shoved it into Tharp's back pocket.

"Now we wait," she said pleasantly, as bright wet snow swirled and drifted all around them.

*   *   *   *

Tay fought the hypothermia that crept deeper into his body core as his skin was assaulted by wave after wave of wind-driven snow. Even if he could have seen clearly across the canyon from his perch on the southern monolith, he couldn't have hit much through the pine boughs that partially obscured Tharp and the Warchez woman. At supersonic velocities bullets reacted to obstacles in counterintuitive ways; he was just as likely to kill Luke or Jennifer. He decided to pick his way down the backside, cross the creek, and find an opening in the trees from down below.

He moved quickly. It would be warmer among the trees, if only slightly.

*   *   *   *

Salia stood alone, eyes impatiently fixed on the slippery ledge as Jack stepped carefully along it. She looked preoccupied and Silas thought he knew why.

"Hey Tharp!" he said, "What say you let us crawl in one of these caves here? It'd be a shame if we froze to death before you got the chance to kill us."

"Maybe," he conceded. "Let me look." Pushing Keetna in front of him, he examined the nearest cavern. "Sure, why not?" he concluded after a cursory inspection. "It might make my life easier."

Luke lifted Cassie into the man-sized entrance of the small space. It was roughly spherical with several inches of fine gravel on the bottom. The dogs jumped in after her. Catalyn followed, then Jennifer and Silas.

"How about you, slick?" Tharp growled in Keetna's ear, "Care to huddle in there with the rest of the rats?"

"Gee, I don't know, Hadrian. Think you can bear to take your hands off me?"

"I'll get by," he assured her. "Just watch yourself—I'd hate to have to kill you."

Luke pulled her in and Silas promptly made a place for her. She turned and kissed his cheek. "Hi, boyfriend. Here we are in the soup again."

"Maybe we'll get out of it this time."

"Maybe," she said.

Tharp watched his captives through the opening for several minutes before becoming bored with the chore. "Bobby? Get your lame ass over here and watch this sorry bunch, will you? And make damn sure Teague doesn't untie your girlfriend."

Bobby hobbled over to the entrance and looked in. Keetna winked at him and said, "Hi there, sugar." Bobby blushed red, his acne scars even redder. He might even have smiled before pulling his head out.

After a moment they all settled in and huddled close to preserve warmth. Jennifer and Cassie closed their eyes. Silas did the same.

It was restful. And enlightening.

Jennifer? Silas?

Yes, Cassie, they both answered.

Let's turn her.

Turn her? Jennifer answered doubtfully. The child's voice rang clear in her head and Jennifer glanced quickly through the opening to see if Salia was picking up on their conversation. Apparently, she had enough to occupy her mind.

Yeah. Turn her inside out.

Let's, Silas agreed.

Jennifer studied Salia for a long moment. She paced back and forth near the dropoff, looking along the ledge every few seconds. She seemed totally preoccupied with something Jennifer could get no sense of. She answered, *Okay, let's do it,* though she had no idea what Cassie had in mind.

*   *   *   *

Jack stepped quickly and silently through the assembled brethren, happy to be off the icy ledge. His presence drew little reaction from any of them as they huddled in a small group on the lee sides of their steeds, hats lowered against the wind. Steam rose in horse-scented swirls from the animals' backs before being quickly swept away by the mounting storm, and Jack enjoyed for a few precious seconds the warmth emanating from the large beasts.

He had nothing to say to the brethren so he walked on, thinking the meeting peculiar in a nagging sort of way. It troubled him to the same degree that his logical about-face on the subject of the COTO anterium protocol did not. Because reason was contingent on data and therefore subject to change, but a man's attitude toward his fellows seldom was.

Simply put: once a wiseass, always a wiseass.

But he'd passed them by without so much as a "Hey, there; nice day for a blood sacrifice, ain't it, boys?"

Whatever. It wasn't worth thinking about. The fact remained that Salia was right, he'd been wrong, and—

And...what? Think this through, Jacky boy, cuz it's a really big fucking 'what' dangling there and you wouldn't want it to come crashing down on your head, now would you?

No. He wouldn't.

Through ceaseless waves of horizontal snow that chewed viciously at his frozen skin, he spied the upturned Hummer and trotted toward it. His disquieting see-saw ruminations could wait.

* * * *

They had formed a triad. Jennifer, Silas and Cassie occupied each of the points, joined equally to one another. Yet each remained distinct. The psychic gestalt thus created was far greater than the sum of the parts, just as a volume of air, a pile of tinder, and a spark are greater.

Together they combined their natural talents with surgical efficiency, weaving a web designed to ensnare Salia Warchez. They sensed she was not as strong as before; she was distracted, like a puppeteer trying to control too many puppets at once. Just the same, she remained the most formidable foe any of them would ever encounter.

* * * *

What the hell was Vara doing? He kept fading in and out like a radio signal from a distant source. It was disturbing; she didn't know if Jack was the cause of the problem, or merely the symptom. Was she losing control over her prize subject?

She rubbed her tired eyes and stole another glance down the narrow trail. At least three inches of fresh snow had accumulated on the smooth rock surface that jutted out from the cliff side and it was quickly crusting over and turning to ice.

She really hoped to be gone from this place before the storm got any worse.

At the far end she could just make out the shapes of the seven brethren huddled in a knot of men and beasts.

Seven is a more prophetic number than eight, is it not? She was attempting to put a favorable twist on the fate of the one lost brother when she realized that *they* were the source of her problem. *Too many irons in the fire, my dear.*

It was draining her to maintain them...or rather, to ensure their continued loyalty through to the successful conclusion of this unheralded coup.

But it just wouldn't do to turn them all loose and let them begin thinking for themselves again. It might be troublesome if their frayed and jumbled emotions reassembled themselves in the form of resentment for being used to perform acts beyond what their sense of morality would allow. So she'd just have to suck it up and draw even more deeply from the well.

She closed her eyes to minimize the sensory input flooding her brain. And though snow and biting cold air swirled around her in ever more persistent gusts and eddies, she was for the moment immune to nature's caprices, comfortably cloistered in a perfectly controlled world of her own making; a world that bent always to her will.

Jack Vara, where are you? Oh yes; she could feel him now, could feel... *what's this? A door?*

It was indeed a door. A door inside a door inside a door.

A million doors, all wide open and lined up in a neat little row. It was like standing in front of a mirror with another mirror positioned perfectly behind you, such that mirrors—or rather, doors—proceeded without interruption into the maw of infinity. The difference was that she herself was not a repeating image but a series of images, each one different.

Memories, she realized, of her childhood.

Intrigued, she drew her attention to the first door. She was a girl of no more than five, crouched behind a short mud-brick wall in the small Polish village where she grew up. She wore a torn dress and her knees were scuffed in the way children's knees always are. On the far side of the wall two of her playmates sat cross-legged in the dirt; shy little Edyta, and her fiery-haired older brother, Marek. They were talking about her in hushed tones.

Oh, yes! I remember this! she thought, *I remember Edyta saying...*

"...She's too creepy. I don't *like* her!"

and Marek saying to his younger sister, "Shhh! She'll hear you, you know. She hears *everything*. And then she'll make your nose bleed. Or worse!"

She smiled to herself, for she had indeed made their noses bleed, made them bleed until...wait. What's this?

The first door became many, replicating left and right, and behind each one another endless series of doors filled space beyond her ability to see. They formed around her in a circle and then a sphere in which she was suspended in the exact center, and through each of these doors she saw things she had done, or might have done, or wanted to do but hadn't. She even saw herself acting in ways the young Salia did not wish to act but did, because it was the moral thing to do.

The troubling part was (*and it was more than a little troubling*) that she had distinct memories of each and every one of these mutually exclusive reactions to her playmates' conversation. Yes, she *had* made blood gush from their noses in great streams; and she *had* run away crying to her father; and she *had*, with due contrition, run through the gate to beg forgiveness from Edyta and Marek.

Just as she *had* killed them both by willing networks of capillaries to burst inside their brains. It was a cruel impetuous act for which her father's mission had been burned to the ground and Salia and Isaiah stoned to death.

Seeing it now and remembering it so clearly, she felt substantially diminished. The knowledge that the unique personality upon whom she had built her identity was but a bit player in the far larger drama of the eternal Salia Warchez humbled her and left her weak in the knees. And yet it shouldn't have; hadn't she known all along? Hadn't she capitalized on the infinite nature of consciousness and the soul to control, belittle and confuse Pryus Gordon Primm and so many others, including her newest toy, Jack Vara? It was the very core of her power.

But until this moment, it hadn't occurred to her that she was subject to the same rules.

* * * *

Baker wasn't dead. He wasn't even seriously injured. He moaned softly, almost somnolently, suspended by the still-inflated airbag with his head to one side as if it were a pillow. The backseat side window had been shattered by gunfire but the front-seat window was still intact. He hadn't been shot, after all.

Blood dripped down the side of his face from a gash inflicted by the lens of the dome light. It was probably what knocked him unconscious. But beyond that, Jack could see no injuries of consequence.

What did it matter? He hadn't come to tend to Baker. He pulled open the back door and retrieved the sheaf of papers from under the seat. Shielding the document from the storm, he quickly thumbed through it to see if it was indeed the protocol for the COTO anterium. Confirming that it was, he fished further under the seat and was pleased to find a plastic poncho rolled up in a small bag which he promptly slipped it over his head.

One last search for anything of value turned up...a gun? Yes. Clutched in his nearly frozen fingers was a snub-nose .32 revolver. Would he need it? What if the brethren turned hostile on his return trip? He stuffed the gun in the small of his back, the protocol in the front of his trousers.

"Good luck, Baker," he said.

He leaned into the storm and trundled back toward the lacuna, recalling how strange it was that Silas should wrap an arm over his shoulder and call him 'old buddy,' even though they had only met briefly. Was Silas being sarcastic?

You should know, oh high lord of acerbic wit, the voice at the back of his mind chattered in his ear. *Of course he was being sarcastic; he was driving little needles into you, hoping to get a reaction.* But the fact was, Jack didn't know that. At least not right away. And he should have.

What's more, he now felt a warmth spreading down his arms and across his face, a warmth originating from his shoulders and the back of his neck, where Silas had touched him. A clarifying warmth. Like the spontaneous regression of a virulent contagion.

The feeling was...confusing.

Before he had the chance to think any further on the matter he was met by one of the brethren, a heavyset man, wandering toward him on foot. Like Jack, his head was lowered against the battering waves of wind-driven snow buffeting him from side to side, and he only looked up when Jack was directly upon him. Even through the blinding snow, Jack saw a haunting sadness in the man's eyes. He said, "Mister? Can you help me? I'm afraid I've done something terribly wrong."

*   *   *   *

The only consolation Tay could find for the steadily worsening weather was that he couldn't possibly get any wetter while wading through the wild waters of Old Scratch. Or so he thought, until he slipped on the mossy rounded stones lining the creek bed and fell into the rushing water. To keep his rifle from plunging into the creek—where water would seep into the action and freeze, rendering the precious weapon unusable—he spun and fell on his back in the swift stream, holding the gun high in his outstretched hands. Icy water washed over and through every part of his body below his upraised elbows, stealing the breath from his lungs and teaching him a new meaning of cold. It only grew more acute as he struggled desperately to his feet, careful to keep the rifle elevated in one hand. Clumsily, he slipped and slid and sloshed to the far bank.

The cold gnawed at his bones like a frozen-toothed rat. He shivered uncontrollably; his teeth clicked and chattered. It distracted him from the immediate tactical problem of finding an opening in the trees from the valley floor to the top of the trail that would allow him a clear shot with minimal chance of collateral damage. It was the sort of thing he'd been trained for, way back when the axles of the world were greased with oil and all the world's immediate problems were directly or indirectly related to that fact.

Rifle slung over his shoulder, he squeezed as much water as he could from his meager clothing, rubbing his arms and legs to warm himself. Then he began to study the terrain slowly and methodically, hoping to finish this messy business before he froze to death. And knowing he might not be able to.

* * * *

Silas and Jennifer sat quietly with their eyes closed, as did Cassie. Her parents, by contrast, held each other tightly as they sat huddled together against the back of the cave. *How curious they are not holding their daughter*, Keetna thought. *Are they not concerned for her welfare?* Intuitively, she sensed something was at work here the parents weren't a part of. But what? Something important.

She was careful not to do anything that might disturb them.

The two dogs rested in the middle of the small cave between the hostages, curled up on all of their feet. The body heat they emanated was welcome and invigorating, enabling her mind to think creatively and productively. Could she take Tharp? No, not without a weapon. But Bobby? He'd be a pushover.

The rock walls of the cave had all been worn smooth by some natural process she didn't understand, making it unlikely that she could wear through the tough nylon rope binding her hands behind her back, either by abrasion or by cutting the rope on the stone wall against her back. But as her restless fingers began to feel around, she discovered she was sitting on a pile of rubble that really didn't belong there. The stones were too smooth to be useful, but she had found one or two with marginally rough edges; rough enough to encourage her to keep digging as if her life depended on it.

After a moment more of clawing through the rough dirt beneath her, she found a suitable shard; a long skinny flake that had been broken off a larger piece. Perhaps it had been produced by a pickax. The granite sliver had an edge plenty sharp enough to cut the ropes binding her hands, but as she cleared the ground around her of dirt and stones that might impede her progress she discovered something else—something flat and metallic, like the lid to a box.

Thinking, hoping, praying it might contain something they could use to better their odds of survival, she decided to take a chance and wake Silas from his meditations. She started to nudge Silas but stopped when the girl's mother met her eyes.

Don't!, the eyes said.

Why am I the only one left out of this silent cabal? Keetna wondered, more frustrated that insulted. She nodded to the mother and went to work on the rope binding her wrists. Silas and the other two had better make it fast. The second Keetna was free she intended to open the box, with or without community approval.

*   *   *   *

Salia was lost in the intimate details of a thousand thousand lives, every one as real and memorable as the one before it.

My God! I have lived them all! Am living them all!

It would understate her quandary to say she was merely overwhelmed; she was drowning in sea of infinitely multiplying permutations on the particulars of her past, present and future, completely incapable of finding a tuft of solid ground on which to stand and get her bearings.

For the moment she had forgotten about the one existence in which she was a hair's breadth from obtaining the one thing that would facilitate her mastery of the world, or at least that part of it she deemed worth mastering. And even if she could have drawn her focus back to that probable/improbable time and place, the thought of acting linearly from that unique point of consciousness was quite impossible, for every action was occasioned by a million equal and opposite reactions.

And that was putting it mildly.

She would've been lost forever—lost a million times over—were it not for Tharp's strong, indelicate hand upon her shoulder.

"Here comes Vara," he murmured gratingly into her ear. "Better quit your daydreaming."

In a breathless dizzying instant brought on by Tharp's touch, a universe of Salias collapsed into one. *This* one.

*　　*　　*　　*

As if awakened by a gunshot, Silas, Jennifer and Cassie were drawn back into the dark cave and the cold wetness that accompanied their premature return. "Shit! We almost had her!" Silas whispered, just loud enough to be heard over the roar of the storm.

"She's weaker now," Jennifer offered. "That makes her more vulnerable."

"I'm going to finish her," Cassie murmured defiantly.

"No, Cassie," Catalyn insisted, "she's too dangerous."

Cassie gave her a look. Catalyn frowned and mouthed 'no.' It was a command Cassie had no trouble ignoring.

Keetna leaned forward with her hands still behind her back, and looked out the opening. Bobby leaned lazily against the cliff face with his head lowered against the blizzard. He was paying no attention to what was going on inside the small cave. On closer inspection, Silas saw that Keetna's hands were free and that she was sitting on the long narrow case that held the cache of weapons.

He nudged Jennifer and pointed downward; her eyes grew huge with surprise. Luke and Catalyn saw it too, while Cassie sat silently with her eyes closed to the world.

Silas chanced a quick look outside and saw Tharp and Salia several paces away, talking and looking in their direction.

It was now or never.

With great effort, Catalyn and Jennifer crawled over the tightly packed throng and emerged from the cave entrance. Sasha and Jazzman jumped out behind them, shaking melted snow off their thick coats now that they'd found enough space to do the job properly. Bobby stood just outside, shivering and disinterested, a layer of snow building on his shoulders and eyebrows and the folds of his shirt.

"It's stuffy in there," Jennifer said to Bobby, holding a hand to her forehead to keep the driving snow from her eyes. "We needed a little air." To prevent him from discovering the seeds of their rebellion, they blocked the cave entrance with their bodies. Predictably, Bobby did not suspect that any-thing was amiss.

Unfortunately, Tharp did.

"What's the matter, kids?" he shouted over the howl of the storm to make himself heard. "Your little playhouse getting too crowded?"

"My husband farted," Catalyn told him, straight-faced.

If it was meant to be funny (and knowing Catalyn, it was a stretch), Tharp didn't get the joke. He lived by his instincts and instinct told him trouble was brewing. He drew his gun and ran quickly to the cave, roughly pushing Jennifer and Catalyn out of the way. He was met by the muzzle of a nasty-looking short-barreled rifle when he peered in the opening. Keetna shoved it in his face, saying, "Back off, Hadrian!" in no uncertain terms.

Hadrian raised his hands and smiled disarmingly. Bobby turned to see what the commotion was all about and Catalyn kneed him in the crotch. The gun fell from his hand just before Luke's arm wrapped around the cave's entrance, holding the twin to Keetna's automatic rifle.

"Shit, oh shit, oh shit!" Bobby moaned, doubling over with both hands cupping his bruised testicles.

"Seems you kids have found some new toys."

"Yeah. Wanna play, big boy?" Keetna asked with a suggestive wink.

Hadrian smiled. "Love to," he said, spinning quickly on one heel. He kicked out with his free foot, sending both weapons flying. Luke gazed into his empty hands, befuddled by Tharp's lightning-fast maneuver. Keetna saw no point in dwelling on it. She launched herself into Tharp's midsection, push-ing him back with what little momentum her small form possessed. Tharp's hands flew out from his body, his right hand still holding the automatic pistol. He had just begun to curl the gun toward Keetna when it flew from his hands and shattered into shrapnel in midair. The sharp *crack!* of Tay's rifle reached Jennifer's ears at the same time a spray of blood erupted in the space where Tharp's middle and ring fingers used to be.

"VILLA!!!" Tharp screamed in a boiling rage, holding his injured hand in front of him to inspect the damage.

As if in reply, another shell whizzed past, removing Tharp's left earlobe before smacking flatly into the granite wall in front of him.

Tay could kill him easily if he wanted to. *But he won't. He's having too much fun taking him apart piece by piece, goading Tharp to come after him, leaving Salia alone. With us. But where is the witch? She must be on the ledge, going to meet Jack—her Jack.* She swallowed hard at the thought but refused to dwell on it.

Tay's gambit worked. In his rage, Tharp had forgotten all about Salia. With his remaining good hand, he grabbed Keetna viciously by the shoulder and sent her sprawling off the side of the trail where she landed hard against the trunk of a towering fir tree and dropped into the underbrush. Luke, still on his knees in the cave entrance, was dumbfounded by Tharp's strength. He got the same treatment, landing in a heap on the edge of the trail.

Freed momentarily from Salia's enchantments, Jazzman prepared to get into the fray, rising to his feet with the thick hair on his back standing straight up. He circled Tharp with his teeth bared, waiting for a chance to strike. Sasha, still mired in a daze, shook her head and rose bleary-eyed to join her mate.

Cautiously, Tharp crouched lower and lower, hands outstretched, blood gushing from the stumps of his two missing fingers. He was slowly working his way toward one of the two assault rifles barely visible in the ever-deepening snow. If he reached it, it would be lights out. Tharp was that quick. But before he could, Silas poked his head out of the cave and fired a short burst just a few inches in front of Tharp's hand from a third assault rifle. "Touch it and you'll be wiping your ass with a stump," he said calmly, meaning every word of it.

Seeing his final option dissolve, Tharp backed away to the edge of the trail where it dropped off sharply for several feet. He said, "By the time *she's* done with you little piss ants, you'll wish I'd stayed." With that he turned and jumped, freefalling ten feet before his boots met with the sloping snow-covered ground on the side of the hill. He slid for a little ways, then gained his feet and disappeared into the trees.

Jennifer assessed their situation. Tharp gone. Bobby disarmed and huddled against the wall, massaging his family jewels. A stash of automatic weapons and two big dogs with their ducks back in a row. *That* ought to be enough to deal with one power-mad sorceress, hadn't it?

Before the thought could settle in, Cassie stuck her head out of the cave and said, "Uh, watch out, everybody. I think I really pissed her off."

*   *   *   *

Salia was still reeling when Tharp ran off to check on the hostages. Her hands shook and her knees trembled. Dear God, she thought, what just happened to me? The totality of the experience was beyond anything she could've imagined and its source remained a mystery, though she had a feeling she might have underestimated her hostages.

A heavy gust of wind slammed hard into her back and pushed her forward, causing her to slide on the icy rock surface. Looking up, she saw that Jack wasn't doing any better; was, in fact, slipping with each step as he made his way back to her, leaning forward on bent knees and hugging the wall as much as he possibly could without leaning into it and risking his feet slipping out from under him.

She had lost contact with him—indeed, with the brethren, too—during her experience with the doors (*oh, it was so much more than doors, my dear*) and hadn't yet gotten her bearings enough to feel her way back to them.

She wove her way into him now, undetected through the backdoor into his mind. What was this? He was having trouble reconciling his actions, somehow. Something…trivial. A joke? Because he had failed to make a joke? Nonsense; she was reading him wrong.

Then something else, something disturbing. Lyman Moran.

So. The pious farmer had fought his way free.

That's understandable, my dear, considering that you stopped his wife's heart while he stood watching, the nagging voice inside her admonished. *You really ought to exercise a little restraint sometimes, don't you think?*

What of the others, the remaining six? Did she still have *them*, for Christ's sake? She thought she did; no, she *knew* she did.

Small comfort.

Through curtains of snow she saw them all huddled together with their horses and their mules, heads down, waiting. Just as they had been for nearly an hour. With a traitor in their midst she'd deal with later.

Jack was her immediate concern. His usefulness would expire the second he handed over the anterium protocol. After that, he could slide off the ledge into oblivion for all she cared. Perhaps she would make sure of it. But for the moment he was the most important person on the planet.

His progress was painfully slow. Too slow. If a strong gust were to take him now…? She glanced quickly at Tharp. He seemed to have things under control so she inched toward the narrow ledge, toward Jack. He raised his head into the storm to meet her eyes and smiled reassuringly, yet she did not sense the degree of control she needed to ensure his obedience.

She had to reach him; to touch him. Even if it meant going out on the slippery ledge.

The voice was soft and playful, no more than the voice of child, but it hit her like a freight train: "Oh, oh, Salia! You're gonna fall off!" Then the child giggled. Damnation! It was the impudent girl! Why hadn't she—?

As if pushed (though whether it was the chaotic wind or the meddlesome girl, she would never know), she slid several feet out onto the ledge. Her feet slipped out from under her and she fell sharply on her hands and knees on the hard, icy rock. "Bye, bye, Salia, you nasty old witch!" the girl tittered with glee, and to Salia's horror, she had begun sliding toward the edge with nothing to grab hold of. She pulled her feet in closer, but the action only hastened her slide. Six inches. Five. One foot slipped over the edge. A leg dangled. Frantic, she dug her fingernails into the ice. They held fast, giving her the grip she needed to hold herself in place, but not enough purchase to fully pull herself back up.

Jack was approaching, one ponderous step at a time. Fifty yards, now; maybe less. She tried to pull herself to her knees and felt a bolt of pain shoot down her legs. "Ohhhhh!! You little *bitch*!!" she screamed. With great effort she dug her nails deeper into the ice and rolled onto her side.

Gunfire. One shot from a high-powered rifle. Another. Too late to think about it. Everything she wanted in this world was right in front of her; Tharp could deal with the untidy details.

Jack hastened to close the gap. Ten paces. Five. Salia felt her strength sapped by the cold; she was slipping away toward the edge with no way to stop herself. If Jack Vara was no longer hers...

Imploringly, she gazed up at Jack as he grasped her arm and pulled her to her feet. In spite of the storm that raged within and without, she forced a gratified smile. "Dear God, Jack! That was close."

"You should be more careful," he replied stiffly.

"So I should," she replied, sensing his coldness. She asked, "Do you have it? Please tell me you do."

He shook his head. "Silas must've had it all along," he said, raising his voice to be heard above the storm. "Did anyone look in his bag?"

No one had.

Again, the voice. "Ha, ha, Salia! Pooh pooh on you!!"

"YOU SNIPPY LITTLE BITCH!!" Salia screamed, and turned so fast she almost slid off the ledge; would have, in fact if Jack hadn't caught her and pulled her back in, saving her life for the second time in two minutes. *Well, at least I know where Jack's loyalties lie.* It was a small comfort.

A quick burst of gunfire. A small rifle this time. Maybe Tharp had killed them all and ended her worries, but she doubted it. It hadn't been that kind of a day.

Casting caution aside, she skated along the ledge, leaving Jack behind her. *Got to get back to Hadrian; got to get back...*

In her desperation, a thought came to her; a very simple thought: *Why should I be hauling around all this dead weight? I don't really need the brethren now.* And like a pointless memory, she let them go, casting them aside to live or die by their own feeble wits. Suddenly everything changed; she felt a great surge of strength flow through her, like a raging river breaking through a logjam, and she the force driving the unstoppable flow of water forward.

The girl: "Careful, Salia! It's slippery wippery!" A pause. Then: "Uh, oh."

Damn right, "Uh, oh," you disrespectful little snit. I have a special death planned for you.

The scene before her when she turned the corner at the edge of the monolith was almost comical. They were lined up as if for a family portrait. The dogs stood in front; crouched behind them were Luke *(killer of Pryus)*, Silas *(the deceiver)*, Bobby *(hell has a special place for traitors)* and the one called Keetna *(this one is indeed a warrior)*, all armed *(with very old guns that could easily malfunction)*. Behind the "warriors," stood Jennifer *(sister of Silas)*, Catalyn *(husband of Luke)*, and Cassie *(soon to be daughter of none)*. They stood with their arms crossed over their chests trying not to shiver or appear weak in her eyes, as the relentless storm caressed them all with icy fingers.

"Why are you all still alive?" she asked, as though it were a perfectly logical question.

No one answered. They were freezing and scared half out of their wits. So she offered an easier query. "Where's Hadrian?" She asked no one in particular.

"Gone to visit an old friend," the Teague woman answered.

Luke added, "But he wanted you to have these." He opened his large hand to reveal a pair of fingers. "He seems to have lost them," he said, throwing them toward her. They disappeared into the snow a few feet in front or her. She ignored them. To Silas she said, "Give me the protocol, Teague, and I will leave you all to your own fates. Just as I would have done with Carlos, had he been more agreeable."

"Sorry, sweetie," came the mocking reply, "but I ain't got it. Your new boyfriend just pulled a fast one on you."

Jack? Impossible! He just saved my life. Why would he…?

She heard Jack behind her and turned to see him rounding the corner holding a small revolver in both hands. It was aimed at her chest. "Salia, darling!" he said, "What a pity we'll never get a chance to kiss goodbye!"

* * * *

Nice save, Jack! Now can the theatrics and shoot this bitch so we can all go home.

Salia, unfortunately, had other ideas. She spun toward Jack in a blur that swept a whirling cloud of snow around herself. Jack aimed his gun and…it misfired. Terror swept across Jack's face as he looked at the gun, then at Salia. Whether or not she physically pushed him was impossible to tell, but Jack flew backward toward the ledge as if hit by a cannonball. With wide-eyed surprise, he leaned forward and pinwheeled with his arms in an attempt to maintain his balance and for a breathless moment it appeared he might regain control. He hung for a moment as if in midair, before falling to the snow-covered rocks below.

"Jack! No!" Jennifer screamed.

Salia turned and faced them. Her humanness had left her, replaced by rage; her features became distorted into a caricature of the beauty she had been only a moment before. The four guns pointed at her only invoked a vengeful sneer.

Maybe Cassie pissed her off, Jennifer thought, *but Jack unraveled her.*

Keetna was the first to pull the trigger, followed by Silas, Luke and finally Bobby. The order didn't matter. Their guns were useless; frozen up, either by ice or sorcery. Luke and Silas exchanged puzzled glances. Keetna grabbed the barrel of her M-16 and launched herself at Salia with a piercing war cry, Jazzman and Sasha right behind her.

Again Salia spun as she had with Jack, creating a vortex of ice and snow that sent all three of her attackers flying in different directions as if spit out of a raging tornado. Keetna crumpled into the webbing of the travois abandoned after Primm's funeral; Sasha was thrown into the side of the cliff. Jazzman was not so fortunate. He was lifted off the ground by the force of her rage and sent flying over the ledge in the same place Jack had disappeared moments before. With legs outstretched and head held back in terror, Jazzman was quickly swallowed by the raging blizzard.

At least they died together.

Satisfied the ill-conceived attack had been thwarted, Salia turned her attention to those who were neither dead nor disabled. She regarded them with a singular focus for a long uncomfortable moment with eyes that had become black and cold. Perhaps she wanted to see them tremble in fear for a little while longer. Or maybe she just wanted time to decide how to make their deaths as painful as possible. No one would ever know for certain what was going through her mind in those few moments, but her countenance had taken on a fearful cast.

Cassie screamed. It was a bloodcurdling sound that sent a blade of fear stabbing down the length of Jennifer's spine. Holding her head as if to keep it from exploding, the girl moaned, "Mom! Make her quit!"

But mom couldn't make her quit and neither could Luke or Jennifer. They were frozen by a queer paralysis that locked their joints as if the ends of all their bones had knit together. But not Cassie; she stood doubled over with her hands pressed tight to her head, continuing to scream.

Behind her Sasha began to stir as Keetna slowly unpeeled herself from the travois' webbing. Jennifer felt a small sliver of hope wedge itself between mounting layers of despair. *Silas,* she whispered, mind to mind, heart to heart, soul to soul, *can we do this without Cassie?*

We'd better try, Silas answered.

No doors this time; no fancy tricks. They needed to blindside Salia by whatever means they could. It meant reaching deep into her tortured soul and awakening...what? Jennifer didn't know what, nor did she care to ponder. She took a deep breath and told herself resolutely, *What is meant to be will be,* refusing to think about her simple sentiment's multifarious implications.

Cassie's screams rose to a new pitch. Droplets of blood began to drip from the girl's ears and nose.

What is meant to be will be.

Jennifer fixed her eyes on Salia and felt Silas do the same. They joined, becoming as two aspects of the same consciousness, wielding a combined strength greater than anything either alone could have mustered. As one they gazed beyond the physical layers of the corporeal Salia, far into the spiritual center from which all life flowed, poking and prodding until they found her weakest point. And from the festering wound in her soul they extracted the thorn that had caused her so much pain and held it before her with such benevolence she might've felt it floating in on a soft, warm breeze.

Salia? Is that you, my precious?

Daddy? She cocked her head toward her shoulder, but did not turn around.

Yes, Salia. I am here.

But...I thought you...had been...killed.

No, child. It was a dream, a terrible, unlikely dream. I am here with you, now.

In a way that defied all explanation, Isaiah was on his own with no help from Jennifer and Silas. It was no less than a crossing of worlds, and it held them spellbound.

Like a little girl faced with the fact that her role-playing game might soon be over, Salia turned to face the image only she could see. Keetna watched in amazement from below the edge of the trail as Salia's features softened and she became radiant and beautiful in the way of an angel. Even Sasha sat quietly on her haunches with her head cocked to one side, enthralled by her strange behavior.

It's time to come home, child, Isaiah told her gently.

Please, Salia, came a second voice, unbidden. It was the sweet voice of child. *There is so much for us to do here. It would be wonderful if you would join us.*

Anna? Is it really...you, Anna? Salia muttered. *But you...died. So very long ago. And I have always missed you so...*

No, Salia, Anna said gently. *I am still at your side. Where a true friend should be.*

Confusion. Then: *But Daddy. Anna. I almost have it, I—*

The bullet from Tay's rifle caught Salia in the side of her chest and spun her to the ground.

DADDY!!!

A terrible force shuddered through Jennifer and Silas, nearly sweeping them off their feet. The pain they felt—Salia's pain—was dark and bottomless.

Still they heard Isaiah: *It's what must be, child. I'm sorry, but it's time for you to come home.*

Then Anna: *Please, Salia. Join us. You have been alone far too long.*

"NO!!" she screamed, rising to her feet. A bright red stain of steaming blood spread across the back of her fur coat. "You tricked me! Both of you! Your treachery has killed me!"

But Isaiah and Anna were silent now, and Salia was dying.

Running wildly in a crouch, she stumbled to the corner of the monolith and ran along the icy ledge, screaming in a pitiful wail, "Lyman! Dear Lyman! Come save me! I...I can bring Ellie back to you!"

Jennifer felt her joints unfreeze and raced with Silas and Keetna to witness Salia Warchez's final moment. It came quickly. Lyman was already most of the way to her, although not with the intention of assisting her in any enterprise that did not involve her immediate death. Like a bull that had just torn through a fence and was carried along by its own momentum, Lyman slipped and slid and ran toward Salia with his arms held out as if to embrace her at a full run. Which is exactly what he did.

"Lyman?" she whimpered in a frail voice. "Lyman, you have to help—"

Bellowing with rage, the stout farmer hit her full on, body to body, and grabbed her in a bear hug. For an eternal instant they tottered together on the icy edge of the deep abyss. Incredibly, Salia had regained *(summoned from the murky depths?)* a considerable measure of her strength. It almost seemed that she—disoriented and mortally wounded—would, through sheer force of will, cast Lyman over the side and return to finish what she'd started.

But nature would not allow it. Like a jet of air expelled from the mouth of a wrathful god, a blast of wind of incredible vehemence swept through the lacuna, laying Jennifer and Silas flat against the ledge. Silas covered Jennifer with his body to keep them both from being swept over the side.

Salia and Lyman were not so fortunate. Jennifer lifted her head and watched as the farmer and the viator, still locked in a fatal embrace, disappeared into the waves of snow that obscured the creek two hundred feet below.

Jennifer collapsed on the icy ground and wept. She wept for Jack, she wept Carmen, and she wept for Jazzman. She wept for all the happy endings that might have been but weren't.

⁑

Death Match

Of all the rigors of war, there is none more physically exhausting than hand to hand combat...

FROM THE UNPUBLISHED MEMOIRS OF CARLOS HERRERA

Tay is waiting for his old nemesis Hadrian Tharp when the stocky outlaw emerges from the woods at the base of hill. They smile at each other like two longtime friends, but there is no common ground of friendship between them, a notion poetically illustrated by the fact that neither can see the other's smile through the blankets of snow whirling around them.

There will be no cat-and-mouse game this time. It will be the match they have always wanted: face to face, man to man, hand to hand. May the best warrior live to tell the tale.

As Hadrian approaches, Tay wills his body to cease its shivering. Any display of weakness will only add to Hadrian's strength. He reminds himself that he will shortly be covered with steaming sweat. And blood.

Tay leans his sniper's rifle against the large stone that marks the grave of Pryus Gordon Primm. Ironically, the stone proved to be the perfect vantage point from which to attract Hadrian's undivided attention and, of course, to end the life of the woman responsible for the deaths of Jack Vara and his own *Carmenita*.

A fresh wound on Hadrian's face makes Tay curious, but not curious enough to ask about it. Instead, he says, "The hand, *Hadriano*, does it hurt?" as Tharp draws close enough that they can speak without shouting.

"It was a good shot, Tay," Hadrian says. By the emotion he shows, he might be talking about a shot fired during a pheasant hunt. Tay sees that

Hadrian has torn a section of cloth from his shirt to stem the flow of blood from the stumps of the middle fingers of his right hand. The flesh above his missing earlobe has stopped bleeding on its own.

"I couldn't let you kill them, *Hadriano*. They are my family."

"And Salia was mine," Hadrian replies, the first hint of anger creeping into his voice. "I saw you kill her, Villa."

"*Asi es la vida, amigo*. And still life goes on," Tay tells him, letting the rifle drop away from his hand as he begins to move in a circle around Tharp.

"Longer for some than for others," Hadrian says, matching Tay's move by tossing his shoulder holster to one side, along with a small revolver he extracts from his back pocket. "Knives?" he asks, dropping into a defensive crouch.

"The rules will be defined by the nature of fight, *Hadriano*. But, yes, I would prefer knives. There is no honor between warriors with guns."

"Tay Villa and his fucking honor," Tharp laughs. "As if it makes any difference in the end."

"For some it does," Tay tells him, knowing that he has already grown tired of talking to this man. Hadrian is also done talking. Without warning, he lunges quickly forward and kicks out at Tay as he goes into a graceful spin with his foot at the level of Tay's chin. Tay was expecting this and steps back before the boot has a chance to connect with his jaw. The momentum alone would've sent Tharp to the ground, but Tay grabs his foot and upends his foe into the sloppy snow.

He backs off as Hadrian bounds back to his feet, telling him, "That one was free, *Hadriano*. The next one will cost you."

Humiliated and angry, Tharp feints another lunge, then spins as Tay reacts to it. This time his foot meets with the hard sinewy flesh of Tay's back and sends him sprawling forward but does not knock him off his feet.

Anticipating Hadrian's next move, Tay drops quickly to the ground in the same instant Hadrian throws himself at Tay's midsection, catching only air. Hadrian lands hard on one shoulder and groans briefly in pain. Tay knows there will be no more easy moves.

It's time to end it.

Before Hadrian has a chance to gain his feet Tay leaps on top of him, catching him in the chest with a knee. He feels the snap of breaking bones and feels the breath go out of the powerful man beneath him. It causes him to relax when he shouldn't. Hadrian, like Tay, is disciplined to work through the pain.

As Tay carelessly withdraws, Hadrian swings his leg and hooks him hard on the side of neck, forcing Tay down onto the other leg. It's a deathly place to be, but before Hadrian can break his neck in a quick scissor motion, Tay plunges an open hand into Tharp's crotch, grabbing for anything his fingers can find.

The action has the desired effect, but Hadrian doesn't give Tay the satisfaction of hearing him cry out in pain. Instead, he kicks Tay in the chest, sending him onto his back in the deep snow.

Tay feels one of his own ribs crack. He draws a quick breath and, though painful, he knows Hadrian has not sent a jagged bone into his lung.

Tiring quickly, they stand and face off again, gasping hard for ragged breaths as steam rolls off their bodies like phantoms nearing a state of opacity. Tay knows it has to end before his body becomes exhausted and can no longer summon the energy it needs to fight this formidable foe.

He sees blood appear at the corner of Hadrian's mouth; different blood, he is sure, than that dripping from the wound across his face. It means that Tay has managed to do to Hadrian what Hadrian has not been able to do to him: puncture a lung. His left lung is filling up with blood and will shortly disable him.

"Give it up, *Hadriano*," Tay says through tattered gasps of air. "Your injuries will kill you if you don't."

Hadrian coughs, spraying blood. "And you will let me live?"

"Perhaps," Tay answers, then reflects for a moment as he draws in a few more precious gulps of air. "But, no," he finally concludes, "I think not. You are a dangerous man, *Hadriano,* and I do not want to always be looking for you over my shoulder."

"You too, Villa. Far too dangerous," Hadrian says. Then he reaches down into his boot and extracts a small-caliber automatic from a hidden pocket sewn into the leather.

Why do I never remember these things? Tay scolds himself. *This man has no honor.* The gun, though small, looks like death from Tay's perspective. He quickly dives into a roll and lands back on his feet as two bullets whiz past the side of his chest.

Enough! Hadrian is in too much pain to move quickly, but Tay can only weave and dodge so much before his luck runs out. He pulls his knife from its scabbard then spins quickly around to Hadrian's backside, taking one slug in the shoulder and another in the abdomen. *That will be the one that kills me*, he thinks without emotion.

Hadrian tries to face him, but his pain is too great; he stops in mid turn and lowers his head. It is the opening Tay needed. He pulls Hadrian into the snow, then comes down hard from the top, concentrating all his weight on the knife that plunges into his heart.

Hadrian's pained and surprised expression lasts for only a second before the air leaves his one good lung and the light in his eyes winks out forever. Tay doesn't even have a chance to say goodbye.

He rolls onto his back in the snow and gropes greedily for air that seems to be in critically short supply. There is no part of him that does not hurt. Just some parts that hurt more. The wound in his gut is the most painful, and he knows he is bleeding inside, perhaps badly.

But as he stares into the sky above he sees a tiny patch of blue; the storm is ending. And he has the peculiar feeling that whether he lives or dies, something terrible has at last come to an end and his part in it has not been a small one. It is more consolation than most men carry with them to their graves, and it brings a soft serenity to his face as he closes his eyes to sleep.

Whether a minute later, or an hour, he is awakened by something warm and wet sliding roughly along his face, and he looks up to see Jazzman standing over him, hot drool dripping from the dog's tongue. Behind him, Jack Vara stands leaning to one side, favoring a leg down which blood flows from an open wound beneath a pant leg that is ripped to shreds. But still Jack is smiling.

"I saw you die," Tay tells him.

"No," Jack corrects him, "you only saw me fall."

Tay smiles back.

Springtime

It is only in retrospect that life's ironies unveil themselves and stand prominently at the fore, as if they were the real reason for all our pain and suffering. And so will we forever struggle with life and with each other; we have too great a passion for fate's poetic twists to do otherwise.

FROM THE UNPUBLISHED MEMOIRS OF CARLOS HERRERA

Sitting in the Daisy Mae at the same table where they ate less than an hour before Sheriff Primm's timely death, Jack stares ardently at Jennifer. She smiles demurely (all of her smiles are demure, he thinks) and reaches across the table to entwine her fingers with his. She loves him still, and completely, and his own feelings are unchanged from the moment he first saw her.

Jennifer has always been his destiny, no matter how much past events have folded, twisted, duplicated and doused the meaning of the word.

He hears a deep drumming outside and turns his head away from Jennifer to find its source. It's Sturm Baker, tooling through Purgatory proud as a prize boar in his refurbished black Hummer.

What a long path it's been from that day to this one...

If Sturm Baker's life was spared as a result of airbag technology and bad marksmanship, Jack's was surely saved by the whims of weather and geology. The countless tons of scree that sloped from the trail on the west side of the monolith to the broad valley below had, over the eons, spread around the corner to the south side, where it quickly dropped off toward the creek in a steep but not entirely impossible slope.

A careful measurement later confirmed that Jack and Jazzman fell approximately sixty-two feet; a considerable distance, but far less than the two hundred feet he would have fallen, had Salia forced him off the edge just fifteen feet to the east. Both the man and dog survived because of the steepness of the scree (think ski jump) and the fact that they had fallen onto the lee side of the embankment, where the driving snow had accumulated in a huge drift that only became discernible to those on the ledge once the storm ended.

Tay's survival was a direct consequence of Jack and Jazzman's auspicious fall. Too weak from injury and exhaustion to make his own way home, he would probably have perished before anyone found him. Fortunately for Tay, the only way back up for Jack and Jazzman was to continue down to the level of the creek and around to the trailhead, a route that led them directly to Tay.

In a way, then, Tay's life was spared by the woman he killed. But still he would have died if not for the timely ministrations of Catalyn and Cassie, who steadfastly refused to let him die, in spite of a feverish rant in which he confessed a desire to do exactly that.

A further unwitting favor was also afforded the survivors by Salia, since it was only by Sturm Baker's powers of obfuscation and his station as head of Desa that the messy aftermath of that day could be quickly tidied up. Baker survived only because Salia Warchez had chosen her band of brethren from among a community of men unskilled in the art of shooting at a quickly moving target (Carmen's misfortune was that she was simply too close to miss). With his own expansive derriere in the hot seat, Baker was compelled to concoct a believable tale in which all the blame for the entire affair was placed on the shoulders of the deceased mercenary, Hadrian Tharp, who had been on a relentless quest for a stash of diamonds that, as Baker convincingly argued, simply did not exist.

The story was made believable by the fact that Baker himself actually thought quite a lot of it was true. As often happens with head injuries, he was unable to remember anything for several hours prior to his accident, and he had no recollection of Salia Warchez's involvement or the existence of the COTO 2.82 anterium protocol.

Bits and pieces of the whole story were known to others, particularly the six remaining brethren and Bobby. But all were reluctant to divulge what little they knew during the ensuing investigation which was, again with Baker's nimble manipulations, brief and cursory. Thus did the brethren return to farming humbly and silently, to avoid being implicated in the murder of Carmen Ortiz. Bobby also returned to farming, at least until his sideline black-market activities proved to be more lucrative in Tharp's absence than they had ever been under his direction.

Because his injuries had not erased his prior knowledge of the hidden diamonds, a portion of them was doled out to Baker in installments sufficient to maintain the portly bureaucrat in a comfortable, if somewhat scaled-back, lifestyle.

And where were Carlos's diamonds? Several thousand carats of loose stones were discovered behind a sizable chunk of quartz in a mine obscured by overgrowth in a heavily forested hillside on Forest Service land. It was miles from the mine where Jennifer thought they would be and the diamonds might have remained lost forever if not for the fact that this particular mine was also the hiding place of a slightly different version of the COTO 2.82 anterium protocol. It was a mine only Tay knew about and the presence of the second protocol was something of a surprise to him, since Carlos had told him he had moved it from there and Tay had not bothered to verify that fact. Had Silas not insisted that the version he'd retrieved was deliberately planted to deceive Salia, they might never have gone looking.

Was Silas's protocol the red herring? No one knew for sure. The only difference between the two version were a few subtle substitutions in several rather lengthy stretches of DNA code. But Silas's suspicions were largely confirmed after Jack came across a memoir hidden in the back of an old filing cabinet; a memoir Carlos had been working on the last few years of his life. In its final pages Carlos made a startling confession:

By the use of intermediaries, both witting and unwitting, I was able to get Isaiah's diary into Salia's hands in such a way that she would feel certain it had come to her by way of one of her faithful. Or, at the very least, an enemy of mine. I knew she would read the diary, surmise the protocol's survival, and attempt to retrieve it from the person most likely to have stolen it from Dobry Robak. As I was the only investor able to sniff out Isaiah and Dobry's true intentions, she would naturally suspect me. All that remained, then, was to plant a carefully falsified copy of the anterium protocol in a place she would eventually discover, by tapping into the mind of one she would have no reason to harm.

It was hardly a perfect plan and I admit it was fraught with danger throughout, not only for Silas Teague, whom I entrusted with the counterfeit protocol's location, but for all those close to him. Yet I felt it was worth the risk if it would, in a manner of speaking, kick the legs out from under Salia Warchez in her moment of triumph, and forever discredit her in the eyes of the deluded who looked upon her as a worker of miracles.

How ironic it is that I shall not live to see the result of my finely crafted plans...

That, at least, is how events unfolded in this particular incarnation of the tale, though threads of fate surely wormed themselves through countless more permutations in which destiny was not so forgiving and felicitous, and Murphy was granted his due with a steely vengeance.

Those were the worlds that seized Salia Warchez in a smothering embrace and nearly drew them all to their doom; worlds denied, not because they did not exist, but were only made to seem imaginary by the onerous constraints of consciousness bound to flesh. Freed of those constraints, as Salia was for a time, anything is not only possible but imperative.

In every sense, she became all that she could be.

As do we all.

As for the peculiar fates of the two COTO 2.82 anterium protocols in this telling of the tale...

*   *   *   *

It had only been a week since Jack sat pensively watching bright tongues of orange and blue flames lick the cool night air as a playful breeze swirled the smoke of the campfire into a tight gray rope ascending to the heavens. Jack appreciated the irony of holding their soirée on the spot where he had found Tay lying in the snow on that fall day many months ago.

Everyone was present: Luke, Catalyn and Cassie; Silas and Keetna; Jack and Jennifer; Jazzman and Sasha. And Tay, who sat unmated, facing them all. Through the dancing flames the scar that ran down his face glowed brighter than the dark skin in which it was embedded. Jack thought it looked like a lightning bolt frozen in time.

Tay took a flask from his flak jacket, poured a couple of fingers of whiskey into the stainless steel cup that served as a lid, then passed the flask around. Each poured a portion into their own cups. Even Cassie, whose part in the drama had not been a small one, treated herself to a few drops of the volatile liquid.

When the flask returned to Tay, he set it on the ground beside him and raised his cup. "To *Carmenita*," he toasted. The corners of his mouth turned up into a smile that was made sad by the mournful cast of his large dark eyes. "*Un espíritu de fuego, siempre libre.*" A spirit of fire, forever free.

They raised their cups together, saying, "To Carmen," then threw the whiskey down their throats. The toast was followed by coughing and quick exhalations and, for Jack and Luke at any rate, quickly downed beer chasers. Catalyn looked worriedly at Cassie; she appeared to have enjoyed her small taste of Tay's hard whiskey.

Jack felt like he should say something then; probably they all did. But what was there to say that Tay had not said already?

Keetna cleared her throat and everyone looked her way. She was certainly more pleasant to look at these days. Jack was impressed with the young woman she'd blossomed into as a result of Silas's companionship and, he suspected, a diet rich in fruits and vegetables. Though she was no less powerful than before (considering her diminutive stature), her sinewy musculature had softened and her skin had become smooth and radiant. She'd discarded her ill-fitting synthetic pants and pullovers in favor of articles of soft cotton, linen and wool. She had also discarded her black beret and allowed her richly blonde hair to lay down naturally against her head and neck, where it now moved naturally and gracefully in the breeze.

Everyone agreed that she had earned her right to participate as an equal in this gathering, and she spoke briefly now. "I never knew her, Tay," she told him with her intense blue eyes fixed on him, "but I'm sure I would've liked her very much."

A small laugh escaped Tay's lips, and he replied, "Yes, I know you would have. She would have driven you crazy—" a few chuckles erupted from the group "—just like she did all of us, but yes: you would have counted her among your friends."

Perhaps to keep the sentimentality from perpetuating to a level that would make him more uncomfortable than he already was, Tay produced from a backpack the two existing copies of the COTO 2.82 anterium protocol and held them up for everyone to see. "We need to decide what to do with these...*cosas*...that have brought us so much misery."

"Burn 'em!" Keetna proclaimed, still feeling she had the floor. "No good can come from them."

Except for Cassie, Keetna was the only one who had no recollection of the days when oil ruled the world. Nor did she fully appreciate that the chaos created by the end of oil was responsible for every hardship in her short life. And yet she was unequivocal in her disdain for the protocol.

"I agree," Luke chimed it. "Cremate them both."

"Jack?" Tay said quizzically. His ambivalence was no secret. And the fact that he had been 'under the spell' of she-who-wanted-the-protocol-to-rule-the-world still carried with it a lingering uneasiness that had only lately ducked beneath the surface. How could he blame them? For a brief time he had been, if not exactly their enemy, at least Salia Warchez's ally. Like the brethren (oh, how he hated the comparison), and his ex-wife (not one damn bit better), he had, as they saw it—all except for Jennifer, who could see the discomfiting truth as no one else could—betrayed them.

But he hadn't; not really.

As he had tried so often to explain, his mind had not been changed. It had instead been transported to a place where everything Salia Warchez believed in made sense to him. And then held there against his will. It was crazy but true. Where or what that place might have been was something his scientific mind still wrangled with. Was it real or delusion? Or illusion? He couldn't say. But as far as Jennifer was concerned, it was as real as icicles in January, ticks in springtime, and love in places where all logic proclaimed it didn't belong. He was in no position to argue. As for the business at hand, he owed his life to Jennifer and he swore to himself he wouldn't let her down.

Reflectively he said, "Oil has caused the world more woes than could ever be counted. It was only after we became addicted to oil that the human population grew completely out of control and we, as a species, began to threaten the existence of everything beautiful on this planet." Approving looks all around. "And, as I recall as a teenager, we reacted to this knowledge as if the obvious solution to the problem could not even be considered because of the economic chaos it would create. In effect what we were saying, in voices that betrayed the very logic they proclaimed, was that we were destined to destroy ourselves because to do otherwise would upset our notions of wealth.

"It was the most pitiable non sequitur ever uttered; no more reasonable than a drug addict rationalizing his habit. And yet we swallowed it hook, line and sinker for the simple fact that it was uttered so often it began to make a hollow sort of sense that everyone—me included—wanted to believe."

"So?" Tay asked, growing impatient.

"On the other hand," Jack went on, amid dubious frowns, "It could be that we have finally learned our lesson. Perhaps, under the proper constraints, oil actually could be used for good...in a limited sense. We should at least allow the possibility, at any rate."

Jack saw Jennifer's eyes flash, and he knew he'd said too much. "That's your old girlfriend talking, my dear," she said pointedly. "Proper constraints? What a joke! Think Hitler. Think Stalin. Think of all the uncounted atrocities of the twentieth century. Then think oil, because that's what mobilized the armies that made them possible. What would Salia have used it for? World peace? Burn the protocols, Tay. Burn them now."

"I seem to recall that the biggest atrocity of all occurred after the oil quit flowing," Jack countered. "Besides, the protocol is worth billions." He cringed inwardly at that last part and wondered if perhaps there was still a scrap of Salia lingering in some distant outpost of his mind.

Catalyn stood and towered over Jack. "All the more reason to rid the world of it," she said looking down at Jack without expression. "The only people who would pay the price it commands are the ones who would use it for all the wrong reasons: to hook us on a drug we broke our addiction to twenty-one years ago. Or to build an army no one could resist. Besides," she said, peering now into Jack's eyes, "We have to remember that we never found Salia Warchez's body."

"Surely you don't think she's still alive, do you?" Jack guffawed. "She fell over two hundred feet after being mortally wounded, for Christ's sake. It's much more reasonable to assume she washed downstream. Or was taken by predators."

"Then where is the body?" Silas asked reasonably. "It should've been next to Lyman's, but it wasn't."

"She was the lighter of the two. The wind would have carried her farther. She must have landed in the creek," Jack replied, infusing his voice with a strained certainty. "It's the only logical explanation."

"Logic doesn't hold much water when it comes to that woman," Catalyn shot back with a mirthless grin. Then, looking at Tay, she added, "I say we burn the protocols. Both of them. Then, dead or alive, the bitch is out of the oil business."

Jack sipped his beer and fell silent.

Tay peered at Silas, who removed a scrap of paper from his jacket pocket on which he had written something. He said, "Because of Carlos's memoir, we now know exactly what went down last fall. But we also know what he loved and revered; what fascinated him and gave him wonder. And most of all, what he hated. Above all he hated the War of the Turning and all the senseless death and suffering that it wrought. But he also hated the reason behind it: the weakness that spread through the soul of humanity once living became too easy. On the last page he wrote, *'If ever men resume the pumping of oil, we can be assured it will be accompanied by a return to the uncounted excesses that nearly smothered all life on the planet in the first part of the twenty-first century; a return to a time when lavishness in all things was considered a God-given right and the wisdom that accompanies life's simplest pleasures is crushed beneath the wheels of progress—all because of the unrestricted use of a form of energy that we would all have been better off without. We have at last cured ourselves of our addiction to oil and we cannot afford to backslide. A man may be strong, but mankind is deplorably weak, for if history teaches us anything, it is only that it teaches us nothing at all.'"*

Silas paused for effect, then said, "I was inside that woman's mind and I know what she wanted the oil for. I say we burn the fucking things so we can all go home."

Without comment, Tay smiled at the youngest member of the group. "Cassie?"

The girl looked in every face before mimicking Silas. "Let's burn the fucking things so we can all go home," she said in her small expressive voice.

"Cassie!!!" Catalyn admonished, but the girl just gave her a smug I-always-wanted-to-say-that smile and Catalyn's disparaging scowl warmed to an acquiescing smirk. Then she chuckled. Along with everyone else.

That left Jack and all eyes returned to him. "This really isn't our decision to make," he said lamely, and quickly saw written on the long faces around him how little credence his argument carried. With a shrug he relented. "What the hell? Burn 'em."

Tay stood, holding the two bound treatises over the hot flames that jumped toward it like a pack of starving dogs vying for a bloody bone. "End of discussion?"

Every head nodded. Jack's last and most reluctantly.

Tay let the first protocol drop from his hand, the one Silas had brought back from Old Denver. The plastic envelope bubbled and blackened, and its contents quickly burst into flames.

Then he dropped the second one; the one they'd found in the mine.

Instinctively and against his better judgment, Jack thought to reach for it before it fell into the flames, but forces born in the universe in the days when mankind was yet a distant probability stole from Jack the chance to betray his only friends. A zealously focused explosion of wind stole along the ground and swept up beneath Tay's fingers the instant he opened them, taking the bound protocol as its own, spiraling it away from the hungry fire to the rocky ground along the banks Old Scratch Creek, far into the woods beyond where Lyman Moran's body was found, broken, battered and alone...

*   *   *   *

Sue, pretty little Sue of the stained dress and the lively hips, brought their food—Jack a plate of rabbit tacos, Jennifer a chicken salad sandwich—and set the plates on the table. Jack drew his focus back in from the street where the dust kicked up by Baker's tires still swirled in small eddies, and saw that she had not yet retreated back to the kitchen.

"Yes?" Jack said, gazing curiously up at her.

"I've just gotta know," she replied, looking at him as bemused as she was hesitant. It was a look that underscored her down-home comeliness.

"Know what?" he asked.

For a moment she stammered and fidgeted and Jack thought this was very unlike the bold and assertive girl he'd first met last fall. Finally she said, "You know...what we talked about the first day you came into town? All those other copies of us? I've been thinking about it ever since and, well...I just wanted to know if you ever figured it all out."

Jack peered across the table at Jennifer and when she lifted her eyes to meet his, he grinned conspiratorially.

Jennifer returned a smile that was anything but demure and said reassuringly, "Pull up a chair, honey. This may take a while."

THE AUTHOR

Rex Ewing's diverse interests have led him from Colorado to Costa Rica to Alaska, working cattle and horses, mining gold, and formulating equine supplements. He now lives at the end of a rough dirt road in the Colorado Rockies with his wife LaVonne and two dogs. There he writes novels and non-fiction books from his hand-hewn log cabin powered by the sun and wind.